MEET ME IN BOMBAY

MEET ME IN BOMBAY

A Novel

JENNY ASHCROFT

ST. MARTIN'S PRESS
NEW YORK

Published in the United States by St. Martin's Press, an imprint of St. Martin's Publishing Group

MEET ME IN BOMBAY. Copyright © 2019 by Jenny Ashcroft. All rights reserved. Printed in the United States of America. For information, address St. Martin's Publishing Group, 120 Broadway, New York, NY 10271.

www.stmartins.com

Designed by Devan Norman

Library of Congress Cataloging-in-Publication Data

Names: Ashcroft, Jenny, 1980- author.
Title: Meet me in Bombay: a novel / Jenny Ashcroft.
Description: First U.S. edition. | New York: St. Martin's Press, 2021.
Identifiers: LCCN 2020035320 | ISBN 9781250270269 (hardcover) |
    ISBN 9781250270276 (ebook)
Subjects: GSAFD: Love stories.
Classification: LCC PR6101.S525 M44 2021 | DDC 823/.92—dc23
LC record available at https://lccn.loc.gov/2020035320

Our books may be purchased in bulk for promotional, educational, or business use. Please contact your local bookseller or the Macmillan Corporate and Premium Sales Department at 1-800-221-7945, extension 5442, or by email at MacmillanSpecialMarkets@macmillan.com.

Originally published in the United Kingdom by Little, Brown UK in 2019

First U.S. Edition: 2021

10 9 8 7 6 5 4 3 2 1

For Molly, Jonah, and Rafferty

MEET ME IN BOMBAY

PROLOGUE

A letter to somebody, from somebody else

Tonight, I cannot recall what year it is. Try as I might, I can't think how long I've been here, in this residential home that's really a hospital—this place of the old, the infirm, the forgotten . . . and the forgetful. I asked a nurse—a young woman with freckles and a quiet voice—to remind me, but she wouldn't. She said I would panic again, that I mustn't fret; time isn't important. And yet, it feels so important to me. I am sure, you see, that I've been in this place too long. I have an awful sense I've been here for very many years.

I know that it was 1915 when I became a patient. I remember that much at least. And that I marked the date in the book I was given then: a leather-bound journal, handed to me during my first session with Dr. Arnold to take note of all the things my broken memory mightn't keep hold of. Anything that comes to you, *Arnold said,* jot it down directly. *His words have somehow stayed with me; for all I've forgotten, I can hear his voice even now, picture the open fire in his study, feel its warmth, quite as though I am still sitting before it, my skin prickling beneath my convalescent blues.* View your past as a puzzle, *he said,* one you must slot together. Don't let any piece slide away. *I haven't seen Arnold in a long time. I cannot recall when or why we parted. Perhaps he gave up on my puzzle.*

Something I can never let myself do.

Today, after morning tea, I fell asleep quite suddenly. It happens like that. I never fight it. My dreams are all I have left of that other world: the one I'm sure I once belonged to. It was full of heat, light, and color; so much life. There was a party, on the banks of a sea. Nothing like the tame affairs we hold here—no finger sandwiches, diluted cordial, and crackers that don't make bangs. It was loud, packed with people; the music of a ragtime band.

A figure, a woman in a silk dress, stood in the darkness with her back to me, gloved fingers touching a chair.

It was you. I am certain it was you.

The sky seemed to explode above. I watched you look up, the arch of your neck. I waited for you to turn, to see me. Something—a memory?—told me that you would.

Cheers filled the night, the opening chords of a song I cannot place, and still, I waited.

Slowly, you dipped your head. Your chin tilted, over your bare shoulder; the hint of your cheekbone coming round.

I held my breath. Even as I slept in my chair, I wasn't breathing.

When I woke, as I always wake before you allow me a glimpse of your face, there were tears on my cheeks.

I have no recollection of what you look like, and yet I know that if I saw you, I'd recognize you instantly. I am certain you are beautiful. I want to think that we were happy together once. I try to believe our story was a wonderful one. But I am here, old and alone, and you are not, so I don't know how that can have been.

To return to you is all I need, yet it feels more impossible with every passing day. Because however often I dream these dreams, however patiently I wait for my broken mind to conjure just one starting clue that might lead me back to you—an initial, the name of a place, just the smallest detail—it never does. I don't know where you're from, who you are to me, or if you're even alive. I try so hard, every hour of every day, to remember, but sometimes I can't even recall that I'm meant to be remembering your name.

And I still have no idea, after all these many, many years, of where I've been, what events took me from you, how I came to be in that hospital in 1915.

Or who on earth I am.

CHAPTER ONE

It always seemed so strange to Maddy how, within the space of moments, life could go from being one thing to another thing entirely—with no hint, no warning sense of the change afoot. After that New Year's Eve of 1913 especially, she'd often pause, bewildered by how oblivious she'd been in those hours leading up to midnight, caught up in the furor of the Royal Yacht Club's party, never once suspecting what was just round the corner. But that night, as the clock edged toward 1914 and the ragtime band struck up a fresh set, filling the club's hot, candlelit ballroom with Scott Joplin, and the vibrating dance floor with couples—a throng of sequined gowns and evening suits, racing across the boards in another sweaty quickstep—she thought of nothing but the heat, the music.

She had absolutely no idea of everything that was about to come her way.

She kept to the edge of the floor. Having danced the last five, she was happy to spectate for now, catch her breath and feel the cool relief of her iced gin and tonic pressed to her cheek. Rolling the glass on her baking skin, she let her eyes move over the opulence surrounding her. It was a lavish party, even by Bombay's standards, and she, fresh from the soft, cozy world of her aunt and uncle's in Oxfordshire, had to keep reminding herself that she wasn't trespassing on a theater set, but actually now belonged in this steamy, foreign land. White-clothed tables fringed the dance floor, groaning beneath platters of curry puffs, naan, and tropical fruits. At the long wooden bar, tureens of punch jostled for space with buckets of champagne. Colored lanterns burned everywhere—on the tables, the walls—casting the paneled room in tinted light; their waxy scent mixed with perfume and hair pomade, the muggy heat that wafted in through the ajar veranda doors. There was no Christmas tree—apparently none could be got in India—but instead an arrangement of mango and banana tree branches had been decorated with baubles and balanced precariously by the ballroom's grand entrance. It was rather an odd-looking construction, certainly like no fir Maddy had ever seen, and somehow succeeded in making it feel less rather than more like Christmas—much like the humidity-dampened paper hats Maddy's father, Richard, had insisted they all wear on Christmas Day. It had felt so incongruous to be eating a turkey lunch out on the villa's sun-baked veranda, peacocks sauntering by.

Richard was wearing another hat now. It was impossible not to laugh at the sight of him across the room—the head of the Bombay civil service, every inch the distinguished colonial servant in his pristine white tie—with a purple polka dot crown tipping jauntily on his graying hair. He was trying to coax Maddy's mother, Alice, into a dance. Alice—who, unlike every other person in the room, still looked as cool as a Pimm's cucumber, fair curls in place, not even a hint of sheen to her porcelain skin—held her gloved hands up, refusing. Maddy wondered if there was even the tiniest part of her that was tempted to do the opposite, say, "Yes. Yes, please. What the devil?" Maddy wished she would. It would be rather nice to see her let loose for once, take Richard's arm and career into the fray with the same happy abandon as everyone else.

But Richard was already turning away, creases of resignation on his weathered face. Maddy felt a stab of pity for him, then again as he pushed his chin up and set off toward the bar. Why couldn't Alice have just danced with him? Maddy, pulling at the damp neckline of her dress, didn't even attempt to answer her own question. For all she'd been in India two months now, back living with her parents after more than a decade in England (she'd gone home for school, like almost all children of the Raj, but also to escape the tropical fevers she'd been so prone to as a child. "We couldn't keep you well," her father had told her sadly, many times. "It was terrifying . . ."), she often felt she understood her crisp, contained mother no better than she had that sweltering October day she'd docked in Bombay and met her again.

"Don't look so serious," came a voice from Maddy's left, making her start, "not on New Year's."

Maddy turned, met the mock-scolding glare of her friend Della Wilson. The two of them had been on the voyage over from Tilbury together, in the same row of cabins as all the other single women on their way to families in India—in Della's case, to stay with her older brother, Peter. They'd bonded over the ship's irresistible high teas, their discomfort at the rest of the passengers' assumption that they were all part of the "fishing fleet," India-bound to find husbands. *Which of course is exactly what my mother is hoping I'll do,* Della had said through a mouthful of chocolate éclair. *It's why she let me come. Not that I'm averse.* She'd swallowed. *I'd just much rather go tiger hunting instead.*

"Where did you spring from?" Maddy asked her now. "I haven't seen you all night."

"I've only just got here," Della said. "You can blame Peter for that, if he ever decides to come."

"Where is he?"

"Heaven knows. He was meeting some friend earlier at the Taj Hotel, but was meant to be coming back to the house to fetch me. I imagine they both got lost by way of the Taj bar." She fanned her flushed face. "I was worried I was going to miss midnight, so I hailed a rickshaw in the end. Don't tell Peter. He keeps telling me off for getting them alone."

Maddy, who'd oft heard Peter bemoan how much simpler his life had been before his irrepressible sister had descended on it, laughed and said, "Poor Peter."

"Poor Peter nothing," said Della. "God," she blew air from her bottom lip, "it's oven-like in here. Come outside? We can squeeze a quick smoke in before he gets here and tells me off for that, too."

Maddy, deciding she could do with one—and without another raised eyebrow from her mother—nodded.

"So who've you been dancing with?" Della asked as, together, they picked their way through the heaving room.

"The usual suspects," said Maddy, naming a couple of army captains, a perpetually sunburned naval officer, and a handful of civil servants who, like Peter, worked for her father in the Bombay offices.

"Not Guy Bowen?" said Della, in an overly innocent voice and with a nod to where he was standing, deep in conversation with some of the other surgeons from the military hospital.

Maddy rolled her eyes. "Would you stop it?" she said. "He's my parents' friend."

"*Your* friend, too. He calls on you often enough."

Maddy pushed the veranda door wide. "He could be my father."

"Not really," said Della. "He can't be much over forty. You're almost twenty-three."

"I'm fairly sure," said Maddy, "that he used to bounce me on his knee when I was a little girl."

"Did he just?" said Della, in a way that made them both burst out laughing.

They carried on into the close, balmy night. As they went, out onto the seaside terrace, the band played on, and the clock in the pulsing ballroom behind them struck eleven: the very last hour of 1913.

It was quieter outside, the sultry air acting as a muffler on the music, the voices of all those milling around, lounging at the tables in the shadows. Flame torches crackled, lighting Maddy and Della's way to the seawall. Not that they really needed it. This was hardly the first time they'd disappeared off for a cigarette together. They'd discovered the hidden spot on the sea stairs at a party not long after they'd arrived and had been using it to escape the watchful eyes of their relatives and the gossiping memsahibs ever since—much as they'd used to slip off to the P&O lifeboat decks on the voyage.

As they walked through the blackness, Maddy opened her clutch, searching out the cigarettes her parents' bearer kept her supplied with. ("I am doing it for a small fee, yes?" he'd said hopefully, the first time she'd asked. "Yes," she'd agreed, handing over the rupees, "yes. And for my sanity, too.") She was still rummaging among her comb, matches, and powder compact when Della grabbed her hand and squealed, "Quick, Peter's coming."

Reflexively, Maddy turned to look in the direction of the grand Taj Hotel, dropping her matches in the process. She bent to fetch them, eyes on the

approaching Peter. He was easy enough to spot, even on the dark promenade; it was his slight build, that ambling walk of his. He hadn't seen them.
He was talking to the other man with him, Maddy assumed the friend he'd
collected from the Taj. She stared, taking in the stranger's outline beneath
the palms. He was taller than Peter—broader, too. She wondered briefly
who he was, but didn't give it much thought. She didn't have time; Della
beckoned her on.

Abandoning her matches, Maddy followed in Della's hasty wake, gathering up her silk skirts to climb over the seawall, then down the damp
stairs to perch beside a breathless Della on the usual step.

It was quieter yet nestled beneath the terrace. The water rippled against
the stone wall, and local children splashed, playing—despite the late hour—in
the Arabian Sea, in and out of the nearby fishing boats. A gentle breeze carried from the city, musty with pollen, dust, and drains, the heat of hundreds
of thousands of people. Maddy felt it cloak her sticky bare back, her upper
arms, and let her shoulders loosen, relishing the calm after the glittering in-
tensity above. Placing a cigarette to her lips, she leaned over to let Della light
it, and inhaled, closing her eyes at the rush of lightness to her head.

"I wonder what everyone's doing back in gray old England," said Della,
in a tone that made it clear how much she enjoyed the thought that whatever it was, it was nothing like this.

"Do you really not miss it?" Maddy asked. "Not even a bit?"

"Not even a smidgen," said Della. She looked at Maddy sideways, a tease
in her round eyes. "You should try it; you'd be much more comfortable."

"Easy for you to say," said Maddy, because it was. Della had an open
ticket to travel back whenever she wanted, family, friends that she knew
she'd see again.

"You were so looking forward to coming," Della reminded her, "on the
boat."

"I know," said Maddy, "I do know." But on the voyage, she'd thought her
trip to India was just a holiday. She'd been excited. With college finished,
it had all felt like such an adventure, one to relish before she took up the
teaching post she'd been offered. And she'd been desperate to see her father
again. Unlike her mother, he'd visited her every couple of years in Oxford,
where she'd been staying with her aunt Edie—his sister. When Maddy was

younger, she'd used to cross off the days until his next trip in her diary, drawing up elaborate itineraries for picnics, trips to the theater, all of that. A long spell staying with him had seemed such a treat. She'd even let herself hope for . . . something . . . with her mother: a relationship beyond stilted letters with foreign postmarks, perhaps. However, somewhere between her P&O liner leaving Port Said and arriving at the chaotic docks in Bombay, things had rather fallen apart for Aunt Edie and Uncle Fitz in Oxford, and Maddy no longer had a home left in England to go back to; no job either, thanks to Uncle Fitz, nor means to set herself up on her own. Just a mother who became ever less talkative whenever she raised the subject of whether she and Richard might see their way to helping her do it.

"It'll get easier," said Della.

Maddy exhaled smoke, making a haze of the stars. "Yes," she said, "of course it will." It wasn't too hard to believe, not on a night like this, well away from her silent days with Alice in the villa, and with music playing above, children laughing below. "Anyway," she said, "I have it on good authority that it takes at least a year to feel settled in a place."

"Whose?"

"My father's."

"Excellent," said Della. "Peter would approve."

Maddy smiled. Then, keen to move the conversation on, said, "How was your Christmas?"

"Ripping," said Della, and went on to give an account of the trip she'd convinced Peter not to tell their parents she'd booked for herself—an organized tour of the waterways of Kerala; so many sunsets, visits to bankside villages, and freshly caught fish cooked over coals each night. It did all sound quite ripping.

"You lucky thing," said Maddy. "Cocktails at the Gymkhana Club was about as adventurous as our Christmas got. Although," she said, "Cook did curry the turkey for lunch."

"How very daring," said Della, laughing.

"Honestly," said Maddy, tapping her cigarette, "I think it was mostly about disguising the taste of the meat." No one had had any idea of how long the unfortunate bird had been waiting, plucked and ready, at the market. They'd all been poorly afterward. ("Par for the course," Richard had said over dried crackers and tonic the next day. "I'm only ever one of Cook's curries away from my ideal weight." "Richard," Alice had said, "really.")

"Did you see much of Guy?" Della asked.

Maddy groaned. "Not this again."

"Come on, tell me, do," said Della.

"Della, he's like my uncle."

"A very attentive uncle."

Maddy made no reply, hoping the look she shot Della would be enough to put her off.

Which of course it wasn't. "I quite like the idea of an older man, you know," Della said. "And Guy does it so well. Rather heavenly, if you ask me."

"No one is asking you."

"A surgeon, too. Think what he can do with his—"

Maddy kicked her.

"Ouch." Della laughed, reached for her shin. "Fine, I'll stop."

"Thank God." Maddy flicked her cigarette out to sea, and looked back, up toward the club, the drifting music of the ragtime band. "Ready to go?" she asked.

"We probably should," said Della. "I'm starting to worry Peter might have gone home after all to fetch me."

Peter hadn't gone home to fetch her. ("What a rotter," breathed Della.) He was still outside, drinking at one of the round tables with his usual crowd. Maddy recognized nearly all of them from evenings and weekends spent at the city's various clubs; the Bombay social scene was as small as it was hectic. She'd danced with most of them that night. There was only one there she didn't know: Peter's friend. He sat just back from the table, his face hidden from the glow of the flickering lanterns. Unlike all the other men, he wasn't in evening suit, just trousers and a shirt, a linen jacket. It made Maddy look twice, wonder afresh who he was.

He turned, as though sensing her curiosity. She flushed, feeling caught out, and switched her attention to Peter, who stood as she and Della approached.

"Della Wilson," Peter said. "I don't even want to know that you were just down there smoking."

"I—" began Della.

"No, I insist you don't tell me. That way I won't have to lie again when our mother wires to ask how you're behaving." He shot Maddy a despairing look. "I've never told so many lies in my life."

Maddy laughed, a little self-consciously; she had the strongest sense the man in the linen jacket was still looking at her, probably wondering why she'd been staring at him.

"I was going to say," retorted Della, "that I can't believe you just left me at the villa."

"I knew you'd be all right."

"I might still be there. I could have missed the whole party."

"And yet," Peter said, "here you somehow are. Maddy, come here." He reached forward to kiss her still-flushed cheek. "You're very warm," he said.

"I'm fine."

"You need champagne," he said, and turned to the table in search of a bottle. "Any New Year's resolutions?" he asked.

"I haven't thought," Maddy said.

"Untrue," said Della. "You're going to try and not be homesick."

"But that's no good," said Peter, handing them both brimming glasses.

Maddy had to ask. "Why not?"

"Because resolutions never stick," he said.

"That's rather negative," she said, and, from the corner of her eye, caught the turn of the stranger's head. He was still too far back for her to see him properly; she more felt than saw his smile.

"Just candid," said Peter. "They really never do."

"Well," she said, one eye on his friend (had he smiled?), "since it's not really my resolution, perhaps it will."

"That," said Della, "makes no sense whatsoever."

"A truth," agreed Peter. "However," he raised his drink, "since it's New Year's, let's forget Maddy said it, and drink up. Oh, look," he said, distracted by a pair of Indian waiters circulating the terrace with trays of kebabs, "sustenance. I'll be back. Be good now. . . ."

And with that, he was off.

As he went, Della declared that she was keen to go herself, see how things were inside. A couple of the others at the table protested ("Stay, have more champagne. Don't leave us here alone"), but Della was unmoved, and Maddy, finding no reason not to, agreed to press on.

"Break our hearts, why don't you?" an officer called after them as they left.

Confident that no one's heart was in any real jeopardy, Maddy felt not a mite of guilt. And it wasn't that officer she found herself glancing back at, on her way across the muggy, dark terrace. It was the stranger in the linen jacket. She wasn't sure why she did it, and she wished she hadn't, because, just as before, he turned, his face a shadow above the white of his clothes, making her look away too quickly, and feel foolish all over again.

"Who was that?" she asked Della, talking through her embarrassment.

"Who was who?"

"That man," Maddy said. "The one Peter brought from the Taj."

"I don't know," said Della, looking over her shoulder. "Why? Was he there?"

"Yes," said Maddy, and then, before he could see Della trying to spot him, "It doesn't matter."

It didn't, of course.

"Typical of Peter not to make introductions," said Della.

"I suppose," said Maddy. Then, as they carried on, back into the humming ballroom, the light, music, and laughter, she let the stranger slip once more from her mind.

The dance floor was, if such a thing was possible, even fuller than it had been before, and hotter. Della disappeared onto it within seconds, on the arm of a sergeant major, and Maddy, glimpsing her father and his polka dots at the bar—remembering how downhearted he'd looked before—made a beeline for him, dragging him onto the sweaty floor in just the same way as he'd tried to drag her mother earlier, assuring him that of course he wouldn't be cramping her style. "Well, perhaps we could do without the hat. . . ."

He wasn't a particularly adept dancer, certainly not what you'd call smooth, but what he lacked in skill he made up for in gusto, swinging them both around the floor. As they dodged other couples, narrowly missed a collision with the banana and mango Christmas tree ("We'll try harder next time," he said), Maddy laughed up into his smiling face and almost managed not to notice her mother on the periphery of the floor, observing them both, her expression unreadable. Baking as Maddy was, she didn't hesitate when Richard asked her to dance again.

From then on, she didn't leave the floor. Men at the party outnumbered the women two to one (as was always the case in India), and a song barely ended before someone else came forward, asking her to do the charitable thing and go again. She danced with Richard's secretary ("Will you risk it, Maddy?"), then more of his staff, and the sunburned naval captain again. Della's card was just as full, and Maddy stopped trying to keep track of all her partners. The band played on, and more and more people moved in from the terrace, packing the glowing room until it felt as though there were no space left for anyone else, no steamy air left to breathe. Maddy's skin ran slick; her hair, loose of its pins, fell in damp waves on her neck—as chaotic, she was sure, as Della's own brown curls had become.

It was at just before midnight that she finally stepped back from the floor, clutched a stitch in her waist, and thought she might just expire if she didn't cool down before risking anything with anyone again. Since Della was still merrily pegging it across the boards, she didn't waste time telling her where she was going, but headed back outside alone.

It was blissfully quiet on the terrace, all the previously full tables deserted. Some of the lanterns had burned themselves out, making it even darker than before. Leaving the music behind her, Maddy walked on, toward the sea, and leaned against the wall, feeling the pressure of the stone through her skirts. She smiled, seeing that the children were still down below, playing. Farther out on the still water, hundreds more boats bobbed; the voices of the people on them lilted across the waves, the scent of food grilling on charcoals, too. Maddy drew a long breath, soaking it all in. She wondered if she had time for a cigarette, decided she did, then cursed, remembering her dropped matches.

Returning to where she'd left them, she crouched on the cobbles, skimming the black stones with her hands. Finding nothing, she knelt properly, bending down to see. But no, they really weren't there.

"How bizarre," she said, and as her voice broke through the night, conspicuously loud in the silence, she realized that the music inside had stopped.

She looked back toward the club's illuminated doors, the silhouettes of the crowd within. Everyone appeared to be facing the clock. She could almost feel the press of bodies, the sweaty anticipation, and, tempted as she was to stay outside, she told herself that it really would be too sad to see the new year in alone, and that she'd better hurry if she wasn't to miss midnight. She gave the floor one last, hopeless scour, and, with a sigh of exasperation, stood and recrossed the shadowy terrace.

She could never say, afterward, what made her pause in her tracks, step sideways, and go by the table Peter had been at. Or why she reached out and touched the back of the chair his friend, the stranger, had sat in, remembering him all over again.

But, as her fingers closed around the wooden frame, she jumped, shocked by a surge of explosions—out at sea, along on the nearby beach, behind her in the city. She looked up, around, eyes on the fireworks everywhere, filling the air with smoke, the sky with cracking flashes of color.

Oh dear, she thought, *midnight,* then laughed anyway. Because it didn't feel sad to be outside, alone, not at all. It was far, far too beautiful for that.

From inside the club, cheers carried; the opening chords of "Auld Lang Syne" quickly followed. She didn't rush to leave, though, to join in. She didn't go anywhere. The fireworks kept coming: her own private show.

Had she noticed him already? Was that part of what made her stay?

She often wondered that, in the weeks ahead.

She didn't know. She wasn't sure when she first became aware of the outline of him there, a hundred or so yards away on the promenade, face toward her, hands in his pockets, linen jacket moving in the breeze.

But with the fireworks still exploding above, she felt her attention move toward him. Slowly, she brought her gaze down, tilted her chin over her bare shoulder.

Her eyes met his through the blackness, and this time she knew he smiled.

He raised his hand in a wave.

Not stopping to think, she raised hers.

It was a space of moments.

But nothing was ever the same again, after that.

CHAPTER TWO

Maddy waited for him to come back to the club's terrace, close the distance between them, let her see his face. *Hello.* She thought, from his wave, the slow way he dropped his hand, that he wanted to do that. She almost set off toward him. She even took a step, felt her muscles tense in anticipation of . . . something.

But then noise flooded the silence behind her, voices and laughter. She jolted, disorientated by the interruption. She'd all but forgotten that the party was even happening. Within a breath, she was surrounded by every-one spilling from the ballroom, their eyes to the igniting sky: no longer her own private anything.

"Maddy," her father called from the terrace doors. "There you are. Hurry over here and wish your old papa a happy new year. I've missed the last fifteen."

She didn't hurry anywhere. Distracted as she was, she barely managed a nod, a quick smile in her father's direction, before returning her attention to the promenade, just in time to see the stranger turn from her, walk away toward the city.

He was going?

Gone?

"Maddy," Richard called again. "What are you doing?"

She stared after the stranger a second longer, sure, even now, that he'd change his mind, turn around.

But he kept walking, into the darkness. Her brow creased.

"Maddy?"

Forcing herself, she dragged her gaze from the promenade, and went to join her father, back into the thick of the hot crowd.

She couldn't help but steal a final, curious glance in the stranger's direction, though. He'd already disappeared. She imagined him, just beyond her vision, pausing in his tracks, looking toward her. She really felt like he might be.

Why did he go?

She couldn't think. Or why it should matter to her so much. She only knew that it did. She didn't attempt to understand it.

It was simply the way it was.

She struggled to get back into the swing of things in the hour that followed. She'd barely been aware of the stranger's presence and yet, now that he was gone, she felt it. She couldn't even find Peter. She went in search of him—just as soon as she'd wished her father a happy new year—impatient to find out whatever he could tell her about his friend (who he was, for instance), but all she could discover was that Peter had left, too, off to another party.

"Social butterfly that he is," said a puce Della, still on the dance floor.

"Is he coming back?" Maddy asked, her voice flat to her own ears.

"I don't think so," said Della, pressing the heel of her hand to her dripping forehead. "He said he'd asked your papa to take me home. Now, are we going to find you someone else to dance with?"

Maddy wasn't sure she had it in her. Her feet suddenly felt too sore in her tight slippers, the heat oppressive.

When her mother came over not long after, telling her that she was going home, but that Richard would bring Maddy and Della later, Maddy found herself saying that if Alice didn't mind, she'd go with her now.

"Really?" said Alice, visibly surprised.

Maddy could hardly blame her. She was rather surprised herself. She did, after all, normally avoid being alone with her mother whenever possible. Those awful silences . . .

But, "Yes," she said. "I'm ready, I think."

She was. And even though one of the usual silences stretched for almost the entire journey home (tense, entirely uncompanionable), for once the awkwardness didn't bother her. Or at least, not as much. As the chauffeur drove them through the dark, tree-lined streets of Bombay's center, past the sandstone telegraph office, the grand British municipality buildings, the hidden alleyways where families lived ten to a room, jammed together in this city that never stopped and had more people than space, she stared sightlessly into the musty breeze, replaying his wave over and over again.

So lost was she in her reverie, it took her longer than it should have to realize that Alice was looking at her, an expectant expression on her shadowed face.

"Sorry," said Maddy, "did you say something?"

"I asked if Guy found you," Alice said.

"Guy?" said Maddy stupidly.

"He was looking for you," said Alice.

"I didn't speak to him all night."

"I think he wanted to dance."

"He didn't say," said Maddy.

"No?"

"No."

"A shame," said Alice.

"Yes," said Maddy.

So polite, both of them.

There was a short pause.

Maddy, thinking that must be it, turned, ready to resume her vigil of the black streets.

But, "Did you enjoy the fireworks?" Alice asked.

"I did," said Maddy, guarded now. Had Alice seen her, out there on the terrace? Seen him?

If she had, she gave no sign. "You used to love them," was all she said, "when you were little."

"Yes?"

"You don't remember?"

"I'm not sure," said Maddy. She'd been so young when she left, not even eight; there was so much that was hazy. "I remember Bonfire Night, in Christchurch Meadows—"

"I wouldn't know about that," said Alice, cutting her off.

It was her short tone, the look in her blue eyes. Maddy realized too late that it had, of course, been a mistake to mention Oxford. She felt like she should apologize.

But before she could, Alice leaned forward, tapped the driver on his shoulder, and told him to hurry along.

Another silence followed. Maddy couldn't ignore this one, or the set of Alice's slight shoulders beneath her shawl. She tried to think of something to say that might soften the new tension, but when she tentatively reopened the subject of the fireworks, asking, "Did we watch them here, in Bombay?" Alice's forehead pinched. "It really doesn't matter, Madeline," she said.

Maddy was relieved when they finally left the city behind and started the gentle coastal climb to the quieter, leafy roads of Malabar Hill, where so many British lived. Her parents' own villa—a cream three-storied mansion that was as beautiful as it was lonely, with wide verandas, balconies at every window, and palm-fringed lawns—was one of the largest, toward the top of the hill. She rested her head against the window, eyes blurring on the still sea below—invisible, but for the reflection of the moon, the stars—and waited to be back there. It didn't take long; free of any traffic, they sped past the other lantern-lit villas nestling in the jungle foliage, the odd late-night rickshaw, then slowed, pulling through the villa's iron gates, along the curved driveway. Alice sighed as they drew to a halt, apparently happy to be home, too. Maddy wasn't sure who, of the two of them, was out of the motor first. Neither of them paused for more than a brief good-night before taking the candles left on the porch and heading to their rooms.

Maddy closed her door, leaned back against it, and exhaled. *At last.* Crossing over to her bed, she set her candle down, drew back the folds of her mosquito net, and fell on the soft mattress. Outside, the cicadas clacked, the trees shivered. She pressed her hand to her rib cage, feeling the give of her corset, and closed her eyes. The instant she did, she saw him there again, on the promenade, as though he'd been waiting, just beneath the film of her subconscious.

Why *had* he left like that, so quickly, without a word?

Ridiculous, probably, that she was thinking of him as she was, when he had. And yet . . . that wave.

Was he thinking of her, too?

Her mind was still whirring when she woke the next morning, a pink dawn breaking through the shutters.

She rolled over, listening to the peacocks call in the garden, the repetitive swoosh of someone sweeping the veranda below. It was early, too early to be awake; she could tell from the muted light, the heaviness in her warm body. She stared through the rose-tinted veil of her mosquito net, considered trying to get back to sleep, then, knowing she'd never be able to, pushed herself up, dressed, and crept quietly downstairs.

Breakfast was already laid out in the shade of the veranda awning: freshly cut fruits beneath a fly net, sliced banana loaf, soft rolls from the local bakery, and bowls of creamy curd, honey, and pistachio nuts. Beyond, on the lawn, the peacocks strutted territorially, safe, for the moment, from the gardener's children, who would chase them later, trying to steal feathers from their tails.

Maddy slipped into one of the wicker chairs, poured herself a steaming coffee, and, realizing how hungry she was (she'd steered clear of the curry puffs the night before: the Christmas turkey . . .), helped herself to the banana loaf, a roll, and some honey.

She'd just taken her first mouthful when Ahmed, the same bearer who kept her supplied with cigarettes, appeared through the drawing room doors, dressed in a pristine white tunic, a paper package in his hands.

"Memsahib," he said.

He always called her that, even though she wasn't married, and had asked him countless times to use her name instead.

She did it again now. "It's Maddy," she said, swallowing, "please. Honestly, I keep thinking you must be talking to someone else."

He smiled (as he always did), then said "Memsahib" again, and held out the package. "This is coming for you."

"Me?"

His head wobbled.

She reached for it, assuming it must be from England, although she couldn't think who would have sent it. Aunt Edie, who had very little money left these days, had already posted talc for Christmas; Maddy's old college friends had clubbed together and sent a care package (fruitcake, custard powder, cocoa, and a box of Jacob's High Class Biscuits). Had Uncle Fitz remembered her? Had he really thought she'd want him to?

It seemed not.

The package wasn't from England at all. There wasn't even a stamp on it. She looked up at Ahmed. "Where did this come from?" she asked.

"A boy is bringing from the station," he said.

"The train station?"

Another head wobble.

"Bombay train station?" she asked. "The terminus?"

"The very same, memsahib."

Even more intrigued, she pulled the paper apart.

Then she felt a laugh break from her, just at the surprise of it. Because her box of matches was inside, a well-worn copy of *A Guide to Bombay*, too, a piece of paper on top.

The first letter he ever sent her.

I overheard your non-resolution for 1914. It's a very good one. I don't like to think of you being homesick. Hopefully this guide will help you enjoy your time in Bombay a little more, as it helped me when I used to live here.

It's a loan, Miss Bright. I shall be back to reclaim it.

And I saw you mislay these matches. I thought you might need them, perhaps they will help with the homesickness too.

Luke Devereaux

She laughed more, reading his words over, looking from them to the book and matches, then back to the paper.

Luke, she thought, tracing her thumb over his writing. *Luke Devereaux. I like it.*

She liked that he knew her name, too. That he'd found it out, found out where she lived. Heat spread through her skin as she realized that he must have asked someone—Peter, probably—even before he'd waved at her on the promenade. That he'd noticed her drop her matches, cared enough to collect them.

Seen her right from the very start.

Hand trembling, she turned the note over, wanting to see if there was an address, any clue as to where he'd gone.

There was nothing.

I shall be back, he'd said.

"When?" she said. "When will you be back?"

Ahmed looked at her warily, as though she were running mad.

She didn't care. All she could think of was that his name was Luke Devereaux. That he'd surprised her. Done this.

That he hadn't just disappeared.

He'd been thinking about her, too.

CHAPTER THREE

She became even more desperate to speak to Peter, of course. There was so much now that she wanted to know: how Peter knew Luke Devereaux, where Luke Devereaux was from, what train he'd taken . . . The list went on, multiplying. She'd see Peter that afternoon, she was sure. There was an officers' cricket match between the Hussars and the Gurkhas at the oval: a large, very British expanse of green surrounded by poinciana, palm, and banyan trees, adjacent to the university. She hadn't been particularly excited about the match, or a long afternoon in the middle of town shielded from the cooling sea breezes, but now couldn't wait to get there. She could talk to Peter then.

He wasn't there.

Everyone else from the party had come, lethargic on the rattan loungers lining the boundary, parasols propped on shoulders, flanneled legs crossed, clapping lazily at each four and six, but not him.

"Sick as a dog," said Della.

"The curry puffs?" said Maddy.

"The champagne, I suspect," said Della, who looked quite pale herself. "What do you need him for, anyway?"

"Nothing important," said Maddy. A lie, but, much as part of her yearned to confide, talk about it all, another, bigger, part held her back, even with Della, afraid that if she started picking over everything, it would ruin it. Besides, what was there really to tell? Just a wave, a parcel . . .

She thought about that parcel all through the sunbaked afternoon. She sat by Della's side in a deck chair, slowly cooking in her tea dress, and pictured it on her bedside table, rereading Luke Devereaux's note in her mind;

she already knew it by heart. The cricketers played on, knocking the ball around the yellowing grass field, but she wouldn't have been able to say who, of the Gurkhas or Hussars, were batting at any one time. She barely remembered to speak when Guy Bowen, dapper in a cream suit and boater, stopped by to say hello, cool lime sodas for her and Della in hand, and asked if they'd both had fun the night before.

"A little too much," said Della.

"I'm sorry I didn't get a dance," he said to Maddy, gray eyes crinkling.

"Next time," she said.

"I'll hold you to that," he called over his shoulder as he returned to where he'd been sitting, beneath the swaying cloth punkahs on the pavilion. "Already looking forward to it."

"Just like an uncle," said Della, stifling a yawn.

"Drink your drink," said Maddy.

For once, Della did as she was told. Luckily, she was too preoccupied with her own tiredness to go on, or expect much in the way of conversation for the rest of the match.

"Early nights all round, I think," said Richard, when it at last came to an end. (Who had won? Maddy hadn't the faintest; all she could think about was that she was within touching distance of returning to her room.)

She collapsed on her bed as soon as she got there, not even stopping to remove her hat, kick off her boots, before she started on Luke Devereaux's book. She had to put it down again for a bath, to dress for an early supper, but read it cover to cover that night, her head on the soft pillow, the shutters open, dragonflies fluttering invisibly in the darkness beyond. She turned the pages slowly, lingering over the tantalizing descriptions of temples and markets, seeing them in her mind's eye. She thought how strange it was that he must have done the same once. That she now had his book, and knew nothing about him, hadn't even met him.

Not yet.

She finished the final page and let the book fall shut on her chest. Eyelids heavy, she told herself that it didn't matter that she hadn't managed to speak to Peter. She was always seeing him, she wouldn't have to wait long. Her eyes closed. She could talk to Peter soon.

But the very next morning, before she was even fully dressed, her father stopped by her room to tell her that he'd had word from the viceroy: he was needed for business in Delhi, from there for a goodwill tour of the independent princely states. "There's been a lot of change with our residents lately," he said. "We need to smooth things over, keep 'the kings' onside. I'm taking Peter, too. I've just been to see him. He's meeting me at the terminus. We'll be gone a couple of months."

Maddy stared, hairpin halfway to her head. Was he joking?

He didn't look like he was joking. In fact, he was looking at her like it was all about to get worse.

"Della's going to tag along," he said.

"What?" said Maddy.

"I'm sorry."

"You're all going?"

"We'll be back before you know it."

"No you won't." She dropped her hairpin on the bureau, the full enormity of two months ahead, just her and her mother, sinking in. There'd be no prospect of her father coming home each evening to look forward to, no Della. . . . "Can't I go as well?" she asked, slightly desperately.

"Your mama would prefer you stay here."

"Why?" Maddy asked, baffled.

"She missed you, darling, all that time you were away."

"She never visited," said Maddy. "Only once. . . ."

"I've told you, she had her reasons."

Maddy didn't ask what those reasons had been. She'd done that enough over the years. Richard would never say, nor would Aunt Edie. *It's not my story to tell.*

"I can't believe you're all leaving me here," she said.

"I'll miss you," said Richard, "but honestly, you don't want to come to Delhi. It will be chilly at this time of year, very dull."

It's absolutely ripping fun, Della wrote, several days later, days in which, with the city in a post-Christmas lull, Maddy hardly left the house, then only for evening drinks with her mother and Guy at everyone's favorite watering hole, the Gymkhana Club, and, out of desperation, back at the club again for a sweltering morning tea of scones and stale cucumber sandwiches on the long, lower terrace with Alice and her fellow memsahibs.

(So much moaning about one's servants, the cost of flour, and the constant battle of keeping food safe from the red ants. "Table legs in water," said a wife from the army cantonment, Diana Aldyce, "it's the only way. If I've told Cook once, I've told him a thousand times." If Maddy had heard it once . . .) *We're staying at the viceroy's house,* Della went on, *which is essentially a palace. He throws the most marvelous drinks parties and dinners for us every night, with more brandy and gin than even Peter can drink. We're leaving for Rajasthan tomorrow, first stop a hunting lodge in Ranthambore. There's talk of a tiger safari. Tigers, Maddy.*

Maddy wrote by return.

You're very heartless, she said, *but tell me more, anyway, so I can live vicariously.*

She watched the silver post tray each morning for Della's reply, or something from Aunt Edie, one of her friends back in Oxford; anything to break the hot monotony of her days with her mother. The two of them echoed around the too-large villa, coming together only for meals, where—but for the occasional comment on the growing heat (Alice), ponderings as to what everyone must be doing in the north (Maddy)—they spoke very little. Unable to bear it, Maddy spent most of her time wherever Alice was not, moving from her room to read on the veranda, play the piano in the drawing room, outside for yet another walk among the butterflies and peacocks in the garden. The nights were hardly better. Although the usual round of Bombay soirées, music recitals, and dances picked up again, and she went along, if only to be doing *something,* they weren't the same with everyone gone. Whenever she escaped for a cigarette at the Yacht Club, she missed Della more. Each time she took out her matches, she turned them slowly in her hand and thought of Luke Devereaux. Sometimes she considered taking his advice, using his guidebook to get out and explore—her yearning for England, the green parks, warm, buzzy cafés, Aunt Edie (even, in her lowest moments, Uncle Fitz) was only worsening—but she kept telling herself, *I'll go tomorrow.* As the days rolled by, though, pushing New Year's further into the past, she didn't go anywhere. The second week of January became the third, and gradually she started to doubt Luke Devereaux ever would come back to reclaim his guidebook. It was far easier, in the baking loneliness of the villa, to believe that he must have forgotten all about her.

It was on a rare cloudy Monday toward the end of the month that she drifted down to breakfast, went to check the post, then paused, seeing a sepia postcard on the pile of embossed envelopes. It was a picture of a dirt street, women in saris, rickshaws, and a cluster of elephants. She picked it up, turned it over to check who it was from (she assumed either Della or her father in Rajasthan), then squealed in disbelief.

Hello from Secunderabad,
I find myself wondering if you're putting my book to good use, Miss Bright. I hope so. I'm looking forward to a full report. Go down to the tank at the base of your hill if you haven't found it yet. It has water from the Ganges in it, and the Hindis meet to scatter their loved ones' ashes. Or, for something a little less deathly, try the spice markets.
 Meanwhile, here's a taste of somewhere else for you to discover one day.

              Luke Devereaux

She held the card to her bodice, then tipped it away again, looking back down, just to make sure it was real.

It was.

It really, really was.

"You look happy," said Alice, coming out of the drawing room.

"I am," said Maddy, forgetting for a moment who she was talking to, too ecstatic for inhibitions. "I'm just about over the moon." She read the card once more—*I'm looking forward to a full report*—and, on an impulse, said, "Could I borrow the motor?"

Alice reached for the coffee. "What for?"

"To explore."

Alice filled her cup, then added milk, freshly squeezed from the kitchen cow. "Explore where?"

"Bombay," said Maddy.

"I realize that, Madeline, but where in Bombay?"

"I don't know," said Maddy, who'd remembered now who she was talking to, and that it wasn't someone who invited confidences, least of all about Luke Devereaux's book. "There's so much I haven't seen."

"You can't go out alone," said Alice. "I could go with you . . ."

"Or Ahmed?" said Maddy, too quickly.

Alice didn't appear to notice her haste. In fact, she smiled. It was one of the truest Maddy had seen from her. It suited her, softening her delicate face.

Maddy almost smiled, too.

But then, "How about Guy?" Alice said.

Exploring with Guy was hardly what Maddy had had in mind. She suspected it wasn't what Luke Devereaux had intended either. Alice was adamant, though. She even suggested they invite Guy for dinner that night. "We can ask him then."

"It's really not necessary," said Maddy. "No need to go to the trouble of dinner."

They ate in the candlelit dining room, the windows ajar, balmy air wafting in.

Guy had come straight from the hospital, but had still changed into evening tails. He nodded along as Alice told him that Maddy was in need of a guide, listening in that gentle way of his. Maddy, examining him in the glow of the flickering candles, couldn't deny that with his dark pomaded hair, fine-boned face, and closely shaved jaw, he looked well; there'd be many besides Della who'd think him on the heavenly side. Not that she'd ever concede that to Della, who'd have a field day with the admission (if she ever returned from her ripping fun hunting tigers). Maddy didn't really like to think about it. She wasn't sure why she was. She jostled her shoulders, shaking the awkward musing away.

Guy smiled across at her. "Maddy," he said, "I wish you'd said something before. I'd love to show you around. We can go in the mornings, before it gets too hot."

"You're so busy," said Maddy.

"It will be my pleasure," he said. "There are some perks to being in charge. I'll juggle things around."

"Really," Maddy insisted, "it's too much to ask."

He called twice weekly from then on, pulling up in his open-topped motor, glass bottles of boiled water in the trunk, their itinerary for the morning ready-planned. He told her that, truly, she didn't want to visit the nearby water tank—"I'm afraid the men can't be relied on not to disrobe before wading in with the ashes"—and took her to the most British of landmarks instead: the Victoria Gardens, Flora Fountain, the esplanade— all places she'd been to with her father, not one of which was referenced in Luke Devereaux's book. Guy didn't ask if there was anywhere else she wanted to visit. In fairness, he probably assumed that, having been back so short a time, she didn't have many ideas. And he'd gone to such lengths to help her, she was loath to hurt his feelings by telling him how much he missed the mark with his excursions. So she went along with him, said how marvelous it was to be out and about, listened to his tales of the hospital, laughing in earnest when he told her about a snake who'd got into the operating theater, how he'd had to finish an appendectomy, one eye on it curled up in the corner, and chatted in turn when he questioned her about her friends back in Oxford, whether she'd eaten at the Lyons Corner House on St. Giles (absolutely), or gone to the moving pictures (once or twice; her aunt Edie was an avid Calamity Anne fan). She didn't *not* enjoy the mornings out. They just weren't anything like what she'd hoped to do.

She resolved to take matters into her own hands. (If you want something done, and all that.) Every Monday, her mother left in the motor for one of her memsahib teas, which lasted a good few hours. It was enough time to do something. Maddy had only ever occasionally accompanied Alice before, so it was hardly out of the ordinary for her to elect not to do so now. She waited for her to leave, then pinned her hat into place, asked Ahmed to hail her a rickshaw (for a small fee), and off she went.

The first outing, she didn't go far, just a few minutes down the road to the water tank, which she'd pictured as a tiny affair hidden in the trees, but was as wide as a river with long sloping steps framing it, the sea just beyond, and shrines all around. Men (who did indeed have a tendency to disrobe) were having their hair shorn beside it, she presumed as part of their grieving ritual. ("Yes, memsahib," said Ahmed later, "it is a way to make sacrifice.") More were in the water itself, scattering their urns while hundreds of women and children watched from the stairs. For herself, she kept well back, sharply aware of not belonging there, unwilling to intrude, holding her breath at the otherworldliness before her, feeling, for the first time since she'd arrived back in October, the thrill of being in *India.*

Buoyed by the wonder of it, she planned to go farther afield the following Monday, take a rickshaw to the tram, from there into town and the spice market.

It wasn't a success.

She'd gone out alone all the time back in England. Aunt Edie had never been the kind to insist on a chaperone, and at college they'd all been left to it by their tutors (who were far more concerned with who was attending the next suffrage rally than whether social niceties were being observed). But the broiling, unfamiliar streets of Bombay were hardly the cobbled alleyways of Oxford; to her mortification, she didn't get much farther than the central tram stop. She hailed another rickshaw there, but after a minute of the driver weaving hectically through the camels, carts, and motor horns, she gave in to her nerves and told him she wouldn't go all the way to the markets after all, she'd visit a nearby mosque instead. Flustered as she was, she felt horribly conspicuous as she stepped onto the heaving pavements outside the ornate domed building, too painfully conscious of her pale skin, blond hair, and cream dress. It got worse as she walked around the mosque's gold-painted walls. She peered through the archways at the bald Jain monks praying within (*Very good,* she thought, *you've seen another something new*), pushed on around the walled gardens—countless eyes on her as the women, who sat in the shade eating rice from betel leaves, scrutinized her like the interloper she was—and somehow lasted a half hour.

Her corset was soaked with her own anxious sweat by the time she returned home.

Ridiculous, she told herself.

She made it to those spice markets on her next trip. She had to draw a resolute breath before ducking through the low-beamed doorway into the cavernous warehouse, but duck in she did. She looked up from beneath the brim of her straw hat, eyes adjusting to the dim light, her ears to the intense noise: vendors shouting their prices, hundreds of locals haggling. The air was dense with trapped sunshine, a heady cocktail of paprika, saffron, turmeric, and cardamom. A shirtless boy hared past, barrow full of sacks, and she stepped back clumsily, only just avoiding being mown down (*Not entirely less deathly,* she wanted to tell Luke Devereaux), then, gathering herself, walked on, down the first pungent alleyway of stalls, full of bags brimming with chilies, feeling the heat catch at her throat, her lungs. Her eyes streamed, and she started to cough, fighting for air. The vendors laughed and, realizing what she must look like, she tried to laugh, too, but coughed more. One older man grinned and held out a chili, gesturing for her to come forward. "It good," he said, "no fire, this one." She went, hesitantly, and took a small bite, fully expecting to lose the lining of her mouth. But, "It *is* good," she said, hearing her own relief. "Yes," she smiled, "good." Others called out to her, offering cinnamon, aniseed, allspice. She tried it all, thanking them, *dhanyavaad,* and found herself wandering on, farther and farther into the furor, stopping to buy a chittack of saffron for Edie, ginger for Cook.

She stayed longer than half an hour.

And this time she counted the days until her next adventure, to Elephanta Island in Bombay Harbour: *Gharapuri,* Luke Devereaux's book read, *the city of caves. Catch a boat from the quay and leave the heat of the city behind as you enter into these dark, echoing chambers of stone deities.* She wasn't the only European this time; they filled the cool caves, commenting with cut-glass consonants on Shiva's many carved faces, how different it all was to anything one had seen before. Maddy, lost in the beauty of the statues, the thought of the sculptors who'd stood where she stood, all those hundreds of years before, forgot they were there.

The next week, she went to the tomb, Haji Ali Dargah. *Make sure to arrive at low tide, when a narrow causeway will appear, taking you to the* dargah. She walked across the strip of rocky earth, rammed between jostling, sweaty hordes of other pilgrims, the sea all but touching the hem of her skirts. The white domes of the mosque sparkled, stark against the blue sky, the green palms surrounding it. Children ran up to her, some shyly eyeing her and then scampering away, others asking to touch her gown, her hair. She stooped, letting them, laughing at their astonishment, their excitement. The week following, she visited the huge outdoor laundries at Dhobi Ghat, staring herself, at the men, the dhobis, who worked without stopping in the sunshine, bent over the deep stone baths, scrubbing and slapping the mountains of linen: the vibrant garments of wealthy Indians, uniforms from the army, bedding from Bombay's hotels and hospitals.

She ached to write to Luke Devereaux and tell him about all she was seeing. *It's helped, so much.*

Thank you.

She had no address, though. Her letters, her thanks, remained in her head.

He kept writing to her, though. Every week or so, a new postcard arrived, making her catch her breath with delight. A long sandy beach in Pondicherry (*I think one of my favorites in India. You haven't lived, Miss Bright, until you've eaten a freshly baked pastry, watching the sunrise here*), then, in early February, locals making flower garlands at a stall in Madras (*If you were here, perhaps I'd have bought you one. Would you have liked that, I wonder? Why do I keep wondering such things?*); later in the month came a majestic government house in Calcutta (*Note the ubiquitous cows outside, reminding everyone who this country really belongs to*), tigers in Bengal followed (*How are you getting on with your tour?*).

Della wrote as well, full of tales of elephant treks, feasts in kings' palaces, their wives (*plural*) hidden behind screens, as did Richard (less effusively, always hopeful that Maddy was all right, getting along with Alice, full of apologies that the trip had been extended, *it will be late March at least before we're home*), but it was the possibility of another card from Luke Devereaux on the post tray that made Maddy wake earlier each morning, dress hastily, then pick up her skirts and jog down the stairs, eager for the day when one would arrive telling her something of himself, why he was on these cross-country travels, and when, oh when, Bombay was going to be his next port of call.

February gave way to March, and the heat built by the day, toward the summer monsoon. Guy took her for another walk in the gardens, warned her off eating kulfi from a street vendor, and then for a trip to see some very sad-looking animals at the zoo.

"No," he agreed, "they don't look like they're having much fun. I'm not sure we are either. How about a long glass of something cold at the Gymkhana Club?"

March crept on, edging toward April. . . . Maddy went to the docks to see the ground being prepared for the new Gateway of India—hundreds of sweating workers hauling rocks, dark skin gleaming in the dusty sunshine—avoided the Taj's Sea Lounge and drank chai at a corner shop instead (*The best you'll find in Bombay*), then visited more neighborhood mosques, the coriander-scented alleyways of Crawford Market. She kept checking the post, always hoping, feeling a little flatter every time the words she'd been waiting for failed to arrive.

Until, at last, they did.

On the back of a postcard from Poona: camels by a palm-fringed lake.

As you can see, I'm a lot closer now to Bombay. I would like, very much, to see you, Miss Bright. Would you meet me? There's a small coffee shop not far from the terminus (the start of chapter five, if memory serves). I shall be there at noon on Tuesday.

Will you?

CHAPTER FOUR

King's Fifth Military Convalescent Hospital, Surrey, 1915

He arrived just before luncheon, on an arctic November morning. The ambulance that brought him progressed cautiously up the winding, icy driveway, wipers flipping back and forth, clearing snowy semicircles on the windshield. Sister Emma Lytton, who'd come onto the hospital's front stairs to wait for him, jigged on the spot, rubbing the sleeves of her Queen Alexandra's uniform in a futile effort to keep warm. She was a seasoned nurse—fifteen years now in the service, as many months of which had been in this hideous war—and ordinarily, in these final few minutes before a patient's admission, would be focused on nothing but them, running through their notes in her mind. Today, though, all she could think about were the roaring coal fires inside, and that she'd left them a little prematurely.

"Come on," she instructed the lumbering vehicle, her voice leaving her in a cloud of fog. "Do come on."

The ambulance maintained the same sloth-like speed.

She consoled herself that the patient's room would be cozy, at least. She'd had one of the VADs stoke the fire, put a ceramic hot-water bottle between the sheets. A new girl herself, the VAD had wanted to know how they could be sure this patient—Officer Jones, they were to call him, Officer Tommy Jones (it wasn't his name; no one knew his name)—wasn't a spy.

"What if he's lying about his memory?" she'd said. "What if the Boche has sent him here to find out our secrets?"

"Our secrets in Surrey?" Emma had said. "Silly girl. The poor man's just lost."

The VAD had turned scarlet, spoken not another word as she refolded the corners of Officer Jones's sheets.

Emma wished now she hadn't snapped. It was the long nights, the men waking constantly, screaming at their ghosts, then the short winter days trying to coax them into walks, conversation. And now this cold snap, which had frozen the old hospital's pipes solid . . . Emma realized there were a lot more having to put up with a lot worse (she remembered them every evening in her prayers), but still, it all took a toll. She resolved to find the VAD later, take her some fruitcake from the sisters' larder and apologize; it was hardly her fault she was so naive. Comforting really, when one stopped and thought, that the girl had managed to retain some innocence in this world run mad; that she'd still been green enough to believe espionage likelier than a catastrophic head wound.

The ambulance crunched to a halt, interrupting Emma's sad thoughts. She gave her arms one more vigorous rub, and watched the driver—another young woman, this time in the belted khaki jacket, calf-length skirt, and cloth cap of the First Aid Nursing Yeomanry—climb down from the cabin.

"Good morning," Emma called.

"Is it?" the FANY replied, rather curtly, lending weight to Matron's oft-aired theories about the type of girl one might expect to operate a motor vehicle. "Too damn cold."

"Nothing a cocoa won't fix," said Emma, wincing inwardly at her own jolly tone, the same one she always found herself using with her most morose patients.

The FANY wasn't won over. (The patients never were either.) "I feel like my toes have fallen off," she said, and stomped her feet, presumably to reclaim feeling, then made off round to the back of the ambulance to open the red-crossed doors.

She swung them wide and said something indiscernible to the patient inside. Emma clasped her hands in front of her and waited for him to appear, but there was a delay. Emma felt a brief stab of panic. What if Officer Jones was less mobile than she'd been led to expect? She didn't have a bath chair with her. Matron had assured her one wasn't needed, but what if Matron had been wrong? Mistakes *did* happen. What if this man's head wound *had* affected his movement? She would have to leave him in his freezing cabin with this taciturn driver while she went in search of an orderly. What a start. Why on earth hadn't she erred on the safe side? *Be prepared for every eventuality.* It was her motto, one she passed on to all her probationers, and now here she was, not prepared at all.

She was still berating herself when Officer Jones appeared at the doors in an army greatcoat, his back to her, perfectly agile. She permitted herself a brief, icy exhale, but before her relief was halfway out of her mouth, he turned, looking up at the hospital's sandstone façade, and she stopped, staring, even though she knew one should never, ever stare.

It took her a few seconds to realize she was even doing it.

Then a few more for her to understand why.

It wasn't about his face, certainly. Perfectly drawn as his handsome features were, she wasn't one for going weak at the knees over such things. (Not anymore.) No, no. It was something quite different about this officer that took her aback.

Slowly, it came to her. Exhausted as he evidently was (she saw the telltale bruises shadowing his strong face, all too clearly), he didn't look ill. Not at all. Not in the way her other patients did, with their eyes that had seen too much, shoulders that sagged and hunched, that waxiness to their skin. Officer Jones, he seemed so . . . so . . . *alive.* His spine was straight, his shoulders square, and his fists clenched in a way that spoke of so much vigor that she, who prided herself after fifteen years in the service (fifteen years!) of being nigh on unshakable, almost blurted out that he must have come to the wrong place.

The FANY coughed pointedly, making Emma realize just how long she'd been staring. She felt heat spread through her frozen skin at her own lack of professionalism, then even more as she caught the FANY's smirk, and realized the conclusion she'd leaped to.

I swear it's not about that, she yearned to correct the girl, *there's nothing left in me for any of that.*

She said nothing, of course. She'd made quite enough of a spectacle. (What would Matron think?) Sternly reminding herself that she was a nursing sister, Officer Jones her patient, and, whatever his appearance, anything but in the pink of health, she returned her attention to him. *A hemorrhage of the mind,* Dr. Arnold always said, *can be just as critical as one of the blood.* She repeated the words silently, then again for good measure, willing her embarrassment away. *Pull yourself together.* She took a step toward Officer Jones, who after all had served, given so much, and deserved the same care and compassion as all her other boys. The kind she hoped her darling fiancé, Freddie, had been given before he was taken at the Marne.

The sort she needed to believe her younger brother, Billy, had known in his casualty clearing station at Loos. (No lying unattended, thirsty and in agony on a stretcher; please, not that.)

She drew a sharp breath against the torturous, always ready images, and forced her attention onto Officer Jones instead, watching as he grasped the ambulance's doorframe, jumped down onto the icy gravel, his posture proud. With her mind still half clinging to Freddie and Billy, she felt her heart swell for the soldier before her, this lonely, suffering man.

"Officer Jones," she said.

He winced. She wasn't sure why. The long journey getting on top of him, maybe. *Nothing a cocoa won't fix.* She took a step forward, ignoring the snow that seeped through her nurse's hood, the shoulders of her cape, and held out her hand in anticipation of taking Officer Jones's arm, leading him inside.

The poor man's just lost, she'd told that VAD.

Not anymore, she assured herself now.

He'd found her.

She'd look after him.

He was quiet as they left the driveway, talking only to thank the ambulance driver in a low, well-spoken voice, and then to assure Emma that he didn't need her hand for help, really, and he could carry his own small bag. "I insist."

Emma, well used to brevity from her patients, was also well practiced in filling silences. As she led Officer Jones into the hospital's warm, paneled entranceway that smelled of smoke, bacon from the basement kitchens, and Jeyes Fluid, she chatted, saying what a tonic it must be for him to be out of that cold ambulance. He didn't reply. Thinking he probably hadn't had much in the way of companionship from that driver, she decided he'd benefit from some light relief before his initial session with Dr. Arnold. She was meant to be taking him straight there, but . . .

"Why don't we go on a little tour?" she said.

"A tour?" he said.

"Yes, why not? Leave your things here, yes, just by the stairs. I'll have them sent to your room."

"I can take them. . . ."

"No, no need. Now, if you come this way."

She walked on, skirt swishing across the large front hall, past the burning oil lamps and open fire, to the dining room, with its mahogany table to seat twenty. "There are three sittings for every meal," she said, "and we mix them up to keep everything sociable." She didn't add how little anyone talked at dinnertimes, or how many subjects had had to be banned from conversation (France, Belgium, Kitchener, the Boche . . . really anything to do with the war); plenty of time for him to find that out. Pressing forward, she took him to the drawing room, full of armchairs, landscape paintings, a handful of patients in their blues, and a silent gramophone. She told Jones they had to keep it off whenever certain patients were downstairs, and stopped, distracted briefly by the most damaged of them all: a tragic captain who wore a mask over his poor jaw and skull, wept whenever his mother visited, never wanted to let her go, and shook uncontrollably all the time.

"What happened to him?" Jones asked, following her gaze.

She hesitated, then lied, telling him she wasn't sure, loath to upset him with the grim detail. With a sigh, she moved them quickly on, to the library. "See, we have a billiards table. Do you play?"

"Billiards?" he said, and the muscles in his cheeks tensed, she wasn't sure whether in the start of a smile or a frown. "I don't know."

"Of course," she said, cursing herself for her insensitivity. (It had been a frown, it must have been a frown.) "Well," she said, "I'm sure we can find a friend to teach you."

He looked at the table, the bookshelves, appearing to ruminate.

"Would you—" she began.

"I wonder," he said, cutting her off before she could offer to take him to the arts and crafts room, "might I go to my room? It's been a long morning."

"You must see Dr. Arnold first," she said, "but I was going to show you the—"

"Dr. Arnold?" For the first time, he looked straight at her. "Now?"

"Well, yes," she said, "he's waiting to meet you."

"Then please, let's not keep him."

"Of course," she said, "of course."

She offered her hand again, but he didn't notice, so she let it drop and led the way across the library, through the far oak door, toward the doctor's rooms.

Officer Jones was quieter yet as they progressed down the hospital's back corridors, his attention fixed on the foggy, lead-lined windows and falling snow outside. Afraid that his thoughts might be running to the maudlin (why wouldn't they? poor man), Emma tried to distract him with some history, and told him that the building had been a manor in Elizabethan times, but had been made into a military hospital the year before, specifically for head wounds. (She omitted to mention that it had previously been a lunatic asylum for hysterical women; as with the dearth of dinnertime conversation, it seemed for the best.)

She came to a halt outside Dr. Arnold's door. "Here we are," she said, unnecessarily. "The doctor will ring for me when you're finished, and I'll take you upstairs."

"Thank you," Officer Jones said, "you're very kind."

"Not at all," said Emma, and, despite his distracted air, felt another swelling in her chest. "It's my absolute pleasure."

He watched her bustle away, taking her chatter, her well-intentioned smiles, and her talk of manor houses with her. (He knew the hospital had been a lunatic asylum; the ambulance driver had told him. "There's talk it's haunted," she'd said, with merciful disregard for his shattered nerves.) Once he was certain Sister Lytton was gone, he breathed deep, steadying himself with the silence, then raised his fist to knock on the doctor's door. Exhausted as he was, he was happy to be doing it. He'd been waiting impatiently for his space at the King's Fifth ever since his doctor at the London General had told him of Arnold's reputation as a miracle worker.

Jones (he loathed the name, but he'd learned to think of himself by it; to accept the unsettling sense of its wrongness, having no idea what was right) needed a miracle. He wasn't sure how he was going to endure living in this morose, echoing place—the way those men in the drawing room had slouched in their chairs; the one who'd been shaking—but he had to believe that Arnold would help him leave, to mend.

Remember.

He needed, so desperately, to remember.

The door opened. A lean, elderly man peered out. He had neatly combed white hair, an even whiter mustache, and wore slacks, a bow tie, and a waistcoat, a knitted cardigan over it all. He smiled, tipping his head so that he could look over the top of his spectacles. "Here you are," he said, "I've been watching the clock." He stepped back and extended his arm into the book-lined study. "In he comes."

He hadn't called him Officer Jones. Or Tommy. Or Tom.

Jones liked him for it instantly.

Arnold gestured at the armchair to his left, next to the fire. Jones crossed over to it. It was warm in the room, such a contrast to the drafty corridor, the snowy outside. His skin, still acclimatizing, prickled beneath his convalescent blues.

Arnold poured them both tea. "Have you worked out how you take it?" he asked.

Jones gave a small smile. "Just milk."

"Same as me," said Arnold, "excellent. Now let me tell you about what we're going to do. . . ."

He said that their session that morning would be brief, not even an hour. Subsequent ones would be longer, but he didn't want to exhaust him. "I know you must be very, very tired."

Jones was. Tired was all he could recall being.

"I'll do most of the talking today," Arnold went on, and was true to his word. He told Jones that all fifty-two men at the King's Fifth were suffering from neurological disorders. Some had lost part of their memory, some—like Jones—all of it; others held on to far too much. "I can't decide which is the lesser of the two evils," Arnold said.

"Perhaps they're both as bad," suggested Jones, who'd shared a room in London with an officer whose mind was locked in France, the trenches. He couldn't leave and woke screaming, all the time, trying to claw invisible rats from his skin.

"Yes," said Arnold. "Maybe I'll write a book on it one day. However," he reached behind him for a leather-bound journal, "this one is for you. As I'm sure you've been told, we operate gently here. No shock therapy, no intervention, just . . . care, coaxing for your mind. The pages here," he raised the journal, "are blank, waiting for your memories." He held it out for Jones to take. "Anything that comes to you," he said, "jot it down directly. View your past as a puzzle, one you must slot together. Don't let any piece slide away."

"I don't have any pieces," Jones said.

"None?"

Jones hesitated.

"What is it?" Arnold leaned forward, cloudy eyes sparking, the springs in his chair creaking.

"They're just dreams," said Jones.

"There's no such thing as 'just dreams,'" Arnold said. "Tell me about them."

"It's hard to describe." Jones stared into the fire, reliving the way he'd wake, covered in sweat, more often than not crying or panting with frustration, his mind a kaleidoscope that never came into focus. "I don't see anything that means anything."

"What do you see?"

"I can't say exactly." How to put word to those anonymous voices, the faceless faces?

"Feel then?" said Arnold, persisting.

"Heat," Jones said. "I think I was somewhere hot."

Arnold nodded, gaze unwavering. "Anything else?"

Another hesitation. Should he say?

Was there any point?

"Tell me," Arnold urged. "What can it cost you?"

Jones sighed. What could it cost him?

He'd already lost it all.

"There was a woman," he said at length. "I'm sure there was a woman."

"Yes," said Arnold, and smiled sadly. "There generally is."

He dreamed of her again that night.

He had his own room. He was grateful for that, for the silence. It was warm, carpeted, with a bureau, a reading lamp, and a view over the snowy front lawns. There was a hot-water bottle in the bed. He'd been in far worse, these past months.

Dreamed in far worse.

After a silent dinner ("I've squeezed you into the first sitting," Sister Lytton told him when she came to collect him, "there's trifle for dessert"), he'd escaped to it, with barely the energy to undress and wash before he fell into his bed. He lost consciousness within seconds. He always did. He didn't know how long it took for the dream to begin, but soon it was all he knew. He left the ice, the dark, and felt heat beat on his face, his shoulders.

He was in a tight street; buildings hemmed him in on both sides, colored canopies obscured the sun's glare. Crowds of people surrounded him. There was a woman, in a lemon dress, a straw hat, buttery waves.

It was her.

He was sure it was her.

He pushed his way toward her. He was trying to run.

She kept walking, faster, faster, disappearing.

He stopped, climbing onto a stone step, chest rising, falling. Then he saw her again. Too far away, a man in front of her, grinning toothlessly. He felt himself open his mouth, fill his lungs. He thought he might be about to call a name, her name . . .

His eyes snapped open. Awake. Blackness surrounded him; a heartless contrast to the color of the place he'd just left. He blinked, trying to recollect where he was now. His skin, beneath his sheets, was soaked. His pulse raced. His toe touched the cold hot-water bottle, and he remembered he was at the King's Fifth.

The dream was already retreating, gone as quickly as it had come.

Shakily, he reached for his journal, and noted down the only things he could recall.

Toothless man.
Noise.
A market?

He let the pencil fall from his hand, and sank his head back on his damp pillow.

He didn't know what any of it could mean.

CHAPTER FIVE

Bombay, Spring 1914

Luke Devereaux's postcard arrived on a Saturday, leaving three days until he'd be waiting for Maddy in that coffee shop. *Three days.* It seemed at once an age, and terrifyingly, thrillingly close. Maddy couldn't make herself believe it would truly happen. Even as she planned how to escape the villa without questions from her mother (she decided to say she was meeting Guy for lunch at the Gymkhana Club; Alice would inevitably discover the lie, but Maddy could worry about that then), it seemed too surreal that she'd truly do it. She tried to imagine how it would be: herself walking into the unknown coffee shop and finding Luke Devereaux there; the two of them at a table, breathing the same air, looking one another in the eye, speaking about . . . what? She didn't know. A shiver of pure nerves shot through her, every time she thought of it.

She couldn't settle to anything that endless, baking weekend. With the exception of church at St. Thomas's Cathedral on Sunday morning, she and Alice spent the entire time at home. There wasn't a polo or cricket match to break things up, no evening drinks nor dinner party to go to. The heat bore down relentlessly from the cloudless sky, scalding the lawn, the palms and jungle beyond, turning the villa's shuttered rooms into so many ovens: all thick golden light and floating dust.

Maddy looked for distractions. She took several baths, enjoying the brief respite of the cool water, the freedom from her corset and stockings. She tried to read, but found herself constantly going over the same paragraph, taking none of the sentences in. She started a letter to Aunt Edie—*How are you, up there in Scotland? Have there been any signs of spring springing? I hate to think of you so alone. I wish you could come out to stay, that you'd let me at least ask Mama . . .* —but ran out of steam before she finished the first, sweat-smudged page. She began another to Della—*When on earth are you coming back?*—then gave up on that, too. Her eyes strayed to Luke Devereaux's postcard on her writing desk, the slant of those words.

I shall be there at noon on Tuesday.

Will you?

Did he realize how little he needed to ask?

She drifted from her desk to her closet, where she spent a shameful amount of time agonizing over which gown would be best for a coffee shop. (What would Sylvia Pankhurst think?) She took countless walks, fanning herself in the dappled shade of the garden's trees, and even, on a whim, went back to the kitchen to see if she could help Cook bake his Sunday Victoria sponge.

"Memsahib," he said, "you are not liking my food?"

"What?" she said. "No."

He stared. "No, you are not liking?"

"No, I am liking, I am. . . ."

He dropped his gaze to the workbench (legs in bowls of water, not a red ant to be seen), jaw set.

"Oh God," said Maddy, "truly, I just wanted to help. I love your food, especially that turkey curry at Christmas. . . ."

He closed his eyes.

She left.

The weekend wasn't a complete disaster. There was one happy occurrence, care of Alice, strangely enough.

It was late on Sunday, just as the scalding sun was dipping toward dusk, bathing the villa's lawn in ethereal light, and the sky behind the palms and dense jungle in a rush of red, purple, and gold. Kites swarmed in flocks from the villa's rooftop to the trees, their battering wings and the clack of the cicadas' chorus mixing with the laughter of the gardener's children playing chase with the peacocks on the grass. Maddy, who'd been watching the three children from the veranda, decided they could do with a distraction, too. Fetching Alice's oil paints from the drawing room, she sent them all in search of white stones, then sat with them on the lawn, covering the stones with color: monkeys, polka dots, patterns of every description. (She hoped the peacocks were grateful.)

They'd worked their way through about half of the stones when Alice came down to see what they were all up to. She approached so quietly that Maddy didn't realize she was there until she spoke.

"I used to paint like this with you, Madeline," she said.

Maddy turned, meeting her eye. She was already dressed for dinner in a high-necked white gown, and had her arms folded as she bent, peering over Maddy's shoulder.

"We always used to do it," Alice went on, talking as much to herself, Maddy thought, as to her.

"I remember," Maddy said, because she did. Unlike with the fireworks, the recollection of her hours cushioned on Alice's lap, Alice's chin on her head, her child's hand guided by Alice's slender fingers, was one she'd held on to. She'd even taken some of the stones they'd made together to England, struggling, the older she got, to reconcile the memory of that lap with the mother who never visited. "You painted orchids," she said. "You were rather good at it."

Alice smiled one of her rare smiles. "Was I?"

Impulsively, Maddy held out her brush. "Why don't you see if you still are?"

She didn't expect Alice to agree. She was sure she'd demur, hold up her hands and refuse in the same way she'd turned Richard's dance down at New Year's.

But Alice reached out for the brush. She gathered up her lace skirts, knelt down on the coarse grass, and asked the youngest of the children to pick her a nice flat stone. "Yes, Suya, perfect." She ran her thumb over it, finding the smoothest surface, then dipped the brush in magenta, and proceeded to paint the most graceful, intricate flower. They all watched her, none of them speaking, the children's breathing heavy with concentration. Darkness fell and the villa's windows began to glow as the servants lit the oil lamps inside.

"There," Alice said when, at length, she added the final detail and turned the stone, examining it in the dusky light. "Not too bad."

"Not too bad at all," said Maddy.

"For you," Alice said, holding it out for her.

Maddy took it, touched and surprised in equal measure. "Thank you," she said.

"You're most welcome," said Alice, and for a second, just a second, she held Maddy's eye, and the corners of hers creased in another smile.

"Make one for me, Memsahib Alice," chorused the children. "For me, for me."

"No, no," said Alice, "it's far too late," but she laughed. Actually laughed; a soft, rippling sound that surprised Maddy all over again, but that the children didn't seem as taken aback to hear.

And even though Alice insisted that it was time for everyone to go inside, before the mosquitoes ate them, and was her usual quiet self again at dinner, Maddy placed the stone on her bedside table before she climbed into bed. She blew her candle out, and closed her eyes thinking of her mother's smile, her laugh.

Strange as both still felt, she was glad that she'd taken those paints into the garden.

The stone was the first thing she saw when she woke the next day. She reached out, touching her fingertips to the now dry paint, and, replaying Alice's laugh, briefly considered offering to accompany her on that morning's memsahib tea. For the first time it occurred to her that her mother might not be as indifferent to her going as she always seemed. She dismissed the idea as quickly as it came. After the drawn-out weekend, and a fitful night fighting to get comfortable in her tangled sheets, she felt perilously close to madness as it was; several hours of good housekeeping with Diana Aldyce and the rest might just push her over the edge.

However, since another day in the steamy villa seemed just as certain a path to lunacy, she resolved to go into town, as soon as Alice left. She stood, crossing to her closet, and pulled out a lemon dress, laying it on the bed. She moved quickly, skin dampening in the already warm room, relieved to have a purpose. She couldn't quite believe how much time she'd watched slip by these past days. Back in Oxford, she'd always had somewhere to be: college, out with her friends, for meetings at the school she'd been meant to work at, on the train to Paddington for the theater, a rally . . . She wasn't sure what had happened to that busy person. Maybe this sultry life was changing her. If she wasn't careful, she'd become just another of those waiting for the sun to pass the yardarm so that her first gin might feel respectable.

"Oh God," she said, her voice filling the airless room, "no."

She reached for her bath sheet and decided that she'd spend the morning at a bazaar. There was one she'd been meaning to go to, not far from the terminus, as it happened. It was hardly the worthiest of pursuits, but would hopefully make the day pass more quickly than it otherwise might. Little wins.

She caught a tram to the Victoria Terminus, pressed into a window seat for the creaking journey into the city. The vehicle was hot, stuffy with stale sweat, and grew even more so as they moved further into the center, swapping the lapping sea, lush plants, and birdsong of Malabar Hill for dusty roads, shanties, and apartment blocks. More passengers climbed in, as many standing as sitting: women in saris carrying baskets of sweet-smelling fruits, laundry, and vegetables; men in loose trousers and tunics, a couple in starched blazers, off to work in British offices. It was a relief when they at last reached the terminus. Maddy ran gratefully down the tram's stairs, deliberately not looking in the direction of her father's nearby office, not wanting to tempt fate into making anyone there spot her.

The sun-crisped streets surrounding the Gothic walls of the station were teeming. Camels and bullock carts vied for space on the dirt roads with rickshaws and automobiles, the *dabba* wallahs who rode bicycles laden with tiffin bags, delivering lunch to the sahibs. Porters thronged at the station entrance, handcarts at the ready, joking and laughing by the statue of Queen Victoria, eyes alert for approaching carriages and motors packed with luggage. Beggars slumped beneath the scant shade of the mango trees; Maddy flinched at their bony limbs, a baby, swaddled in frayed sacking, trying to feed from its staring mother. Most had their eyes closed, heads on their chests, ignored, just as they were at the port, in the gardens, on every city street. *One forgets they're there*, Diana Aldyce had remarked, back at a tea on the Gymkhana Club's pristine terrace, when Maddy had first arrived and naively asked whether something couldn't be done, *much nicer that way*. Alice had given Diana a level look that still made Maddy wonder how much she really liked Diana after all. Alice hadn't pulled Diana up on her coldness, though; no one had, all complicit in their silence. It made Maddy's already hot skin burn. She reached for her purse, dropping coins onto the lap of the woman with the baby. The woman didn't move, or nod her thanks, and Maddy didn't blame her. In her place, looking at her British coloring and fine gown, she wouldn't feel particularly grateful either.

She left guiltily, then paused at the corner of the road, Luke Devereaux's guidebook in hand. She squinted down at the directions to the bazaar, wiping sweat from her forehead, then carried on, around the vaulted side walls of the station. Wheels screeched on the tracks within as a train creaked to a halt; steam billowed out. Through the haze, she glimpsed a young man in a topee hat, on the platform just inside the archway. She cursed inwardly, recognizing him as one of her father's junior secretaries. His eyes widened as he spotted her, clearly recognizing her, too. He took his hat off; he looked like he might be about to call out to her. Not wanting to have to explain what she was doing there, she hastened away, losing herself in the hordes of others walking toward the markets.

The wheels screeched, the delayed train from Poona shuddering to a halt. Luke, who'd been working in the otherwise empty first-class carriage, preparing for the meeting he was already late for, packed away his papers: the lists of the presidency's battalions, the ranks and skill levels, outstanding training requirements, his guidance on mobilizing the Indian troops for war in Europe, should mobilization ever be required. (He hoped it wouldn't, obviously, but after the past decade of rearmament, it felt depressingly likely; half the continent wanted to build their empire, the other half to block them, and if anyone tried to do either, the web of treaties in place could drag everyone into battle.) He stood, flexing his neck, his back, beyond relieved to be back, at last. It had been a relentless three months. He'd only been commissioned to be in India for two, but General Staff in England were jumpy; they'd kept wiring, adding to the regions they wanted him to report on. MOST GRATEFUL FOR YOUR SERVICE AND PATIENCE STOP. He'd lost count of the ghats he'd stayed in, the visits to cantonments, interviews with commanding officers, hours spent observing the local troops, the sepoys, most of whom had never heard of the Balkans, let alone thought twice about which parts of Europe belonged to whom. The more men he'd talked to, polishing his rusty Hindustani, the less easy he'd felt about potentially dragging any of them from their families, their villages, thousands of miles across the sea. He had no idea how the practicalities would even work. Many of the COs he'd met had shared his concerns: how the men would manage if it came to them being led by officers untrained in their language, their religion, customs, and caste system; how they'd cope, after a lifetime of the Indian climate, with warfare in northern Europe. Luke had been tempted, several times, to wire General Staff telling them to leave the sepoys well alone. MOST GRATEFUL FOR YOUR UNDER-STANDING STOP. He would have, if he'd believed for a moment it would have done any good.

For now, he shut the fastening on his attaché and ducked, peering through the carriage's murky window, scanning the shaded, steam-filled terminus for the man Peter had written to say he'd send to meet him. *Fresh off the boat, but spectacularly keen, and useful enough.* The platform was packed; all the passengers flooding from the train's other carriages, their belongings in battered suitcases, sacks heaved under their arms. His eyes moved over them all, then settled on a sun-scorched man in a topee hat, just near the arches, bouncing awkwardly on the spot. Deciding he was a likely suspect, Luke reached up, pulled his case from the overhead racks, and, wrenching the door open, stepped into the crowds. Pausing only to pay a porter to take care of his things, he set off toward his impatient escort.

"Fraser Keaton, I presume," he called, voice raised above the furor.

Keaton spun, exhaling, so visibly, earnestly flustered that it was hard not to smile. "Mr. Devereaux," he said, "thank goodness."

"I'm sorry to have kept you waiting," said Luke.

"No, no, it's not that. I'm happy to wait, of course. I hope I didn't offend . . ."

"Not at all."

"It's just . . ." Keaton darted a look toward the sunlight outside, then back to Luke. "I'm dreadfully sorry," he said, "but might I leave you to go on to the office without me?"

"Without you?"

"I hate to ask."

Luke could see that he did.

"It's just," Keaton went on. "Well, I saw someone . . . I feel I should check. I mean to say . . ." He broke off, as though it was all too much.

Luke advised him to breathe.

Keaton did.

"Right," said Luke, losing his battle against the urge to smile. "Now, what is it you mean to say?"

Another deep breath. "It's Richard Bright's daughter." Keaton widened his eyes. "I think she's out there. All alone."

The light in the stall-packed alleyways was muted, colored by the awnings that spread out from the terraced buildings either side. The air, hot and thick, was filled with the scent of sizzling onion and garlic: pakoras frying in vendors' pans. Maddy's stomach grumbled beneath her tight, sweaty corset. She was half tempted to throw caution to the wind and buy one. She probably would have, had she not been chasing a man some distance ahead of her, a bolt of pink silk on his bare shoulder. She'd seen him within seconds of entering the bazaar, and her unfinished letter to Aunt Edie had popped into her mind. Deciding to parcel up a gift to post with it—a shawl to make Aunt Edie smile, distract her from Uncle Fitz and his new life for a little while (if anything could)—she'd set off after the man. He was moving so fast, though, it was all she could do to keep up; she walked faster herself, dodging piles of manure, half-eaten fruit, and discarded rubbish, growing sweatier the quicker she went, perspiration slickening her skin, pooling in her collarbone.

"Try," the vendor at a bangle stall called to her, waving a red one in her direction. "Perfect fit. Perfect color."

"Later," she said, not stopping, "maybe later."

She carried on, through the clamoring crowds, round a corner, and another, then halted, finding herself in an alley even more packed than the last, bursting with stalls, almost all of them selling fabric: cottons, silks, and muslin, thousands of different shades reflecting the dim light. She stood on her tiptoes, straining to see the man she'd been following. It was impossible. There were simply too many people crammed into the tight space. The shopkeepers all spotted her, though. She hardly had paused for breath before a chorus of "Memsahib, memsahib" broke out. They rushed out from behind their stalls, swatches held up to her face. "You look, memsahib. Look."

"Beautiful," she said, weaving forward, "very lovely."

"I have best in city," the man at the nearest table called, "you buy from me. Best in Bombay. Best in India."

"Memsahib," shouted his neighbor, "you come this way. This way."

Hearing the desperation in his tone, she turned. His black eyes sparked with hope, and he waved at the cloths laid on the trestle before him, then stepped back to reveal more rolled up against the crumbling building behind.

She looked closer. There was a color there like none she'd seen before. A deep lemon, richer than her dress, with luminous thread woven through. It looked almost like sunshine itself, and was quite perfect for Edie and those gray Scottish climes.

"You buy," said the man. "I have many children, big family. Need to eat." He mimed food going into his mouth. "I give you good price. Full-power good price."

Maddy wasn't sure what a full-power good price was, but she liked the sound of it. "I need this much," she said, and drew a line on the trestle. "How many rupees?"

He named an exorbitant sum.

She smiled.

He beamed back at her.

He had no teeth.

"Lower," she said.

He named another price. "My family," he said. "You help my family."

"I'm not buying them a house," she said, still smiling.

It was then that she first heard the shout. She couldn't make out the voice, or even the words, but there was something about it that sent her still.

It came again, louder.

This time she turned, pulse quickening.

It had sounded so much like *Miss Bright*.

And even though there were any number of people who might call her that, a thrill shot through her. She searched the crowds, eyes moving everywhere, but could see nothing beyond the faces of other shoppers, the stallholders, many of whom started calling out to her again. "Memsahib, you look at mine now. Memsahib, you come."

She shook her head. *Be quiet,* she wanted to say, *let me hear.*

She couldn't hear.

Had she imagined it?

"Memsahib?" The toothless man. "Memsahib, you buy."

"Just wait," she said. "Please."

She held her breath.

Nothing.

Then, just when she was about to give up, deflated, feeling a little foolish, she heard her name once more, only it was *Maddy*, not *Miss Bright* after all, which didn't feel right, but she spun regardless, craning her neck, hoping yet, unable to help herself . . .

Then she stopped.

Because she saw the man, plowing his way toward her.

And it really wasn't what she'd been hoping for, at all.

CHAPTER SIX

Luke hung from the step, one hand gripping the brickwork, elated, even in spite of the older man in uniform bearing down on Maddy, simply because, after all this time, she was there, her flushed face somehow even more beautiful than he'd remembered, and because he was almost certain she'd heard him just now.

That she'd wanted it to be him.

He could no longer see her properly, though. He wanted, very much, to do that. But she was facing away from him, toward the man in uniform—a major, from his stripes—her hat concealing her features, her expression.

"Maddy," the major called to her, "Maddy. Stay where you are. I just saw Keaton . . ."

Bloody Keaton.

Luke had told him he'd find her. He hadn't thought twice, back at the platform, before running to do that.

"You can't," Keaton had exclaimed, "we're so late."

"I'm afraid we're going to be later," Luke had replied, laughing, in spite of Keaton's aghast expression, and a little because of it, but mostly because he'd felt so damned vindicated that she was close. All these weeks away, he'd wondered whether he was running mad, so unable to shake the thought of her, and then here she was, somehow right here, just as he returned.

"You're not worried about her?" Keaton had called. "You don't look worried." The accusation, however respectfully toned, had been clear.

"I'm not worried," Luke had said, his mind replaying the image of her scaling that wall for a cigarette. "I'm sure she's fine."

"You know her?"

"Not yet," Luke had shouted over his shoulder. "I will, though. You'll see."

Clearly Keaton hadn't been inclined to see anything. Because now here was this major, apparently sent by him, taking Maddy by the arm.

Luke watched the easy, familiar way he did it, and felt his brow crease. But no. Surely not. The man looked old enough to be her father.

Still, there was something in his expression that made Luke jump down from the grubby step and push through the busy crowds toward where they both stood, unable, suddenly, to wait a second longer before speaking to her.

It wasn't as easy to reach her, though, as he needed it to be. People kept getting in his way. He moved as fast as he could, head raised above the sweaty press, but it took too long.

When he got to where she'd been standing, she was gone.

He cast his eyes around, desperate to spot her, sure that he must, struggling, even in spite of the evidence, to accept that she wasn't there.

"She go with the sahib," the toothless vendor supplied. He was no longer grinning. Quite the opposite, in fact. He seemed to be struggling with the turn of events, too.

"Did you see where?" Luke asked.

The man shook his head. "You buy?" he said, holding the gold fabric up.

Luke expelled a breath of frustration. He couldn't have lost her.

Cursing, because it seemed he had, and because *she go with the sahib*, he told the vendor to give him a minute, and set off toward the bazaar's entrance, retracing the steps he'd taken before, when he'd first come from the station to find her, hoping that she and the major had done the same.

Even more people had massed into the bazaar in the short time since he'd arrived (it was hard not to take against them), stealing the space, fueling the furnace-like air. By the time Luke had fought his way to the entrance, his shirt was sticking to his chest, his shoulder blades; his lungs swelled from the chase. He broke into the harsh noon glare, the clamor of rickshaw bells and motor horns, and, shielding his eyes with his forearm, scanned the pavements, the saris and linen smocks, for her straw hat, a glimpse of her lemon dress.

But it was only Keaton who he saw, advancing toward him with some pace of his own. His pink, mottled face was even more wrought than when Luke had left him, back at the terminus. (A not inconsiderable feat.)

"Keaton," Luke called, "I thought we were friends."

"Friends, Mr. Devereaux?" Keaton came to a halt, clutching his side.

"Friends, Keaton."

"I don't quite follow," Keaton said. "And we need to go."

A truth, Luke knew it. Even so. "Why did you send that man after Miss Bright?" he asked.

"Major Bowen?"

"I assume so," said Luke. "Let's hope it was him, at least."

"Who else would it be?"

"I have no idea, Keaton. Or why you sent him. Which leads me to ask again . . ."

"Why I did?"

"Very good."

"Because he knows her, Mr. Devereaux. You said you didn't. I wasn't sure how you'd find her."

"She's a white woman alone in an Indian bazaar."

"Well, yes," said Keaton, "of course. But since she and Major Bowen are going to be married . . ."

The words landed in Luke's solar plexus. "What?" he said. "Married?"

"So I'm told," said Keaton.

"You don't know?"

Keaton shook his head. Was it a no, or a yes?

Luke couldn't bring himself to ask.

Married?

Married?

"They're over there anyway," said Keaton, and pointed across the wide road, where, a hundred or so yards in the distance, Luke finally saw her, getting into a hoodless saloon motor.

He watched her do it. How she reached down to gather her skirts, slipping into the seat in one fluid movement. He saw her again, as she'd looked at New Year's, the slender cut of her silhouette on that dark promenade, her hand on his chair. The way she'd turned, toward him.

Married?

It didn't make sense.

He couldn't make it make sense.

He kept his eyes fixed on her. He realized that he was waiting for her to look around, just as she had beneath those fireworks, see him again.

But she didn't.

The motor roared away, with her in it.

He stared after its dusty wake, still just about able to make out her hand holding her bonnet to her head. She'd been holding something before. He frowned, thinking of it. He was sure she'd been holding something. . . .

"We really do need to hurry," said Keaton. "We're beyond late. If you'd just come with me. Oh no, Mr. Devereaux. *No.* Where are you going now?"

Maddy reached up, hand to her hat, just in time to stop it flying off as Guy sped them away, rickshaws swerving to let them through. He was driving a deal faster than normal, with several degrees less courtesy. He'd propelled her fairly rapidly to his motor, deaf to her protestations that she wanted to stay, or at the very least buy the silk she'd been looking at. (That poor stallholder and his family. Poor Aunt Edie.) "Maddy, *please*," he'd said, when she'd pulled back, telling him to wait, "I'm meant to be in theater."

"Go then," she'd said, unable to keep the impatience from her words. It was his assumption that she needed a rescuer, her disappointment that he wasn't who she'd thought. Her irritation at herself for hoping. (Why had she done that?) "I can manage perfectly well myself."

"Of course you can't," he'd said, gently, conciliatory, very much as though he were breaking bad news to a patient.

It had made her even crosser.

"Why on earth shouldn't I?"

"You're too clever to ask that question," he'd replied, steering her toward a side alley. "Now come this way, it's quicker."

She'd given in, not because she was mollified (she wasn't), but because it had been clear he wasn't going to, and because of the thought of the anxious soldier waiting on his operating table.

"I'm so glad I found you," Guy said now, his voice raised above the engine. He clunked the gears. "I almost didn't drive this way. Think of it, I wouldn't have seen Keaton."

"Just think," she said, jaw set at the quirk of fate, and the thought that, for such a large city, Bombay really was impossibly small.

"I can't imagine what you were thinking," Guy went on, "coming out like this."

She almost snapped again then. *For God's sake, I am not a child.* But she stopped herself, because she wasn't a child, and because it was Guy she'd be snapping at: kind Guy, who always had bottles of boiled water for her in his trunk, and who was, after all, only doing what he thought right. However grating that might be.

"Promise me you won't do anything like this again," he said.

"Guy . . ."

"Please, otherwise I'll have to talk to your parents."

She turned her head on the seat. "You'll tell on me?"

His lips twitched, and she almost wanted to laugh, because she liked that he was able to find it funny, but couldn't, because she was still a bit cross.

"Just promise me," he said.

"If you like," she said with a sigh, burying the niggling guilt that she was planning to use him as her alibi to break her word the very next day.

The very next.

It's not so long to wait, she told herself.

She wished it didn't feel so very long.

Or that she had the faintest idea what she was going to do with the rest of the afternoon now that Guy had taken it upon himself to deliver her home so prematurely.

He made short work of the city streets. Far too soon, the traffic around them thinned, the jungle thickened, and they were back at Malabar Hill. Sunlight sliced through the leaf canopy in shards, reflecting off the palms, the sleepy, silent villas. The occasional Indian servant walked at the side of the road, back from the markets, carrying baskets laden with vegetables and fruit. But for the occasional rickshaw trundling past, theirs was the only vehicle. Maddy, staring through the foliage at the glistening sea below, didn't attempt conversation; she kept replaying that shout in the marketplace, less and less sure, the more she did, that she'd heard anything at all. Guy, seemingly focused on the road, didn't talk either.

It was only when he broke the silence that Maddy realized how long it had been there.

"I'm sorry you're annoyed with me," he said, in a way that suggested he'd been thinking it for some time.

Remembering again all he'd done for her, Maddy forced herself to find a smile she couldn't feel. "I'm not annoyed," she said.

His smile was equally strained. He knew she was lying.

"At least you're home now," he said, turning through her parents' gates.

"Yes," she said, "there's that."

He didn't linger at the villa. She stayed on the porch steps to watch him leave, feeling worse than ever, knowing that he, too, now was upset. Such a mess, the whole morning. She waited until his motor had disappeared up the driveway, the sound of his engine dissolving into birdsong, the lazy rustle of the trees, then made her way inside. Tucking her purse and book under her arm, she peeled her gloves from her sweaty hands, and crossed toward the stairs.

Then she stopped.

She walked backward, arching her neck, looking across the tiled hallway toward the sunlit drawing room door, the figure who was standing there, all brown curls and beaming smile.

And, impossible as it would have felt, even seconds before, she felt her own face break into a grin, an ecstatic exclamation bursting from her.

Della laughed. "Hello, hello," she said, arms held wide. "I thought you'd never come."

They'd all arrived on a train much earlier that morning, Della told Maddy. Richard and Peter had had to go straight to the office from the terminus, but she hadn't been able to wait to come and say hello. "I cheekily accepted your bearer's offer of lunch," she said, as they walked to the back veranda, where the table did indeed hold a half-eaten plate of kedgeree. "I was worried I was going to waste away. You've been rather a long time."

"I might say the same to you," said Maddy. "Why didn't you wire you were coming?" She thought of her mother, at her mem-tea. "I don't think Mama even knows you're back."

"It all happened in rather a rush," Della said, sitting down. "One minute we were going to be away another week, the next we were all haring back for these meetings."

"What meetings?" asked Maddy, reaching for the carafe to pour herself a drink.

"Something to do with the army," Della said, waving airily. "Let's not talk about it; there are far more interesting things. Such as," she shot Maddy a mischievous look, "was that Guy Bowen's motor I saw bringing you back just now?"

"Or," said Maddy, smiling, "everything you've been up to while you've been away."

Della's eyes danced. "All right," she said, "we'll get to Guy later."

"We won't," said Maddy, "but don't ever change."

"Oh, you mustn't worry about that." Della picked up her knife and fork. "Will you eat as well?"

"Are you inviting me to lunch in my own house?"

"I suppose I am," said Della, with another gurgling laugh. "Did you miss me?"

"You have no idea," said Maddy, laughing, too, because she had, and because after the hours that had just been, it felt especially wonderful that she didn't have to do that anymore. "Can you stay the afternoon?"

"I need to have a sleep at some point," said Della. "Those trains. But definitely for an hour or so."

She stayed for four.

Ahmed brought food for Maddy, more drinks. The plates got emptied, the glasses, too, and they didn't stop talking; the more they spoke, the more there seemed to say, to ask. Della filled in the gaps her letters had left, taunting Maddy with her descriptions of the lake in Udaipur, the palaces she'd visited in the blue city, the pink city, safaris taken on elephant-back. Maddy, conscious that her trips around Bombay paled in comparison, nonetheless spoke more about them, laughing about how terrified she'd been at the start. "Still, no tigers or hunting lodges, I'm afraid."

"And you really went all on your own?" asked Della.

"All on my own," said Maddy.

"I'm very proud of you, old thing."

"I'm very glad I've made you proud."

"What made you do it, though?" said Della, folding her napkin. "You never told me when you wrote."

"I . . ." Maddy began, and almost said, finally, about Luke Devereaux. She bit her lip, holding herself short, just as she had in her letters. It still felt too soon, too tenuous to speak of, the entire thing (whatever it was) strangely breakable. She couldn't bring herself to risk jinxing it. "I decided to stop being homesick," she said, giving a different version of the truth, not entirely comfortably.

She felt another kick of guilt as Della clapped her hands happily. "Good for you," she said. "And your mother never suspected?"

"Not that I know of."

"How are things there?"

"Better," said Maddy, thinking of her painted stone upstairs. "Just a little better."

"Clearly I should go away more often," said Della.

"Please don't," said Maddy.

Ahmed cleared their plates and brought out sliced fruit, a piece each of Cook's Victoria sponge.

"I'm not sure I have the room," Della said, leaning back, wincing as she pressed at her waist.

"Eat it," said Maddy, "please. Or I'll have to."

They left the table only once, then for a cigarette at the end of the garden, both of them skulking behind the beds of agapanthus like naughty schoolchildren in case Alice, who had stayed out much later than usual, should return home.

In the event, she came just after Della left, and Maddy was on her way up for a bath.

"Your father surprised me for lunch at the club," Alice said, with a flush to her skin that suggested the surprise hadn't been entirely unwelcome, and which made Maddy wonder what else this strange day might have in store.

Certainly dinner with Della and Peter, since Alice also told her that Richard had arranged it with Peter.

"He won't be back until much later," Alice said. "Apparently there's a man from England over, and they're all tied up with him."

Maddy carried on upstairs and didn't ask more. There were always men over from England meeting with her father. Besides, she was too preoccupied with looking forward to seeing him herself at last, the night ahead, to think about anything else.

She dressed carefully for dinner, with a bubbling anticipation she hadn't known in months. She chose one of her favorite gowns, black, with a low back, and beaded cap sleeves, took her time pinning her hair, threading a sequined band through it, then pulled on her gloves. All the while, she kept one ear tuned to her open window, hoping for the sound of a motor, her father's low voice, more impatient than ever, now that she knew he was on his way, to have him back.

He still wasn't by the time the sun had set in its blaze of color, and Peter and Della arrived, Peter strolling languidly up the driveway in the balmy dusk, fair and slight in his tie and tails, Della bouncing along beside him in a scarlet gown.

Maddy ran out to meet them.

"Ah, here she is," said Peter, "a sight for the sorest of eyes. Your father's on his way," he continued, before Maddy could ask. "Tying up the most *endless* afternoon. He was allowed to escape for lunch, so it was my turn for dinner." He touched his hand to his chest. "A gentleman's agreement."

"Do you think you can come out after dinner?" Della asked Maddy. "We want to whisk you away."

"My idea," said Peter.

"I like your idea," said Maddy. "Where are we going? Don't say the Gymkhana Club."

"The Gymkhana Club," said Peter. "But before you protest, or tell us you're far too bored of it, and how cross you are at how long you've been left," he pouted apologetically, "have this." He reached into his pocket, pulling out a tissue-wrapped parcel.

"A gift?" said Maddy, taking it.

"Not from us, I'm afraid," said Della. "Do open it, though. Peter won't tell me what it is."

"Really?" said Maddy, smiling curiously at Peter, who suddenly appeared rather pleased with himself.

"Go on, Maddy darling," he said.

She did as she was told, pulling the tissue apart.

Then she gasped.

Because the fabric she'd been looking at in the market was inside. Slowly, she pulled it out, the silk spilling over her fingers, her wrist, glowing in the dusk.

"Oh look at that," said Della. "How gorgeous. Who's it from?"

Maddy didn't answer. She raised her eyes to Peter. Her heart was beating uncomfortably quickly in her chest.

"There's a note," he said.

"What note?" said Della.

"Is there?" said Maddy weakly, suddenly back in that bazaar again, hearing that shout, no longer so certain she'd imagined it. Not certain at all.

"There is," he said.

Fingers trembling, she searched amid the silk, in the tissue. *Please*, she thought, *don't let me be wrong.*

Then she saw the paper, the hand on it, and her fingers shook even more. Because she wasn't wrong.

I saw you carrying my guidebook. It made me very happy.
I hope you've enjoyed it.

And that you'll come tonight.

Tomorrow feels like far too long to wait.

CHAPTER SEVEN

Maddy stared at the note, the tissue in her shaking hands, unable to take her eyes from either, only distantly conscious of her own incredulous smile, Della's questions, Peter telling Della to do just be quiet for a second, Della refusing to do any such thing, their voices blurring, Luke Devereaux's writing, too, the ink merging the longer Maddy stared.

He'd been there, really been there.

Seen her.

And she was going to see him. Tonight.

Tomorrow feels like far too long to wait.

"What's even happening tomorrow?" Della asked, louder now. "Who *is* this Luke Devereaux? Maddy? Madeline Bright?" She wrenched the silk from Maddy's grasp. "Are you listening?"

"Now I am," said Maddy, pulling the silk back.

"Good," said Della. "So tell all, if you please."

"There's really not that much to tell."

"I don't believe you," said Della.

"Very astute," said Peter. "I'd give her something, Maddy; she's got that dog-with-a-bone look about her."

"A most put-out dog with a bone," said Della, folding her arms with an exaggerated frown. "I don't like you two having secrets."

"It's not a secret," said Maddy, realizing as she spoke that a secret was exactly how it seemed, and also that Della looked a little hurt, which was the last thing she wanted. "Really," she said, "you mustn't be upset. . . ."

"I won't be if you tell me," said Della.

"All right," said Maddy, "all right," and, wishing now that she'd done it a deal sooner, she made herself go on, recounting New Year's, the guidebook and returned matches, all the postcards—"A nice touch," said Peter, "a very nice touch"—eyes darting back to the silk as she talked, nerves building, rippling through her, because he'd surprised her again, and tomorrow had always been too long to wait, yet tonight was tonight, which couldn't have felt less like not much at all.

"It's the opposite of not much," said Della. "Why on earth didn't you write? Or say something at lunch?"

"I wanted to," said Maddy. "I did. I've just had this . . . superstition, I suppose. . . ." She broke off, her nagging fear that it might all turn wrong there, even now.

Della gave an exasperated sigh. "What about you?" she said to Peter. "You might have said."

"None of my business," Peter replied.

"But you gave him Maddy's address?" Della asked.

"I did," he confirmed, setting off toward the house. "An uncharacteristic interference for which," he threw a smile back at Maddy, "*you* are most welcome. I wouldn't have done it for a lesser lady, or man."

"Wait," said Maddy, remembering, now that the first wave of shock was passing, everything she'd been so desperate to grill him about. "How do you know one another?"

"Have done for years," said Peter, still walking. "Luke used to be based here."

"Doing what?"

"Soldiering, Maddy darling."

"He's an officer?" said Maddy, taken aback. She wasn't sure why. The warmth of all his messages, perhaps. Or the memory of the way he'd lounged at that candlelit table, so at ease, nothing like the stiff lieutenants and captains she'd encountered from the cantonments.

"He left," said Peter, which made more sense. "Or at least, he's still in the reserves."

"The reserves?"

"Mmm," said Peter, "same as me. First in line for the call if we trip into a war. Which hopefully we won't. Anyway, these days he mainly tells General Staff and the rest of us what to do. Can I go now, please? I'm parched. All these *questions.*"

With another teasing smile, he jogged up the porch stairs.

As he went, Della gave Maddy a narrow-eyed look. "For someone so blond," she said, "you're an awfully dark horse."

Maddy couldn't deny it. "Will you forgive me?"

"Eventually," said Della. "I'll need a few minutes to sulk," she held up her hands on the caveat, "but after that I'll endeavor to let it go."

"Thank you."

Della leaned over, peering again at the note. "Are you terrified?" she asked.

"Just a bit," said Maddy.

"Of?"

"Everything."

Della laughed, not unsympathetically.

"What if I mess it all up, Della?"

"You won't do that."

"I might start talking too much. . . ."

"Not likely, given current form."

"Or not enough," Maddy went on, "and he'll just stand there looking at me, thinking, what on earth—"

"Stop," said Della, cutting her off. "I won't hear it."

Maddy drew a shaky breath.

"You're going to be fine," said Della. "I have a *wonderful* feeling about it." She glanced up at the villa, its cream walls shadowy in the twilight. "I suspect this dinner's going to feel rather endless, though."

"I suspect you're right," said Maddy.

It was.

It didn't help that her father took another hour to arrive, delaying the start of the meal until well after dusk had given way to night. Or that Alice joined Maddy, Della, and Peter on the veranda while they waited, mosquitoes swarming around burning pots of citronella oil, gin and tonics on ice, quietly questioning Della and Peter on their trip ("I'm afraid Madeline rather wished she were there with you"), obviously making an effort to be sociable, which Maddy wanted to feel grateful for, but couldn't, because it was torturous to be kept from pressing Peter to tell her more of his friend. Della, not so restrained, kept throwing animated smiles in Maddy's direction; more than once, Maddy caught her mother looking puzzled, as though wondering what Della could possibly be so fired up about.

Richard finally appeared at nine, but not even the happy sight of him ducking through the veranda doors, the feel of his vast familiar hug, could distract Maddy from her apprehension. Although she held him tight, telling him how much she'd missed him, too, she was only semi-aware of the relief of his return. As they all progressed into the humid, candlelit dining room, and sat down to eat, her mind kept flitting, moving from the sound of that *Miss Bright* in the bazaar, up to the silk, hidden in her bedroom, back to the promenade at New Year's, to the ticking clock, Luke Devereaux waiting in the packed bar at the Gymkhana Club, whether he'd still be there by the time they finally were, what would happen if he was, unable to focus, because the more she thought about the possibility that she might really see him so soon, the less she could believe it, and yet she believed it enough that she felt a little like she might be sick.

"You're not hungry?" her father asked, eyeing her untouched bowl of soup.

"Not really," she said, then, knowing how easily he worried (all that typhus as a child), "it's so hot tonight."

"Do you normally find the heat affects your appetite?" Della asked.

Maddy met her smirk. "I do, Della, yes."

Peter snorted into his bowl.

"Should you stay home?" Richard asked, persisting.

"I'm fine," Maddy assured him, "really."

"Or we could come with you?" he offered. "I'm not so tired—"

"No." She practically shouted it.

His eyebrows shot up.

Della grinned.

Lowering her voice, Maddy said, "There's no need, honestly."

"You're sure?" This from her mother.

"Absolutely," she said.

"Have some gin," suggested Della.

"I'd rather she ate her soup," said Alice.

Maddy did try, but it was an inevitably poor effort, swiftly abandoned, as were each of the subsequent four courses Cook had laid on in honor of the sahib's return. She suspected her failure to eat any of them would be the nail in the coffin so far as she and Cook were concerned, but there was nothing to be done.

Della at least helped with dessert. "Pass it over," she said, reaching across the candles, "I think I can squeeze it in."

"Ever the lady," said Peter.

At last, the meal was over, and there was just a nightcap to be got through before the three of them were on their way. More anxious than ever about the time, Maddy knocked hers back with a swiftness that made her mother look twice, and Della nod approvingly ("Bracing," she said, "excellent"), and then they were off, climbing into the waiting motor, driving through the city's dark streets, Maddy fretting the entire way about whether he'd have waited, trying to get her strumming heart under control, failing utterly, but then they were there, and she was standing at the club's garden entranceway, staring toward the lamps burning in the foyer, the long lower terrace where she'd sat so many times for tea with a carelessness that now felt unimaginable. She placed her hand to her liquid stomach, tight lungs full of the musty air, her gown rippling in the breeze. From above, in the bar of the upper pavilion, she could hear voices and laughter, the crackle of the gramophone that was playing the chairman's Harry Lauder recording again.

"Ready?" Della asked.

"I almost wish I'd stayed at home," she said.

"Don't be ridiculous," said Peter, already heading into the foyer.

"Frankly, I'm excited," said Della, following. "I can't wait to see him."

Maddy closed her eyes. *Was* he still here?

Would she even recognize him if he was?

She wasn't sure.

She really wasn't sure.

And Della and Peter had disappeared down the terrace toward the stairs, yet she couldn't seem to move, and now she'd have to go in by herself.

Perhaps she'd just stay where she was a while longer.

Even as she thought it, she walked, her feet seeming to move of their own volition, along the tiled terrace with the empty playing fields stretching to her left, then up the double staircase, past the stained-glass windows and the grandfather clock, toward the hot buzz of the bar.

She paused again on the threshold. The ceiling punkahs swooshed overhead, wafting air over her clammy neck, her cheeks. Lamps burned on every spare surface, scenting the smoky air with oil, turning the room's mahogany paneling a rich golden brown. Her eyes moved, looking for him, or the shape of him, but she was too nervous and couldn't absorb anything beyond disjointed snapshots of the scene before her. One blink showed her men in evening dress playing cards by the shuttered windows, even more lining the bar. Another, Diana Aldyce at a round table, her brunette head thrown back at something a young sergeant was saying, Captain Aldyce fiddling at his mustache beside her. She blinked again, this time seeing couples dancing on the only free space of polished floor, arms around one another, moving to the beat of the music, much slower than her own racing pulse. She turned her head and saw the punkah wallahs lining the wooden walls, their faces blank as they pulled the fans' cords. Then, the sunburned sailor she'd danced with at New Year's; he waved at her from across the room, but Guy, in evening dress, didn't, because he had his back to her, was talking with his deputy from the hospital, and hadn't yet seen that she was there.

Just as she couldn't see Luke Devereaux.

She moved, toward where Della and Peter had stopped at the end of the bar, anxiety growing, but with it a horrible flatness, because he wasn't there.

He really didn't seem to be there.

We took too long, she thought.

Except then Diana Aldyce turned toward her, her rouged mouth still wide with laughter, and seemed to go still at something beyond Maddy's shoulder. Maddy watched the way her eyes sharpened in interest, and felt the hairs on the back of her own neck stand on end.

There was a pause.

She held her breath.

"Hello, Miss Bright," came a low voice from behind, full of warmth, full of fun. And which she liked.

Which she liked very much.

Moving without thinking, because it would have been impossible to do anything else, she turned.

Dark eyes met hers. Deep and bright, they sparked with enjoyment. For a beat, they were everything. Then, so much else followed: his shoulders, lean yet strong beneath his evening jacket, the slant that she remembered so well; the way he stood, hands in his pockets, just as he had on the promenade, so relaxed, so near. His skin, tanned by the Indian sun, the cut of his jaw, his cheekbones; his face, which she knew, and which she saw now she'd have known anywhere.

And which she liked.

Which she liked very much.

He stared, taking her in as well, making her wonder what he was seeing, what he thought. "It's very nice to meet you at last," he said.

Somehow, she managed to reply. "It's very nice to meet you, too, Luke Devereaux."

His lips moved in a smile.

She felt hers do the same.

He's here, she thought, *really here.*

This is happening.

The silence between them stretched, at once wonderful and unbearable, her smile growing the longer it went on, skin becoming hotter, until, compelled to break it, she thanked him for the silk, his guidebook, and postcards, talking every bit too much (she almost wished Della were there to hear it), the words rushing from her. "I haven't given you anything, though," she said. "It all feels rather one-sided."

"Not at all," he said. "I hope it was the right silk?"

"It was," she said.

"Good," he said, and smiled again, the muscles in his face moving easily, as though used to his doing that. "I wanted you to have it."

"I love it," she said, and didn't tell him it was meant to have been for her aunt. "What were you even doing in the market, though?"

"Trying to find you," he replied, so plainly, so unapologetically, that she was glad she'd asked. And, as he went on, telling her how worried Fraser Keaton had been, how late he'd made himself chasing her, she found herself laughing, in spite of her nerves, loving that he'd done that.

"I wish Fraser hadn't told Guy as well," she said.

"I wish he hadn't either," he said.

"You should have shouted louder," she said.

"I should have, Miss Bright."

"You can call me Maddy, Luke Devereaux."

Another slow smile. "I'll bear that in mind," he said.

The gramophone petered into silence. For that moment, with the music gone, it was like the club went, too, and it was just them, looking at one another.

She realized how much she wanted it to be just them.

But, as someone reset the needle, filling the room with song once more, Della and Peter came over, all noise and chatter, very much there, Peter wondering if the pair of them had any intention of moving at some point, congratulating Luke on surviving the afternoon, "Apologies for Aldyce. He does go *on*," Della insisting on being introduced. "I would tell you I'd heard lots about you," she said to Luke, "but," arch look at Maddy, "I'm afraid it would be a lie."

"No," said Luke.

"Yes," said Della, "isn't it too awful?"

Maddy drew breath, to say what she didn't know, but then even more people were there: Peter's crowd, wanting to know what was keeping Luke ("Oh hello, Maddy darling"), shaking Peter's hand, kissing Maddy and Della, inquiring as to whether they'd been offered a drink.

"Not a sniff of it," said Della. "I might have to return to the north."

"No," came the chorus, "don't do that."

"You mustn't," said Diana Aldyce, sashaying over, predictably unable to stay away. (Now she was here, Maddy was amazed she'd waited so long.) "You're very naughty for abandoning us."

"I'll be sure to ask your permission next time," said Della.

"Good girl," said Diana.

"I wasn't being serious," said Della.

Maddy hardly heard. She was too distracted by Luke's gaze, the way he was watching her.

"Oh God," said Peter, "here comes the husband."

Anyone else? Maddy thought.

"Devereaux," said Captain Aldyce. "I must just bend your ear."

"Must you?" said Luke, still looking at Maddy.

"I really must," he said.

But he didn't get to, because one of Peter's friends interjected, suggesting they all reconvene at the table, "No shop talk, though, Aldyce. All work and no play makes Ernest a dull boy," and everyone was off, across the room, pulling out seats, pouring glasses of champagne, Ernest Aldyce telling Luke to sit, really, what he had to say wouldn't take long ("I've heard that before," said Luke, not sitting), the sunburned sailor asking if he might join them, Guy looking over as though he was thinking of doing the same thing, and suddenly Maddy, not sitting either, knew that she mustn't, that if she did, the night, already more than half over, was going to be gone and she and Luke wouldn't have had another chance to be alone again. No one was going to let them.

"Mr. Devereaux," said Diana, as though further evidence were needed, "are you ever going to take me for a turn on the floor?"

It was like she and Ernest were in cahoots.

"I'll dance with you, Diana," offered Peter, falling on his sword.

"I've danced with you a hundred times," said Diana.

"Why not make it a hundred and one?" said Della, with a tight smile.

Maddy was fairly confident Diana wasn't going to make it a hundred and anything. She suspected Peter, already topping up his glass, knew it, too. She didn't wait to find out. Stopping only to catch Luke's eye, let him see her meaning, she turned, away from Diana, away from them all, and, unable to quite believe she was doing it, left.

As she walked across the crowded room, her breaths came a little quick, a little shallow, nerves back in earnest. Her skirt skimmed the tables of others, and she felt that everyone must be watching her, that they knew what she was about: Guy, Peter's friends, Diana. Their attention prickled, needling at the flushed skin on her bare back, her arms.

Her steps didn't falter, though. She walked on, faster, through the doors, back down to the terrace, toward the playing fields beyond, and cared about only one thing: that Luke had understood just now, that he saw where she was going.

And that he followed.

The fields were deserted, the dry grass baked hard, uneven from the hooves of the polo ponies who galloped over it daily. The shadowy palms on the periphery shook, leaves rustling, a soft accompaniment to the muted music playing on in the club behind, the distant thrum of the city's horns and rickshaw bells.

Not wanting to linger too near to where everyone else was, she walked on, her skirts wisping on the parched lawn, toward the rattan loungers on the farthest side of the pitch. As she came to a halt, she sneaked a backward glance toward the clubhouse. The grass behind her was still empty, still silent.

Drawing another ragged breath, she sat. Bats hovered in the still blackness, wings flickering; dark on darker. Cicadas nested all around. Such a world away from England, Oxford, and she couldn't remember ever having felt less homesick.

She wished, though, that she'd thought to bring a glass of champagne out with her. Or brandy. *Bracing.* She didn't really want a cigarette, but, too jittery to do nothing, she reached into her purse anyway.

Then stopped.

Were they footsteps?

She sat quite still, listening.

They were.

She swallowed, not moving, almost too afraid to look in case it was Guy coming to ask what she was doing out here all alone, or Della. *He's gone home; I'm sorry.*

She knew, though, that it wasn't Guy, or Della. Her heart quickened, knowing it, too. She stared at her lap, picturing him coming toward her. When she turned, needing to see after all, he was even closer than she'd imagined, so close that she felt the shock of his eyes meeting hers, saw them flash in a look that was half amusement, half challenge.

"Was this a test, Miss Bright?" he said. "To see if I could find you?"

"Well, you passed," she said, and couldn't believe she managed to sound so normal.

He came to a halt. "I was going to get us away from the table, you know."

"You were?"

"Yes," he said. "I was going to ask you to dance."

She arched her neck, looking up at him, adjusting, still, to his being there, really there. "And after that?" she said.

"Another dance," he said.

"Then?"

He gave a low laugh. "Another."

"Yes," she said, still marveling at her own composure. "I see where this is going."

"Peter told me how clever you are."

It was her turn to laugh. "So, we'd have just kept dancing," she said. "To Harry Lauder. I warn you, they keep playing him."

"I'd noticed," he said.

"And it was so hot in there."

"Yes," he said, "I'd noticed that, too."

"Hmm," she said, cocking her head to one side. "I think I prefer my plan."

"I think I do, too," he said. "But we won't be left alone for long."

He sat, his knee almost touching hers.

"No?" This time she heard the tension in her voice.

"No. Peter was worried. Something about your reputation."

"It's not safe with you?" she said, speaking without thinking, feeling her cheeks flame at what had come out.

He smiled back at her. *I'm not entirely sure,* he seemed to say.

I'm not entirely sure I mind, she found herself thinking.

His smile deepened, like he'd heard.

The moment went on. She had to fight not to drop her gaze.

He didn't look away either.

At length, he said, "Since we don't have much time, we'd better not waste it."

"Best not," she said.

"We don't know each other."

"Not at all," she agreed.

"Shall we do something about that, then?" he said.

"Yes," she said, "I think we should."

So they did.

He started, asking her how long she'd lived in England before she returned to Bombay. "Peter told me you were born here."

"Yes," she said, silently absorbing how much he and Peter seemed to have spoken about her, enjoying the thought. "I left when I was seven, fifteen years ago."

"A long time," he said.

"A very long time," she said, and went on, haltingly at first, getting used to the idea of her words in his ears, talking of the stories she'd been told of her childhood illnesses, her foggy memories of soft hands on her forehead ("Your ayah's?" he asked. "I'm not sure," she said), the little monkeys that someone had sewn into her mosquito net, then the voyage to England, how little she recalled of it. "Just the cold, as we'd got closer. And playing quoits on deck with my father."

"Your mother wasn't there?"

"She didn't come. I don't know why."

"Too hard for her?" he suggested.

"Perhaps," she said, thinking of those fireworks, the painted stones.

"You're not sure?"

She shrugged. "My mother's not a simple person to read."

"But you're trying."

"I think we're both trying," she said, realizing the truth of it as she spoke. "It's not easy."

"Because you don't want to be here?"

She gave a wry smile. "I certainly didn't plan to be," she said, and found herself going on, without really meaning to, just because he was so very easy to talk to, relaying the shock of her holiday becoming permanent, the news of her lost teaching position in Oxford, even speaking of Edie and Fitz's divorce, Fitz's marriage to her old school friend. "The daughter of one of the governors at the school I was meant to work at, in fact."

His steady gaze didn't alter. She could tell he already knew about Edie and Fitz, probably also about Fitz's new baby, due any day. She wasn't surprised; most people did. But she liked that he wasn't embarrassed, or making a fuss.

"Your father must worry about your aunt" was all he said.

"He doesn't talk about it," she said, "but he must." Thinking of Edie all alone in Scotland, she did then admit that the silk had been meant as a gift for her.

Luke stared, and she laughed, feeling some of the seriousness that had been building between them dissolve. "I'm sorry," she said.

"What are you sorry for?" he asked.

"I don't know exactly," she said, still laughing.

He smiled. "I think we'd better find her something else," he said.

"Yes," she said, liking that *we*, "I think we should."

And, not wanting to go back to speaking of sad things, she changed the subject, saying she felt like she'd talked more than enough, and it was his turn now.

"What do you want to know?" he asked, leaning back, lighting a cigarette, the flame illuminating his tanned skin, the firm lines of his face, and offering it to her. She took it absently, finally asking him what he was doing in India, how long he'd been here before, why he'd stopped being a soldier, and what had made him become one in the first place.

He pulled another cigarette from his case and lit it. "That's a lot of questions, Miss Bright."

"Fine," she said. "Why did you join the army?"

"Because I was eighteen, and had no idea what else to do."

"Why did you leave?"

He exhaled smoke, like it was a long story, and then made fairly short work of it, saying how little he'd liked the rigidity of the life, the insularity of the cantonments, and had given it up as soon as he could. "The only thing that ever felt right, was leaving."

"You were with the Indian Army?" she guessed. There were hardly any British regiments in India; almost all British officers were here to lead the sepoys.

"I was," he said.

"So you speak Urdu?"

"You have to."

She nodded. She knew that. Unlike other colonies, the native soldiers here weren't expected to speak English, even if they were barred from commanding themselves. "And you still work for the army now?"

"Not directly. I've been at Whitehall, for five years now. But I was asked to do this project."

"Which is?"

"Classified," he flicked ash, "and quite uninteresting." Then it was his turn to change the subject, asking her to tell him what she'd been doing while he was gone.

She almost kept probing, but stopped herself. It was obvious he didn't want to dwell on his work, and she didn't want to ask him to, not if it would make him uneasy. Already, she only wanted to make him happy.

So instead she said, "Exploring, thanks to you," and told him how much she'd enjoyed reading his book, laughing at her abortive trip to the spice market, telling him of the mosque she'd visited instead.

"I'm not sure I've heard of that one," he said.

"I'm not sure anyone has," she said ruefully.

"But you got to the spice market in the end?"

"I did," she said, and, realizing her cigarette had gone out, she set it down and talked of how she'd shocked herself by staying so long, then of the children at the *dargah*, the crowded trams; the amount of money she'd lost bribing Ahmed into cooperation.

"And you never felt unsafe?" he said. "I hope you didn't."

"Not once," she said.

"Good," he said, finishing his own cigarette, "that's good."

He told her more of his own travels: the years he'd spent in Bombay, his experiences of the same places she'd been to, others that she hadn't. He spoke of a stretch of coast, not far away, where every year, around this time, turtles hatched with the full moon.

"I'd love to see that," she said.

"Yes," he said, smiling, as though he'd love her to, too.

The music continued behind them. Occasionally a burst of laughter, a shout, fractured the sultry air, reminding her of the clubhouse, everyone still in it. Mostly, she didn't think about them at all. She watched his face as he talked, his every turn of expression, feeling the energy in him, an answering beat in herself, the urge to reach out, touch him, stronger with every minute. He leaned toward her, closer, feeling it, too, until only the barest slice of air separated them. One move, and it would be gone.

They fell silent. She wasn't sure, anymore, how long they'd been talking. He looked across at her, like he was seeing her for the first time. *I like him,* she thought. *I like him so much.* A soft gust of wind snaked through the trees, the grass. She felt her chest rise, fall; the sense of something coming.

"Did you ever worry?" he asked.

"Worry?" she said.

"That we might be wrong," he said.

"No," she said, "not really."

"No," he said, "I didn't either," and, hearing his quiet bemusement, she was glad, that it was strange for him, too. "I don't feel like I've only just met you," he said.

"No," she said softly.

"Can I still see you tomorrow?" he asked.

"You know you can," she said.

"I'm with your father, first thing. I'd better tell him."

"It's not my father you have to worry about," she said, barely aware of her words.

He smiled. "I'll come and collect you," he said. "No more bribing your bearer."

"For coffee?"

"Not for coffee."

"Where then?"

"Does it matter?" he asked, his lips all but brushing hers.

"No," she said, "I don't suppose it does."

His eyes blurred in hers.

She wasn't sure she breathed.

"Maddy," came Peter's voice from the terrace, making her start. "Time to go."

For a second, neither of them moved. Then Luke dropped his head. He looked up at her, gave a short, silent laugh. She smiled, self-conscious now, at what had so nearly happened.

"Maddy." Peter again. "If your father dismisses me, I'm suing for recompense."

With a reluctant sigh, Luke stood. He offered her his hand. Reaching up, she took it, feeling his fingers close around hers, the warmth of him through her glove.

She still felt it, even after he'd pulled her to standing, had let her go.

"Madeline. Madeline Bright. I really don't want to have to come and find you. It's *dark*."

Luke smiled down at her. "Until tomorrow," he said.

"Until tomorrow," she echoed.

It wasn't so very long to wait.

CHAPTER EIGHT

He slept; the consuming sleep of deep night. He was outside, a black expanse of lawn surrounding him. She was there, too, walking away. He watched her steps, so slow, lingering. He felt like he might be smiling. She wore a dark dress. He saw how it dipped, low, forming a V on her spine, the hem trailing on the grass. Her blond curls, silver in the night, dripped from her headband, skimming her neck.

At last. The voice, a man's, came through the night. It was familiar, pleasantly so. *Diana's been having a field day.*

His eyes snapped open. Awake.

He stared at the shadowy ceiling cornices above, breaths coming nauseatingly quickly. *Where am I?*

Who am I?

It took him less than a second to remember that he didn't know who he was. Then, as the rest followed—how he'd woken, lost in a soundless forest, no jacket, no identity tags, then gone from there to that frantic casualty clearing station, on to Dieppe, the freezing journey across the Channel to the ward in London, the hospital he was in now—he punched his fists down on his sweat-drenched mattress, and yelled in anger, because it was either that or weep.

Who was Diana? *Who?*

Scrambling, he reached for his journal, and wrote the name down before it, like the woman in his dreams, could disappear.

He didn't sleep again that night. He didn't try to. It wasn't that he wasn't tired. He was still exhausted, all the time. It was that he'd never yet managed to return to the same dream, and he couldn't face the disappointment of his own failure. He wanted to be back wherever he'd been too much. So he rose, lit an oil lamp, read through the nonsense in his journal, and then pushed it away, because in the darkness before the dawn it always felt especially hopeless.

By the time Sister Emma Lytton came to his door, the inevitable mug of cocoa in hand, he was dressed, had opened the thick brocade drapes at his window, and made his bed. It never ceased to unnerve him that he knew how to do such things, yet couldn't remember who had taught him. A mother, he was sure. He'd pushed himself, many times, to recall her. He wondered constantly if she, and his father, were still alive. He felt like they were; he didn't know why. He realized they must believe him dead. ("And how do you feel about that?" Arnold had asked. "I hate it," he'd said, feeling their pain, such needless pain, all through him. "I can't put words to how much I hate it.")

"I expect you're ready for breakfast, Officer Jones," Sister Lytton said. "I saw your light burning at four."

He didn't ask her why she'd been up so early. Arnold had told him of her dead fiancé, her brother. ("Another bruised soul," Arnold had said.) She herself had admitted that she struggled to sleep. "Not that I'm complaining, of course."

"You're allowed to," Jones had told her.

She'd laughed, like he'd made a joke.

"Oh, Officer Jones," she said now, "you've made your bed again." She gave him a despairing look, as she did every morning.

"If you keep doing that," said the VAD with her (Poppy, she'd told Jones to call her), "I won't have an excuse to come and see you." Her lips pursed in suggestive smile. "And then where will we be?"

Again, it wasn't the first time Jones had heard the quip. Was this one of

Arnold's tricks, he sometimes wondered, asking the staff to repeat themselves over and over again? Sister Lytton's disapproving frown at Poppy certainly came on cue. Even he played his part, telling Poppy he was sorry about the bed.

"I'll forgive you, Officer Jones," she said, with another smile.

He didn't smile back. He never did.

He stood to go downstairs with Sister Lytton, leaving his journal on his bed, and hardly noticed the way that Poppy watched him leave, dimples deepening.

The breakfast room was busy by the time he and Sister Lytton reached it. Not noisy, because no one really talked (every bite of toast, clink of cup, and sugar cube dropping in tea could be heard), but full. Several other nurses were there, supervising proceedings—they were always supervised—and almost all of the seats around the mahogany table were occupied by Jones's fellow patients, hunched and pale and wearing the same stiff blue uniform he had on.

Spotting a free seat beside the captain he'd seen in the drawing room when he'd first arrived at the King's Fifth, the one who wore a mask on his shattered face, he made his way toward it. As he sat, he readied himself for the stuttered introductions. Unlike him, this captain forgot each day the second it passed. Jones had by now met him two hundred and three times—each day marked in his journal. Sister Lytton had told Jones, on one of the walks she liked them to take together ("Loneliness is no one's friend"), that she made sure she was always by the captain's side the second he woke each morning, ready to tell him where he was before he could start screaming in panic. There was a wife somewhere, too, but she never visited, only the mother. The longer she stayed with her son, the less he'd shake.

Awful, though, how he cried when she left.

"Hello," Jones said to him now.

"G-G . . . m-m-m . . ."

"Morning," said Jones.

"I . . . I . . ."

"Don't think we've met," said Jones, saving him the torture of getting the words out, shifting in his seat as Sister Lytton leaned between the two of them and reached across to the silver serving dishes with a waft of starch, lavender water, and carbolic soap. She fetched the captain's bacon and toast, optimistically leaving them on his plate for him to eat, even though his shaking was so bad he struggled to cut his own food.

Jones declined her offer to serve him, and as soon as she'd left, her nurse's hood swaying as she circumnavigated the table, surveying what was and was not being eaten by everyone else, he reached for his companion's plate, forced a smile in reply to his stuttered thanks ("S-s-such a b-b-buffoon t-t-t-today"), and sliced his bacon for him, buttered his toast, too, then cut it all into bite-size mouthfuls. He stared out through the dining room window as he worked. Winter had passed. Spring, too. The garden's lawns were lush, dewy with the misty summer rain that had been falling since dawn.

He slid the man's plate of bacon and toast back to him. Gently, he took his cold fingers, feeling his dry skin, his bones, and placed them around his fork, then shifted his mask slightly so his food might reach his mouth.

"There," he said to him, "you're all right now." He didn't know why he always said that.

They were all of them anything but.

"He for one will never get any better if you keep helping him," Arnold scolded Jones, later that same day as they sat together in the orchard.

The small, wild corner of the grounds was Jones's favorite part of the otherwise neatly landscaped gardens. The grass, in contrast to the hospital's long, trimmed lawns, was earthy, unkempt, cluttered with leaves and fallen apples. The trees were heavy with many more of them, ripening pears, too, and the hedgerows plump with green and purple blackberries. There was a stream, tiny—more a trickle, really—but Jones loved the sound of it, the sense of it there; just like that voice before in his dream, the water felt familiar, comforting.

The rain had started again. It dusted his woolen blues, Arnold's tweed jacket and glasses. It was so thin, so fine, Jones felt as though he were breathing it. He arched his neck, staring into the white summer sky; the cool brush of moisture on his face.

"Hardly rain at all, is it?" said Arnold.

"No," agreed Jones, and felt the oddest compulsion to compare it to something else, only he didn't know what. His brow creased. He tried to think. It hurt, physically hurt in his head to do that, and it got him no-where. But before he could vent the unbearable frustration of it, he heard a low grumbling in the sky. It wasn't thunder. Arnold, who'd taken to speak-ing with him lately of France and Flanders ("You can cope with it, and one of these days I'll happen upon a word or name that will mean something to you, I'm determined"), had told him that the noise came from the heavy guns at the Somme, and the battle that had been waging there since the first of July, already killing far too many.

Jones closed his eyes, listening to the bombardment, thinking of the trenches he couldn't remember, hoping the same rain wasn't falling there. He imagined muddy rivers, men and boys sheltering beneath scraps of tar-paulin, bullets whistling by, and felt a tightness in his chest, of grief, of anger.

He told Arnold about it. "I don't know what makes that happen."

"Love," said Arnold. "For your men."

"But I don't remember them," Jones said.

"Not consciously," said Arnold. "No."

"Not at all," said Jones.

Arnold said nothing.

There was a short silence. A bird hopped among the windfall apples. The sky growled on. *Howitzers,* Jones thought, and couldn't recall whether it was Arnold who'd told him that's what the guns were called.

"The nurses have taken a shine to you," Arnold said, seeming to change the subject. "Sister Lytton, especially."

"She takes a shine to all her patients, I think," said Jones.

"She's told me you make her think of her younger brother," said Arnold.

"Really?" said Jones, surprised and saddened in equal measure. How inadequately he must compare. "I wish she still had him."

"As do I," said Arnold. "She has too good a heart to have lost so much."

"Yes," agreed Jones, and resolved to be kinder the next time she sug-gested a walk.

"There's that VAD, too, of course," said Arnold.

"The VAD?" said Jones.

"Hmm," said Arnold, "the one who looks like she's always on the edge of mischief."

"Poppy?"

"Yes, Poppy," Arnold said. "She's very pretty. Makes me think of a dairy-maid."

"I'm not sure she's as wholesome," said Jones.

"Do you think her pretty?" Arnold asked. His tone was too careless. He was digging.

Jones looked sideways at him, curious now as to where he was going. It was always somewhere. "I really hadn't thought about it," he said.

"No?"

"No," said Jones, truthfully.

"I can assure you," said Arnold, "she is uncommonly pretty."

"Well, then," said Jones, at a loss to know what else to say.

"But you don't think of her in that way," said Arnold.

It wasn't a question, but Jones answered it anyway. "No," he said, seeing again that black dress, those blond curls. "I don't."

"You must have come across many nurses by now," Arnold went on.

"Yes."

"And you've never felt . . . tempted?"

"Not once," said Jones.

"There you are then," said Arnold, who hadn't changed the subject at all. "Love."

"Love," echoed Jones.

"Yes." Arnold's eyes glinted behind his spectacles. "You remember plenty, my friend, I assure you. We just need to find out where it's all hiding."

CHAPTER NINE

Bombay, Spring 1914

Maddy woke late the morning after that first night with Luke, still absorbing that it had happened, smiling into her pillow because it had, replaying it all over again, the way he'd looked, opposite her in the darkness, that almost-kiss, *I don't feel like I've only just met you*, biting her lip on the thrill that she was going to be with him again in just a couple of short hours, not quite able to absorb that either.

From the silence in the house, she guessed her father was already at the office, perhaps with Luke even now. Luke wouldn't have to tell him he was coming to call; she'd already done that for him. Richard had still been up when she'd returned home, waiting on the front porch in his dressing gown, despite his professed exhaustion, it being well past midnight. *I wanted to make sure you're really all right.* He'd been as accepting as she'd known he would be when she'd said Luke was taking her out; surprised, but not unpleasantly so, telling her Luke had struck him as a good sort that afternoon.

"Yes," she'd said, "a very good sort."

Richard had smiled tiredly. "Peter certainly holds him in high regard," he'd said, picking up his candle. "Am I right in assuming you don't want to take your mother with you as chaperone?"

"Quite right," she'd said.

"Hmmm," he'd said, with another smile. "I'm not sure what she's going to think about that."

Maddy wasn't either.

She turned on her pillow, looking sideways at the painted stone on her bedside, mood dipping, just a little, at the prospect of going downstairs, finding out. Even given the recent thaw in Alice's manner, Maddy wasn't looking forward to speaking to her about Luke. She could have done it the night before—she'd seen the light burning in her window, known that she, too, was awake—but, after Della making her talk the entire way home ("Don't even try telling me that you're too tired," Della had said. "I want to know *everything*." "Oh God," Peter had groaned. "Must we?"), the draw of disappearing into her bedroom, being alone with her own spiraling thoughts, had been too strong to resist. Besides, it was her mother; aside from that one interlude painting in the garden, Maddy couldn't remember the last time they'd spoken about anything more personal than the heat.

However, since there was no other way around it, she rose, too quickly, feeling the warm room spin, and, seeing the time, registering how little she had left, *until tomorrow,* went to her closet, impatient now to dress, get the inevitably stilted exchange over with.

After a breathless half hour bathing, pulling stockings onto her damp legs (never easy), pinning her hair, fastening a white lace tea gown (Would Luke like it? She didn't know, she just didn't *know*), she found Alice embroidering in the shade of the veranda. The breakfast table had been cleared; only a plate of food remained, waiting for Maddy beneath a fly net. (She wondered if it meant Cook was still talking to her.)

She hovered awkwardly, unclear why she was thinking about Cook, listening as Alice stiffly remarked on how surprised she'd been to learn Maddy had a new acquaintance.

"Father told you?" Maddy asked, even though it was patently obvious he had.

"Yes," said Alice. "He said he's a friend of Peter's."

At her clipped tone, Maddy wondered what else Richard had said to her, whether he'd warned her not to be difficult about letting Maddy go out without her. Alice, expression closed, tensely moving her needle in and out of the cloth, was certainly doing a good impression of someone who'd been told they mustn't make a fuss.

Was it just about Maddy refusing to let her be chaperone? Maddy didn't think so. She didn't ask either. She suspected it was as much to do with her going anywhere with someone other than Guy, but would rather not have it confirmed. She'd been working, very hard, to ignore her creeping misgivings about what her mother had started to hope for there. Just as she preferred not to dwell on the possibility that Guy really had come to think of himself as something more than an uncle (all those bottles of boiled water).

And now Alice was talking again, saying that she'd like Maddy to reconsider her plans for the afternoon and remain at home, let Luke have tea here.

Maddy told her that she had no intention of reconsidering anything.

"You can't just run around like we're nobody in this city," said Alice. "Think of your father. His position."

"He really didn't seem worried," said Maddy.

"There'll be gossip," said Alice.

"There's always gossip," countered Maddy, well used to it in any case. (Thank you, Uncle Fitz.)

Alice's forehead pinched, like she might be thinking of him, too. She didn't say, of course. She never spoke of him, or Edie.

She simply snapped her thread, then folded her sewing, standing. "I have a headache," she said. "I'm going to rest. I won't come down when he gets here."

"What?" Maddy stared, nonplussed. She hadn't expected that. "You won't even meet him?"

"It's clear you want to be left alone," said Alice.

"But—" Maddy began, then stopped.

Did she want to be left alone?

Part of her did. But there was another, surprisingly larger, part that didn't, that wanted her mother to say hello when Luke came, perhaps even smile. Like she'd smiled the other evening, painting in the garden.

It hurt, actually, that she wasn't going to at least try.

But before Maddy could say that, Alice turned from her, told her to make sure to eat something before she went anywhere, and left.

Mouth open, Maddy watched her go, too disorientated by the speed of her departure to call her back. By the time she realized she wanted to, it was too late.

She dropped into the chair nearest her. What had even just happened? She had no idea. Or why she should feel so deflated. Had she really been foolish enough to hope that Alice might be curious about Luke, want to know who he was, where he was from? Be pleased, even, that she, Maddy, was happy?

Sighing, at herself more than anyone, because she had, and she really should have learned by now, she reached out, lifting the net from the plate of fruit and bread, only to drop it again without taking anything. She couldn't manage a bite.

Trying to push Alice from her mind, *don't let her ruin this,* she leaned back, peering through the doorway at the drawing room clock. Less than an hour to go. She drew a nervous breath, picturing Luke in one of her father's polished boardrooms, handsome in a shirt and a waistcoat, talking about those classified things (getting the Indian Army ready for a war, if one should happen; Peter had told her on the drive home); she saw him leaving the office, running down the grand front steps, out onto the chaotic street, getting into a staff car, on his way to her. *Her.*

She stood, without knowing she was going to, and with no idea of what she wanted to do. But she couldn't just sit where she was, staring at the inedible food. She left it, sending Cook a silent apology, and went back indoors.

Depressingly well-versed by now in the art of making endless minutes pass, she set to her usual activities: a lackluster spell at the piano, filling the steamy villa with her clunky chords; into the study to find, then abandon, a Brontë; up to her room, to check her hair; past Alice's room, to listen at her silent door.

With only a quarter of an hour left to go, unable to bear another moment's drifting, trying not to stew over her mother, waiting for the sound of a motor that felt like it would never come, she pinned on her hat, pulled on her gloves, and went to sit on the villa's terra-cotta front steps.

It was hot, too hot really to be outside without any shade. Insects screeched everywhere. The long dusty driveway blurred in the haze.

Where is he now? she thought, and instantly felt more nervous. She pressed the backs of her hands to her burning cheeks. *Calm,* she told herself, *just be calm.* Birds pecked at the lawns, enviably nonchalant. Even the poor, persecuted peacocks, over by the hibiscus beds, looked more relaxed than she felt.

She wondered again where he was going to take her.

She closed her eyes against the glare, sweat beading on her forehead, and hoped, really hoped, that wherever it was, he'd get here to take her soon. She wasn't sure how much longer she could bear to wait.

He saw her, sitting pensively on the sunny steps, white dress reflecting the light, before she saw him. He stopped by the gate, stilled by the sight of her, the strange reality that she, hands clasped in her lap—hands he'd held, however briefly, the night before—was waiting for him. *Him.*

All that morning, he'd been so impatient to get to her. He'd sat in her father's office, Ernest Aldyce going on and on, rationalizing why he mustn't be sent anywhere near Europe, in *any* circumstances, but was needed in Bombay ("We're meant to be discussing current reserve numbers," Luke had reminded him, more than once), seeing her in his mind's eye, thinking of her voice, her laugh, all the countless things he still didn't know about her—what she liked, didn't like, read, all of that—more desperate to leave with each passing hour.

Her father at least had been very genial, very straightforward, not giving any argument when Luke had told him where he wanted to take her. "Peter's vouched for you," he'd said, "and my daughter clearly thinks you're none too bad. That's all I need. So long as she's happy, so am I."

There'd been a lightness in his voice; relief, Luke thought. He hadn't been entirely surprised to hear it. Peter had, after all, told him how much Richard had been worrying over Major Guy Bowen's interest in his daughter. That had been the day before, when Luke had asked Peter why Fraser Keaton thought Maddy engaged to Guy.

"Probably because Keaton hasn't yet learned not to believe everything he's told here," Peter had replied, before going on, saying that Keaton had better be careful not to repeat the gossip in front of Richard. "Alice kept writing while we were away, telling him about these trips Guy's been taking Maddy on."

"He doesn't approve?" Luke had said, not approving much himself.

"He just doesn't think it's right," Peter had said, "for Maddy."

Luke hadn't pressed him to say more. He hadn't wanted to talk about Guy Bowen, or what was right, or not right.

He certainly didn't want to think about him now, standing at the head of Maddy's driveway, looking in at her, oblivious, in the sunshine.

He still hadn't moved.

It came to him that he was waiting, just as he'd waited at the bazaar yesterday, for her to look up, notice him.

This time, she did.

He saw, even from a distance, how her face broke into a smile.

It did something to him, her smile.

Not holding back, not anymore, he walked, faster, closing the distance, unsure, now he was on his way, how he could have waited at all.

She stood as he approached, straightening her skirts with shaking hands, eyes moving, taking him in: the first time she'd seen him in daylight. He wore a gray suit, and had his jacket open, the top button of his shirt undone. His waves, beneath his panama, were darker than she'd thought; his skin was fairer: a light tan, rather than the deep burn of so many here. His face, though, his face was the same, just the same.

Calm, she told herself, *do just be calm.*

She wasn't calm at all. She heard it in her own taut voice as she called a hello.

His in return was low and warm, carrying through the sticky gold air. "I wanted to bring flowers," he said, drawing to a halt. "But I'd have been late."

"Then I'm glad you didn't bring flowers," she said.

He smiled, the skin around his eyes creasing. It did something to her, his smile. She felt the tension in her ease. Just a little.

"Are we going in?" he asked, looking up at the villa.

"Only if you want to," she said, thinking again of her mother; she'd forgotten her there for a second.

"We don't need to," he said, and she, replaying what she'd said to him the night before—*It's not my father you have to worry about*—wondered if he was thinking about Alice, too.

If he was, he didn't say.

He asked her if she was ready to leave.

"I think so," she said. "I still don't know where we're going, though."

"Then let's find out, shall we?"

There was no motor waiting for them on the road. No rickshaw or carriage either. Luke didn't stop on the road at all, but carried on, toward the dense trees on the other side, holding a branch back for her to pass under, into the vegetation.

She hesitated, brow creasing: half smile, half frown of bemusement. "*Where* are we going?" she said.

"Only one way to find out," he said.

She stared a moment longer, then, more curious than ever, ducked down, feet sinking on the thick bed of leaves.

It was much darker, beneath the canopy. The branches obscured the light; the air smelled green, of heat and damp earth, a hint of salt from the sea below. He walked on, and she followed, becoming breathless as they clambered down the rugged incline toward the beach.

"I think there might be snakes," she said.

"Yes," he replied, grinning over his shoulder, "we'd better be quick."

There was no one else there; the only sound came from their shoes sliding on the loose dirt, the birdsong, and their voices as she asked him about his morning, whether he had to return to work that afternoon, feeling her excitement grow as he said that no, no he didn't.

"Peter's told me what you're doing here," she said, slipping on a steep bit, stopping herself from falling just in time.

He caught her elbow anyway, grip strong, firm, and she felt all the muscles in her arm tense.

"Then now you know," he said, not letting go. "Like I said, very uninteresting."

"I think that's a matter of opinion," she said.

"Perhaps you'd feel differently," he said, pushing back another branch, "if you'd just spent the morning with Aldyce."

"I spend enough time with Diana," she said.

He laughed. She liked his laugh so much.

They were almost at the beach. The soft lapping of the water carried up from the shore. She bent over, peering through the lush foliage at the sand.

"Are we having a picnic?" she asked, the idea occurring to her.

"Not here," he said.

"Somewhere else then?" she said.

"An excellent guess," he said, jumping down the last drop, onto the beach.

She jumped, too, leaving the shade, squinting at the rush of sunlight. Hand shielding her eyes, she looked out to sea, blindingly blue in the glare, then along the coast, toward the city, wondering where he meant to take her.

"Are we going to swim there?" she said, trying for a joke to cover her befuddlement.

"If that's all right?" he said, smiling, playing along.

She smiled, too. "How far are we going?" she asked.

"Only a mile or so."

This time, she laughed. "Oh," she said, "just a mile."

"I knew you'd be game," he said. "But just to be safe, I've also borrowed a boat." He gestured down the sands, past where some fishermen in cropped trousers and salt-crusted shirts were laying their nets to dry, toward a small sailing dinghy bobbing at anchor a few yards from shore. *Quite* a few yards. She took them in, then glanced dubiously down at her skirts, thinking of her boots, her stockings beneath.

It took her a second to realize he was watching her, seeming to fight another smile, as though thinking of them, too.

"Don't look so worried," he said, sitting down on the rocks, removing his shoes, rolling up his trousers, "you'll stay quite dry."

"You're going to pull the boat in?" she asked, willing the burn in her cheeks away.

"We wouldn't be able to get out again," he said.

"But . . ." she began, then stopped as he stood, setting off toward the sea, and it dawned on her what he meant to do.

"Are you coming?" he asked.

"Yes," she said, gathering her wits, "of course."

He went out to the boat first, dropping his shoes and hat into the hull, then taking off his jacket, throwing that in, too. She waited by the water's edge as he rolled up his shirt sleeves, his eyes cast down on his cuffs, the sun making a silhouette of his dark profile. Then he turned, and she swallowed, trying to force her body loose as he waded toward her.

"Ready then, Maddy?"

It was the first time he'd called her that. It was very distracting. Before she could say anything in response, or her heart had had a chance to miss its beat, he slipped his arm around her waist, his other beneath her legs, and scooped her up. She reached around his neck reflexively, tensing even more at the shock of his skin.

"Is the water warm?" she asked, for something to say as much as anything.

"It's beautiful," he said. "You haven't been in?"

"No."

"We'll have to do something about that," he said.

She didn't think he meant now. But he tipped her, making her squeal, and then gathered her back to him, letting her know he'd never have let her go. He waded on; she felt the rise and fall of his chest, and found herself thinking back to her mother's suggestion they stay in for tea, freshly incredulous at the idea, the possibility that she might have missed this. Let the gossips do their worst. All she cared about was that she was in Luke's arms. All she wanted was to let her head drop against him, feel the beat of his heart. She was aware, so very aware, of how much she wanted to do that.

Far too soon, they were at the dinghy. He set her down, and she wished he hadn't, but then it didn't matter, because he climbed in beside her, asked her if she'd ever sailed before (she hadn't), and then told her to consider this her first lesson. He showed her how to unfurl the sail, tie the rope, explaining something about the wind, and the tiller, which she didn't follow ("Useless," he said, "where's your attention?"), and she laughed, her attention every bit with him, then exclaimed, falling back as he pulled the tiller round (so that's what he'd been trying to tell her), sending them off, scudding across the swell.

"Fun?" he said, shouting above the wind, the spray. "Yes?"

"Yes," she shouted back, hot air rushing over her face, into her eyes. "Yes."

Her hat blew free; she reached out in vain, trying to catch it, watching as it floated, so much slower than them, up, then down, dipping into the sea. She leaned over the edge, peering into the deep blue, at the hundreds of fish swimming beneath the surface, racing them. She looked up once more, at his smile, his shirt billowing, holding her hair back with both hands, tilting her face to the beating sky.

"You'll get burned," he warned.

"I don't care," she shouted back.

"Take my hat," he said.

She shook her head. "I never get to not wear a hat."

They hugged the land. The city sprawled to their left, that other world of heat and bustle, sewers and dust. To their right was the haze of the horizon, the silhouette of yet another P&O liner moving languidly toward England. She caught the way Luke looked at it, the sudden seriousness in him, and thought maybe he was thinking about his own voyage home. She didn't want to know if he was. She never wanted *this* voyage to end. She loved that he'd taken her on it, that they weren't now sitting in the back of a stuffy staff motor, stuck in Bombay traffic.

She thought he was probably taking her for lunch back at the Yacht Club. Or the Taj Hotel. Both were by the water. But they passed first the grand domes of the hotel, the Sea Lounge's tables on the shore's edge, then the red roof and yellow walls of the club, the stairs she'd sat on at New Year's, and he kept their course set straight.

It was only when she'd given up ever knowing where they were going that he called for her to duck, then changed the sail, steering them back toward land, a long stretch of beach. Its sands were packed, absolutely teeming with people from shore to road; even from a distance she could hear the vast thrum of voices, the carrying sitar music, the steady beat of street drums. As they got closer, she saw that in between the patchwork of saris and tunics were blankets bearing jewelry, sweet-smelling incense, ornaments, rugs and fabrics. It was another market, only like none she'd seen before. Smoke rose from vendors' charcoals: grilled vegetables and paneer, sizzling fat. Boats hugged the shallow waters, overflowing with vegetables, bags of rice, huge bunches of coriander and curry leaves, soaked in sunshine.

She turned, meeting Luke's smiling eyes, smiling herself, because of the way he'd obviously been watching her, waiting for her to speak.

"This isn't in your guidebook," she said.

"I wanted to bring you somewhere new," he said. "And we need to get your aunt her gift."

"It's incredible," she said, looking around once more, amazed, now that they were here, that she'd ever thought they might go to the Taj. She pictured the carriages and saloons lined up at the entrance, the formal dining room inside—the expressionless punkah wallahs, hot, stale air, clinking crockery, and polite, tinkling laughter—and couldn't have felt sorrier for everyone who was in it.

She felt that more and more as the afternoon passed. They went ashore, stopping at the stalls to buy Edie a woolen shawl, then kebabs rolled in naans, which they ate on a wooden jetty, the stallholders splashing through the shallow waves asking them to come, look, buy, buy.

"Later," they both said, "later."

They talked, so much, the words coming effortlessly, freely, just as they had the night before. In response to her prompting, Luke told her more about how he and Peter had become friends, the polo they'd used to play.

"Peter plays polo?" she said.

"He plays Peter's version of it," said Luke, "which, if it hasn't been banned yet, should be."

He described his house in Richmond, tone becoming wistful as he talked of the peace of it, even so close to London, how the Thames ran by the bottom of his garden, the boat he kept, and went out in whenever he could.

"Hence you being so handy with a sail," she said.

"No, actually," he said, "that I have my father to thank for. I grew up in Sandbanks; he used to take me out on the Solent. Still does, when I go to visit."

She smiled, enjoying the image of him with an older version of himself, in thick woolen jumpers, out on the cold, choppy sea.

They finished their kebabs, fetched kulfi. She didn't say how Guy had warned her off eating the ice creams. She didn't think of Guy at all. She spoke more of the small Oxfordshire village she'd grown up in, holidays in the Lakes, her time at Somerville, all the rallies in London.

"Were you ever arrested?" Luke asked.

"No," she said.

"Don't sound so disappointed," he told her.

One hour turned to another, on and on, the intense heat ebbing, mellowing, until, without either of them stopping to acknowledge it was happening, the crowds thinned, the waters emptied, the boats all packed up, on their way home.

He arched his neck, brown curls brushing his collar as he looked up at the darkening sky, then across to where the sun was bleeding into the horizon, stare narrowing, as reluctant as Maddy felt.

"We have to go?" she said.

"I promised your father we'd be back by nightfall," he said. "He didn't seem to have much faith in my ability to sail in darkness."

"No?"

"No."

"Such a worrier," she said.

He smiled. "Wait here," he said, "I'll bring the boat to you."

The journey back in the deepening dusk was, if possible, even more beautiful than the one out had been. Slower, too. The wind had changed direction, leaving the sea calmer, inky, filling the sail just enough to push them softly along. They sat next to one another. Luke showed Maddy how to work the tiller, guiding her hand with his. She stared down at their fingers, hers pale, his dark, marveling at her earlier nerves, her coyness; it seemed like something someone else must have felt. The city's lights came on one by one, glinting on the shoreline, and she dropped her head against his shoulder, breathing in the trace of the beach's charcoals on his shirt, his scent of soap and heat. She closed her eyes, relishing the breeze, warm on her burned face, and the vastness of the sea, stretching all around.

The stars were out by the time they reached the beach. All the fishermen had gone home. Luke dropped the anchor, jumped into the sea, and turned, pulling the boat toward him.

She placed her hands on his shoulders, felt his come around her waist.

She looked down, her hair loose, falling forward. "Thank you," she said.

"For what?" he asked.

"This day," she said.

"You know I planned it," he said, "just for this excuse to hold you."

"I thought as much," she said.

Slowly, feeling each beat in her chest, she dipped, toward him.

This time, there was no Peter to interrupt them. There was no one.

She thought she knew what was coming. It wasn't her first kiss, after all. There'd been boys back in Oxford; a handful of stolen moments in dark hallways at balls, college parties.

Only, they'd been different.

This was different.

His lips brushed hers, then again, and she felt herself fall, from the boat, into his arms, with an abandon that shocked her. She didn't question it. He kissed her more, scooping her close, and she didn't think at all. She pressed into him, the strength of him holding her tighter, the kiss going wonderfully on and on.

She wanted to be nothing but entirely happy. She almost was. But, as they pulled apart, and she rested her forehead against his, her skirt dipping in the shallow sea, she saw the way he looked at her, the movement of his thoughts behind his dark gaze, and, out of nowhere, was reminded of how he'd watched the P&O liner leave earlier, only this time it was impossible to push the prospect of his going aside. Instead, eyes in his eyes, she found herself thinking of what had brought him to India in the first place—this war that she wanted to believe could never come, only she'd read too many articles on the arms race in Europe, the lands everyone wanted off one another—and felt the spike of her old fear return: that this happiness, so unexpected, so surreal, wouldn't last; a shadow, moving over the perfect day. *Don't trust it.*

He held her tighter, as though he guessed some of what she was thinking.

He didn't ask her about it, though. Just as she hadn't asked him, when they'd seen that liner disappear before.

He kissed her again, and she tried to let her fear go.

What was the point in holding on to it?

There, in the blackening darkness, the sea rippling, silence all around, keeping the world out, and them, just them, in, she told herself that there was no point, no point at all.

It's all going to be fine.

CHAPTER TEN

It's all going to be fine.

Alice told herself that as she waited by the drawing room window, pained eyes on her daughter and this Luke Devereaux, barely visible in the now deep night, coming through the gates, meandering up the leafy driveway, toward the house. She rested her fingers on the window, watching the slow way they walked, hand in hand, their heads tipped toward one another, so oblivious to everything else around them, and even in spite of her reservations (which were legion) felt her heart pinch, the start of the saddest kind of smile: part memory of what it felt like to walk that way with a young man; part grief, that this was the happiest she'd seen her daughter since she'd arrived in India; part fear that Luke would leave (Richard had said he had less than a week left in the country), either compelling Madeline to follow, or hurting her horribly.

She pressed her hand harder against the warm glass, brow creasing as she realized Madeline was wearing no hat. Her blond curls were disheveled, falling down her back. She'd been sailing, of course; Richard had told Alice that, too, when he'd got home from the office an hour before. Alice had been furious with him, for not trying to stop her.

"Our daughter's been out on a boat?" she'd said. "All day?"

"There are worse things, Alice."

"Are there?" she'd said. "Do I really need to tell you what people will say?"

"Who gives a damn?" he'd said, pouring them both brandies. "Let them talk. What does it matter?"

"It matters plenty," she'd said, "whether it should or not."

"She's a grown woman, whether you like it or not."

"Perhaps I'd like it a deal more if I hadn't had her childhood stolen—"

"No," he'd cut her off, "no. I am *not* doing this again."

He'd turned, gone upstairs, leaving their brandies untouched. The lead-crystal glasses were still sitting on the sideboard; a fly had landed in one, drowned in the alcohol. (It seemed a happy enough end. *There are worse things*.) She hadn't seen Richard since. She wanted to be angry at him still (it was a familiar battle), especially now, seeing their daughter in such a state of disarray. And yet, as she continued to watch her approach, sun-kissed and happy, she couldn't manage to be. She found herself picturing Madeline out on the waves, head thrown back—that gurgling laugh she, Alice, had been so terrified of forgetting every day of the past fifteen years—and felt the pull of another smile.

"Are you ready?"

She started at Richard's voice, breaking through the humid silence. He was by the doorway, dressed for supper in white tie. She could tell from the softness in his weathered face that he'd caught her smile.

"You're talking to me again?" she said.

"I'm always talking to you, Alice."

He crossed the room, running his arms around her waist. She stiffened, but didn't pull away. Whatever her resentment toward him, she never really wanted to do that.

"It's like I keep telling you," he said, "Guy's not the right man for her."

"He's the *perfect* man for her," said Alice.

"No. He's just not going to leave. That's not the same thing."

"He'd look after her, Richard, you know he would."

"She has two perfectly good parents."

"I don't think Guy wants to be a parent."

"I'm not sure I want to think about that," he said.

Alice sighed.

"He's nearly the same age as you," said Richard, "almost twenty years older than Maddy."

"You're almost twenty years older than me," she said, which he was. He was sixty to her forty-four. They'd become engaged when she was twenty-one and heartbroken (thank you, Fitz; thank you, Edie). Richard had been on home leave in Oxford. He'd taken her on walks along the river, for teas in Oxford's cobbled alleyways, convinced her everything could be all right again. They'd married quickly—he'd said he was terrified of her changing her mind (which she'd never had any intention of doing)—and, to her parents' lasting fury, had set sail for Bombay the very same day. Madeline (a name Alice had always loved, and could never bring herself to shorten) had been born ten months later, the only one of her treasured babies to survive a pregnancy; all that mattered, from her very first breath.

"Was I wrong to marry you?" she asked Richard now.

"It was the cleverest thing you ever did," he said. "But Maddy isn't you."

"She'd be happy with Guy," she said. "He thinks the world of her."

Richard said nothing.

She returned her attention to the window. They were almost at the house. Hidden by the shutters, she studied Luke as she hadn't been able to earlier that day, when she'd tried to make him out from her bedroom. He was much younger than Guy, thirty perhaps, and undeniably handsome, with the kind of face one noticed. That alone didn't worry her. Guy was handsome, too, albeit in a fairer, somehow more gentlemanly way. It was the warmth in this stranger that unsettled her, the almost . . . *magnetic* vitality. The way he was looking at Madeline; how she was looking at him. . . .

A fresh spike of dread shot through her. "I can't lose her," she said to Richard. "Not again."

He didn't tell her it was too soon to worry about that. He didn't insist that she'd be able to go, too, to England, if it came to it. He'd been with her, after all, that one time she'd gone back. That awful summer after he'd first taken Madeline.

"Stop pushing her away then" was all he said. They both turned, hearing footsteps coming into the porch, along the tiled hallway. He squeezed her shoulders. "Invite Luke to dinner," he said. "Try."

She nodded slowly, swallowing on her nerves. So odd, to be shy with one's own daughter. But she would do as Richard said. Much as she hoped that the entire affair would end as quickly as it had begun (with as little pain as possible), she knew she needed to. The other night in the garden, when she'd painted that stone, Madeline's smile had meant . . . everything.

She'd kept peeking into Madeline's room ever since, just to check the stone was still there on her bedside table. They'd been getting somewhere, the two of them. She'd ruined that, with her feigned headache earlier. She couldn't risk doing that again.

She had to try. She *had* to.

It's all going to be fine.

She turned to the door, eyes moving over Madeline's face as she came into the room, suffused with joy. *You look like you've had a lovely day,* she meant to say to her.

She wasn't sure why "You seem to have lost your hat" was what came out.

"Was she angry?" Della asked Maddy the next morning.

Maddy had come to call on her, as she'd promised she would, at Peter's house: a small villa in between Malabar Hill and the city. They were having a breakfast of soft rolls and honey in his postage-stamp garden, trees hemming them in on every side, mercifully blocking the already hot sun, but not the noise of traffic and tram bells, the thick buzz of voices carrying from the streets.

"About the hat?" said Maddy.

"About any of it," said Della.

"Disappointed, I think," said Maddy, swallowing her mouthful.

"Oh no," said Della. "That's always worse."

"Isn't it, though?" said Maddy, feeling fairly disappointed herself. To think she'd actually been glad to see her mother waiting there in the drawing room; relieved, that she'd been willing to meet Luke after all. "You should have heard the way she asked him to stay for dinner," she said to Della. "She might as well have been inviting him to pull her teeth."

"And he didn't stay?"

"No, he had to be at one of the cantonments for nine. He's coming tonight, though."

"For dinner with your parents?"

"No, they've got something for Papa's work. He's taking me out; I don't know where."

Does it matter? he'd said when she'd asked him before he'd left, the two of them alone in the driveway.

No, she'd said as he took her hand, pulling her close, pushing all thoughts of Alice's curt manner aside, *I don't suppose it does.*

"You're smiling," said Della. "Like a lunatic. And your face is very burned, by the way."

"I know," said Maddy, touching her sore cheekbones tentatively. "I'm just hoping it fades before I see Diana Aldyce again."

"God, yes," said Della.

"*Let's hope we don't get freckles,*" they both mimicked, and burst out laughing.

"She'll be chomping at the bit to see you," said Della, reaching for the pot. "She was *full* of questions about how you and Luke know one another when you disappeared the other night. Not that I said anything."

"Thank you."

"A pleasure," said Della. "Frustrating Diana might just be my new favorite sport. You realize she's going to have all sorts to say when she gets wind that you went out unchaperoned."

Maddy shrugged. "If it wasn't that, it would be something else."

"And is your mother so relaxed about it?"

"Hardly. Which is rich, as she never had an issue about me going anywhere with Guy, and apparently used to go out unchaperoned with my father all the time." Richard had said as much over dinner, when Alice had tried to make a fuss again about Maddy's doing it now. Maddy was still absorbing the revelation. "I've never pictured her doing something like that."

"I quite like the idea," said Della. "Alice, the rebel."

Maddy raised an eyebrow. "I've asked her to trust me anyway. And promised that we'll be back by midnight."

"The fairy tale witching hour," said Della.

Maddy didn't laugh at the quip. Neither did Della, who was suddenly eyeing her with what looked like concern, making her feel fairly wary herself.

She asked her what was wrong.

"It's just . . ." Della began. "Well, Peter said . . ." She sighed. "Has Luke told you he's leaving?"

"Oh," said Maddy flatly. (So that's what it was about.) "Yes." He'd spoken to her about it on their walk home from the beach. "It's not long, is it?"

"Not long at all," said Della.

Maddy's brow creased. "I don't want to think about it."

"Best of luck with that," said Della. "And are you not thinking about Guy either?"

"Very good," said Maddy. She'd been carefully not thinking about him all morning. Just as she'd been determinedly ignoring the strangeness of Fraser Keaton telling Luke the two of them were engaged (another thing Luke had passed on during their walk home. "What?" she'd said, stopping in her tracks. "*What?*"), not to mention whether Guy knew about the rumor, if he'd done anything to correct it, or if he'd been hurt that she'd failed to even say hello to him at the Gymkhana Club. (Also, all those bottles of boiled water.)

Della stirred her tea. "I expect Guy will be steaming when he hears you and Luke went sailing."

"I'm not sure Guy gets steaming," said Maddy, struggling to imagine him, so gentle, ever being angry, feeling instantly worse, because he really was so very, very kind. "Can we speak about something else?"

"All right," said Della. "Since it's you."

As she talked on, trying to guess where Luke would take Maddy that night ("A restaurant? Or another beach? No, that would be too much for nighttime; you'd be *ruined*"), Maddy felt herself relax once more, readily distracted by the tantalizing thought of being ruined by Luke, repeating to Della what she'd told him the night before.

She didn't care where they went.

Which she didn't. She really, really didn't.

Not that night, which wasn't a beach, or another boat, rather a drive just the two of them in Luke's borrowed motor to the old Portuguese part of town. They parked in a tiny cobbled side street, beautiful European houses with latticed shutters and balconies on both sides, and ducked through the low doorway of a tenement. Luke took Maddy's hand, leading her up a narrow stone staircase toward the scent of curry leaves and steamed rice, laughing over his shoulder at her intrigued smile, then opened another door, revealing the most beautiful rooftop restaurant, all burning lanterns, incense and smoking tandoors, Indians dressed in their finest silks, women dripping in bangles.

"Do you like it?" he asked.

"Like it?" she said, amazed he could ask. "I love it."

They sat at a low table, a single flickering wick in a saucer of paraffin between them, the burr of Urdu all around. The owner—a portly middle-aged man in a linen tunic and trousers—brought them soft naans, platters of spiced vegetables, which they must have eaten, only Maddy wasn't aware of them doing it. She couldn't recall taking a bite afterward, once she was home and alone in her bed, replaying each second of the night (smiling, like a lunatic); all she could remember was how it had felt to hold Luke's hand when they'd climbed the stairs, the moment he'd held her stare, asked her how she'd feel about him wiring his contact at General Staff, staying in Bombay longer.

"You can do that?" she'd said, scared to even ask, to believe he might.

"I don't see why not," he'd said, eyes shining, happy, it felt like, that she was so happy. As though she could have been anything else. "There's plenty of work still to do."

"Oh my God."

He'd laughed. "Is that a yes, you'd like me to stay?"

"Of course it is," she'd said, laughing, too, at the relief, the shock, the wonder that he really would. But, "You don't want to get back to your river in Richmond?"

"Very much," he'd said. "It's not going anywhere, though."

"But what if they don't want you to stay?"

"Then I'll take a holiday," he'd said, laughing more, as though trying to make sense of himself. "You are not very easy to leave, Miss Bright."

He didn't need to take a holiday. His contact wired by return, saying General Staff would be glad to keep him on in Bombay. He drove over the next day between meetings to tell Maddy, surprising her out on the veranda, where she'd been agonizing over when they'd know, also having tea with her mother (who herself had been acting rather surprisingly by bringing the tray out in the first place, then quizzing Maddy, albeit stiffly, on her meal the night before. "It sounds very . . . interesting. Was the food quite safe?").

It was Alice who asked Luke how long he'd be staying on now for, talking for Maddy (who'd momentarily lost the power of speech).

"I don't know," he said, his eyes holding Maddy's. He wore another dark suit, a crisp white shirt. A smile played on his lips. "I think it all depends on what happens. Certainly another month."

"A month?" Alice said.

A month, Maddy thought, heart pummeling. *A whole month.*

Luke went on, saying it could be longer, and Alice asked him if that meant his stay was indefinite.

"No," he said. "I will go back. Certainly by the summer. I'm afraid I'm not cut out for life in the Raj."

Alice stared, as though not quite comprehending.

Maddy comprehended. Much as she'd started to enjoy her time in India—the past couple of days especially—she wasn't cut out for a lifetime here either. Loath as she was to get ahead of herself (that old superstition again), she was already picturing a soft lawn beneath a willow tree, a boat bobbing on a summery Thames.

Meanwhile he was staying on, truly, truly staying on. For her. *Her.*

"A month," she said, rediscovering her voice. She wanted to get up, throw her arms around him, kiss him like she'd kissed him in the sea.

His eyes sparked from across the room. He held his whole body still, like he was containing the urge, too. "At least a month," he said.

She beamed, squealed, looked from him to her mother (not beaming), then straight back to him. "Is this madness?" she said.

"Probably," he said, laughing.

Alice sighed. "I think you'd better come to dinner tonight," she said.

He did.

And it was fine. Nothing like as relaxed as the hours they'd now spent just the two of them, but perfectly . . . fine. Despite Alice's all too clear reluctance to even think of starting to like Luke, she did go to an obvious effort, even making a special trip to the Taj's kitchens to fetch oysters fresh enough to trust for the first course, then dressing the dining table herself. And she was polite when he arrived, thanking him for the flowers he brought ("And you weren't even late buying them," said Maddy quietly. "I didn't think that would be the best idea," he said), offering him a drink.

She just didn't speak very much from then on. Luke tried to draw her into conversation several times through the meal, asking her about everything from her childhood in England to places she'd visited in India, but she gave only the barest minimum by way of reply. She told him she'd grown up in Oxford (information Maddy already knew and had passed on), had been to lots of places in India, but no, she wasn't sure she had a favorite, although she liked the cool of the hills.

"You used to love sledging with Maddy," said Richard. "You'd do it for hours."

"I remember," she said.

"Maddy," he turned to her, "do you?"

"She'll have been too young," said Alice.

"I think I do remember, actually," said Maddy. She didn't say it to be kind. Or at least, not just for that. Now that she tried, she was sure she could recall trudging up a slope, hanging on to long woolen skirts, hearing a breathless voice. *One last time.* Or had that been Edie? Maddy had had so many more winters with her in Oxford, it was hard to know.

"Do you go up there these days?" Luke asked Alice, interrupting her thoughts.

"I haven't been since Madeline left for England," said Alice. "Now, has everyone finished?"

"It's not you," Maddy said to Luke as they walked together to his motor once the meal was over. It was baking, despite being almost eleven. Her evening dress stuck to her damp skin. The nights were getting ever hotter; the air was laden with the scent of the day's sun on the earth, the steamy perfume of the garden's overflowing flower beds. "It's just the way she is."

"Is it?" he said, glancing over his shoulder at the house, seeming to think about it, his strong face contemplative in the darkness. "Do you notice the way she looks at you?"

"Looks at me?"

"It's like she can't quite believe you're there," he said.

"No," she said.

"Yes," he said. "She watches you, all the time. She adores you, Maddy."

Maddy laughed, because it was such a strange, if sweet, thought. "She barely came to see me in Oxford," she reminded him. "Only once."

"Have you ever asked her why?"

"I asked Papa, Edie . . ."

"But not her?"

"I—" Maddy began, then stopped. "She wouldn't tell me if I did."

"Maybe you should try her," he said.

"Maybe," she said, noncommittally and with no intention of doing it.

He gave her an exasperated look, then turned to open his door. "I shall see you at seven tomorrow," he said.

She smiled. "Where will we go?"

He smiled, too. Stealing another look at the house, he ran his hand around her neck, sending tremors right through her. "Does it matter?" he said.

"No," she said, leaning forward for his kiss, "I don't suppose it does."

He took her to a dimly lit curry house on the outskirts of the city, at the end of a lane so dark as to be almost black. It was full of locals who stared when they arrived, but otherwise ignored them, caught up in their own laughter, their meals, which they ate with their hands, and their noisy, indiscernible chatter. Maddy's evening gown brushed the earthen floor as she followed Luke to one of the few spare tables ("You seem to have ruined your hem," said Alice, who was waiting up when she returned). She breathed in steamed rice and spices, the kerosene used to fire the stoves, and the musty throng of bodies, the cows who lurked, waiting to eat everyone's banana-leaf plates. They ordered dal and roti, chai in murky cups, and he told her of his day, the many things he was working on ("I've decided you're not a spy after all," he said. "Excellent," she said, "then I'm doing my job well"), how hard it was to track the reserves in such a vast country, to know their skill levels, then the additional railway and ship transportations needed on standby, training requirements in India, at grounds in England. "It's endless," he said.

"And hopefully pointless," she said.

"Hopefully," he said, and she wished he could have sounded more convinced.

"I wish I could, too," he said.

The following night, as a concession to Alice—who was still far from happy about them going out so much alone—they took Peter and Della with them and went to the restaurant at Watson's Hotel, not far from the cricket oval. There were other British there this time, but mainly tourists, and no one that any of them knew. They all sat in a corner of the buzzing dining room, talking, laughing, eating until Maddy felt as though her stays might burst ("I think mine already have," said Della), the hours flying by. In response to Maddy's quizzing, Luke spoke more of his own family, how his father was a lawyer, his mother a doctor.

"Oh, a doctor," said Maddy. "I feel even worse now for not being anything."

"You're not nothing," he said.

Later, as they left Peter and Della behind and walked slowly up Malabar Hill, hand in hand, the motor parked at the bottom, just so that they might have some time together with no one else watching, Maddy spoke more of Oxford, confessing how she'd always liked to think of her mother growing up there, when she'd lived in Edie and Fitz's village. "It made me feel closer to her, I suppose."

"Are her parents still there?"

"No," she said. "They died when I was young, I barely knew them. Edie did. She said they were always very strict with my mother."

"She and Alice were friends?"

"Good friends," said Maddy, "once. Edie said they drifted apart after school. I'm sure there's more to it."

"Is this another thing you haven't asked your mother about?"

"Aren't you clever?"

He smiled. "Did your father know your mother back then?"

"No, he was already working here. Edie said he came back on leave when she and Mama were eighteen and fell head over heels, but Mama didn't want to know. It was only when he came again, three years later, that she agreed to marry him."

"And then you came along."

"As you see."

"Well, thank God for Alice agreeing," he said, and slowed, pulling her to him, face serious, dark eyes dancing. He raised his hand, touching her cheek, and she turned, pressing her lips to his palm, hearing his intake of breath. He leaned down, closer: another kiss she never wanted to end.

One week ran into the next, each passing faster than the last. They went again to the rooftop restaurant, more curry houses, and while there were other occasions when Peter and Della came with them ("Leaves for plates," said Peter. "Such larks." "Do be quiet," said Della), mostly they kept it just them, losing hours in hidden garden restaurants bursting with mango trees and frangipanis, giving the Aldyces and their friends plenty to talk about. ("They're all electrified at the club," said Della, "although of course keep very quiet whenever your parents are near. I wish you could hear them, though, Maddy.")

On the weekends, Luke came to the villa, persevering with Alice, talking to her of Bombay, how much it was growing, the noise that was so easy to forget when not here, and did anyone want to stop those children torturing that peacock?

"I'll do it," said Maddy, setting off toward where Suya was standing between her siblings, little legs akimbo, the squawking peacock's tail in hand. "Suya. *Suya. . . .*"

"Suya," called Richard, following in Maddy's wake, "what did that bird ever do to you?"

Suya didn't respond. She kept tugging at the peacock's feathers, her angelic face tense with effort as it screeched and battered its wings.

"Stop," called Maddy.

"Enough," shouted Luke from the veranda, half laughing, half scolding.

Suya beamed back at him. With her brother and sister delightedly egging her on, she gave one final yank, and, just as Maddy and Richard reached her, hooted in victory, released the terrified bird, and raised her stolen feather to the beating sky.

"Jesus Christ," said Richard.

Other times, Maddy and Luke went for walks up to the Hanging Gardens at the top of the hill, where they'd stroll around the manicured lawns, dragonflies filling the air, birds circling—vultures among them, lured by the bodies the local Parsi community left out for them at their nearby Towers of Silence.

"No," Maddy said, horrified when Luke told her about the tradition.

"Yes," he said, laughing at her face.

"Well, now that's all I'm going to be able to think of when I come here," she said.

"That's no good," he replied. "Let me see if I can distract you."

They stopped to talk as briefly as possible with the other people they ran into there ("Goodness me," said the sunburned sailor, "Maddy. You're becoming a rarity. What an honor"), and sat in the shade of the palms, her head on his shoulder, hand in his hand, both of them staring at the sea and city stretching beneath.

I never want this to end, she thought.

Please, never let this end.

They returned to the beach they'd sailed from, taking a picnic Maddy had asked Cook to package up (attempting to charm him with the Hindustani she'd asked Luke to pass on. "Perhaps you are talking now in English," Cook said. "So I am understanding"). The fishermen were all back, lining the shore. Luke paid them for fresh snapper to have with their saffron rice and tomato salad, and made Maddy laugh until her eyes streamed by trying to light a fire to grill them on, failing abysmally, until she dug in her bag and produced the matches he'd posted back to her after New Year's, and which she'd kept all this time.

He narrowed his eyes. "Did you really not know you had them?" he asked.

"I forgot," she said, still laughing, "I swear it. Don't use too many of them, I want to keep them."

"I only need one *now*," he said, kneeling again in the sand.

As April moved toward May, and no word came from England asking him to return, he left the Taj Mahal Palace Hotel and moved into private rooms by the water, near the docks. He told Maddy he preferred the privacy, the certainty that he wouldn't run into the Aldyces of the city in the lobby. ("One sympathizes," said Richard with a sigh.) Maddy didn't visit him there. She feared that to be caught disappearing into his apartments would be a step too far, even for her. She was sorely tempted, though. She was desperate by now to be alone with him for something more than a few stolen moments before they returned to the villa, back for a midnight that always came too, too soon. Each time they kissed, it was harder to pull away. She could tell, from the tense way he forced himself from her, that he felt it, too.

"Maddy," he said, "I'm not sure what you're doing to me."

She wasn't sure what he was doing to her.

May passed. The temperature soared, edging the mercury ever upward. She struggled to sleep through the broiling hours until dawn. She thought of nothing but him, whether he was lying awake and restless, too. What it would feel like, to be by his side.

Every night, she wanted him to go on, for them to go on.

She didn't know how to tell him that, though.

Was there even form for asking a man to ruin you?

"No," said Della as they took tea one steamy morning. The heat sat like a damp blanket over Peter's drooping trees, the dead grass. "Unequivo-cally, no."

"You're no use," said Maddy.

"Sorry about that," said Della, taking a bite of a cardamom bun. "Maybe you shouldn't take my word for it anyway. I have absolutely no experience of all this."

"Neither do I," said Maddy.

"I'm not sympathizing," said Della. "I'm far too envious. Talking of which, Diana was asking about you last night, complaining that she hadn't seen hide nor hair of you or Luke in far too long. I think she'd rather like a bit of ruination care of Mr. Devereaux herself."

"She can make do with Ernest," said Maddy.

"Ugh," said Della, spraying crumbs, "just imagine."

Maddy really didn't want to.

"Back to your conundrum," said Della, chewing. "In my view, you either need to brazen it out, this is the twentieth century after all, or wait for him to do it for you."

Maddy's brow creased, replaying his words. *I'm not sure what you're doing to me.* "I think he might be waiting, too."

"Well then," said Della, "you know what to do."

He had been waiting.

He'd been driving himself to distraction, waiting. Twentieth century it might be, but he knew how the world worked, and they were causing enough of a stir as it was. (Peter had kept him well abreast of the gossip: "The mems can hardly believe their luck. Alice and Richard's *daughter . . .*") Luke couldn't have cared less for himself, but he cared for her: whether it would, eventually, upset her; if for him to ask for more would be too much.

Night after night, he thought about nothing but her. He lay sweating and sleepless in his bed, the waves lapping the walls of his building below, and replayed every minute they'd shared: the sound of her voice, her laughter, each turn of her head, her every look and smile—thousands now, filling his mind.

He didn't know what they were going to do. He couldn't stay on in India, of that much he was certain. He'd been happy enough to come back, to have this second taste of everything he'd fallen under the spell of back when he was an army captain—the vast beauty of the country, its raw life, heat, and color—but a handful of months had been more than enough to remind him of why he'd been so desperate to leave then. Nothing else but being with her could have compelled him to stay so long in the frenetic chaos, the entitlement everywhere. The thought of getting to her each evening was all that kept him going through the endless days of meetings, the drills in exposed, fly-infested parade grounds, the hours consumed sweating in traffic, being civil to people who were all too often anything but to their hosts.

He wanted to take her to England with him, of course he did (however horrendous he felt about what that would do to her mother, and he felt awful. "So you should," said Peter. "Poor Alice. Richard says she's beside herself"); he'd wanted to do that from the moment he'd returned to Bombay and caught sight of her in that packed bazaar. But it had only been a few months. He didn't want to rush her, rush anything. Not when he didn't need to. No one was putting him under any pressure to return to England, after all (quite the opposite; MOST GRATEFUL FOR YOUR SERVICE STOP); it felt for the best to hold off asking her.

And if he was holding off asking that, he surely shouldn't ask anything else either.

So he'd been waiting.

Not wanting to rush her.

On the early June evening that he borrowed another boat from the Yacht Club, planning to take her, as promised, to the beach he'd spoken about at the Gymkhana Club, see if they could find those turtles hatching, he hand on heart had no thoughts of doing any more than going for another sail, sitting side by side with her on the sands.

It made him happy, of course, that she had other ideas for the evening. It made him bloody ecstatic. But he had no intentions himself.

Not really.

Not seriously.

No, he didn't.

("Liar," she said afterward.)

She was oddly keyed up from the second she ran out to meet him in the driveway. Her cream skin had an unusual heat to it, her smile a devilish slant. He didn't read anything into it, though, or that she was quieter than usual on the walk down to the beach, then again as they sailed across the pink-tinged sea, the sky aglow with the setting sun. He was too caught up in watching her watch the water, blond curls loose, her chin pressed to her shoulder, bare but for the capped sleeves of her dark evening dress.

They arrived at the beach just as the sun was disappearing. The sands were deserted. Aside from the gentle break of the waves, the swooping gulls, it was silent. Only the smoke rising from the thick vegetation behind, carrying the scent of charcoal and grilled spices, gave away that there was anyone else nearby at all.

He steered them on, toward the shore. She leaned over the boat, peering down, biting her lip. It had been another boiling day. The heat on the horizon was still as fierce as any European noon. He could almost feel her temptation.

"You should go in," he said.

"How warm is it?" she asked.

"Like a bath," he said. He swam every morning, from the cove by his rooms.

"A bath," she echoed.

She peeled off her gloves. He watched her do it. He couldn't look away. Her fingers trembled as she dipped them into the water.

She was nervous. The realization struck him. He didn't immediately understand why, but his chest contracted, seeing it. He didn't want her to be nervous. Not with him. Not ever. It was the last thing he wanted for her. Just as he hadn't been able to stand the thought of her homesick. He'd barely known her five minutes before he'd never wanted her to be anything but happy.

And now, right now, with his own back prickling with perspiration beneath his shirt, he wanted her to know what it felt like to have the Arabian Sea drench the sweat from your skin, to not sit a second longer cooking in stockings and corset and God only knew what else.

"That's not going in," he said.

"No?" she said, turning; that slanted smile.

"I think you know, no," he said, still not entirely clear what he was about to do, but going to her, the boat rocking beneath him, laughing at the way she burst out laughing, her eyes wide, incredulous. "You definitely do know how to swim?" he said.

"I do," she said, "but—"

He didn't wait for her to finish. He pulled her up, into his arms, feeling her laughter all through her body, loving how that felt, and, ignoring her protests about her dress, his clothes, threw them both in, not letting her go, not even when the water rushed up, surrounding them.

He was still laughing when they came up for air. So was she, her hair plastered over her cheeks, face as incensed as it was delighted.

"I can't believe you did that," she said. "My mother's going to *kill* you."

"I don't want to talk about your mother," he said, kissing her. "Stop talking about your mother."

She laughed more, kissing him back, stronger, more insistent than he'd known her; the same urgency he felt. He held her tighter, half carrying her against the weight of her gown pulling her down, feeling her lips give beneath his. Her hands ran down his back, skimming his sopping shirt, the muscles either side of his spine, each one tensing in turn. He kissed her throat, her collarbone, tasting salt, the night's heat on her skin. Moving without thinking, he reached around her back, about to undo the clasps on her bodice, then paused: one last hesitation.

She looked at him, the sky turning black behind her. She dipped forward, her lips to his ear. "You have my permission," she whispered.

He groaned inwardly, and knew he wasn't waiting. Not anymore.

"Am I brazen?" she asked.

"You're an absolute harlot," he said. "But I love you for it."

"You love me?" she said, a smile in her voice.

He kissed her more. "You know I love you."

They stayed in the water a long time that night, taking off their clothes, throwing them into the boat, never letting one another go, not even for an instant. "Like a bath," she said, breathless. He kissed every part of her, in the way he'd been aching to do, slowly, savoring each second, not rushing her, not rushing anything. He felt her every movement, every touch, and wanted nothing more than for it to go on, on and on.

They never did see any turtles hatch that night. He forgot they'd come to see them at all. They swam back to the boat, the life jackets as pillows beneath them, her head on his chest, hand in his hand, and he forgot everything but her. Nothing else mattered. There was no mother who didn't want her daughter stolen. No kaiser. No sepoys. No bayonet practices, or broadsheets talking of the intensifying European climate, how Germany, Austria-Hungary, and indeed everyone except Britain needed to keep their imperial ambitions in check.

It was just them.

All they needed.

He was always glad, afterward, that they had that. That for those hours when they lay together in the swaying boat, talking for the first time of a riverside in Richmond, and a house that would feel far too empty without her in it, they'd been oblivious to how much of a fantasy it all really was. That they'd been happy, so unreservedly happy.

With no idea of just how soon that was all going to change.

CHAPTER ELEVEN

King's Fifth Military Convalescent Hospital, 1917

The drawing room was busy, bustling in fact, filled with nurses, several orderlies, and all the patients, too. The fire roared in the grate. Lamps of varying shapes and sizes burned on the coffee tables, the windowsills and mantelpiece, warming the watery, gray light.

It was winter.

Again.

And it was snowing, just as it had been that November day Jones had arrived.

Earlier, he'd wrapped himself in a greatcoat, pulled on boots, and trekked with some of the orderlies through the thick drifts, out to the surrounding forests to cut down a fir. He'd walked briskly, savoring being out, losing his breath; becoming, for just one short hour, something other than a patient. This was the third time he'd made such a trek. His third Christmas at the King's Fifth.

He'd hoped so much he'd only see one. ("We all hoped that," said Arnold sadly.)

On clear days, they could still hear the guns, not at the Somme these past months, but Passchendaele. The battle, now drawing to a close, had cost hundreds of thousands more lives. Jones had met one of the men who'd been out there. The man had spoken, before Sister Lytton had interceded to stop him upsetting himself, of the way the Ypres soil had turned to swamp in the rain, men falling and drowning in the mud.

"Yes," Jones had found himself saying, "I remember that," and then stopped, hearing his own words, *I remember*, heart quickening in wonder, anticipation of . . .

Nothing.

Nothing else had come. He'd never been able to think what had made him say it in the first place. It had been a tease: a memory of a memory, but no more than that.

That soldier had already left, home to his wife in Portsmouth and a local doctor Arnold had referred him to for the condition he called shell shock. So many others had left, too; hardly any of the patients in residence when Luke had first arrived were still with him. There had been many who'd become well enough to be cared for by their families. Several had got completely better, seemingly overnight (a miracle Jones couldn't help himself hoping for, even if it would mean going back to the trenches). A couple the year before had given up and left the hospital in another way, which had made Jones so desperately sad; selfishly afraid, too, that he could end up like that.

"Not you," said Arnold. "You have too much to live for, my man."

Sister Lytton had taken their deaths very hard, saying again and again that she'd let her boys down. After the second one had gone, just after the Somme the year before, she'd left, too, for an entire month.

"A spot of leave," Arnold had told Jones. "She'll be back with her cups of cocoa before you know it, you'll see."

"I hope so," Jones had said. Exhausting as he sometimes found Sister Lytton's cheeriness, it had been awful to see it leach from her.

He'd told her that, when she'd returned that October.

"You missed me, Officer Jones?" she'd asked, and had looked so happy at the idea of it, that he'd said, "Yes, of course I missed you."

He had, he supposed. As much as he had it in him to miss anyone.

"What's been happening here while I've been away?" she'd asked, and he'd told her about the masked captain's wife visiting—an aloof, overly manicured woman—and how he, Jones, had only seen her fleetingly as she'd departed, sweeping out through the hallway with the VAD Poppy, both of them seemingly oblivious to the sobbing wreck of a man they'd left behind. He'd barely paid the pair any attention. He'd been too preoccupied with consoling his strange friend. ("D-D-Di . . ." the captain had said.

"No," Jones had assured him, "you don't want to die. There's been enough of that.")

"What did VAD Reid say she was like?" Sister Lytton had asked.

"She didn't say anything, really," he'd replied, not going into the cross words they'd shared afterward.

"Well, that's hardly like her," Sister Lytton had said. "It might surprise you," she'd gone on, "but she was much meeker when she first started, before you got here."

It had surprised him.

He struggled to believe it now, watching Poppy in the drawing room, anything but meek, rather *instructing*, skirts swishing back and forth as she moved before the Christmas tree, telling the orderlies to move it to the left, no the right, back to the left, no, no, not too close to the fire.

"What do you think, Officer Jones?" she said, throwing him one of her arch looks. "Am I getting it all wrong? Do I need a *hand*?"

Somehow, she managed to make it sound suggestive. Jones didn't raise a brow, though, as she seemed to be waiting for him to do.

Nor did he keep looking when she grabbed for a bauble, turned, hitching her skirts to climb onto the stepladder, exposing thick woolen stockings.

He closed his eyes. As always, they fell easily. He was even more tired than normal after that walk. Would he ever stop being so tired?

He leaned back in his chair. Heaviness drooped over him, the suck of sleep approaching. Dimly, he felt a flicker of anticipation: the coming of a dream.

But this time, it wasn't one he wanted to be in. There was no color, no light, nothing warm or familiar at all. Black shapes moved before his eyes: oval leaves swaying in a threatening sky; a thick density of storm clouds behind.

That was all there was. Such darkness.

Darkness, and an overwhelming sense of grief.

CHAPTER TWELVE

Bombay, June–July 1914

They had a fortnight before the news came of the Austro-Hungarian archduke's assassination. A fortnight when the clouds built, thickening in the sky ahead of the rains, the Aldyces went on summer leave back in England, so many others prepared for a break in the hills, and Maddy and Luke continued to let Maddy's parents think they went out each night to restaurants, curry houses, and markets, but stole instead to Luke's rooms on the water's edge, which he finally took Maddy to the evening after their trip not seeing any turtles. She walked around in the lantern light, that first time, acutely conscious of how little she should really be there, loving so much that she was. Her feet padded on the warm terra-cotta floors, her eyes moved, taking in the ornately carved doors, the latticed shutters at the windows, the silvery sea, just visible through the pattern, and she thought she had never been anywhere more beautiful.

"I can see why you prefer this to the Taj," she said.

"Yes," he said, kissing her ear, her neck. "There are other reasons, too, of course."

When they were cocooned in those rooms, the rest of the world disappeared, and the two of them were untouchable, invincible. They worried over nothing. While they spoke from time to time about whether they really shouldn't be more careful about chancing a baby, neither of them ever *did* anything about it. Maddy wasn't sure she really wanted to. In truth, she hardly thought about it. All she thought about was Luke.

Whenever they got hungry, he'd fetch their dinners from a nearby street vendor, pulling on trousers, a shirt. She'd wrap herself in a sheet while he was gone, pour warm champagne into ceramic mugs. They ate by candle-light, nestled lazily together in the bedroom window seat, hidden from view behind shutters open to the humid breeze, the sea rippling blackly below.

It was the night before the archduke was shot, as they lay on his low bed, his hand on her waist, hers on his tanned shoulder, fingers lazily running over the dip and curve of his arm, that he told her he had something for her.

"Hmm?" she said drowsily.

"Hmm," he said, far more awake. "I do." He turned on the pillow, lithely reaching down to the floor below the bed.

She watched him, more awake herself now, but not suspecting, not straightaway.

He lay back down, facing her, a velvet pouch in his hand.

She eyed it. "That's not a guidebook," she said slowly.

"No," he said, eyes reflecting the candles' glow, "it's not."

"Or silk," she said.

"Or silk," he agreed, holding it out to her: such a tiny little parcel.

She stared, not touching it, suspicion growing, feeling the nudge of a smile.

"Is it earrings?" she said.

He laughed at that. "Look, why don't you?"

So she did, sitting up, taking the pouch. Fingers far from steady, she pulled the drawstring, smile growing; the heat of his gaze on her skin. She peeked in, eyes widening at the handful of diamonds, loose and spar-kling inside.

"I suppose they could be earrings," he said, "or a brooch."

"A brooch?" she said. "I don't want a brooch."

"Good," he said, grinning, too, "because I was thinking, a ring."

She looked across at him, laughed, almost sobbed, then laughed again, taking his face that she loved in her hands, kissing him, not stopping.

"Is that a yes?" he said.

"It's a no, obviously," she said, then squealed as he swooped her up, dropping her back down on the bed.

They planned so much that night: the wedding, which they wanted to have as soon as possible so that they might spend at least some of the summer in England; the honeymoon they'd take on the voyage, stopping off in Port Said, perhaps even visiting the pyramids ("I've always wanted to do that," she said, excitement growing with each breath); then how they should get back to her parents' villa, tell them, then wire his, first thing Monday since it was Sunday the next day.

"Edie, too," she said, "we can't forget Edie. And Della will kill me if she's not one of the first to find out."

"We'll call at Peter's tomorrow," Luke said.

"Guy will want to know, too," she said, mood flattening temporarily at the thought of his reaction. She'd barely seen him in weeks. He'd stopped calling at the house. Whenever she ran into him—which she sometimes did, at church, up at the Hanging Gardens, then on the couple of occasions she'd gone with Della for lunch at the Gymkhana Club—he never lingered for more than a brief hello, a gentle, guilt-inducing smile. ("Oh, that *smile*," Della said. "I feel riddled myself, and I haven't even done anything. If only he'd let me.")

"Guy will be fine," said Luke.

"Will he?" Maddy said.

"Probably not," he said, and she reached across the bed, punching him. "I'd be beside myself," he went on, laughing, rubbing his arm, "if you were marrying him instead of me."

"As if I could ever do that," she said.

"Will you tell him?" he asked.

"No," she said. "I'll let my mother do it. Call me a coward."

"I won't. I'm strangely fine with you not having an emotional tête-à-tête with Guy Bowen. Although," his brow creased, "your mother's not going to be easy to talk to either."

She sighed, knowing it.

She'd realized by now that her mother was scared of her leaving. She wasn't sure why it had taken her so long to see how afraid she was ("No," Luke had said. "Remind me again where you went to university?"), but ever since Luke had spoken to her about the way Alice watched her, she'd started to watch her, too, in a slowly changing light. Lately, she'd finally come to notice the softness concealed, but not hidden, by the sharp blue of her mother's eyes; the tension in her stillness, then how her composure slipped, just for a second, whenever she, Maddy, caught her gaze. Much as her failure to visit in Oxford still upset Maddy, badly—she just couldn't let that go—she'd begun to *not* leave rooms whenever Alice walked into them. She'd started making more of an effort to talk to her—about anything: Luke, Della, all her mishaps with Cook—and was sure she didn't imagine that Alice had started smiling more. ("No," said Richard, with a smile of his own, "I've noticed it as well.") Unimpressed as Alice had obviously been when Maddy and Luke had returned from not seeing the turtles, their clothes damp and crumpled, Maddy's hair tangled with salt ("You fell in," she'd said, stare moving over them. "Both of you?" "Both of us," Luke had said, "my fault. Don't be angry with Maddy." "I'm not," she'd said), she hadn't made a scene. Really, she'd seemed more resigned than anything. She'd been almost . . . sweet, ever since, waiting to take breakfast so that she and Maddy might eat together, remarking on what a relief it was that so many in Bombay were disappearing now, saying how much she loved the quiet.

"You don't miss Diana now she's gone?" Maddy had said.

"I'm bearing it as best I can," her mother had replied, and there it had been: that smile.

She'd even suggested, just that afternoon, that she take Maddy to visit the small local school the gardener's trio attended. "They always need more help," she'd said. "I realize you're hoping . . . well, for Luke to . . ." She'd paused, taken a short breath, as though gathering her nerve. Maddy had felt her throat swell with sadness. "If there's a chance he might stay," she'd gone on, "I think the children would be very lucky to have you."

Oh God, Maddy had thought.

"It will be fine," she told Luke now.

"Will it?" he said.

"Probably not," she said.

And it wasn't. Not at all.

It was her father who exclaimed his congratulations when they showed them both the diamonds, nodding as they spoke of the wedding, the August honeymoon they'd like to have. He rose from his drawing room chair, shaking Luke's hand, hugging Maddy for a very long time (making her throat swell all over again), saying how sad he'd be to see her go, heartbroken in fact, but he understood, of course he understood, and he'd be over to visit, just try and stop him. "You'll be sick of the sight of me, you wait."

"And you, Alice?" Luke said. "Will you come?"

"I . . ." Alice began. "I . . ." She couldn't seem to go on. "Excuse me, will you?" she said, then stood, so quickly she knocked the side table bearing her and Richard's drinks, and left.

Maddy stared after her, at once desperate to run, catch her, and unable to move, to even think what she might say.

It was her father who went. "You leave this with me," he said, squeezing her shoulders, then making for the door. "Please, don't either of you worry."

Maddy turned to Luke, feeling even worse for the compassion in his dark gaze. "How can I not worry?" she said.

He didn't reply. He just crossed the room, pulled her into his arms. She dropped her head against his chest, closing her eyes at the rise and fall of his deep, slow breath.

"We don't have to go to England," he told her, even though she knew how desperate he was to return, what it must cost him to say it.

She loved him even more, for that.

But, "We do have to," she said, her mind flooding with everything waiting for them there (riverbanks, willow trees, and violet dusks; all of that). "I can't not go," she said. "I want it too much."

"Then we'll visit here," he said. "If she really won't come to us, we'll come here."

She raised her eyes to the ceiling, picturing her mother crying upstairs. "I don't understand why she won't come," she said.

"You need to ask her," he said.

She nodded. She did.

But it was her father, not her mother, whom she spoke to the next morning, since Alice, pleading a stomach ache this time, didn't come down to breakfast.

"Don't even think of trying to put me off," Maddy said to Richard, before he'd had a chance to reach for the coffee. "It's too important."

He paused, hand hovering inches from the pot, frowning across at her.

His lined face was weary. Maddy didn't know what time he'd been up until. He'd still been awake, talking with her mother, when she herself had gone to bed.

"I don't want to put you off," he said. "You have no idea how much I wish you could understand . . ."

"Then tell me what the matter is," she said.

He sighed.

"Please, Papa," she said, sensing that he was wavering, feeling the truth within touching distance. "Why won't she travel?"

"Oh, darling," he said heavily, "it's not a question of *won't*. She can't."

She felt her brow crease. "Can't?"

He gave her another long look, as though weighing up whether to go on.

She leaned forward in her chair, willing him to.

But he shook his head, as though remembering himself, and said, "You need to talk to her. I've given her my word it won't come from me." He reached for the coffee again, pouring it this time, apparently needing it. "Leave her for now, though, please. She's resting."

"But—" Maddy began.

"Please, darling," he said, widening his eyes, entreating.

She hesitated a second more. He stared back at her. He really did look so tired.

Slowly, she nodded, giving in.

What else could she do?

"I'll talk to her when she's better," she said to Luke when he arrived, not long after, to take her to Peter and Della's.

He leaned on the steering wheel, looking sideways at her. "Promise?" he said.

"I promise," she said.

"Are you sure you still want to go to the Wilsons'?"

"Absolutely," she said. "Otherwise I'll just be sad all day."

He smiled a small smile. "Well, we can't have that," he said.

"We absolutely can't," said Della, after they'd arrived at Peter's and told them both their news. "I'm absolutely *over the moon* for you, cock-a-hoop. It really is about time."

"It certainly is," said Peter, pushing his hair back from his beaming face, seizing Luke's hand, kissing Maddy, ushering them all into the stuffy drawing room, where he cracked open the windows, then a bottle of champagne. "Does this mean you'll go back too now, Della?" he said, turning to his sister. "Can I return you to Mama as an empty?"

"Sorry, no," Della said. "I'm digging my nails in for another season, and don't pretend you wouldn't miss me if I went."

He narrowed his eyes, neither confirming nor denying it, and topped up everyone's glasses.

"What about church?" said Della.

"Let's be late, then miss it," said Luke, who always did anyway. "I'm sure God will understand."

Maybe he didn't.

Or perhaps he was annoyed at someone else (Franz Ferdinand, for example).

But that very night, as they reconvened again, this time for engagement drinks at the Gymkhana Club (Richard insisted; Alice, still claiming to feel unwell, hadn't come along, although had surprised Maddy by coming down to say goodbye before she'd left. "I want you to be happy," she'd said quietly, standing in her dressing robe on the stairs. "I hope you know that." "I do," Maddy had replied. *I just wish it made you happier*), the news came from the viceroy's house that Archduke Ferdinand had been shot by Serbian nationalists.

Not everyone was worried. Della, for one, professed herself at a loss to understand what the fuss was about. "What does this archduke mean to us?"

"Hopefully nothing," said Peter, sounding less than convinced.

Maddy wasn't convinced either. She turned, looking at Luke, seeing the sudden sobriety in him. She knew what he was thinking. They'd spoken too often of everything going on in Europe for her to be in any doubt that he was as concerned as she that Austria-Hungary, long hungering for an excuse to attack Serbia and gain strength in the Balkans, had just been given that very thing. If they did attack, then Russia, who'd pledged to support Serbia, would be dragged in, too. France would follow, since they had a treaty with Russia, then Britain as well (thank you, Triple Entente), and Germany with them (they were allied with Austria-Hungary). She closed her eyes, feeling the full enormity of what might unfold dawn on her. *It's all set up like a game of dominoes,* she'd said, just the other night. *Only, not fun.*

"It might not happen," she said now, speaking to reassure herself more than anything.

"Let's go with that," Luke said. "I'll drink to it."

They all did that.

And the evening wasn't ruined; far from it. Almost everyone still in Bombay for the summer had come (with the exception of Guy, who'd sent his apologies by way of a card. *I'm afraid I must work this evening, but wish you only happiness.* "Are you riddled?" Della had asked Maddy. "Utterly," Maddy had replied); the candlelit clubhouse was packed, the sticky air vibrating with Harry Lauder, clinking glasses, and the buzz of happiness. Maddy danced with Luke, and he twirled her, dipping her to the floor, making her laugh until her sides hurt. They teased, and smiled, and spoke once more of all the summer held (the wedding, their honeymoon; that Richmond riverside), but not of his work, or how it probably wasn't going to have all been pointless after all. Richard called a toast to the future, and everyone cheered and raised their glasses.

No one wanted to dwell on assassinated Austrian royalty. Not that night.

But it felt like the last time anyone didn't. From that day on, to talk about whether Austria-Hungary would or would not retaliate on Serbia became as commonplace as discussing the weather. No one seemed to question anymore whether a war could happen.

Overnight, it had become a question only of when, and Maddy couldn't stand it.

CHAPTER THIRTEEN

Everything happened so quickly after that.

The very morning after the archduke was shot, Maddy's father called on the bishop of St. Thomas's Cathedral, persuading him that the reading of the banns absolutely could be managed in short order, and booked the ceremony for 3 August. That same afternoon, Luke dropped by at the central telegraph office to wire Edie and his parents of the news (*Thrilled to my very heart*, Edie wrote in reply. *Utterly wonderful*, said Luke's parents, *so looking forward to meeting our new daughter-in-law*), and he and Maddy went to the port, the packed P&O ticketing bureau, booking their 7 August passage home.

"Barely even a month," said Maddy as she sat at the clerk's polished desk, writing her details on the passenger form (biting her lip as she used *Devereaux* for the first time). "Not long."

"Not long at all," said Luke, grinning.

She looked up at him, pen hovering. "Nothing will happen with the Serbians before then, will it?" she said. "It couldn't happen that fast. . . ."

"No," he said, "no."

But on 6 July, just as the wedding invitations came back from the printer's—an embossed stack of cards that Maddy opened impatiently, smilingly, a thrill of excitement shooting through her—the laden Bombay sky tore and cracked, sending rain spilling over the city in rivers, and Richard returned home with the news that Germany had issued a blank check to Austria-Hungary, confirming its support in Serbia.

"It still doesn't mean there'll be a war," said Della, also there to admire the invitations.

"That's the spirit," said Richard.

Only no one else seemed to share Della's optimism. In fact, rather a lot of people seemed to hope she was wrong.

"Fraser Keaton's absolutely champing at the bit to get into uniform," said Peter that night as they all—with the exception of Alice, who was still, worryingly, claiming to be unwell—assembled in the humid, candlelit drawing room to finalize the small guest list. "Keeps saying how much he wants to do his bit."

"What does he think his bit will be, exactly?" said Luke, lighting a cigarette.

"Wearing a smart jacket, of course," said Peter.

"Well, I can get him one of those from the Army and Navy store," said Richard.

"I'll give him a jacket," said Luke. "I'll tell him to let that be an end to it."

He never did speak to Fraser, though. He didn't get the chance. With everyone (except Della) now believing the need for an Indian army in Europe nigh on inevitable, he became busier than ever, back and forth to Poona, training with one of the first divisions earmarked for mobilization. While he and Maddy grabbed every opportunity they could to be together when he *was* in Bombay, he missed almost all of the wedding preparations (Maddy rather envied his avoidance of the endless discussion on table plans, the benefits of fruit versus sponge cake. "I don't mind what cake we have," he said, kissing her in bed one evening. "Does that help?" "No," she said, "it doesn't. Can we swap jobs?"); he was constantly in and out of meetings—with shipping officers, army quartermasters, company COs—preparing transport plans, munitions and supply requirements, temporary accommodation for the floods of troops who'd come to the city if the situation got much worse, ready to sail out.

There was a shortage of officers, though. With more than a quarter of Indian Army COs on home leave in England, there weren't enough left to lead the sepoys on the parade grounds, let alone off to war.

"It's absurd," Luke said to Maddy as they sat on his window ledge in the middle of the month, the rain falling in sheets through the black night, hammering the invisible sea. "I don't know what's going to happen. . . ."

"It won't affect us, though, will it?" said Maddy, feeling a creeping foreboding that it might. He was in the reserves, after all. *First in line for the call if we trip into a war,* Peter had once said. The words came back to her coldly. "You won't have to stay here to lead anyone?" She sat up, turning to face him. "We've booked our voyage . . ."

"Don't," he said. "It hasn't happened yet. Della's right, it still might not."

"Oh, Luke . . ."

"No, seriously. So long as France keeps out of things, we can, too."

But France, of course, didn't keep out of anything.

In the third week of July, the French president, Poincaré, visited Russia and pledged France's allegiance in defending Serbia against Austria. Maddy, now starting to dread that war might break out before she and Luke could even be married, thought of little else but how rapidly everything seemed to be running out of control as she went for her final dress fitting at the tiled seamstress's shop in the basement of the Taj Hotel. Her mother was with her; she'd insisted on coming to all Maddy's appointments, even though she hadn't stopped complaining of her stomach, and was looking paler every day. Maddy had, on one of the motor journeys over, finally spoken to her, as she'd promised Luke—and herself—that she would. Mouth dry with sudden apprehension, she'd asked her why she was so averse to visiting Richmond, what had stopped her from coming to Oxford all those years, and—the words rushing from her, voice catching on the relief of letting them free—why she hadn't come on that first voyage, to take her, Maddy, to Edie and Fitz's. *I think it broke your heart, to send me.*

Alice hadn't replied, not at first. She'd stared, blue eyes wrought, almost afraid, as though these were questions she'd long dreaded, making Maddy start to wish she'd never asked them.

Even more so when Alice had spoken, each syllable taut, forced; an agony. "It did break my heart, Madeline," she'd said. "It was the hardest thing I ever did. I wanted so much to go with you."

"But . . ."

"It was impossible," Alice had said. "It felt impossible."

"Impossible?" Maddy had echoed, as confused as ever. "Because of Edie?" she'd hazarded. "You used to be friends. Did you row?"

Alice had sighed, which Maddy had taken as "yes," but before she could think how to press her mother to say more about the long-suspected disagreement, Alice had gone on, assuring her that Edie had had nothing to do with her not sailing. "Nor did Fitz. I would never have let something like that stop me."

What happened between you, though? Maddy had almost asked.

Only then Alice had moved, touching her hand to her waist, brow denting in what had looked like another pain. Assuming it was, and feeling awful for her—guilty, too, certain that she'd somehow helped cause it—Maddy simply hadn't been able to bring herself to add to her upset.

To Luke's, and Della's, frustration, she hadn't raised any of it again.

Just as she didn't now, as she spun on the spot, looking past her simple white lace gown at Alice's ashen reflection in the condensation-smeared mirror—"Perfect," Alice said quietly. "Like a picture"—feeling a churning in her own stomach at what Poincaré had promised, and the terrifying unpredictability of what was coming next.

"I want them all to stop," she said to Luke, "I want to go over there and *order* them to stop."

"You should," he said, kissing her throat. "I'd really rather not be a soldier again, and they'd listen to you, I'm certain."

But she didn't go over, obviously, and on July 23, Austria-Hungary issued an ultimatum to Serbia dictating that they should be given free rein to carry out an inquiry into the archduke's death, which Serbia rejected out of hand.

And then, with just a few days left until the ceremony, the dominoes fell.

On July 31, after Maddy had risen before sunrise and gone with Ahmed and Della to Bombay's fragrant, glorious flower markets—the three of them sheltering beneath bowed umbrellas amid the early-morning throngs, jostling their way through the groaning stalls to select cartloads of damp, sweet petals for the church—the grim news arrived that the Russians had mobilized in support of Serbia.

"It doesn't mean . . ." began Della, then stopped.

Even she couldn't try and pretend it wasn't happening anymore.

They still sent the flowers off to the cathedral, though. They all told each other that nothing else could really happen until *after* the wedding. Surely not.

But the very next day, while Maddy was in the villa's kitchen, making all the right noises about Cook's quite genuinely breathtaking wedding cake (fruit, not sponge), Luke arrived to break it to her that the Germans had moved into neutral Belgium.

"We're still getting married," he said, once they'd retreated to the privacy of the empty drawing room. "Nothing's going to stop that."

"But afterward . . ."

"Is afterward," he said, pulling her to him. "We'll manage it then." His eyes met hers. "It will be all right."

She sighed, sinking against him, gladly letting herself be convinced—for the moment at least. "You're not running off anywhere now, are you?" she said.

"I have to be at the cantonment."

"I'd rather you stayed with me," she said.

"I'd rather that, too," he said, with a lingering kiss. "And that's my plan, just as soon as this mess is over. I intend to do nothing else."

"And will that really be by Christmas, like everyone says?"

"Maybe even sooner," he said.

She hoped to God that he was right.

She hoped it again the next day, when France and Belgium began full mobilization. She went to collect her dress from the Taj, stopping to stare at the broadsheets on display in the lobby—the pictures of happy English bank holiday crowds, the headlines declaring that the country, in the grip of a heat wave, was ready for battle—and silently prayed that all of this would be nothing more than a short interlude of madness.

Inevitably, Britain issued an ultimatum to Germany, commanding them to move out of Belgium or face a declaration of war. By the time the morning of the wedding dawned, all British and Indian troops, active and reserve, had been placed on standby. Luke and Peter were, inevitably, among them.

Beside herself as Maddy was (and she was terrified), she still woke far too early for the wedding, a smile stubbornly tugging at her cheeks, full of unquenchable euphoria at the day ahead, the thought of Luke waking up in his rooms, and the shivering, wonderful reality that within hours they'd be married.

Married.

Her excitement took over as she bathed, dressed in her white gown, and shakily pinned her hair. Her fear over everything else retreated as she drove with her father to the church, held his hand with her trembling one, then took his arm and ran through the driving rain to the doors of St. Thomas's, veil trailing behind her on the slippery front steps. She stood at the head of the marble aisle, looking down toward Luke at the altar—so handsome in his morning suit (not uniform, not yet), so happy as he stared up at her, *her*—and thought only of him, and what they were about to do. She took a step, dizzy with her own short breaths of excitement, and her mind emptied of the reserve mobilization points that were being pulled up all over India. She forgot the empty vessels steaming, even now, to Bombay, ready to carry the army away. She didn't think of which army was moving across which forbidden border, or how grim her mother looked in the wooden front pew, or that Guy had sent another card declining to attend the wedding. *I'm sure it will be quite wonderful without me.* She came to a halt at Luke's side, her veil falling around her shoulders, and he leaned toward her; the touch of his low voice against her ear. "This is it," he said, and she felt like she had never been so happy.

She hardly listened to the bishop's welcome. She felt Luke's arm beside hers, the warmth of his presence, and kept sneaking looks at him, just as he did at her, both of them trying to suppress smiles that couldn't be suppressed. The bishop announced the first hymn, the organ's chords rang out, and as everyone shuffled to standing and sang about amazing grace, Luke leaned over again, and told her how much white suited her.

"Thank you," she whispered back.

"You're welcome," he said. "You look very pure."

She felt her smile grow. "Do I?"

"Yes," he said, moving closer to her, "I might almost be deceived . . ."

She laughed, winning a disapproving frown from the bishop, which deepened as she laughed more, just because of the way the bishop was looking at her.

"Stop," said Luke, dark eyes dancing, "you're getting us in trouble."

Della read from Corinthians, beautifully ("She's been practicing," said Peter afterward), they all sang another hymn, this time of hopefulness, the bishop gave his sermon (mercifully short), and then asked if anyone knew of any just reason why Luke and Madeline shouldn't be lawfully married, and no one—not even Alice—spoke.

They exchanged their vows, not taking their eyes from one another as they promised to love one another until death did them part, and ran from the church in a flurry of monsoon-dampened confetti, on to the small wedding breakfast back at the villa; all they'd wanted. With rain drenching the lawns, the palms, and a string quartet playing beneath the veranda awning, they cut Cook's magnificent cake, drank champagne, danced and laughed and spoke not a word of war, then, with darkness falling, headed out into the weather again, in a flurry of kisses this time, back to Luke's apartment.

"I'll love you forever," Maddy said to him, as he carried her from the motor, into the hot, silent shelter of his rooms. "I'll love you even longer than that."

"Good," he said, lowering her to the floor, his words on her lips, her neck. "I intend to hold you to it."

CHAPTER FOURTEEN

Alice really hadn't felt well enough to go to the wedding. She hadn't felt well enough to go to the dress fittings either, but she'd have as soon missed those as she would have watching Madeline walking down the aisle; even as she'd sat in the pew, that seamstress's shop (*my daughter*, she'd thought, eyes on her beloved face, *my daughter*), she'd known she was forming memories to join the thousands of others she stored, ready to be replayed endlessly in the months and years ahead. In her most hopeless moments, she almost wished Madeline had never come back; it would have been easier, in some ways, not to have had to lose her all over again.

She'd struggled to keep her composure in the church, then again through the afternoon at the villa. (She'd been so relieved when Madeline had asked they make it a low-key affair, no pomp, no fuss. *No fuss*, she'd thought, *I can manage that*.) She hadn't danced. She'd barely managed to sit up straight. Her stomach pains these past weeks hadn't been a pretense, or an excuse to hide her grief and fear behind (although they had also been that); they'd been very real, and growing worse, her nausea with them. She'd thought it all to do with anxiety.

"No," Guy said softly when he came late the next evening, "your appendix."

Richard had called for him. That was after Alice had spent the entire day in bed, feverishly dipping in and out of consciousness, dreaming of the wedding, Madeline as a little girl crying and begging her, Alice, not to make her go to England (*I don't want to go, no thank you. I'll stay better, I promise*), then again as an adult, gone, walking up the gangplank of another ship, a ship that Alice was so very certain she'd never be able to bring herself to set foot on. As the hours had passed, the agony in her stomach had intensified, her whole body had started to shiver uncontrollably with heat, the villa around her an oppressive island, swaying in the clattering Bombay rain.

"You should have come to see me, Alice," said Guy, his kind face tired, creased by concern. He pulled out a needle from his case, told her it would help with the pain, and then pierced her arm.

She closed her eyes, feeling the opioids ooze through her, blissfully blanketing feeling, and moved her head in a heavy nod. She should have.

He moved away. She heard him speaking with Richard just outside her bedroom door, their hushed voices only just audible above the rain. Something about moving her to Guy's hospital, operating. Groggily, she thought she should be afraid of an operation. She floated past the feeling. Really, so long as the pain stopped, what did it matter?

"It's ruptured, I think," said Guy. (Perhaps that mattered.) "I'd like to do the surgery myself, with your permission."

"Of course," said Richard, "of course."

Even in her deadened state, Alice registered their stiffness. They'd spent so little time in each other's company lately; none of their dinners, or drinks. She herself had only written to Guy of Madeline's engagement, then again to invite him to the wedding. They'd been avoiding each other. *Had to,* she thought. They all knew too much of how the others felt, most of it unspeakable, so (as Alice often found to be the case) it really was easier not to try and speak at all.

Not that she could speak now, even if she wanted to. Her lips were full of weights, her face, her limbs, growing denser by the second. Hazily, she realized Richard had returned to her. The room pitched and spun as he picked her up, carrying her downstairs; the always surprising gentleness of his vast arms. Then she was lying on the warm leather backseat of the motor, her head in his lap, his hand on her hair. How many such midnight dashes had they made? All those babies . . .

They lurched into motion. She must have lost consciousness, because when she opened her eyes she was being lifted once more, placed on a bed that moved and made an odd noise on the tiles below. *A trolley,* she thought, *we're at the hospital.* It was a muted kind of knowledge. Even her panic

when a man placed a mask over her face and told her they were taking her
to theater now, Major Bowen was waiting there, seemed to live somewhere
other than inside herself.

All she knew with any clarity was that Madeline was going to leave,
very soon, and she wanted her to stay. She wanted her daughter. She wished
she'd been able to tell Madeline that, to say how much she loved her, and
explain . . . everything.

It was her final thought as liquid dripped down onto her mask.

That, and that someone else in the room might have just said that
Britain had declared war on Germany, but the mask had started to taste
very strange; the voice disappeared. She was swimming, not in water,
which she hadn't been within touching distance of in many years, but in
blackness. Only blackness.

The rain-sopped messenger came in the early hours of dawn on August 5,
hammering on Luke's door, waking Maddy and Luke, who'd been asleep
on the low bed, the bedsheets tangled beneath them, the mosquito net limp
in the heavy, damp heat.

Maddy lurched to sitting, heart reverberating at the wrench into consciousness, her blood chilling in the instant as her mind caught up, telling
her what the intrusion must mean.

They'd been waiting for it.

Reluctant as they'd been to leave the apartment, even for a minute,
their worry about how long they were going to have with one another, and
whether Germany had responded to Britain's ultimatum, had been too
strong to ignore. The evening before, they'd driven to the colonel's office in
the main cantonment to find out what he knew, hoping, desperately, that it
was that Germany had withdrawn from Belgium.

"Afraid not," Colonel Whittaker had said with a sigh, pulling a bottle of
rum from his desk drawer, "and they only have a few hours left."

He'd offered them a tot to drink. They'd refused, already turning for
the door. When Whittaker had tried to insist, saying he and Luke really
did have a deal to talk about, specifically that Ernest Aldyce and numerous

other officers had left several hundred men a CO short, Luke had tightened his hold on Maddy's hand and told him, "Tomorrow. We can do that tomorrow."

They'd escaped through the steamy rain to the motor, Luke driving fast through the downpour, in silence for the most part, neither of them talking about what came next (and that it almost certainly wasn't going to be their voyage home), Maddy for one feeling like she might choke if she even mentioned it. As soon as they'd got back to the apartment, they'd turned to one another, kissing, pulling their soaking clothes free, letting them fall on the trunks they'd left by the door, ready, heartbreakingly ready, for their trip. They hadn't made it as far as the bedroom. Neither of them had slowed, not with time now the most precious of luxuries.

Their clothes were still draped over the trunks. Luke, in a hastily pulled-on pair of trousers, passed them on his way to the front door. Maddy, fingers to her throat, watched him move through the dark room, the black shapes and shadows, the sultry silence. He opened the door, letting the noise of the storm in, the telegram from London, too. She saw how he took it from the messenger, read it, then, with a few short words of thanks in Urdu, closed the door and leaned forward, hand on the wood, as though for support.

She hardly needed him to turn, to see his set face, to know what the telegram said.

She really didn't need to read the message for herself.

But she did anyway. As he came back to her, kneeling beside her on the mattress, offering her the soggy paper, she took it with cold hands.

```
Britain at war with Germany STOP Do not return
to England but report to Colonel Whittaker
STOP All officers on ground in India needed
STOP Congratulations on your wedding STOP Most
grateful for your service and patience STOP
```

"So we're not going anywhere," she said, and the words felt strange, far from real, and so deeply wrong.

Luke said nothing.

She looked up at him. His eyes were bright, livid with anger.

"Do you know," he said, "how many times I've told people like Colonel Whittaker to cancel all home leave for officers?" His voice was low, only just controlled. "If they'd listened," he said, "there'd be plenty of officers here. I could go home with you, enlist there, but instead I'm having to look after Ernest Aldyce's men while he's in Dorking with his feet up, and a wife he bloody loathes."

She laughed then, a strange, strangled sound that was trying too hard not to be a sob, and surprised her by coming out at all. It was the thought of Ernest and Diana trapped together in Dorking, how much Diana must hate not being surrounded by staff, perhaps even having to butter her own toast. Luke continued to stare at her, not laughing, because nothing was funny, and then she wasn't laughing either, but crying, really, really crying.

"Don't," he said, pulling her to him. "Please . . ."

"I can't help it." She buried her head in his chest, feeling his warmth, his heart, the awful breakability of him. "You're going to be a soldier again."

"I am," he said.

"I should have spoken to Poincaré."

"You should have," he said.

"I can't bear it," she said, the tears still coming. "I can't." She couldn't wrap her head around it. There'd be no voyage for them, no cabin just the two of them, or August in Richmond. He was going to fight, perhaps be hurt, or . . . "I'm scared," she said. "I'm so scared."

He held her tighter, saying nothing. She thought perhaps he was scared, too, and it made her feel even worse. All this time, she'd thought she was prepared, ready—that awful, needling sense that everything would turn wrong; *don't trust it*—but she wasn't ready at all. Somewhere along the line, she seemed to have started trusting in everything, and now her excitement, her happiness, was bleeding from her, and she couldn't stop it. She didn't know how to.

"You can still travel back," he said, trying for them both. "I'll be here to see you off, there's no plan for the Bombay divisions to go anywhere yet. That's only Poona, Lahore . . ."

"Then I'll stay with you."

"No," he said, "sail. I don't know how long passenger ships will keep running. I'll be just behind you." He kissed her, pushing her back so that they were looking at one another. "The sepoys need training," he said. "We'll do that in England, I'm certain. I'll get leave, come to see you. It might even all be over by the time we're ready to fight. This doesn't have to change anything for us."

She nodded, swallowed on her tears, and said nothing.

It felt horribly like it was going to change everything.

It was nicer not to say that out loud, though.

Peter, too, had been ordered to report to Whittaker. He came to tell Maddy and Luke, just after the sun had risen, its rays barely breaking through the thick, black clouds.

He'd already spoken to the colonel. "It's why I'm here," he said, stepping through the door, shaking off his umbrella, shooting Luke a pained look. "I'm to fetch you to the cantonment, my friend."

"Whittaker wants me now?" Luke, only just dressed, said.

"Yes, but let's wait and blame the traffic. I'm in no rush to get back." He pulled out one of the chairs and sat, hair flopping over his forehead. "Whittaker says you're not to waste time trying to convince him you need your honeymoon," he said. "Apparently my Urdu is worse than his four-year-old son's, and you've been promoted to major already. So well done."

Luke wanted, very much, to punch the wall.

"We should have got married last week," said Maddy, clutching a cup of cold tea too tightly. The skin on her knuckles was pale, taut; Luke had never known hands could look so anxious. It made him ache. He wished he knew how to fix it for her, for them, but he couldn't. He couldn't think what to do. "We'd be on a ship by now," she went on, "sitting in sun chairs on deck."

"Stop," said Luke. "Please, stop."

"I'm afraid it gets worse," said Peter.

"How, worse?" asked Luke, barely wanting to know.

Peter grimaced. "We're not staying in Bombay."

Luke stared. "Where are we going?"

"Karachi," said Peter. "Tonight."

This time Luke did belt the wall.

Peter sighed, like he sympathized, then told Luke what he already knew, but had never imagined would affect him: that the Third Lahores, one of the bigger units designated for immediate dispatch, were even lighter than the Bombay divisions on officers.

"We're to fold in with them," said Peter, "sail with them from Karachi."

"What about the men here?" asked Luke, grappling for a way out. "Aldyce's . . . ?"

"We're taking half with us," said Peter, "leaving the others for Whittaker to manage. He's not very happy."

"He should have fought it," said Luke.

"I suggested as much," said Peter. "He reminded me I'm in the army now."

"Christ," said Luke raggedly.

"Where will you sail to?" asked Maddy. "England?"

"Probably," said Luke, with more conviction than he felt. What he felt was sick. He had no idea where the Lahores would sail to, only that, unlike the Sixth Poona Division, it would at least be somewhere in Europe, not the Persian Gulf.

Peter went on, saying he hadn't told Della yet, but obviously couldn't leave her here alone. He turned to Maddy, asking if she could travel home with her on the seventh.

"Yes," said Maddy flatly, eyes fixed on Luke, "of course."

He stared back at her, trying and failing to picture leaving her, tonight, *tonight,* combing his mind once again for a way out of it. There was no way, he knew. None at all.

She came to him, wrapping her arms around his waist. He moved instinctively, pulling her closer, muscles easing at the touch of her body, the comfort, mind reeling that in just a few short hours he wasn't going to have that anymore. They hadn't had long enough, the two of them. It wasn't enough. It could never be enough. . . .

"We'll be sailing at the same time," he heard himself saying, to himself as much as her. "In a fortnight, we'll be together again."

"A fortnight," she echoed, looking up, her eyes bluer than ever; like glass.

He summoned a smile, willing her to smile back.

She tried to. He saw that in the movement of her cheeks. But it wouldn't come. It was the first time he'd ever seen that happen to her, and it broke him.

Had she known then, what was coming?

He asked it of himself, so many times, in all that followed. Asked it of her, too, in his letters.

No, she wrote back, *how could I have known?*

They planned that he'd go to the cantonment to see Whittaker, then come back so that they could spend the afternoon together, just as Peter was spending his with Della. ("I'm rather sad to leave her," Peter said, "although obviously don't tell her that.") Whittaker, who wasn't an unsympathetic man, had granted all of the men with families nearby time to say their goodbyes. "You sail to Karachi at eight," he said. "Just be back for the transport to the port."

Luke didn't want to think about the transport to the port. He wanted only to lie in bed with his wife, his wife he wasn't sure he'd ever be able to accept he could be lucky enough to have, and forget the uniform Whittaker had handed to him, the major's stripes being sewn into the sleeves, the kit bag, rifle, and bayonet that all now bore his name.

The last thing he'd thought to find, when he walked through the door of his rooms, was Maddy gone, and a hastily scribbled note saying that her father had taken her to Guy Bowen's hospital. He'd never for a second imagined the two of them would spend the rest of the day side by side in a busy corridor, sitting in uncomfortable wooden chairs, waiting anxiously for Alice to regain consciousness, both trying to stay calm even though no one knew if Alice was going to be all right, and it felt like the world was turning on its head. They stared at the door of Alice's room, the heartlessly turning clock, holding each other's hands because that was all they could do, both wanting to be anywhere but where they were, the silence laden with the dread of their parting.

Guy came. Luke had to hand it to him, he behaved impeccably, calmly telling Maddy she wasn't to worry, Alice's surgery had gone as well as it could have, speaking in the same unabashed manner Luke was accustomed to his own mother using when talking of medical matters. (He kept thinking of his mother. She'd be terrified today, he knew. She'd started her career as a nurse in the First Boer War, and had a horror of battlefields. Seeing her was the only silver lining he could find in his imminent departure.) Guy went on, saying how sorry he was to hear that Luke was leaving that night, truly seeming to mean it. Luke might almost have liked him, had he not been so sure he was in love with Maddy.

"I'll be going myself, soon," Guy said, "but I'll be here a while longer to take care of you all, Maddy."

"Excellent," said Luke.

"How long will Mama be in hospital for?" asked Maddy.

"It depends," said Guy. "The main thing is to keep her free of infection." He looked back toward her room. "We don't want a repeat of . . ." He stopped, appearing to check himself.

Now why had he done that?

Maddy, brow creased, was obviously wondering it, too. "A repeat of what?" she asked.

"Nothing," Guy said. "Forgive me, I've been up all night. I'm not sure why I said it."

"Can you say more now?" said Luke.

"Really, no," Guy said, turning. "And I must get on. . . ."

"Wait," said Luke, his impatience audible to his own ears.

"Guy," said Maddy, in much the same tone, "please."

"I'm sorry," said Guy. "Do call for me if she wakes."

And with that, he was gone.

Maddy stared after him, expelling a noise that was half resignation, half frustration.

"Do you want me to go and make him tell you?" Luke offered.

"It's tempting," she said. Her red-rimmed eyes moved back to Alice's room, Richard keeping vigil by her bed. "I'll ask Papa, though, once she's awake."

She still wasn't by the time dusk fell. Luke, grimly conscious of his ship waiting in harbor, could put off returning to the cantonment no longer, not if he wasn't going to end up shot as a deserter. (Hardly ideal.) Besides, he had men now, hundreds of them in his charge; men who were leaving their families, too, their homes. A reluctant soldier he might be, but that was hardly their fault. They'd be waiting for him.

"Making do with Peter's desperate Urdu," said Maddy, with another agonizing attempt at a smile, as together they set off, with the slowest of steps, through the hospital's darkening corridors, out to the front porch.

"What are you going to do?" he asked. "I don't think you're sailing anywhere yet."

"I don't think I am either." She looked over her shoulder, back toward Alice's room. "I'll do it as soon as I can."

He drew a long breath, deliberately not repeating his earlier warning that they didn't know how long passenger ships would continue to run. He couldn't ask her to leave her mother. He *wouldn't* ask her to do that. Instead, he told her that he'd do his very best to be at the dock when she arrived in England. Even if he couldn't be, he'd make sure to have his parents waiting for her. "They can show you the house. I'm sure they'd love you to stay with them if you like. . . ."

"I'd rather you were there," she said.

"If I can, I will be," he said.

They reached the hospital doors. He pushed one wide, incredulous that he was putting one foot in front of the other when it felt like the worst kind of lunacy to do anything other than stay precisely where he was. Still, he held the door open, holding it back as she walked through.

The rain was as torrential as ever. It bounced from the dirt driveway, splattering the tiles, their feet. The palms loomed tall against the blackening clouds, their oval leaves bowed with water. He narrowed his eyes at them, and, from nowhere, felt a grim punch of foreboding; the thought that once he went, he might never see such trees again.

"Luke," she said, as though she could sense his sudden fear. "Luke . . ." She touched his neck, drawing his attention back. He felt his stare soften as he met hers. She didn't blink, or look away, as loath as he felt to do that. Her hair was messy, tangled with how many times she'd run her hands through it, chaotic with the humidity. Her skin was flushed, with heat, with grief, and he wanted to see her happy again. He wanted to make her happy. And he wanted to wake tomorrow and be with her. He wanted to be with her every day; talk to her, look at her, never not know what it felt like to do that.

But since he couldn't, he kissed her, and told her he loved her, again and again.

She kissed him back. "I love you, too, I'll love you forever. And I'll see you soon."

"Soon," he echoed. "Very soon."

He rested his forehead against hers, hands either side of her face, re-playing that moment he'd first seen her: a beautiful stranger on the dark, Bombay promenade. He saw himself beneath the vaulted ceilings of the terminus's entrance foyer, crouching on the mosaics, packaging up her matches, his guidebook, all the happiness still ahead of them. His mind filled with every look and word they'd shared since, and then, because that felt far too like a life flashing before his eyes, he pushed the images away, and promised himself there were more to come. Many, many more.

"I'll see you in England," he said. "I'll see you at home."

"Home," she said, and this time her smile was real. "Yes."

He smiled, too, beyond grateful that she had, that he'd seen that again.

There was so much more he wanted to say to her. But there wasn't time. He knew there wasn't time. And for now there really was only one word left that was possible.

He just wished, so much more than he'd ever wished for anything, that it wasn't "goodbye."

CHAPTER FIFTEEN

She couldn't bring herself to cancel her passage to England. She couldn't even face returning to Luke's rooms to fetch her trunk. The idea of entering that empty space, seeing the bed they'd slept in, the cups they'd drunk from, the window seat they'd lost all those many, many hours in, was too agonizing to bear. Della, without Maddy saying anything, understood; it was she who arranged for the trunk to be taken back to Maddy's parents'. "I packed everything else up," she said, when she found Maddy in the hospital room the morning after Luke and Peter had left for Karachi. "Dropped the key next door. I hope that was all right."

"Yes," said Maddy, even though nothing was all right at all. "Thank you."

Della looked at Alice, sleeping again, far from restfully. "Is there really nothing else they can give her?" she asked, face creased by concern.

"Nothing," said Maddy, who'd asked the same question herself, terrified by the high, mottled color in her mother's skin, the way her dry lips kept moving soundlessly, eyelids flickering. "She's had all the morphia she's allowed. It's the fever that's the problem." It had started in the small hours: an infection not even Guy had been able to keep away. He'd said, just an hour before, that there was nothing they could do now but wait, hope for it to break.

"Hope?" Maddy had said, her eyes raw from exhaustion, anger building, because it was too much, it was all too much.

"Hope," he'd echoed helplessly.

I thought you were going to take care of us. She'd almost shouted it. She'd swallowed the awful impulse just in time. It wasn't his fault. None of it was. He'd done his best, tried to help.

She knew now that it wasn't the first time he had.

She'd asked her father what Guy had meant before, back in the corridor when he'd spoken to her and Luke. *We don't want a repeat of . . .* She hadn't immediately remembered to do it. When Richard had found her in the hospital porch, after Luke had disappeared up the sodden driveway, he'd folded her in a tight embrace, restraining her from running after him (*it won't help, it* won't), and she'd sobbed, too consumed by sadness to think of anything else. But later, drained of tears, as she'd sat with Richard by Alice's bed, watching her mother's breaths go in, out, Guy's strange words had returned to her.

Her father hadn't seemed surprised when she'd spoken of them. He'd simply continued staring down at Alice, sighing, as though he'd already been thinking of what had happened himself.

He hadn't told her very much. More than he ever had before, though, shocking her with the revelation that her mother had had to have a surgery on the voyage home to India, after that one time she'd visited Maddy in England. "It was . . . horrendous," he'd said, eyes distant, reliving it. "She was in hospital when we got back here, for a long time. This hospital. Guy was a very junior doctor then, but he helped her."

"What was the surgery for?" Maddy had asked.

He'd shaken his head. *I've given her my word it won't come from me.* "Ask your mama," he'd said, "once she's better. Make her tell you."

"I can't *make* her."

"Of course you can," he'd said. "Darling, she'd give you the moon if she could."

She thought about those words now, as she stroked her mother's hand. She hadn't held her hand in such a long time.

"Where's your papa?" Della asked.

"At the office," Maddy said, "telling them he won't be in for a while." Her voice shook. "He's asking Fraser Keaton to cancel my ticket."

"Oh," said Della, moving round the bed, "come here."

Maddy did just that, feeling her friend's arms come around her, beyond grateful for the comfort, *needing it,* trying so very hard not to think of how it would be to sink into those other arms, arms now at sea, hugging the coast to Karachi, then crying again anyway, because she hadn't slept in nearly two days, and she had nothing left in her to fight it.

"I'm not going to sail until you do," said Della. "I don't know if that helps."

Maddy tightened her hold. "Of course it helps," she said.

He's asking Fraser Keaton to cancel my ticket.

Alice heard Madeline say it, felt her daughter's sadness, her awful disappointment, and raised her hand, reaching for hers, wanting to grasp those fingers again, fingers that had used to slip so effortlessly into her own (every day, *every, single, day*), but found only humid air.

Don't cry, she tried to say to Madeline. *Please, don't cry anymore.*

Was she listening?

Was anyone listening?

It didn't seem like anyone was. Madeline was talking to Della. Something about Della coming to stay at the villa. That would be nice. The house had always felt too empty, too quiet, its rooms missing several heartbeats: Madeline's, for too many years; all those babies'.

Stop, she told herself, *don't.*

She couldn't help herself. It was being in this hospital again. She'd never thought to come back, but now that she had, and her senses were filled by the scent of disinfectant, sickness, and sweat, the metallic trundle of the trolleys, the nurses' voices, the sticky heat of the rubber sheet lining her bed, she could think of nothing but what had brought her the last time. The little boy she'd almost believed she could grow into life, but that the ship's surgeon had told her was yet again coming too early, and the wrong way. *You're going to have a little sleep now, Mrs. Bright. When you wake, it will all be fine.* They'd used chloroform then, too. She'd forgotten the taste of it. Such an awful taste.

No one had let her see him. By the time she'd woken, he was already gone. *Buried at sea*, Richard had told her, and she'd screamed, screamed and screamed, refusing to let him come near her because he'd let them do it; she'd blamed him, she hadn't been able to help herself.

She'd blamed herself, too. Of course she had. He'd warned her against traveling to England, after all. *It's too much, too tiring.* The summer before, when he'd first taken Madeline and she'd been carrying another child, she'd listened to his caution that it was impossible for her to travel and stayed in Bombay. She supposed a small part of her *had* been relieved at the excuse not to see Edie and Fitz—to have to look Edie in the eye while she stole something else of hers—but it was a tiny, meaningless part; mostly she'd regretted not going, from the second Madeline had left. Even more when she'd miscarried anyway, while Richard was still gone.

Two children lost, that year.

Every day that had passed after that, she'd looked forward to the moment she'd board a ship of her own, imagining how it would be to hold Madeline again in her arms.

Only, Madeline had kept running to Edie when Alice had arrived in Oxford, choosing her, just as Fitz (the first person to kiss Alice, give her a ring) had chosen her. The grief of watching Madeline hide in Edie's arms, her little face peeking tearfully over Edie's shoulder. The hideousness of Edie insisting on explaining Madeline's behavior to Alice; her own daughter. *It's just because she knows me now.* The awkwardness of Fitz, handsome, entitled Fitz, looking at Alice as though he pitied her. All. The. Time. *Don't pity me,* Alice had wanted to scream at him, *don't you dare do that.*

Her own mother hadn't pitied her. She'd still been furious at her, for losing Fitz, then running off to India, *no care, no heed.* She'd been so frosty the one time Alice and Richard had taken Madeline to visit that Alice had wished they'd stayed away.

"You'll never convince me you've made my daughter happy," Edna had said to Richard as a parting shot. "Look at her. Sadness ages one, you know, Alice."

Alice's father, already declining with the lung illness he'd eventually died of, had said nothing, just looked so horribly sad and old himself.

That was the day Madeline had hugged Alice for the first time without

Alice having to ask her. *I don't like them either.* After that, she'd shown no interest in Edie, or even Richard, but had wanted only Alice, coming into her bed every night (that warm little body), begging her to take her back to India. *Please, Mama, please.*

"Can't we?" Alice had said to Richard. "She's bigger now; she might not get so ill. . . ."

"She's bigger because she *hasn't* been ill," Richard had said. "You know that, Alice."

She had. Deep down. She'd never have given in otherwise. As with their little boy at sea, though, it had felt easier to blame him.

Had it been her fault that he'd died? Had she let herself become too tired, too overwrought?

No, Guy had told her at the time, *of course it wasn't your fault.*

It had felt like her fault. But no one talked about such things. After she'd left hospital, no one had even mentioned that there'd been a child at all. She'd known she was meant to forget, but she'd never wanted to do that, because then it would be as though his little kicks, his hiccoughs inside her, had never happened.

She never had been able to get on another ship. She'd tried, many times. In those first years, she'd asked Richard to book her passage after passage. But the second she'd set foot on a gangplank, felt the sway of the boards beneath her, the press of the other passengers, and smelled the steam, the salt, she was back in that surgeon's room, screaming again, thinking of that tiny body somewhere out there, *buried at sea.* She'd back away, turn and make for the edge of the quayside, breathing, but not breathing, barely seeing, dripping in sweat.

Eventually, she'd given in to her own terror, given up on going to the quayside at all. By then, she'd already lost so much time with Madeline, years of her life; it had been easier, in some ways, to believe there was no point anymore in her hopeless attempts to get to her. So she'd stopped, feeling Madeline inch farther away from her with each birthday and Christmas, gradually becoming as distant as her brothers and sisters.

Until, she'd come back.

And now she was here, no longer talking to Della, but sitting again, holding her hand.

Tell her. Richard had said it to Alice, countless times. *She'll keep blaming you until you do.*

Could she do it? Tell her?

All this time, she'd convinced herself she was protecting Madeline with her silence, from the sadness.

She realized now that she'd really been protecting herself.

From her shame.

Slowly, she became well again. Very slowly. On the seventh, she was still in the throes of her fever, and Maddy—stiff and exhausted after another night failing to sleep in her chair—barely thought about her liner pushing back from Bombay's dockside, building speed, moving farther out to sea. She stared at Alice with sore, dry eyes, petrified at how she seemed to have left her own hot body, trying not to let in the very real possibility that she was dying. She struggled to be comforted by Guy's assurances that he'd seen this many times before, it always got worse before it got better; now that it seemed that she truly might lose her mother, all she could think of was the sound of her laugh, and how she hadn't given her nearly enough reasons to do that. She wanted to hear her laugh again.

"We all want that," said Richard.

She didn't laugh the next day, but she did become cooler, and lucid enough to open her eyes and meet Maddy's. (*You're here, Madeline,* she meant to say to her. *I'm so happy you're here.* She wasn't sure why "You look like you need a bath" was what came out.)

In spite of her sadness, Maddy smiled. "Hello, Mama," she said.

By the next day, her temperature was normal again, and the swelling around her scar had eased. Guy, who took Maddy and Richard out into the corridor to warn them of the possibility of secondary infections, said that he wanted Alice to stay in hospital for at least another fortnight, until the scar was well healed.

"But the danger's passed for now, though?" said Richard.

"For now," said Guy, and sounded almost as relieved as Maddy felt.

"Thank you," she said, impulsively reaching out to hug him, pulling away just as quickly when his whole body went stiff.

"I really didn't do anything," he said, his tanned face a color she'd never seen before.

"You did plenty," said Richard.

That afternoon, Maddy returned to the villa for the first time, taking the bath she so sorely needed, and changing her clothes—which were, thanks to Della, already unpacked, back in her closet. She stood in front of the wardrobe, heavy with tiredness, the reality of being back in the room she'd left so happily just a few mornings before, and let her mind—liberated of some of her fear for her mother—move to Luke, her longing for him.

She was still at the villa when his wire came; it was almost as though he'd sensed how much she needed to hear from him. He told her that he and Peter had arrived safely in Karachi, giving her the address of the hotel they were boarding at while they waited for the Lahore troops, all of whom were traveling overland across monsoon-flooded ground.

```
Write please write STOP We're not going anywhere
yet STOP
```

She did it then and there, telling him everything that had happened since he'd left, and most of all how much she missed him. *I'm coming, too, just as quickly as I can.*

The next day, with Alice's temperature still stable, Richard started going in to the office again; they were short on staff with so many summering away, and several others, like Peter and Luke, already in uniform, but the presidency still needed governing. There were trade contracts to be approved, goods licenses and building tenders under review, wage disputes, water shortages, rail repairs.

"I can't but wonder if all we've brought to India is red tape," he said wearily, when he returned to the hospital that evening. "I'm missing Peter already."

"I suspect he's missing you, too," said Della, with a smile that was more brave than amused. "I *cannot* picture him as a soldier."

"Well, quite," said Alice.

And they all exchanged looks, needing to be sure that the others had heard, too wary to believe that she really *was* sounding so much like herself again.

For the first time in almost a week, they left her alone that night, and Maddy went to bed in her old room. She didn't dwell on the sadness of being back there this time; she didn't even close her mosquito net after she'd collapsed on the soft sheets. She looked at Luke's telegram, next to her on the pillow, listened for a second to Della moving around in the room next door, then closed her eyes and slept. Slept and slept and slept. She couldn't remember the last time she'd done it so deeply, or for so long.

It was the same for the nights that followed. She'd thought that with all her anxiety, she'd struggle to go off, but the opposite happened: she couldn't keep her eyes open. She escaped to bed earlier and earlier, often (to Della's chagrin) as soon as she returned from her day at the hospital. Sometimes she didn't even last that long and nodded off at her mother's side, her head resting on her folded arms.

"Rest," Alice, who never woke her, said. "You obviously need it."

She didn't sleep all the time she was there. She talked, too, and so did her mother, both conscious of how close they'd come to not being able to do that again, neither inclined to waste this second chance. (*Thank God for that*, wrote Luke, *I only wish I was there to see how relieved it must be making you, and her. I wish I was there for quite a lot of reasons.*) Perhaps it was partly thanks to the opioids, but without Maddy asking, Alice even raised the subject of her prior stay in the hospital; that surgery at sea.

"I was here before, you know," she said, the first day after her fever broke. She didn't lift her blue gaze from Maddy as she spoke. It was obvious she was making herself do it.

"Yes?" said Maddy, quietly, not wanting to risk anything that might make her stop.

"Yes," said Alice, and left such a long pause that Maddy feared she'd leave it there.

She prompted her. "Papa said you were unwell on the voyage from England," she said.

"Unwell?" said Alice, and her cheeks twisted with pain. "No, Madeline, I wasn't unwell."

It didn't all come out as one admission, no single outpouring of the many things Maddy only wished she'd known long ago. Rather, after that first tearful revelation that Maddy had once almost had a baby brother ("Oh," choked Maddy, "oh, Mama, I am so sorry"), Alice divulged it piecemeal, over a course of days, each loosened secret seemingly freeing the next. That tiny little boy, *buried at sea,* and Alice's long weeks in hospital afterward. "The ship's surgeon wasn't . . . experienced. I was never able to . . . hope, for another, after that." How Fitz and Edie had been unable to have children themselves, but had had her, Maddy.

"If I'd known . . ." said Maddy, without any idea of how to go on, or what she could have done, only that she wanted desperately for it to be something.

"You were too little," said Alice.

"I'm glad you picked Papa instead of Fitz," said Maddy.

"He really picked me," said Alice. "But I'm glad, too."

Then, the other babies, eight in total, who'd never been; one the same summer Maddy had first gone to England. ("You should have told me," said Maddy, understanding about why her mother hadn't come with her finally washing through her, pressing on her heart. *It was impossible. It felt impossible.* "I didn't know how to," said Alice.) The long years Alice had tried so hard to leave Bombay, never managing it.

"Your letters," said Maddy. "They were always . . ." She broke off, wiping her tears with the heel of her hand. "You never seemed to . . . care."

"Oh, Madeline." Alice's blue eyes swam. "I am so sorry, for that."

It wasn't all miraculously changed between the two of them. They'd spent so long locked in awkwardness, it was a difficult habit to break. And Maddy, stricken by how much Alice had been through, couldn't let herself relax, slip and speak of anything that would hurt her more—not least how much she was still determinedly planning to travel back to England, *home,* start her life with Luke there.

But they read together, ate the tiffin Cook sent care of the *dabba* wallahs, worked on several crosswords, talked about Luke, how much Maddy missed him, how scared she was about him fighting, then sometimes just sat, in a silence that slowly ceased being something to fear. The days passed and, before Maddy's very eyes, Alice regained some of the weight she'd lost; her awful pallor faded. Guy assured them that, if she kept it up, she'd be ready for home by the end of the month.

"Thank God," Alice said.

Thank God, Maddy thought.

News trickled in from Europe: battles between French, German, and Belgian forces on the German-French frontier, then of German advances, and the landing of the British Expeditionary Force, which everyone said would end the war within days, only the Germans kept beating them, too, pushing the line back from Mons, toward Paris, mile upon mile of French land slipping into German hands. *The troops are all here now in Karachi,* wrote Luke, *although half of them are sick with malaria, and no one has winter uniform. We embark tomorrow, and I hate that I'm sailing in the opposite direction to where you are. Maddy, I'm so sorry, but we're not going to England. I can't tell you where we'll be, only that it's somewhere in France.*

Somewhere in France, Maddy wrote back, desolate. *I can't tell you how that terrifies me.*

"It terrifies me, too," said Della, no longer even attempting to smile at the idea of Peter as a soldier, not in the wake of all the defeats in France. He'd written himself, joking about them all arriving in Europe in tropical kit, even though it would be almost October by the time they landed and it really wasn't funny. "I don't have a nice feeling, Maddy."

"No," said Maddy, who didn't either, and was feeling an ever stronger compulsion to ignore the pull to remain with her mother, and travel to England, as soon as possible. Even with Luke in France, she was sure she'd feel better once she was back. It wasn't just the thought of getting to their home in Richmond. It wasn't even mainly that. It simply felt so very important that she should be there.

"Just wait until your mother's out of hospital," her father said.

"I'll go when you go," Della told her.

The broadsheets brought fresh news daily of the ongoing retreat from Mons: a race to the sea that no one wanted to talk about, because it was such a very unspeakable phenomenon for the British to be pushed anywhere.

Troops arrived by the trainload in Bombay, ready to embark and lend their weight to the defense. The Taj Mahal Palace Hotel was overwhelmed with officers, all in the same uniform Luke would now be wearing, only none of them were him. Maddy, who went for tea at the Sea Lounge with Della—a welcome break from her long days in the hospital's unforgiving chairs—caught herself sitting up in her rattan lounger a couple of times, spine lengthening, thinking, for just a fraction of a second, that she might really have glimpsed his dark hair, the hint of his profile turning a corner, into the hotel, then sagging, because of course she hadn't. It was unbearable. She watched them all, smoking and laughing in the foyer, out on the lounge's sheltered veranda, and wondered if they were only pretending to be so gung-ho about whatever came next.

"Not at all," said one of the many who offered her and Della something stronger than tea (a prospect Maddy found increasingly nauseating). "It's like I tell my men, it's all a grand adventure. Just hope it's not all over by the time we get there."

"I'm going to hope the opposite," said Maddy, "just so you're aware."

At the port, vast rows of tents were set up to house Bombay's temporary residents. Maddy could never look at the canvas village, so gray and bleak in the rain, without thinking that Luke must have had something to do with planning it, perhaps even signed it off. Those who didn't sleep in the tents were housed in the port's warehouses, or in cabins on the lumbering ships waiting in the glassy monsoon sea. Each day, as Maddy drove to the hospital, she saw the sepoys out on hastily organized sightseeing tours of the city—hundreds of them holding hands, staring in wonder at the trams, the traffic—and thought that if she hadn't been so very tired (and female), she could have volunteered her services. Della, who *was* volunteering (in a gender-acceptable position at one of the port canteens), made her smile with a story of a Gurkha regiment who'd never seen the sea before and had tried to wash in it. "Apparently they couldn't understand why their soap wouldn't lather," she said, "or why the water made them even thirstier."

"We actually had a couple of them in here," said Guy, who was in Alice's room reading through her chart when Maddy related the tale. "Salt water doesn't just make you thirsty."

Maddy turned her lips, imagining the taste.

"Well, Alice," said Guy, looking up from the chart. "I think you're about ready for home."

"I am?" said Alice, pushing herself up on her pillow, blond hair loose on her shoulders, making her look so much younger. "Guy, thank you."

"You're most welcome," he said. "I'm glad to see you better before I go."

Maddy didn't ask when he was going. She didn't tell him she'd miss him, which she would. Someone in the hospital had started cooking rice and the steamy smell had just hit her, pushing her over the edge the thought of drinking that seawater had taken her to. She only just made it to the room's large enamel sink before the need to vomit overwhelmed her.

She clutched the basin with both hands, her breakfast of yogurt and mango reappearing, so utterly grim that it made her heave and heave again, then cry, because she always did cry when she was sick, and Guy and her mother were both mortifyingly there, watching, and she wanted Luke. She *wanted* him.

"Madeline," she heard her mother say from the bed, "Madeline . . ."

"Oh my God," she breathed, wiping her mouth.

"Madeline," said her mother again.

Knowing she'd have to do it sooner or later, slowly, she turned.

"Did you eat something?" said Alice.

"I don't know," said Maddy, which wasn't exactly true, but she wasn't ready to voice her suspicions, not yet. They were too precious, too wonderful. *Don't jinx it.*

Guy, though, was staring at her very strangely. He wasn't smiling anymore. He moved, as soon as he realized she was looking at him, telling her he'd fetch her water, but not before she'd been shaken by his stillness, his taut expression.

It was almost like she'd been watching something in him break.

To her sadness, he left for Europe three days later, sailing on the first convoy from Bombay, along with almost all of the men who'd drunk champagne in the Taj, the ones who'd slept in the canvas village, too. The sudden emptiness wouldn't last for long; already, the next wave of men were entraining around India, ready to come to Bombay and embark.

Before Guy went, he called at the villa to say goodbye. He was for France, too, tasked with setting up one of the new casualty clearing stations being established along the emerging front line. They all told him to take care, *be careful,* and Maddy ached because she couldn't imagine what he was going to, and he really was so very alone.

She saw him out to the porch. At the door, he slipped her a card: the details of a doctor.

"He's the best," Guy said. "Don't see anyone else."

"Guy—" she began.

"Please," he said, cutting her off before she could make them both die inside by apologizing for something neither of them wanted to acknowledge, "don't travel. Not when you don't need to. The rain might have stopped, but the water will still be very rough."

"I hope *you'll* be all right," she said, not agreeing to anything, and thinking, too, as always, of Luke; how he and Peter would be managing with their already ill men on the bashing seas.

"I'm made of stern stuff," said Guy, and she knew he wasn't just reassuring her about the waves.

She stood on tiptoes, kissing him lightly on the cheek. "I'll miss you," she said.

He didn't tell her he'd miss her, too.

He paused only to give her one last, brief smile, then turned, hastening through the porch to his motor. That motor that had carried all those bottles of boiled water.

She still intended to travel herself. While she hadn't been able to bring herself to broach the subject with her mother, she'd told her father that she had to be in England by the time Luke was given his first home leave; she'd spend the rest of the month with Alice, then get a passage out, and come back to visit just as soon as she could.

But on September 5, the first German U-boat attacked and sank the British battleship HMS *Pathfinder.* Not long after, with the Battle of the Marne waging in France, finally stopping the German advance at the River

Aisne, several other British warships went down in quick succession. Maddy hardly needed Della and her father to tell her that sailing any-where would be sheer lunacy. All she cared about now was that Luke would reach France safely, Guy and Peter, too. But although to her, and every-one else's, shuddering relief, telegrams did eventually arrive from some-where in France, reassuring them that they all *were* safely on land, it was hard to feel happy, not now the casualty lists from the Marne had been pub-lished. More than one boy Maddy had known at university was on them; killed in action, wounded, missing and presumed . . . It crushed her to think of them gone, just like that. She wanted to believe it wasn't real, that there'd been a misprint and they still existed somewhere as she remembered them—cycling around Oxford, scarves flapping, cheeks flushed with summer sun as they drank warm beer in riverside gardens—but the world felt emptier, so much sadder.

There was only one piece of truly good news, delivered by the rather elderly, highly distinguished, and wholly gentlemanly Dr. Tully whom Guy had told Maddy to see.

"He apologized before examining me," Maddy, fuchsia with the ordeal, told Della, once she returned to her in the waiting room. "I don't think I'm ever going to stop cringing."

"But . . . ?" said Della.

"But," said Maddy, and her cheeks pulled, a smile overtaking her, of dis-belief that she really *did* have this little person growing within her (*their* little person), and utter, overwhelming joy. "I'm going to be a mama, Della," she said, laughing, opening her arms for her friend's hug. "I'm going to be a *mummy*."

Even with all her happiness, she was nervous about telling her parents. Knowing all they'd suffered, she felt conspicuous in her euphoria at what was happening inside her, almost guilty. Her legs shook later that same eve-ning as she walked beside Della out to the veranda, where they were both having aperitifs by the light of scented citronella lamps. The citrus oil caught at her throat; she was still feeling very sick ("A girl, I wager," Dr. Tully had said, "with no scientific reason, other than they always seem to make their mamas the most poorly"), and she had to swallow before speaking, but, with Della's elbow nudging her side, she forced words, not vomit, out.

"I hope you're not going to be busy in March," she said.

"Why's that?" asked Richard.

"Because, and you especially seem too young for this, Mama, you're go-ing to be grandparents."

And, their faces. Their *faces*.

Richard hooted, actually hooted. Alice gasped, placed her hands to her mouth, looked from Maddy to Della to Richard, back to Maddy. "A baby," she said. "Here?"

"I think so," said Maddy, who wouldn't now dream of chancing the U-boats, and had started to accept that, however much she hoped for the opposite, nothing was going to be over by Christmas. She wasn't sure how she could have coped with the agony of it, were it not for the wonder of her growing little bundle.

And it was almost worth the pain of staying to see her parents' happi-ness, the tears in her mother's eyes. She loved that she'd given that to them. She *did*.

But she still would have traded it in a heartbeat, not to have had to tell Luke he was going to be a father by wire.

As it was, his smile, his joy at the news, would only ever now exist in her imagination.

The wire didn't reach him until mid-October, chasing him from base camp in Marseille to Orléans, where his batman—a young sepoy who'd traveled, along with him and Peter, from Bombay—handed it to him in the middle of a wet, windswept artillery practice ground. All around the wire fences, locals gathered, braving the weather for yet another look at the sepoys; a novelty they couldn't seem to get enough of. The men themselves, who'd mostly recovered from the malaria that had made their long crossing to France even worse than it might otherwise have been, were lined up in rows on the stone flagging, their thin uniforms sodden in the drizzle, their turbans dripping, unloading and reloading their rifles, hands moving fast, despite the cold, firing at the strung-up sandbags as their captains, a shiver-ing Peter included, shouted the order.

Luke watched Peter as he bent, helping one of his men to unjam his rifle. He breathed ice as he talked (doubtless murdering some more Urdu); it was freezing for October. They were all freezing, still wearing their Indian uniforms, despite Luke's repeated requests to the quartermasters for great-coats and thick serge khaki. He arched his neck, staring into the misty sky, feeling the moisture on his face, and frowned at the thought of the weeks ahead in the boggy fields of Ypres. A line of sorts had been formed there—part French, part Belgian and British forces—trying to keep the Channel ports from falling into German hands. It was working, but only just, and with no other trained British troops yet in France, it had fallen to the In-dian Army to dig in and help. Colonel Whittaker, also now in Orléans, was going, too. They'd entrain the next night, to God only knew what carnage. Orléans had seen its fair share of men come through, fresh from fighting. Luke had been shaken by more than one tale of companies decimated by machine-gun fire, the power of a howitzer's shells. . . .

All of that left his mind, though, as his batman came running and handed him the flimsy telegram. He tore at the paper, knowing it was from her, craving her words, any words, like an addict. With the staccato of rifles and Urdu commands all around, his eyes moved across the typed message.

```
Aren't we clever STOP Little boy or girl getting
ready for a spring arrival STOP Now you have
another reason to stay safe STOP
```

He drew breath: a gasp of elation that not even Maddy's imagination had been able to do justice to. A child. *Their* child.

"My God," he said, reading it again, smiling, laughing, not believ-ing it. He pictured her, in the Bombay telegraph office, in one of her pale dresses, skin flushed with the kind of heat that taunted him, writing, smil-ing, too, and for a second, just a second, he was there, with her.

He wanted to be with her. He felt the need in every part of him.

Stay safe, she'd written.

Stay safe, he told himself, then started as a bullet from a misfired gun wisped too close to his face.

"Sorry," called Peter. "Still jammed."

Luke refocused, returning to the ground, the drizzle and cold, the men who never complained, and who tomorrow he'd march into battle for the first time.

Stay safe.

He had to do it. Somehow, he had to, and get back to her, this baby; their family.

Nothing had ever felt so important in his life.

CHAPTER SIXTEEN

The Germans didn't reach the Channel ports that winter. Day after day, the shells screamed, bullets rained, but despite relentless attacks and counterattacks by both sides across Ypres's plains of flooded, impassable land, the line barely moved, and all that was achieved was devastation. During scarce breaks in the fighting, Luke entreated the men to lay down their bayonets, rest; still in tropical kit, they huddled for shelter beneath smashed trees, trying to sleep in freezing mud baths and forget the bodies, everywhere, the heavy guns that might at any second point their way, do to them what had been done to their brothers, their friends; the invisible, always-watching snipers. *This is not war,* wrote a havildar, in one of the letters home Luke censored each night, crouched in a shell hole, his mac raised to shield the paper from the rain, *it is the end of the world.*

Men kept dying, every day, in ways Luke could never have believed permissible had he not been there with them—screaming at them to move, just a split second too late; holding them as they went.

"It's the look in their eyes," said Peter, clutching a cigarette one stormy night, the lighthearted façade he wore like a shield for once slipping. "The way they stare." He stared himself, at Luke; a naked despair that made Luke reach out, squeeze his soaking arm, as though such a thing could help. "I don't want this to be the last thing I see," Peter said.

"Then for God's sake, let's not let it be," said Luke.

"You have a plan?" said Peter.

"It's evolving," said Luke, who of course didn't, and had become grimly certain by now that surviving this travesty came down to nothing more than a macabre game of chance.

Peter sucked on his cigarette, knowing it, too. But, "Keep me updated," he said, and dredged up a smile, since he was Peter, and that was what he did.

The days ground on, each impossibly worse than the last. How they kept managing it, Luke didn't know, but he, who felt sick at the hand he'd played in dragging everyone over here, and wanted only to send them home (himself included), was ordered to drag his companies wherever support was most needed by the BEF, moving constantly up and down the salient, thrown from fight to fight. They rarely slept; they were always freezing, always hungry, living off tins of cold bully beef. Luke's own CO was badly burned by an exploding shell and sent to one of the new plastic surgeons in Blighty. ("Plastic," he said, mumbling through melted lips when Luke said goodbye to him at the heaving field hospital. "Sounds like torture.") The rank COs—men Luke and Peter had traveled with from Karachi, men who'd drilled and trained and kept the troops going; men with families of their own, lives and hopes—they disappeared. *I've been made a lieutenant colonel,* Luke wrote to Maddy, *there's no one else left to do it. Peter's now a major. Promotions come quickly on the Western Front. I don't know how we're both still alive. It's begun to feel like we're each other's lucky charm. Hardly any of the captains who came over with us are left, and it kills me. We've been given new British NCOs, but their Urdu is even worse than Peter's. They're trying, but no one can understand them, and we're losing them, too. Maddy, most of them were at school this time last year, little more than children. The snipers target all of us. They know officers wear peaked caps, not turbans.*

For God's sake, she wrote back, in late October, *start wearing turbans.*

It was, of course, an excellent idea.

"A plan, in fact," said Peter. "Well done, Maddy."

All of Luke's officers replaced their caps before they set off on their next attack, charging at dawn across the cratered floor of Nuns' Woods, or Non Bochen; another frantic, smoke-filled advance, this time to push the Germans back from their attempted grab for the Menin Road. Whittaker didn't like the change in uniform, and he refused to wear a turban himself. *You're in the army now.* But then he got killed, too, taken down by a sniper in that same attack, even though he wasn't meant to be involved, but had insisted on lending his weight, saying the men were entitled to hear the order to charge in their own tongue, dammit. He was shot before they'd even had a chance to reach the German position, take the hypothermic soldiers there prisoner. ("*Danke*," the men stuttered. "*Danke*.") Luke wrote to Whittaker's wife later that day, as he and the rest of the uninjured men collapsed in the stone ruins of a chapel, the eerie glow of searchlights arching overhead. His pen moved on the damp paper, repeating the same useless platitudes of bravery and quick ends that he'd already said far too many times before.

Maddy wrote as well, constantly: daily letters that arrived in bundles that always took too long, and lifted him from the horror with talk of the life he craved, and that she spoke of as though they were beside one another—on a beach, at a restaurant, in bed—as if she, too, was imagining that was where they were. She described the movements of their growing, still unbelievable child, told him, at his request, of each of her appointments with Dr. Tully (*He keeps speaking about the baby—who's apparently rising very nicely—as though it's one of Cook's cakes. Cook who, by the by, is not only speaking to me again, but speaking in Urdu. Urdu! I'm sure he's feeling smug because his chutneys helped so much with the sickness*), and how she'd started teaching, at the local school her gardener's possessed children attended, where there were no ridiculous rules against female teachers who were married (or related to those who were divorced).

I'm so glad you're doing that, he wrote. *Are you enjoying it?*

Very much, she said, *I should have started long ago. Mama comes sometimes, too.*

How is your mama? he asked.

So different, she said, *I can't tell you. All better now, and still quiet (Papa says he thinks she's forgotten how not to be), but softer, less . . . furtive, so really rather nice to be with, and much easier to talk to—even Della thinks so—especially when it comes to anything to do with the baby. She's embroidering him or her a brand-new mosquito net, covered in the most wonderful stars and moons. Now I know who sewed all those monkeys on mine! She is, of course, astonished I've remembered those. I'm starting to see just how much she adores children, and feel so desperately sad that she didn't have more than me. Whenever she comes to the school, she says it's only to make sure I'm not tiring myself out on the walk, but the second she enters the class-*

room and the children ask her to paint with them, she agrees, quite as though
she wasn't intending to stay all along . . .

And do the children know you're expecting a baby? he asked.

They do, she said. *They like feeling it wriggle and kick.*

What would Diana Aldyce say? he replied.

What wouldn't she say? she answered.

I'm jealous, he wrote back, rain bouncing off his shoulders, seeping
down his neck. *I want to feel those kicks.*

It got colder. Luke's mother, who'd never been one for baking, sent him
a greatcoat. *Take good care of it please. No tears. No holes. We're with you
every second. Never forget that you hold our lives in your hands, too. You're
all we have.* Luke lent the coat to his batman, who before this hell had never
known a temperature cooler than a Bombay night. His batman asked if he
might let his brother, one of the privates, a naik, in Peter's company, wear
it, too, and after that the men all took turns; savored moments of warmth.
It wasn't until late November, with the year's battle for Ypres finally at a
fizzling, inconclusive end, and the salient stilled by a broken silence, that,
with white coating the obliterated landscape, thick serge winter uniforms
finally arrived. There were too many of them. Almost half of the men for
whom they'd been issued were gone, buried in the frozen ground, never to
return to the heat of India they'd so longed for.

I haven't forgotten it, Luke wrote to Maddy. *I feel it sometimes, in my
dreams. I can never see you, though. Will you please get your photograph
taken? I need so much to look at your face.*

She did as he asked, sending a sepia portrait Richard had taken of her on
the veranda. It found Luke in a new position up the line, near the German-
held town of Neuve-Chapelle, where his new CO—a harassed colonel from
Ipswich—had ordered him to march the battered remnants of his division to entrench for the winter. It was a quieter sector, although there were
whispers of a spring offensive. More livable, too (everything being relative),
with deep trenches built by the engineers, boarded walkways to keep their
feet from the icy puddles, and small luxuries like sandbags to protect their
heads from sniper fire. Dugouts, too, where they could sleep out of the rain,
the wind.

Luke lay on his bunk to open Maddy's letter. Above him, the ceiling dripped soil from the shellfire they exchanged each day with the Boche (just to remind everyone, as though they could forget, why they were all there). In the corner of the earthen room, a group of naiks, his own batman included, played a game of dice. At the table, Peter and a couple of other NCOs dealt a hand of rummy and argued over whether rat racing would or would not be a morale-boosting sport to introduce to the troops.

"The fact that you're arguing about this at all," said Luke, slicing through the envelope, "tells me we've been here too long."

He pulled out the contents of the envelope, his fingers touching the paper hers had touched, and took her photograph in his cracked, mud-crusted hands. *Papa's bought a Brownie box camera,* she'd written, *so we'll send pictures of the baby, just as soon as he or she is born. Your parents have requested ones, too, and Edie can't wait either.* He stared at her picture, his eyes blurring with the effort of absorbing every last detail. She wore a pale dress, no hat. Her hair was all curls, several loose, touching the smooth skin of her neck. She looked directly at the camera, smiling, right at him. He saw the neat curve of her stomach, and felt his jaw clench with the pain, the unbearable pain, of not being where she was. On the table next to her was a half-drunk glass of water, a plate of sliced fruit. He imagined her swallowing the drink, setting the glass down. He heard her voice. *All right, go on, I'm ready. No, wait. . . . Should I smile? Is that allowed in photographs?*

Thank you, he wrote back. *I can't tell you what it's meant, getting this.*

One of you now, please, she replied.

And he sent her a picture his batman took of him and Peter, with a camera borrowed from the local tobacconist when they were out on a week's rest leave in a nearby hamlet, both standing in the cobbled street, wearing the sheepskins they'd bought from a local farmer over their khaki.

Very stylish, she wrote, *you wear them well. In case it helps, I'm also sending socks and gloves. The children in my class helped knit them (very excited at the break from arithmetic). A few of them have older brothers and papas at the front, too, so we do it for an hour every day now. An industrious classroom. We're all busy. Has Peter told you Della's no longer at the canteen, but volunteering at Guy's old hospital instead? She's met a rather sweet dental surgeon there, actually, Jeffrey, but assures me that's not the only reason she goes. Everyone's short on staff these days, and neither of us can stand sitting and waiting at home. I keep thinking about how this time last year I was about to see you for the first time at the Yacht Club. I haven't been since you left. I can't. They're not holding a party this New Year. It wouldn't feel right, and the last thing anyone wants is to dance. Not that I could dance. Thanks to Cook (who's assured us there'll be no turkey curry for Christmas), this baby's most definitely a bonny one. . . .*

I'd dance with you, he wrote back. *If I were there, I'd take you back to our beach, and dance with you on the sand. . . .*

Now isn't that a nice thought, she said.

In the middle of December, new troops arrived to replenish those they'd lost, some much-needed Urdu-speaking officers among them. Fraser Keaton, fresh from Bombay, was in their number. *Keep an eye on him, will you?* Richard wrote to Luke. *He simply wouldn't hear of staying, and seems far too young to have gone.* Ernest Aldyce came as well.

"Oh Christ," said Peter, burning lice from the seams of his shirt, "it really can always get worse."

He was a quieter Ernest, though. Depleted. He'd been at Ypres, too, with the BEF, since he was on leave in England when they were mobilized, and one of the few of his company to come through. If you could call it coming through. Physically, everything about him had thinned: his hair, his body; even his waxy skin hung, wafer-like, on the ill-defined lines of his face. He no longer held his head straight, but at an angle, chin to his bony shoulder, eyes darting constantly, as though afraid to settle in any one place. Such a different man from the assured Indian officer who'd worn Luke out with his endless talk and questions in Bombay. Had Luke not seen his papers, he wasn't sure he'd have recognized him.

"He didn't want to come," Luke reminded Peter. "Do you remember, how adamant he was he should be left in Bombay?"

"Smarter than I gave him credit for," said Peter, not unsympathetically this time. They were all shaken by the change in Ernest. Afraid, too, not that anyone admitted it; that unutterable terror that what had fallen on him might come for them next.

"I'm beginning to think I should have stayed in Bombay after all," said Fraser, wincing at the vibrations of distant shellfire during his first night in the trenches.

"That's only just occurred to you?" said Luke with a sigh.

He kept both men close to him, placing Fraser directly under his own command, and Ernest in the length of trench between himself and Peter. It gave him ample opportunity to see how much time Ernest spent just sitting on the floor of the trench, staring up at the pyrotechnics in the sky, wringing his hands. His sepoys saw it, too. They came to Luke asking to be reassigned.

"I could take them," said Peter. "Happily. They're good men. . . ."

They were. Luke wished he could move them under Peter. But, "I can't," he said wearily. "I'd have to report it if I did." He knew too well what would happen to Ernest then. They'd all heard the stories. Given Ernest had no outward injuries, he'd be court-martialed for cowardice, probably shot.

Luke resolved to do his best for Ernest himself, build him back up by taking him out on some minor operations, help him salvage some resilience before asking him to fight in a more serious engagement. There was a raid planned for December 30, the last of 1914. Just a small affair to knock out a series of observation points in the opposite German position. It wouldn't even make dispatches. He'd take him on that.

"Let's bring Keaton, too," said Peter. "It's terrifying me, how green he is. . . ."

They went early, long before the sun was up. Luke, who'd led countless such expeditions, barely broke a sweat of adrenaline as he crawled up the jumping-off ladder, waving at the others to follow. He wasn't expecting any trouble. They'd had a cease-fire of sorts over Christmas—nothing as amicable as the football matches he'd heard talk of in other sectors, no singing of "Silent Night" across the wastes of no-man's-land, but a stilling of the guns, enough peace for all of them to sleep a bit, write more letters home, and Luke to stare at the wintry sky, pray to a God who seemed to have taken leave of his senses that this would be the last Christmas he'd spend in France. ("That's the wrong bloody prayer," Peter had said, punching him. "You could end up somewhere worse." "Where's worse?" Luke had asked. "I'm sure 1915 has something up its sleeve," said Peter.) They'd all lived and let live, and the Boche wouldn't be anticipating a fight that morning. It was pitch-dark; as long as they all kept low, no duty sentry would spot them coming. All being well, they'd throw their mortars, disable the observation posts, and get the hell away without any casualties.

There were fifteen of them in total. Four officers—himself, Peter, Ernest, and Fraser—then a handful of battle-hardened engineers, and several naiks who'd survived Ypres and all knew what they were doing. Luke didn't need to tell them to keep silent as they crawled across the icy, pitted ground, toward the Boches' trench. It didn't even occur to him that he'd have to warn Ernest, who was always so silent anyway, to hold his tongue.

But as they drew closer to their target, close enough to smell German coffee brewing, the sizzle of bacon fat, Ernest started making a strange sound, something between a bleat and a wail, interspersed with breathless sobs.

Aghast, Luke hissed at him to be quiet. The other men did the same.

"For God's sake," said Fraser, voice shaking with fear, "can someone shut him up?"

"Aldyce," said Luke, starting to panic now himself, "you have to stop."

He didn't stop. He started weeping, and buried his face in the cold earth, maybe in shame, maybe just to muffle himself. It was horrendous to see. If Luke could have, he'd have picked him up then, carried him back to the trench, shot him in the hand if he had to, any excuse to get him to safety, home.

But to stand would be suicide. So he shuffled backward, alongside him, gripping his heaving shoulder. "Aldyce," he said. "Come on."

"I can't," Ernest said to the ground. "I can't, I can't, I can't, I can't . . ."

He was getting louder.

"Let's move," Peter said, "drown him out with the mortars, then you get him back."

But before Luke could agree, Ernest threw him off, with a strength that surprised him, and stood, in the middle of no-man's-land, screaming. The rest of them stared, horror-struck, for what felt like forever, but was in reality probably only seconds, and then the Boche opened fire with a machine gun, and they were all standing, Luke yelling at everyone to go wide, run. One of the engineers ignored him, with a bravery that would get him a Distinguished Service Medal, and carried on, up to the line to throw the mortars, taking out the gunner. In the same instant, Luke grabbed Ernest, throwing him on his shoulder, not noticing how flaccid his body had become, and ran in the wake of his men, lungs bursting, back to the safety of the trench.

Thanks to the engineer and his mortars, none of them were killed. Fraser received a bullet graze to the cheek that at least got him out of the line for a spell. The engineer with the mortars took several more bullets in his shoulder. He wrote to Luke from the Indian Convalescent Hospital in Brighton, telling him he was being sent home to his wife and children in Lahore, and thanking him, actually *thanking* him, for being his lieutenant colonel.

You'd have had more cause to thank me if you hadn't been shot, Luke said.

Even you cannot be controlling the bullets, sahib, he replied. *We would not have been having anyone but you.*

Ernest would have been having someone, Luke was certain. If it hadn't been for him, he'd never have been out there in no-man's-land, standing, screaming, until that shrapnel had blown off half his face. Luke hadn't even realized he'd been injured, not until he'd seen the blood pouring from him when they'd got back to the trench, and finally registered Ernest's limpness. "No," he'd said, reaching down, pressing his hand to what was left of his jaw, "no, no, no . . ."

The stretcher-bearers had taken him to a dressing station, from there to one of the many casualty clearing stations flanking the line, on to London, a facial-reconstruction unit, and, finally, a mind hospital in Surrey, the King's Fifth. Luke wrote to them, desperate to know he was all right. One of the sisters wrote back—Sister Lytton, she was called—kindly telling him that Ernest wasn't all right at all; he had no memory left, *not of his past, or even each day, but please know that we're looking after him as best we can. He loves his cups of cocoa, and the weekends especially when his mama visits.* Luke felt sick when he read that letter. He clenched it in his fist, creasing the paper, shame coursing through him at what he'd done to Ernest. To be left breathing, functioning, trapped in your body like that with no face, no life, no memory . . . Peter was right, there was something worse than France after all. Worse, almost, than death.

"It wasn't your fault." Peter said it to him time and again.

Maddy wrote it, too. *You must know that,* she said. *If you want to blame anyone, blame the gunner. Or Ypres. Blame Ypres, the generals, this whole hideous war. Please don't blame yourself.*

But he couldn't help it. February turned to March, and the days lengthened but grew no warmer, just damper, flooding the trenches, leaving the men tortured by swollen, blackened feet as well as frostbite. He did his best to cheer them up with promises of spring leave that he only hoped would be granted, all the while replaying his decision to take Ernest out that December dawn, the way he himself had just lain there when Ernest had stood, not moving fast enough to drag him back down.

In the second week of March, Fraser Keaton returned from hospital, hundreds more troops poured into their part of the line, extra munitions and heavy barrage shells arrived, and they were all ordered over the top for the long-rumored offensive to retake the town of Neuve-Chapelle. It was another bloodbath, for both sides, with casualties in the tens of thousands— men and boys mown down, left to lie several deep on the battlefields until the shell and machine-gun fire subsided, and those of them that were left could run out, give them water, attempt to drag them back to safety—but dispatches lauded it a success. *Neuve-Chapelle back in British hands, and the line now forward by more than half a mile.*

"Half a mile," said Peter, when they finally stood down, and marched into the demolished town to bunk in whatever building was still standing for a six-day rest. "Half. A. Mile. How many casualties would that be per yard?"

"A hundred," said Fraser, who had mercifully come through the carnage, and had apparently already done the grim calculation.

"A hundred," echoed Luke. He let his gritty eyes move over the snaking line of those still standing, their turbans and uniforms spattered with mud and blood, awed, as always, by how they carried themselves so straight, despite their trench feet, the cold and lack of sleep, the men they'd buried and shot and seen shot. How long would they be able to keep going like this, keep falling in with the relentless orders? Some of their letters had grown angrier lately, laced with a fury that he understood, and would never report. Could their days of subservience be numbered? He decided probably yes, and then, because Ernest was never far from his thoughts, wondered what he would make of it all, if he still had his right mind. And would he still be here, too, on the other side of the three days they'd just endured, if he, Luke, had only allowed him more time to mend?

I should have found a way to get him home, he wrote to Maddy, just before the battalion moved again, back, to his horror, toward Ypres, where another battle for the Channel ports was rumored. *I can't stop thinking of him in that hospital.*

You must be due home leave soon, she wrote by return. *Go to the hospital, see him there.*

I will, he said, *I need to.*

The thought of doing it, though, setting foot in that hospital, it terrified him.

If Maddy were in England, she'd go for him. She'd visit that hospital all the time, if it would only help him feel better. She'd be to and from the King's Fifth, where she'd sit with Ernest, hold his hand and speak to him of all the things that might jog his memory—the Gymkhana Club, polo on dusty grass, gin and tonics at sundown—then write to Luke and reassure him that Ernest had had company that day, he was being cared for. *You did the best for him that you could.*

She'd tried to get in touch with Diana, who was still marooned in Dorking. She'd written to her back in January, telling her how sorry she'd been to hear of Ernest's injuries. Diana hadn't replied. It was now almost April, and Maddy, propped up on pillows in her bedroom, the shutters open in a futile attempt to invite a breeze into the hot room, had accepted she wasn't going to. Too upset, perhaps.

"Too sorry for herself, I'd wager," said Della, not scrubbing bedpans at the hospital that day, or sharing tiffin with Jeff, but sitting beside Maddy, staring adoringly at the precious little bundle in Maddy's arms. "Let it be, Maddy. You've got other things to think about."

Maddy, who had barely lifted her own eyes from the perfect tiny human she was holding, didn't need to be told. Her and Luke's daughter had finally arrived the night before, more than a week after Dr. Tully had said they might expect her, coming, like Maddy's lost brother, the wrong way. Dr. Tully, who'd warned Maddy she was breech, and nodded sympathetically when she'd paled, and Alice had expressed her horror at the news, had given all of them his solemn word that no one was going to be cut open this time; he'd delivered many healthy breech babies *in the traditional manner,* and wasn't in the least worried, they weren't to be either.

Maddy had had her moments in the excruciating, sweat-soaked night that had passed. She was sure that her father, who'd paced around the villa, knocking on the door for news every half hour, had, too. She was certain that her wrought mother, and even Della—neither of whom had left her side, but had knelt by the bed, repeating that it was all going to be all right, it was, and they wished Luke were here, too, they did, but she just had to keep going—had had several. Dr. Tully, though, had been as good as his word, never once appearing to panic, calmly telling her to breathe, then push, then relax, then push, and breathe, and push, and on, and on, until there little Iris had been, all glossy black curls and giant dark blue eyes, warm and soft in her shaking arms. "Thank you," Maddy had said to Dr. Tully, choked with tears of joy and gratitude, silently thanking Guy, too, who'd known just what he was doing when he'd told her to see no one else.

"She really is the image of Luke," said Della now. "Other than her eyes, I'm not sure you've had a look-in, Maddy."

"I don't mind," said Maddy, who wanted only for Luke to see her for himself, this beautiful daughter of theirs. Her mother had already gone to the telegraph office to wire him, his parents, too. It had been a mark of Alice's euphoria (and relief) that she'd also offered to wire Edie.

"I could do it if you prefer," Richard had said.

"No," Alice had replied, stooping to drop another kiss on Iris's downy head. "I think I can manage to share this."

Maddy wished she knew where Luke would be when he received the wire. *Safe,* she thought, *let it be somewhere safe.* He'd sent several of his own in the past fortnight, from somewhere in France or Flanders, never, to her agonizing frustration, able to tell her which part, only that he was thinking of her constantly, waiting for news. PETER ALSO BESIDE HIMSELF WITH IMPATIENCE STOP. She was similarly beside herself, waiting for the news that they'd both been sent to England for leave. Tantalized by the prospect of surprising Luke when he arrived, she'd become increasingly tempted to go, too, despite the U-boats. She'd even offered to pay Ahmed to fetch a schedule from the P&O office. He'd gone, but refused to take her money. "Memsahib," he'd said, eyes troubled as he'd handed her the paper,

"I am not recommending this." He'd been right. She'd have to tell him that. *I'm not going anywhere.* She stroked Iris's soft, pink cheek, pushed the muslin swaddle back from her chin, and was appalled she'd even contemplated putting her in that kind of danger. Just the thought of taking her out on the Bombay roads made her shudder. Impossibly painful as it was, she'd have to wait to be with Luke. They both would.

Della reached over, taking her hand, seeming to know what she was thinking about. "He'll have the photograph," she said.

Maddy nodded. They were taking it that afternoon, in the garden; a picture that would have to do until Luke could cradle Iris for himself, in those arms that she, Maddy, hadn't felt around her for too many months, and missed so very desperately.

"He'll be all right," said Della gently. "He's not going to let himself die over there. Neither of them are."

"I know that," said Maddy, but wasn't sure why.

Neither of them, of course, knew any such thing.

He wasn't all right. He was in Ypres, a hell that the long winter had done nothing to improve, and which managed to be even grimmer flooded in April sunshine than it had been drenched in November rain.

"Poetic," said Peter, beside him in the hastily dug ditch that they, Fraser, and several hundred others were crammed in, bayonets fixed, waiting to go over the top for the second time that day.

"I'll put it on a postcard," said Luke, looking at his watch, then placing his whistle to his mouth, ready to give the signal to move.

Overhead, shells flew, bombarding what they were all praying was the German position they were about to attempt a charge on, although it could just as easily be empty woodland. They'd been fighting for two days now, both sides firing constantly, retreating, advancing, retreating again, until no one knew where anyone was. The officers who'd gone to reconnoiter the land ahead of this attack had failed to return, and the howitzers were shooting blind. Luke could only guess what direction they were supposed to bloody run in. He hadn't met half of the men he was now leading until an hour before. The battalions had become hopelessly mixed, British and Indian scrambling in the chaos of the fighting, running in panic from the gas the Germans had started using for the first time, digging in wherever they found themselves. None of them had gas masks. The only strategy for surviving the clouds was to get below them, or preferably away from them, as fast as humanly possible. "That," Luke had said to them all, "is the plan."

He pressed his hand to his jacket pocket, feeling the crinkle of Maddy's letter inside. He'd got it the morning before. Anxiously as he'd watched for it to come, ever since Alice's wire had found him on a brief rest stop in Poperinghe and made him shout, punch the air with happiness—BEAUTIFUL IRIS IS HERE STOP PHOTOGRAPH ON ITS WAY STOP MADELINE DID WONDERFULLY STOP YOUR FAMILY IS WAITING FOR YOU STOP TAKE GOOD CARE STOP—he hadn't opened the envelope to look inside. He'd wanted to leave it waiting while he was still here in Ypres, so that he had something to get through for. Now, though, now . . . He dropped his whistle, swallowing dryly, and shifted up, against the chalky earth wall, peering through the smoke, the cacophony of fire and guns toward the distant trees, whatever was waiting there, and felt his heart pummel too hard in his chest. Moving without realizing he was going to, knowing he had only seconds left to do anything, he reached into his pocket, grabbed the envelope, and tore it open.

"No," said Peter, realizing what he was doing, "you don't need to, not yet . . ."

He ignored him. He ignored everything. He didn't breathe, just stared. Because there she was. His daughter. His *daughter*. A sepia wonder, nestled in Maddy's arms, palm leaves casting shadows on Maddy's downcast lids, her cheekbones, and Iris's perfect, *perfect* eyes, her miniature lips, her tiny foot that poked, free of the swaddling, her mess of dark hair. He couldn't believe he'd held himself back from seeing her. How could he have thought it would be bad luck to look at her, to look at both of them? He pressed the image to his lips, and for the first time in months felt filled with hope, strength. He felt invincible.

"You're not," said Peter, shouting above the bombardment. "So while she's as beautiful as she was always going to be, you be sodding careful, because she'll want a papa."

"She has one," he said, stealing a final look at the picture, then taking back his whistle. "I'm not going anywhere."

"Just over the top," said Peter, raising his bayonet.

"Just that," said Luke, and blew.

For a while, almost an entire minute, the advance was textbook. They scrambled up in good order, progressing slowly toward the trees in long stretches, keeping well behind the protection of the artillery barrage that wouldn't lift until they reached the woods. There was no answering fire from ahead. No one fell, or screamed, and then they were almost there, at the tree line. Luke glanced sideways at Peter, saw Peter look back at him. *Can it really be this easy?*

That was when the pellets began to rain from the blue, cloudless sky, plopping soundlessly in the grass, releasing a burning yellow vapor that turned the sunlight opaque and filled their eyes, their noses, their lungs . . .

Choking, Luke ripped off his jacket and pressed it to his mouth, sending his identity tags scattering in the process. He saw Fraser Keaton stoop, fumble to pick them up, and yelled at him not to worry, for God's sake, but his voice got lost because their guns were still blazing, and the Germans started up, too, pounding the field with shells, machine-gun bullets with them, only from the side of the wood, not within it as they'd thought, mowing through the grass, the men, taking them down, sending them running blindly, randomly, into the exploding shells, the raining earth and blood, unable to see or breathe.

Luke doubled over, sinking beneath the rising gas, hands to his throat, gasping. He saw his batman less than twenty paces away, struggling to get his suffocating brother's jacket off, and he half ran, half crawled toward them, yanking the jacket free, pressing it to the boy's face, shouting at them to keep low, run for shelter, *now*. It was as they went, disappearing into the haze of smoke and gas, that he spotted Peter, one arm over his mouth and nose, limping, obviously hit.

"Peter," Luke shouted, "Peter, get down . . ."

He saw his friend look around, eyes wide, settling on nothing. Out of nowhere, Luke remembered his words the winter before. *I don't want this to be the last thing I see.*

"Get down," Luke yelled again, coughing on the effort.

"Luke?" Peter shouted back. "Luke?"

"Get *down*," Luke shouted a final time, then cursed, because blood was pouring from Peter's leg and it was obvious he wasn't in any state to do anything. Men everywhere were collapsing, and they were all going to get killed, in this place. This *place*. Some, like Luke's batman and his brother, were making a break for the trees, but Peter went nowhere. He jolted, then dropped, hit again.

"*Peter,*" Luke yelled.

Still struggling for breath, eyes pouring, he stood and made a run for him, dodging shells. As he went, Fraser stumbled in front of him, seemingly out of nowhere, jacketless, his shirt nothing but torn scraps, and his school-boy features horrifically shot to a pulp. He no longer wore any tags around his own neck—which was as ravaged as his face—but was still, perversely, clutching Luke's set. It was the only way Luke was able to tell it was him. Aghast, he moved toward him, grabbing him by the waist as he slithered to the ground. He crouched, threw his own jacket over him for warmth until he could get back to him, then, choking more than ever, raced on to Peter, who was unconscious, but just about breathing. Pulling him onto his back, Luke ran, panting, for the trees.

He was almost there when the shell landed.

He didn't hear it. But he felt a sudden stillness, and his blood turn cold in sickening foreboding, before a wall of heat struck him, slamming into his face, his head, his spine and blood. He flew up, on and on into the Ypres sky. The last thing he was conscious of was Peter on the grass floor, opening his eyes briefly to stare up at him, a look of horror spreading over his pale face.

The last thought he was aware of was his love for his daughter and Maddy; the picture of them that he'd left with his jacket on top of Fraser's faceless body.

And how glad he was that he'd looked at it.

CHAPTER SEVENTEEN

When he came to his senses again, he was limping on a leafy floor, stooped over, clutching his arm, trees all around. He looked up, at the movement of the branches, and heard no rustle, only ringing. Beneath his torn, bare feet, the ground vibrated. He wasn't sure what made it do that.

He wore only trousers, a ripped vest. *I should have a jacket,* he thought, and it felt important, but he didn't know why, or where his jacket could be. When he touched his head—which hurt, very much; almost as much as his arm, his ribs and feet—his hand came away red.

Blood, he thought. *I'm bleeding.*

Again, he couldn't think why he was doing that.

Or what was making it so very hard for him to breathe.

His arm didn't hang properly from his shoulder. He held it to stop it falling. He had gashes all over his hands. He could taste blood in his mouth as well. His vest was covered in it. *I need to find someone to help me,* he thought, and kept on stumbling forward, for he didn't know how long, until darkness fell, and he came to a soundless road that was jammed with other bleeding, stumbling men, and vehicles bearing red crosses, out of which jumped a tired-looking woman who looked him in the eye, caught him as he fell forward, and yelled for a stretcher.

She's helping me, he thought. *Good. That's good.*

Where am I?

"What's your name?" the woman asked him. He watched her lips form the words.

He stared.

She asked him again.

He shook his head, awful realization dawning on him.

He didn't know his name.

To his horror, he had absolutely no idea who he was.

The telegrams arrived at once in Bombay, just as the whole family was sitting down to lunch on the veranda, a sleeping Iris in her perambulator included. They were all subdued. Richard had heard, barely an hour before, that sweet, keen, eager-to-please Fraser Keaton had been declared as missing in action, presumed dead. Much as they were all trying to reassure him that there *was* still hope (*if they've found no body, how can anyone know?*) he couldn't seem to muster any, but instead kept berating himself for not managing to persuade Fraser against enlisting.

Even with the sadness of poor Fraser, though, Maddy suspected nothing when the telegraph boy arrived at the villa. He came so frequently, after all, with wires for her father, and for her from Luke. She felt no real disquiet as Ahmed showed him out through the drawing room doors, only a lift of anticipation, foolish hope, that Luke had written again.

But the boy asked for Della, not her. Della, who was expecting Jeff to join them for lunch any minute, and who never got wires, but whose mother had assured her by letter that she'd send one the second there was any word of Peter.

Della stood warily, pushing her chair back, taking the paper from the boy. Maddy watched her every movement, a slow shiver of fear snaking down her spine. Her parents, too, sat very still.

Fumbling, Della opened the telegraph. She looked down at it, reading. "Oh," she said, round eyes filling. "Oh God . . ."

"What is it?" said Alice. "What's happened?"

"He's lost his leg," Della said. "He's in hospital, in France."

"No," said Richard. "Oh, Peter . . ."

Della went on, voice shaking, saying it was all right, he was alive, getting better, moving back to Blighty soon.

"He's out of it at least," said Richard. "That's something. . . ."

Maddy knew she should speak, too, go to her friend, hold her, tell her how desperately sorry she was for Peter—which she was, she *was*—but the telegraph boy had turned to her, and he had another paper in his hand, only this one was a different color, and it had come direct from the army.

"I don't want that," she heard herself saying. Her voice didn't sound like her own. It seemed to come from someone else entirely. "You can take it with you. Please."

Dimly, she was aware of her parents turning, Della, too, tearfully looking from her to the boy.

"Memsahib," the boy said, "you must be reading it," and he placed it on the table, then grimaced at her apologetically, and backed gratefully away.

Maddy stared at the wire. They all stared. Such a small piece of paper.

Iris stirred, pushing her swaddling free, eyes flickering to open, as though she'd sensed the sudden dread in the air. Maddy went to her, picking her up, realizing as she did how much her arms were shaking, then turned, looking once more at the telegram.

"Do you want me to open it?" her father offered.

"I can," said Alice.

Numbly, Maddy shook her head. She studied the paper a few seconds longer, willing it to say anything but what she most feared. Then, knowing that no amount of waiting could change what was already written, and that the boy had been right, she must be reading it, she passed Iris to her mother and, fingers trembling more than ever, tore the paper open.

She didn't move. She didn't breathe. She just read the words, then again, and again, only they couldn't feel real.

Her parents' anxious voices came, Della's, too, asking questions. Out on the lawn, one of the peacocks called, and upstairs, a door slammed. It all happened in another world, a world he apparently wasn't in anymore. *Killed in action,* it said. Not *missing,* like Fraser. Not *being treated for injuries.* But, *Killed.*

She didn't believe it.

She *couldn't* believe it. He couldn't be gone. He just couldn't be. She'd have known, guessed . . .

She let the paper fall to the ground, and turned to her mother, taking Iris back into her arms, which weren't shaking, not anymore.

"Madeline?" Alice said. "What's happened?"

"I need to write to Luke's CO," Maddy said. "There's been a dreadful mistake."

Guy visited Peter at the Quai d'Escale base hospital, a converted train station in Le Havre, the first opportunity he had, which was nonetheless almost a month after Peter was injured. He'd heard what had happened to both him and Luke from a naik in Peter's company. The Indian private had been admitted to his casualty clearing station—a hospital of tented wards and operating theaters in a field just back from the Ypres line—with shrapnel wounds to the chest and gas inhalation; he'd spoken, to Guy's grief, of the lieutenant colonel whose shrouded body the stretcher-bearers had brought in, then thrown into the ground for burial, and the major who'd been shot in the leg. The naik had tried to bat the anesthetist's mask away as they'd attempted to put him under for surgery, raging on the table at this war, the guns, the daughter the lieutenant colonel had just been so happy to have news of. *He had the photograph with him, it was with him . . .* Guy had tried to console him, badly shaken himself. In his mind's eye, he'd pictured Luke and Peter as they'd been in Bombay—not recently, but years before, when Luke had first lived there, and both he and Peter had laughed and acted the fool down at the Gymkhana Club, racing each other on the polo field. All that happiness, gone. *Gone.* In the end, he'd asked one of the other surgeons to do the operation for him, not trusting his own hands. It had been almost a relief, how upset he was—that even in his wretched jealousy, he'd felt such sadness at Luke's death, nothing but desolation for Maddy, poor, poor Maddy . . .

He'd wanted to send her his condolences, for whatever they were worth. Pass his love on to little Iris, too, who'd now never know her papa. But Alice had got in touch with him first.

I hate to trouble you, she'd written, *especially with this—I can only imagine what you must be contending with there—but I'm too worried not to. Madeline won't accept he's gone, you see. She won't cry, or grieve, but keeps writing letters, first to Luke's CO, then General Staff, telling them they have to find him. She's even asked her aunt Edie to travel to London, visit all the hospitals, which Richard has told her there's no point in, making her as angry as I've ever seen her. Guy, this doesn't seem normal. Should we take her to see someone? Does she need help? She's only just had Iris after all, and I'm scared it's all been too much. . . .*

Guy had written by return, telling her how grateful he was that she *had* troubled him, that she wasn't ever, ever to worry about doing it, and that he was afraid to tell her there really was no chance Maddy could be right; he himself had met one of the privates who'd been at Luke's burial. *Please don't rush into taking Maddy anywhere, though,* he'd said, balking at the thought of her being sent down that particular track. *Let her be a while longer. I am sure this is all quite natural. How is she with Iris?*

Besotted, Alice had written back, *we all are. That child is the only person who can make her mama smile.*

Then I really believe you have no cause for concern, he'd replied, heart pinching as he pictured Maddy with her daughter. *My advice is she spend as much time as she can with the baby. I'm sure she'll accept everything else once she's ready. Please tell Della that I'm going to visit her brother, tomorrow. I'll send him her love.*

He stood in Peter's ward now, which still bore the clocks and vast glass windows of the station waiting room it once was, but was filled with patients instead of passengers, rows of beds surrounded by screens. Peter was at the very end of the cubicles, in the far corner. For all the thousands of amputations Guy had done, it jarred painfully to see the neat flat space where Peter's left leg should have been. That memory of him larking on the polo field . . .

"How is he?" he asked the nurse in charge, Sister Owen. ("Very pretty," said Peter mournfully, once Guy joined him. "Far too lovely to be in a place like this.")

"Devastated," said Sister Owen. "He keeps talking about a Luke."

"They were friends," said Guy. "Good friends. Here together from the start."

"He's definitely dead?" Sister Owen asked.

"Yes," said Guy wearily, thinking again of that naik's words, and Maddy, all her letters. "Why do you ask?"

She looked toward Peter's bed. "He keeps saying he thinks he saw him."

It didn't surprise Guy. He'd had too many men through his hospital who'd imagined brothers and cousins in the beds next to them to read anything into it. It only broke his heart that the ghosts were never real.

"He just seemed so real," Peter said, a few minutes later, as Guy sat beside him. Someone had washed his fair hair, combed it in a side parting. He wore a pair of smart striped pajamas, presumably sent from home. They were too big; he'd lost a worrying amount of weight. "He was killed, right in front of me," Peter continued. "The men buried him with his picture of Maddy and Iris, but I still saw him getting into an ambulance on the Menin bloody Road."

"How much blood had you lost by then?" asked Guy.

"I didn't measure it."

"A fair amount, is my guess."

"He saved my life, Guy." A tear ran down Peter's wasted cheek, then another. "He didn't need to die."

"I'm so sorry," said Guy, wishing there were something more, something better, he could say.

Peter's face folded. Guy didn't flinch at his tears, or tell him to toughen up, as some other doctors might. He did the only thing he could, and sat there by Peter's side, letting him know he wasn't alone, waiting until he was spent.

When he was, Guy asked him what he would do now.

"Not go back home so my mother can look after me," Peter said, and his lips twisted, in a macabre approximation of his old smile.

Guy, who couldn't have felt less like laughing, nonetheless mustered up a short one, realizing it was what Peter needed. "Then?"

"It's a rehabilitation hospital in London first," Peter said, "as soon as they're happy I won't hemorrhage on the boat. I'll visit Ernest Aldyce, once I learn how to walk on wood. Luke would want that."

"Yes," said Guy, who knew all about Ernest. Diana had written, asking him if it was really as hopeless as she'd been told. *Darling Guy, is there anything you can do to help? It's so very lonely for me now. I feel like a widow. And I keep thinking of poor old you all by yourself somewhere in France. Perhaps we could meet when you come back on leave, and you could give me some wonderful advice.* He'd read her letter on a break from a particularly bad day in theater, and been rather short in his reply. *Count yourself lucky you're not a widow,* he'd said. *I can't advise, I'm afraid it's not my area of expertise. But Dr. Arnold has an excellent reputation. Please give your husband my best.* Diana hadn't written again. Clearly it hadn't been what she'd wanted to hear.

"Della's still in Bombay," Peter went on, "and not going anywhere, if this Jeff character is sensible."

"He is," said Guy. "Alice told me about him and Della. I don't know him well, he only arrived as I left, but I liked what I saw."

Peter nodded, as though that at least was good news. "Richard's said my job's waiting," he said. "I might risk the U-boats, go back and give little Iris her father's best. Be there for poor Maddy."

"You won't tell her, will you?" said Guy. "About thinking you saw Luke." That would be all she'd need.

"No," said Peter, "I wouldn't do that." He turned, the pillow crackling beneath him, staring at the ceiling. "Della's written about all her letters."

Guy nodded slowly. "Maddy'll be glad to have you back," he said, and this time it was his voice that was unsteady. Fool that he was, he couldn't help but wish that it was he who was going to her. "You can talk to her. Help her . . . believe."

"Yes," said Peter, his cheeks working again.

"Tell her how sorry I am, will you?" said Guy. "I'm so sorry, Peter."

"I know," said Peter, and choked on it. "We all are."

Guy couldn't stay long after that. He had to be back on duty for the night shift, and had been late arriving, as the train that had brought him had had to stop constantly for shellfire. He remained long enough to take a quick look at Peter's stump, assure himself, as well as Peter, that it really was healing well, and promise Peter that he'd take him for a drink, just as soon as he, too, was back in Bombay.

"I'll hold you to that," said Peter, and raised his hand.

Guy shook it, forcing himself not to betray his shock at the frailty of Peter's grip.

He spoke to Sister Owen again on his way out. She stopped him just before he reached the ward doors, handing him a piece of paper with the address of a CCS on it, not too far from his.

"What's this?" he asked.

"It's where Peter was," she said. "I've been thinking . . . Well," she flushed, "well, that perhaps you could stop by, ask them if they had any admissions matching Luke Devereaux's description."

Guy gave her a long look. Was she being serious?

She colored more, but held his eye, certainly seeming to be.

"Sister Owen . . ." he began.

"I know, I know." She held up her hands. "It's probably hopeless."

"More than probably. He was killed, Sister Owen. I met the man who buried him."

"Peter sounds so sure sometimes. . . ."

"I don't think he's sure at all," Guy said.

"But is there any harm in asking a few questions?" Sister Owen said. "Just this morning, a sergeant who we all thought was going to be well enough to travel home to his mama tomorrow, he died. A clot none of us knew was there." She stared up at him. "In all this hideousness, wouldn't it be nice to think there might still be some good surprises left?"

He hesitated, weakening.

"I gather Colonel Devereaux had just had a daughter," she said, pushing her advantage. "Would you do it for her?"

He wavered a second longer.

She continued to stare.

"All right," he said heavily, pocketing the address. "All right."

He really did have every intention of doing as he promised, pointless as he knew it was. But when he got back that night to his own CCS, it was to find that there'd been a fresh assault on the British line; he had to pick his way through the queues of chugging ambulances, horse-drawn carts and stretchers, just to get back into the grounds. He didn't leave theater that night, had just a few hours' sleep, then didn't leave again the next day, or the day after that. He worked without stopping, sharing the canvas theater with three other surgeons, his eyes dry, legs fluid with the effort of standing for so long, up to his arms in spleens and ruptured livers, torn lungs and intestines, hands moving, repairing tears, tying arteries, doing whatever he could before the next man was placed on his table. By the time the rush of wounded finally quietened, and he got a spare hour to call at the mobile unit Peter had been at, it had already moved, to Artois, preparing for the inevitable casualties of the next planned offensive.

He stayed on in Ypres that spring and summer. There was no major action, but still artillery fire between the trenches every day, and a steady stream of bullet and shrapnel wounds, hemorrhages and amputations to keep him grimly occupied. In September, they were all sent to Loos, a vast attack that was whispered to be the beginning of the end of the war, but that failed to end anything, other than tens of thousands of lives, too many of them on Guy's operating table. As autumn drew in, and rumors abounded of brewing mutiny in the Indian ranks—units who refused to fight, or abandoned their positions; men who'd finally had enough of being led to their deaths, losing the officers they trusted and being placed instead under the command of boys who didn't understand their language or anything about them—the generals decided it was too much after all to ask the sepoys to endure another freezing winter. Much better send them to Gallipoli. Guy went east as well. He boarded a ship for Egypt, a hospital in Alexandria, in November, seven months to the day after he'd visited Peter. Only by now he'd forgotten all about Sister Owen.

In the horror and exhaustion of the summer that had been, he'd ceased to remember they'd ever talked of such a thing as good surprises, or that he'd been handed a piece of paper by her at all.

CHAPTER EIGHTEEN

He arrived just before luncheon, on an arctic November morning, all the agonizing operations in France and London to repair his broken body, his battered skull, mercifully behind him. Physically, he'd been pronounced fit. Only his mind needed fixing now.

"These roads," said his ambulance driver, gloved hands like vises on the wheel, her face pressed so close to the icy windshield that her breath fogged the glass.

"You're doing very well," he said.

"You know there's talk it's haunted," she said, eyes fixed on the sandstone building ahead. "Used to be a lunatic asylum."

He raised a brow. "I gather it still is."

Her chilled cheeks twitched in a smirk. "You have a welcoming party anyway," she said, and pointed through the semicircles left by the wiper blades, toward where a frozen nursing sister waited on the hospital's front stairs. "Looks the worthy sort, I'm sure she'll be having you making friends and playing billiards in no time."

"Excellent," he said, and rested his head against the cabin wall, tired, so very tired. . . .

They ground to a halt.

"Thanks be to God," his driver said, pulling up the hand brake. She got out and exchanged a few words with the nurse.

"Nothing a cocoa won't fix," he heard the nurse say.

Definitely worthy, he thought.

"I feel like my toes have fallen off," said his driver (not worthy at all).

He stood as she came to throw the doors of his cabin wide, sending icy air rushing in.

"Ready?" she asked him.

"I don't know," he said.

"No," she said, "I'm not sure I would be either."

He nodded, grateful for her candor.

"I hope you're not here too long," she said.

"So do I," he replied, making his way out of the cabin. She wished him luck, and he took it with thanks. He'd take anything, if it would only mean this place would work.

He paused on the cabin step, arching his neck, staring through the snow at the hospital's dusted walls, refusing to consider the possibility that it mightn't. He couldn't let himself do that. If he did, gave rein to his dread that he'd find himself one day old and alone, still chasing his dreams, waiting hopelessly for his broken mind to help him back to the life he'd so carelessly lost, he was afraid the fear would destroy him.

So he stepped down. And although it jarred when Sister Lytton called him Officer Jones (he couldn't abide the name), he said nothing; it was obvious she was kind as well as worthy, and he didn't want to make her uncomfortable. When all was said and done, what else was there for her to call him? He went along with her tour, found himself staring at the masked captain in the drawing room ("What happened to him?" he asked Sister Lytton. "Ernest?" she said. "I'm not sure"), managed not to react when she showed him the billiards room, and then, at last, met Dr. Arnold, whom he was relieved to find he liked a great deal.

He took the journal Arnold gave him, picked at a silent supper, not even attempting the trifle, then went to his bed with its hot-water bottle inside, and slept. When, in the middle of the night, he woke in the blackness, sweating and panting, desperate to return to the woman in the lemon dress he'd just left, he reached for his journal and wrote in it for the first time (*toothless man; noise; a market?*), then threw his head back on the pillow because he had no idea what any of it could mean.

November passed. He went for walks, escaping into the white gardens, sometimes for hours at a time, then sat by the fire, feeling his cold skin sting in a way that made him nostalgic, although for what he still couldn't say. "Patience," said Arnold, whom he saw for an hour every day, "patience." He didn't play billiards, because he hadn't forgotten his driver's jest, but did (much to Sister Lytton's hand-clasped pleasure) make a friend of sorts, with poor, stuttering Ernest. It wasn't that he enjoyed their stilted daily introductions, or Ernest's agonizingly enunciated, oft-repeated comments on the noise of the fire, the difficulty of eating soup with his mask, his damned shaking hands. He simply felt compelled to keep him company whenever he spotted him sitting alone.

"You don't need to spend all your time with him," the VAD Poppy said, one December morning, flumping down beside them in one of the drawing room chairs. "You could always come for a walk with me instead." She leaned toward him, whispering confidentially. "I promise to be much more fun than Sister Lytton."

"I'm fine," Jones told her, "we're fine."

"D d do I kn-kn-know you?" Ernest said.

"How about a nice cup of cocoa?" said Sister Lytton, sweeping across the room. "Ernest, I'll fetch you a straw."

Christmas came. No one played any carols, because of Ernest, but in the arts and crafts room several patients made paper chains to decorate the hallway and drawing room. While Jones refused to be lured into the festive cutting and sticking (on the principle that he mightn't know much, but he did know that he wasn't a child), he wrapped himself in his greatcoat, pulled on some boots, and went with four of the orderlies—all too old, or flat-footed, to fight—for a hike into the mist-shrouded forests to cut down a fir. He went for the exercise, for something to do; he didn't expect to enjoy it.

(Truthfully, he fought enjoying anything at the King's Fifth. "Why?" said Arnold. "It would be like accepting I'm staying," he said.) As he and the others trekked across the fields, the oldest of the orderlies cursed because he'd forgotten to order the Christmas turkey for his wife. Jones offered to mark a reminder for him to go to the butcher's in his journal, to which the man laughed and said, "Better yet, let's make a detour now, and stop by the Bull for a drink, too."

The village pub was packed, woody with smoke from the open fire, warm and noisy, full of men who had sons at the front, saw Jones's blues, and insisted on buying him beers. He protested at first, "I have no money to buy the next round," but they all told him he'd paid more than enough already.

"Take the beer," the turkeyless orderly hissed, smiling through the side of his mouth, "take it."

So he did. And got drunk. They all got blind, and didn't return to the King's Fifth until nightfall, dragging a fir they lopsidedly hacked down on their way back, falling over themselves as they clambered back into the hospital's echoing, oil-lit hallway.

"You look perky," said Poppy, coming down the wide front stairs, as though she'd been watching, waiting for them at the top. "We got word from the pub you were having a nice time."

"No repeat performances, please," said Sister Lytton, once she, too, had appeared from the drawing room, and scolded Jones for how worried she'd been before the pub's landlord had telephoned. (For which he told her he was very, *very* shorry.)

"Take me next time?" said Dr. Arnold the next day, not scolding, rather happy, pronouncing it a good sign that Jones had made such a break for freedom.

I don't know if it's a sign at all, Jones wrote, not in his journal, but on a piece of paper: one of the many letters he'd now written to the woman he was trying so desperately to remember.

It's a relief, though, to have had a different day in this place that is so relentlessly the same. I felt myself, being out like that. I felt as though I knew who I was for the first time since I got into that ambulance on the Menin Road.

I remember that road. I can see the driver who helped me. I can feel the ruts beneath the ambulance wheels. I can picture the CCS I was taken to, and taste the blood in my mouth, my fear as I lay in the middle of that stretcher-covered field, wondering whether I was going to die, or remember. A nurse came, and she put a tag on my shirt, then sent me straight to a train, the hospital in Dieppe where they were kind and tired and removed the shrapnel in my skull, my body, and set my broken ribs. I know all this, because it has all remained in my mind. Yet I don't want those memories. I don't need them.

I need you.

Where are you this Christmas? Are you sitting outside, with heat on your face? Your face I can never see. Are you smiling? Are you happy? I want to think that you are.

Are you waiting for me, though, as I am waiting for you?

Are you thinking of me, in this moment?

He set down his pen, and sank his aching head in his hands.

Are you even there at all?

Maddy stared up into the bright Indian sky, the sun on her cheeks, cradling a now eight-month-old Iris on her lap. She held Iris's hand absently, restraining her from pulling at the lace neck of her gown, and thought of Luke, as she always did. Her eyes watered in the glare of the afternoon light, and she tried, really tried to do what everyone kept telling her she must, and believe that he was gone.

"I'm meant to have given up," she whispered to their daughter. "I don't know how to do that."

Iris, finding some unfathomable humor in her words, laughed.

"Heartless," said Maddy, kissing her. "Quite heartless."

It was Christmas Eve. Tomorrow would be Iris's first Christmas, and despite Maddy's promises to her parents, to Della and Peter—who'd thankfully evaded the torpedoes and arrived safely back in September, working again in his old job, staying in the villa, too, since they had plenty of room and no one could stand to think of him by himself—she kept fantasizing that a message would arrive from Luke saying that he was alive after all, on his way back to them. Better yet, that he'd appear on the veranda, hands in his pockets, handsome face turned toward them in the garden. *Did you really think I would miss another Christmas?* Maddy looked toward the veranda, just in case. . . .

But no. He wasn't there.

He never was.

The last letters she'd sent to him at the front had been returned to her; the envelopes containing her descriptions of Iris's every smile and mood and gurgle had been unopened, heartlessly marked: Killed in Action. She'd thrown them out, hating them. And she'd finally stopped trying to find someone who'd admit he might be alive. Not because she believed it was hopeless to try, but because she'd run out of people to write to. ("Thank God," she'd overheard her father say to her mother before dinner one night, and had only just restrained herself from going into their dressing room, telling them both how much their words hurt. *Just let me believe, why can't you?*) The letters had got her nowhere anyway. Luke's CO had been the first to crush her, replying to her entreaties that he admitted there could have been a mistake with softly worded assurances that there absolutely hadn't been, hideous advice that she move on with her life. *I wouldn't want my wife to waste hers waiting for me.* Enraged, she'd thrown that letter away.

She hadn't been able to do that with the reply from Luke's old contact at General Staff, though, because he hadn't sent one. Nor had his superior. Or his superior's superior.

"Won't you pull some strings?" Maddy had implored her father.

"Darling," he'd said softly, "the strings you need don't exist."

The secretaries at all the base hospitals had at least responded to her, but with form letters saying there were simply too many injured men for them to address relatives on a case-by-case basis. *Please accept our sincere condolences.* It was the same with the secretaries in London. If Maddy had only been in England, she'd have visited the wards herself, but the U-boats were still at large and she was as unwilling as she'd ever been to expose Iris to the danger. Edie had refused point-blank to carry out the inquiries for her (*I don't want to give you false hope, sweetheart, I agree with your father on that*) and now Maddy didn't know what else to do.

"Let it lie, darling Maddy," Peter had said, when he'd first returned, pale, quiet, and far too thin.

They'd been walking in the garden, just the two of them, braving the last of the monsoon rains. Della had been out for a Sunday luncheon with Jeff, whose services thankfully hadn't been requested by the expeditionary force—"Teeth are the least of their worries," said Peter—and Maddy's parents had been minding Iris inside.

"I can't let it lie," Maddy had said. "I just can't."

"But you have to," Peter had said. He'd stopped, standing crookedly on his prosthetic leg beneath his umbrella, white face pinched with pain. "He's gone. I'm so sorry. . . ."

"What if he's like Ernest Aldyce?" she'd said, interrupting. "What if he's forgotten, and is waiting for me to—"

"He's not waiting for anything," Peter had said, in a quiet voice that had made it almost impossible not to weep. He'd gone on, reminding her that he'd been to see Ernest at the end of August. Luke hadn't been with him. "I even asked the goddamn nurse if she'd seen anyone like him."

She'd seized on that. "Then you think he could be alive, too. . . ."

"No. *No.*" Peter had turned his face to the pouring sky, fragile jaw clenched. "I just . . . want to. I miss him. Every day. And I feel so guilty that I'm here, and he's not. The nurse said people write all the time, hundreds of letters every month, asking after people they can't let go."

"But . . ."

"No." He'd almost shouted it. "No buts." He'd reached out to her with his free hand. She'd tried to pull away, scared to let him touch her, lest he start to convince her. He'd taken her fingers anyway. "I was there, Maddy."

"Did you see him dead?" she'd asked, and to her horror really had started crying then. "Did you actually see him?"

"I saw it all," Peter had said, tears falling, too. "Don't make me tell you what I saw. . . ."

"What?" she'd said, the words breaking from her against her will. "What did you see?"

"I saw him die."

"No," she'd said, and even as she had, she'd seen Luke herself, not in uniform, not in France, but in a linen jacket on the promenade, in evening dress at the Gymkhana Club, opposite her in that rooftop restaurant, at the front of St. Thomas's Cathedral, holding her in the sea. . . .

"He was blasted up into the air," Peter had said, slicing through her memories, hand still clutching hers. "Maddy, you have to trust me."

"That's not the same as dying," she'd tried to reply, but she hadn't been able to, because she'd been sobbing too much.

"They found him," Peter had said, "buried him, with the photograph of you and Iris on his chest. He has a grave," and she'd cried, cried and cried, and he'd thrown their umbrellas to the floor and hugged her, both of them becoming soaked until Alice had run down from the villa, soaked herself, insisting that they both come back inside. "This is no good, it's no good for you. . . ."

Everyone had assumed after that that she'd accepted Luke was dead. She'd let them, because in the end it felt kinder not to have them remind her constantly that she needed to do it.

She cried more now. She did it most nights, after Iris had gone to bed and couldn't hear her (she never let her hear, terrified that the sadness might somehow blight the happy innocence of her existence); she cried because although she still couldn't believe he was where everyone said he was, he wasn't with her either, and she missed him. She missed him so much.

"I need him," she murmured under her breath.

This time Iris didn't laugh. She reached up, dropping Maddy's lace collar, placing her chubby hand against her cheek, lips to her lips, drooling a kiss.

"Oh, that's lovely," said Maddy. "Thank you." More drool. "Iris, thank you. Aren't I so lucky that I have you?"

"You have more than just Iris," her mother said to her, much later that night, as, with Iris fast asleep in the nursery, they worked by flickering lamplight in the drawing room, wrapping the rattles and stacking blocks and new stuffed animals they'd scoured Bombay's small handful of toy shops to find, ready to nestle, waiting for the morning, beneath the banana-branch

Christmas tree. Della was out, at the Gymkhana Club's Christmas Eve do with Jeff. Peter and Richard were having nightcaps on the veranda. "You're not alone, Madeline," Alice went on softly. She left the ribbon she'd been tying and looked across at Maddy, her blue gaze bright in the lamps' glow. "You're surrounded by people who . . . care . . . so very much."

"I know I am," said Maddy quietly, feeling her eyes prick, because of course she knew, and was endlessly grateful for it, but it still meant so much to hear her mother say it, to see the love in her face; a love she still, after all this time, couldn't quite take for granted.

"I want you to . . . smile, this Christmas," said Alice. "I want to know how to help you do that."

"I'll be fine," said Maddy.

"Oh, Madeline . . ."

"I will," said Maddy. "So long as Iris enjoys herself. That's what matters. . . ."

"No," said Alice. "Not just that."

"Mama—"

"No," Alice said again. She reached out, taking Maddy's hand. "You're *my* Iris," she said, squeezing her fingers. "You matter, too."

Saddened by her mother's words, her worry, Maddy did try to smile more that Christmas. She did it for everyone. Moved by the effort they all put into making the day jolly—the stocking her parents left hidden at the foot of her bed, full of books, bath salts, and imported (not-too-melted) Cadbury's chocolates; the noisy merriment Peter, Della, and Jeff determinedly filled each hour with, fussing over Iris, cramming into the motor to go to church, eating Cook's (vegetarian) feast on the veranda, wearing Richard's paper hats—she did her best to play along. She was acutely conscious of being far from the only one who'd suffered that year (poor Peter, Fraser, Ernest . . .), and was loath to act as though she was. If Peter, with his lost leg, and all his grief, could throw himself into the festivities, surely she could summon the odd smile, too.

But it was so very hard. Try as she might to remain present in the day, her thoughts kept wandering—to wintry European wards, a proper Christmas fir in an unknown hospital; a bed he lay in, waiting for her to find him—and too often she'd realize with a start that she'd failed to reply to someone's question, react to a joke, or pull a cracker. While she exclaimed, like everyone exclaimed, when Iris crawled over to the banana-branch tree and tugged it, sending baubles scattering for what felt like the hundredth time that year ("Oh, *Iris,*" they all chorused), all she could think about, as she cuddled Iris close, was how much Luke would enjoy seeing this havoc caused by their little adventurer, and how much he was missing of her life. When she sat her on her knee to open the gift his heartbroken parents, Nina and Theo, had sent (Nina and Theo, who'd written weekly, ever since Maddy had been forced to send them that agonizing, impossible-to-word letter of their son's supposed death), she pulled out the engraved rose-gold locket they'd so carefully parceled up, *to our beloved granddaughter,* and couldn't even attempt a smile. It was all she could do not to fall apart.

"It was all any of us could do," said Della, once the sun had finally set on the exhausting day, and the two of them were returning from putting Iris down in the nursery. "But since no one else can see you now, could you do with a quick cry before Jeff insists on party games?"

Maddy felt more able to face the rest of the evening, after that cry. And fortified by the generous brandy Jeff poured her (*bracing*), she even managed to mime out *The Old Curiosity Shop* for Peter to guess in charades.

"I actually got it after 'old,' " he said, "but it was far too much fun watching you do 'curiosity' to say that."

Still, she exhaled a long breath of relief when, well before ten, her father suggested they call it a night. She suspected—from the ready agreement of everyone else that yes, it really was getting on—that she wasn't alone in being glad the merrymaking was over.

And she didn't go to the New Year's ball her father's office hosted at the Taj, in aid of the war effort. Charitable cause or no, it would have been too hard—far, far too hard—to be where other people were on *that* night of nights. She wasn't sure she could stand to hear, let alone see, a firework. So while Della and Jeff went, her parents, too, since they could hardly not, she remained at the villa. Peter stayed home, too, with Richard's blessing.

"He's been through quite enough as it is this year," said Richard to

Maddy. "The two of you can keep each other company. Your mother and I will feel much better about not being here that way."

They planned to do nothing more than have dinner on the veranda, and a mandatory glass or two of champagne. For much of the evening, that was exactly what they did. They talked about Luke, endlessly. With the cicadas clacking, the trees whispering, Peter told stories from long before Maddy had even met him: all the tales of polo matches, yacht races, drunken nights, and disciplinary hearings for getting locked out of the cantonment that she could never get enough of. Maddy in turn spoke of Luke's letters from the front: how often he'd talked of Peter, how much he'd depended on him.

"It was mutual," said Peter, "believe me."

With the champagne bottle emptying, the balmy night deepening, they reminisced about that Yacht Club party, two years before, laughing as they replayed Della's indignation over Peter not going home to collect her (*what a rotter*), and Maddy's hopeless search for her matches.

"Do you still have them?" Peter asked.

"Of course I do," she said.

Perhaps it was the champagne, or all the talk of the Yacht Club, but, as midnight approached, Maddy realized that she actually *would* like to see the fireworks after all.

"You're sure?" said Peter.

"Yes," she said, "I think so."

Stopping only to check on Iris with her ayah, and fetch fresh champagne, they clambered down to the bottom of the hill—slowly, because of Peter's leg—back to the jungle-fringed beach Maddy had visited so many times with Luke, and which she hadn't set foot on since he'd gone. She paused as they reached it, hesitating amid the palms, stilled by the memories rushing in. The moonlit sands were exactly as she recalled them. The black, rippling shoreline, heartbreakingly the same.

"We can go back," said Peter gently, his pale face taut with concern in the silvery light. "We don't have to stay."

"I want to," she said, quite truthfully. "I want to be here."

She almost felt as though Luke was, too.

How could she walk away from that? From him?

Midnight wasn't far away. They had only time to fill their glasses, and then the fireworks came, exploding above the distant city skyline. They held each other's hands, watching, neither of them speaking.

Together, they raised their glasses.

"To Luke," said Peter, and tipped his head back, gaze moving directly up, to the heavens hidden behind the starlit sky.

Maddy didn't follow his stare. She kept her own eyes fixed on the city, the living pulsing earth, clinging to her silent belief that he was still on it. Awake, she hoped.

Not too hurt, she prayed.

Just somewhere safe, somewhere warm. Somewhere breathing.

Somewhere *there*.

A good half of the patients stayed up at the King's Fifth to welcome 1916, but not Ernest, which meant the gramophone could be on, and the nurses were allowed to sing. As they broke into "Auld Lang Syne," some of the men joined in—the ones who'd begun to put on weight, talk more, jump less, and whom Arnold had said he'd have no choice but to certify fit for active service again soon—but Jones remained silent, not because he didn't know the words of old acquaintance being forgot, but because he *did* know them. They coursed through him, and every one of his nerve endings leaped. Images flashed through his mind. He was deaf to Poppy offering him a glass of elderflower wine; blind to Sister Lytton smiling at him curiously. Thinking only of his journal, he turned, ran up the stairs two at a time, and wrote everything down. The lyrics, the sense of heat he'd been struck with, the picture of himself crouching on a mosaic floor (*a train station?* he wrote), and the slender gloved hand reaching out, touching the back of a terrace chair.

"This is good," Arnold said, the next morning. "Very good. This might be our year."

But it wasn't.

January passed into February. Winter became spring. Spring became the summer. They heard the heavy guns at the Somme, and Jones felt full of despair for the men still over there in the trenches. Exhausted as he was, he struggled with insomnia, his fragmented, meaningless dreams, and when, one morning in September, Poppy came to make his bed—even though he always did it himself—and gave a silly laugh, remarking that she really was going to give him a good scolding one of these days, "and what would you make of that, Officer Jones?," he snapped, shouting that Jones wasn't his bloody name, and she could scold him as much as she bloody liked.

He regretted his temper instantly. He'd long had an abhorrence of becoming that kind of patient, and turned, ready to apologize. But when he looked again at Poppy, she didn't appear remotely chastened, just disconcertingly flushed. Deciding she could probably do with less rather than more attention, he said nothing further at all.

Later that month, to everyone's horror, two officers killed themselves in quick succession. One had been about to leave the hospital, back to the trenches.

"Sister Lytton's blaming herself," Arnold said, polishing his glasses that didn't need polishing, "but I feel it is I who have blood on my hands."

"It's not your fault," said Jones, and was struck by the certain sense of someone having said something similar to him before.

"It is," Arnold said, with a deep sigh. "I've sent Sister Lytton away, anyway. A spot of leave . . ."

It was while she was gone that Ernest's absent wife came to the hospital. Jones, who'd been up in his room for most of her visit, oblivious to her presence, only saw her fleetingly, brushing past her on his way into the drawing room as she left it hurriedly with Poppy. He turned, staring after her black hair, her rouged, pointy face, then frowned, wondering what had made him look twice.

But then he heard Ernest sobbing in his chair. He went straight to him; that familiar urge to protect, console him. He didn't pay any attention to the way Ernest's wife glanced back toward Ernest. He was too preoccupied with picking up the pieces she'd left.

"D-D-Di," said Ernest.

"No," said Jones, "you don't want to die. There's been enough of that."

Gradually, he deduced that Ernest had been asked by his wife to sign some forms, and that she'd got angry when he couldn't manage it. He felt angry himself, at Poppy for allowing Ernest's wife to approach him without Arnold there, and not intervening sooner.

He told her as much, later. "What were you thinking? Did you not see the way he was crying?"

"Where were you?" she said. "Writing another of your letters?"

"What the hell do you know about my letters?"

She stared back at him, not answering, biting the insides of her cheeks, whether against tears or a smile he frankly couldn't tell and cared even less.

"You have nothing to say?" he asked.

"Not as much as you," she said.

Was she joking?

He didn't ask. "Stay away from my things," he said, turning from her.

He made no note of the whole sorry incident in his journal. He knew he'd remember it all too well.

It wasn't the present he struggled with, after all.

It was the past. Only the past.

Diana's strange note arrived at the villa on a sunny, breezy morning at the end of 1916. The house was quiet. Richard was at work. Della and Peter had moved out earlier in the year—Della, happily married to Jeff, to live just a few hundred yards down the road; Peter, who'd grown better at walking, and put on just a little weight, back to the old government bungalow at the base of the hill. He still came to the villa most evenings, though, for dinner and to talk about Luke with Madeline, read stories to Iris, partly because he loved them both, Alice was sure, but also, she felt, to atone for Luke's death, which he'd never accept wasn't his fault. Just as Luke had always blamed himself for what had happened to Ernest.

Ernest, whose wife had written.

Alice's brow creased, seeing the slope of Diana's hand on the envelope. She picked it up from the silver post tray cautiously. It had been more than two years since she'd heard a whisper from her. What could she possibly want now?

Sympathy, it seemed, for her lot as a *widow in all but name.* Approval, too, for her apparent plan to divorce poor Ernest and remarry.

Just as with Edie and Fitz, Diana said, *I'm hopeful of a new start of my own. I know so many can be sniffy about these things, especially at the club (I may have been guilty myself in the past), but feel sure that with your own sister-in-law a divorcée, you won't judge. Glass houses, and all that. I am still so young, and have a whole life ahead of me to share. My thoughts had turned to one old friend, but I was reminded that your daughter has many admirers.*

Alice set her teeth in irritation. Was she talking about Guy? An *old friend*? Guy had never had any time for Diana. Surely even Diana realized that.

In any case, Diana went on, *I've met a rather lovely man in Whitehall who would be very keen to sample life in our Raj, should Richard be amenable.*

So now they got to it. Alice almost set the letter aside. She had absolutely no interest in helping Diana return to Bombay.

But then a word caught her attention. A name: *Luke,* at the end of the page.

Frowning, more wary than ever, she read on.

Honestly, this man was the image of him. One never imagines they'll encounter a face like that twice. I even asked the VAD about him, the resemblance was so stark, but she assured me he had no wife or children. She rather gave me the impression there was an understanding between the two of them. Lucky Poppy Reid, I say. How funny, though.

Finding nothing remotely amusing, Alice clenched the paper, the words creasing before her as she read them over. *One never imagines they'll encounter a face like that twice.* Mouth dry, she looked out, down the garden to where a newly pregnant Della was with Madeline, both of them clapping and exclaiming as eighteen-month-old Iris pointed at the trees, leaves, and peacocks, naming them in turn. Madeline crouched, the shorter skirts so many women had started wearing exposing her stockinged ankles, and scooped Iris close, tickling her tummy, making Iris throw her glossy black curls back in delighted screams.

"Monkey," said Madeline, laughing, too: that beautiful laugh, which Iris, and Iris alone, could draw from her, and which the rest of them still heard far too little.

It had been torture, watching her become such a shell of herself this past year and a half. Alice couldn't remember ever having felt so powerless, so heartbreakingly unable to help her own daughter. She'd savored every second of their growing closeness after she'd come out of hospital back at the start of the war—the mornings at the school, their hours decorating the nursery, their walks, their talks, then the utter joy of Iris being born—but it was as though she'd been given Madeline back only to lose her after all.

They'd all lost her there for a while.

Although she was doing better these days, much better, Alice was certain she hadn't given up on Luke. She saw the hopeful way she still looked to the gate every time the telegraph boy arrived with a message for Richard. She never went to any party or club—too terrified, Alice was sure, of enjoying herself, or being asked to dance by another man.

She was waiting.

Alice hated it for her. However much she'd dreaded her leaving, she'd give Luke back to her in the blink of an eye if only she could. But Peter had seen him die. They'd been sent his bullet-torn jacket, his letters, his papers and cigarettes. He was gone. *Buried* by a man Guy, *Guy*, had met.

She looked again at Diana's crumpled letter. It would be too cruel, surely, to tell Madeline about it. Alice had wasted so many years of her own life grieving for losses that could never be changed, how could she encourage her daughter to do the same?

She pushed the letter slowly back into its envelope, and, not wanting to let herself weaken, sat down to reply to Diana then and there.

I'm sure Richard would be glad to help your friend. I ask only one thing. This man you saw at Ernest's hospital could not have been Luke. It's impossible, Diana, and I simply cannot allow Madeline to hope. The disappointment would kill her. I need you to promise that you will never breathe a whisper of what you saw to anyone, least of all her.

Diana's reply came less than a month later.
Absolutely, darling Alice, she wrote. *My lips are sealed, you have my word.*

FOUR
YEARS
LATER

CHAPTER NINETEEN

Bombay, 1920

It wasn't until the end of September 1920, almost two years after the armistice finally ended the war, that Guy, who'd remained in Alexandria to help with the casualties of the disastrous Middle Eastern campaign, came back to Bombay.

It was a sadder place. Too many of the men who'd drunk and smoked at the Yacht Club's New Year's party at the start of 1914 had disappeared: the sunburned sailor, almost all of Peter's friends; that drawling officer who'd told Maddy and Della they were breaking his heart. Of the one and a half million Indian troops who'd left to fight, more than sixty thousand never returned. The city felt changed without them. *India* was changed. It wasn't only the sense of loss, everywhere; after the high casualties, there was a new edge to the hot, eastern days, a festering tension that Maddy couldn't remember being there before. Even before the hideous losses at the Dardanelles, her father had been back and forth to Delhi for emergency meetings on how to subdue the growing number of protests and demonstrations against British rule, but she'd been too caught up in her grief for Luke, caring for Iris, to pay close enough attention. While her father had spoken of his concerns over the new measures eventually implemented through the Defence of India Act, enabling government to imprison without trial or warrant any Indian suspected of threatening the Raj, it wasn't until provincial officials started to abuse their powers, making too many arrests and causing even more discontent and violence, that she fully absorbed why Richard had been so worried. It had got worse the year before, in 1919, when, with those like Mahatma Gandhi calling for independence, the vice-roy's council, panicking, had voted to extend the Act, despite the war being over, causing uproar everywhere, in the very highest levels of Indian soci-ety, and nowhere worse than Punjab, where hundreds of rioters had been killed by British fire.

"Women and children, too," Richard had said brokenly, when he'd come home with the news. "We should all be hanging our heads in shame."

"And yet," said Peter, who was still in his old bungalow, still working as Richard's deputy, "there's only one kind of hanging going on."

They deserved all the animosity they received, Maddy was grimly con-scious of that. It amazed her that more weren't hostile. But the schoolchil-dren, whom she'd started teaching again back when Iris was three, were as exuberant as they'd ever been, their parents every bit as smiling and grateful. The gardener's trio, too old now for chasing peacocks, played with Iris as if she were their little sister. Cook, who'd gone to such pains to help Maddy with her morning sickness, and then to tempt her into eating prop-erly again after Luke had vanished (making her the curries and kathi rolls he'd somehow got wind Luke had helped her develop such a love for), had, against the odds, slowly become a friend, Ahmed as well; they often drank chai together in the kitchen, arguing in Urdu over whether Hardy's books were depressing or beautiful, talking politics, Cook's and Ahmed's families in Goa and Poona, the heartbreak of the younger brother Cook had lost to Gallipoli. . . .

Still, out on the streets, there were enough accusatory looks and hard stares thrown around that Maddy couldn't feel as comfortable as she once had going anywhere alone.

"Then stop doing it," said Della. "Please. For your own sanity, if nothing else."

She couldn't stop. All these years on, she still spent hours sitting alone amid the dragonflies and brimming flower beds in the Hanging Gardens, on the bench she and Luke had once shared, imagining the heat of his body next to hers, hearing his voice (*let me see if I can distract you*), staring out across the sea toward the city he'd left so empty and that she was becoming increasingly, brokenly afraid he'd never return to. Some nights, unable to sleep, she crept out of her parents' villa, down through the steamy, nesting forest to hail a rickshaw to his old rooms, tracing her fingers along the windowsills, peering through the shutters at the vacant silence within, then sitting on the front steps, often until sunrise, just because he'd touched those steps, too.

It's the same for me, said his mother, Nina, who still wrote all the time; long, warm letters that somehow brought Luke closer, for the time Maddy was reading them.

I'm sure I've mentioned this, but he came for lunch, just before he met you in India. We had the most wonderful day, walking Coco on the beach, drinking too much wine by the fire. Luke fixed a broken cupboard for me. I'd been asking his father to look at it for weeks. Luke didn't do it properly—all that wine—and it still hangs crooked. Sometimes, I can lose a whole Sunday morning, looking at that door. I hope you come and see us. We'd so love to meet you, and finally hold little Iris.

They were going soon. Edie, who'd given in and let Fitz buy her, out of guilt, a cottage in Sussex, had written, too, asking if Maddy and Iris might like to visit for Christmas.

"It's time," Maddy had told her mother. "It will just be a holiday. You know I'd never take Iris from her life here. I wouldn't leave you."

"I know," Alice had said. "I do know that." She'd managed a smile. "You sound excited."

Maddy was: about seeing Edie again, sleeping in Luke's house, breathing the air of the rooms he'd grown up in, meeting his parents, walking his spaniel, Coco, on that beach. . . . It was the first time she'd looked forward to anything in such a long time. She was planning to take Iris to see a show in the West End, buy a toy at Hamleys. She'd visit Ernest at last, too. Poor Ernest, whom Diana—returning to India herself in the new year—had just that month finally managed to divorce.

"He won't know you, I'm afraid," Peter had warned her.

"That's all right," she'd replied. "I'll know him."

"Your passage isn't for a couple of months, though," said her father, the hot, airless evening after Guy had docked.

Maddy, just down from tucking Iris in for the night (she'd left her nodding off beneath her starry mosquito net, and the watchful eye of her grandmama), agreed that it wasn't.

Richard reached for his cigarettes on the veranda table. "Why not channel this newfound energy into some fun here," he said. "Twenty-nine is too young to live as a recluse."

"I'm almost thirty," said Maddy.

"Quite ancient," he said dryly, flicking his lighter. "Go to the club tonight, please."

"Yes, do," said Della, who'd come with Peter for dinner. Jeff was on his way; he'd been on a late shift at the hospital and was dressing at home, kissing his and Della's two daughters good night: three-year-old Lucy, who was the picture of Della with her wild brown waves, round cheeks, and round eyes, and one-year-old Emily, who had (as Jeff was the first to lament) inherited Jeff's strong bones and oversize chin. ("We're hoping she's got my sunny personality, too," said Jeff, "which will obviously make up for everything.")

"If you hate it, Maddy darling," said Peter, "I'll escort you straight home."

"She won't hate it," said Della.

"You just want me to see Guy," said Maddy, who was oddly nervous about doing that. He'd written to her a couple of months after Luke had vanished, telling her how sorry he was. She'd replied, thanking him, saying how much she hoped he was well and keeping safe—which she had hoped, very much—but hadn't admitted how much it had meant to receive his letter, or asked him to write again. Tempted as she'd been to lean on the comfort of his friendship, it would have felt like a betrayal, to all of them, to have done that.

She'd heard nothing from him since. It had been so long. Would he even want to see her again, now that he was back?

"Us wanting you to come out for once has nothing to do with Guy," said Della.

"He's working tonight anyway," said Richard, exhaling smoke.

"Oh," said Della flatly, giving herself away.

"A shame," said Peter. "He owes me a drink. I need to let him know I haven't forgotten."

"Guy aside," said Della, "when was the last time you set foot in the club after dark, Maddy?"

It wasn't really a question, and Maddy didn't answer it. They all knew she hadn't done it in years. Why would she? She'd only end up looking over her shoulder; that aching whisper of hope he'd surprise her again.

"Time to rip the dressing off," said Della. "You're coming, and that's that."

She didn't go, so she wasn't there when Peter, Della, and Jeff arrived at the bar to find that Guy had dropped by on his way home from the hospital after all. She didn't see Guy look up, spot Peter, and smile slowly, or smile herself as he strode across the room and pulled Peter into an embrace. ("You would have," said Della. "I almost sobbed.") She didn't hear Guy congratulate Della and Jeff on their marriage, their children, and ask after her, Maddy. She didn't notice him glance toward the door, as though checking to see if she was going to come through it. ("It was obvious," said Della.) Nor did she look at the new lines around his eyes, the definition in his jaw, and feel a bit weak because he'd become even more handsome with age. ("Honestly, Maddy, utterly like heaven.") She was resettling Iris, who'd woken from a nightmare—and feeling relieved that she was there to soothe her—when that all happened.

It wasn't until the following afternoon that she saw Guy herself for the first time.

She'd left Iris wrapped in a giant apron, making pistachio biscuits with Cook, and had walked slowly up the hill to sit on her usual bench in the Hanging Gardens. The post-monsoon sun was blazing, beating down on the garden's red-dirt paths, the green lawns and pink flowers. Beneath her cloche hat, she was sweating. Her loose dress stuck to her silk stockings, her back. She closed her eyes, thinking of the English December waiting for her, how nice it would be to feel cold for once, and to have a respite from sitting alone on this bench, replaying the same worn memories over and over again. She told herself, as she always told herself, that she should go home now. *This is doing you no good.*

It was then that she heard his voice, just behind her.

"Hello, Maddy."

She started, turned, shocked from her reverie, a silent *oh* forming on her lips as she saw that it was him.

He smiled down at her. That gentle smile, which showed those new lines that Della had mentioned, and made her heart soften, despite her shock at his appearance, because she could only imagine what had put them there.

Squinting, she raised her hand to the rim of her hat and slowly took the rest of him in. He wasn't in uniform, but a white blazer and flannel trousers. He held his panama by his side. He looked leaner, and there were shadows in his cheeks, but he was still the old Guy. She saw that from his smile, the affection in his eyes. Apprehensive as she still was—almost more so, now that he was suddenly here—she smiled with him.

"What a lovely surprise," she said, for something to say, but also because she meant it.

"It's not a coincidence," he said.

"No?"

"No. Peter told me you like to come here." His gaze held hers. "I'm tempted to tell you that you shouldn't be walking around alone, but I still remember what happened the last time I tried that."

She laughed sadly, remembering it, too; how he'd intercepted her in that packed bazaar. She still kept the golden silk Luke had bought her in her bedside drawer.

"I'm sorry I was so cross," she said.

"I think I probably deserved it," he said. Then, "It's so good to see you, Maddy."

"It's very good to see you, too," she said.

"And you're a mama now," he said.

"I am," she said. "Iris is five. And a half, she'd tell you, if she was here."

It was his turn to laugh. As he did, he took a step toward her. "Can I sit?" he asked.

She hesitated. *It's Luke's seat,* she almost said.

But she didn't. Because it was Guy, whom she'd hurt enough. And because she really was so very tired of sitting sadly by herself.

"Yes," she said, making room on the bench. "Of course you can."

CHAPTER TWENTY

King's Fifth Military Convalescent Hospital, 1920

The King's Fifth was closing, the following summer. Luke had only recently returned to the hospital. He'd grown increasingly desperate, back at the start of 1918—angry at his own failure to recover—and had persuaded Arnold to refer him to a different kind of institution: less kind, less comfortable, but (he'd hoped) effective. Arnold had tried to dissuade him against such places, warning him of the brutality of medical electrics, the dangers of more surgery, but Jones had insisted.

He'd gone that spring of 1918, to a converted Hertfordshire priory, and the care of Dr. Gibbon. It had been hell. Two years of hell, which Jones had been beyond relieved to leave behind when—after all the excruciating procedures to relieve the pressure beneath his skull, the countless rounds of shock therapy and hypnosis—Gibbon had told him he'd done his best, all he could, and was optimistic, it was time for Jones to go back to Surrey, wait, see, *be patient.*

Sister Lytton had come to collect Jones in the ambulance. She'd never stopped visiting while he was away, arriving on her fortnightly days off, a thermos of cocoa in her bag. As time had passed, she'd taken to bringing the ever-lengthening missing-persons advertisements, too. Together, she and Jones had scoured them—the tragic pleadings of parents and wives looking for their loved ones—waiting for a name to leap out: his name. But there were too many thousands to go through, in so many different broadsheets; it had been impossible to look at them all. All they'd ever found in those pages was sadness.

The trips Arnold had suggested Jones and Sister Lytton go on, whenever Jones wasn't in recovery from treatment, had been happier. The two of them had caught trains into London, out to different parts of the country, down to the coast, all in the hope that they'd stumble across a sight or sound or smell that would spark his memory back into action. He'd felt close to . . . something . . . recently, in Windsor. They'd walked by the river, the grassy banks and willows bathed in summer sunshine; he'd stared at the rowing eights crews, their blades slicing into the water, and had felt filled with the warmest sense of belonging.

"Yes?" Sister Lytton had said eagerly, her pink face full of excitement beneath her straw hat. "Anything else?"

He'd wanted there to be, almost as much for her as himself.

But there hadn't been.

And now here he was, back at the King's Fifth.

Waiting.

Arnold hadn't broken the news of the hospital's closure to all the patients yet. When he told Jones about it, as the two of them sat in his study one rainy afternoon, he asked him to keep it to himself, so that no one became unduly alarmed.

"Everyone will be taken care of," Arnold said, shifting creakily in his armchair to reach for his tea. "We've almost a year before it happens, and no one's going to find themselves turfed out on the street. There'll be plenty of hospitals left open. I'm off myself to Swansea," he peered at Jones over his cup, "and hoping I won't be taking you with me."

Jones hoped it, too.

"What about the nurses?" he asked, thinking not of Poppy (who'd eventually given up on him just before he'd left in 1918, then been dismissed when she was caught in flagrante with a cavalry captain who might have forgotten how to ride a horse, but hadn't forgotten everything), only of Sister Lytton, who he now knew had no parents as well as no brother or fiancé, just a bed-and-breakfast in her hometown of Norfolk where she'd admitted she stayed for her solitary leaves.

"We'll find them jobs, too," said Arnold. "And Sister Lytton is not your responsibility."

"She feels like my responsibility," said Jones. It wasn't only how much she'd done for him, these past years (grateful as he was for it); no, it was the thought of *why* she'd done it. *She's told me you make her think of her younger brother,* Arnold had once said. Jones had never forgotten it. And the better he'd come to know Sister Lytton, the more he'd grown to hate how very alone she was. He couldn't stand to think of her uprooted now, having to start again somewhere else, taken from this place that was as close to a home as she had. She, with her cocoas, her heart, her early starts to help poor Ernest—her spots of leave whenever she couldn't cope with the sadness of more death—deserved so much better.

He wished he could give it to her. She'd as good as told him she wished it, too, on the train back from that trip to Windsor. He'd been quiet in the upholstered carriage, still straining to think what it was about that river that had so resonated, and she'd stared across at him, brow furrowed, chapped hands clasped, swallowing, frowning, swallowing again, until at last he'd asked her what was wrong, and she'd spoken—in a rushed way that made it obvious how nervous she was—saying that she didn't want to upset him, she didn't, and she wanted him to remember, she did, she *did*, but had he ever thought there might be a chance he could be just as happy, or at least happy enough, starting again?

"Starting again?" he'd said.

"You're still so young," she'd said, her gaze earnest, full of compassion. "I know what it's like to . . . lose . . ." She'd raised her hands to her chest. ". . . but I just hate to think of you losing any more . . ."

"Sister Lytton—"

"You could find a job," she'd said, talking over him, seemingly unable to stop now she'd started. "I'd help you. I have money, I could buy a . . . cottage, or whatever you like. We could be each other's . . . companion. Nothing more. Just . . . dear friends."

He'd waited before saying anything further, choosing his words carefully.

"I can't do that," he'd told her softly. "I can't give up. Your fiancé, he wouldn't have, I'm sure."

"He's dead, Officer Jones."

"And I'm so sorry for that," he'd said, "so deeply, deeply sorry. But I'm not. I have people; they're waiting for me to remember."

"Yes," she'd said, shaking her head too quickly, swallowing again. "Yes, yes, of course. Silly of me."

"Not silly, Sister Lytton."

She'd drawn a wobbly breath, he'd been sure on embarrassment, disappointment, and he had ached for her.

"You have people," she'd said, repeating his own words stoically, "people you belong to." She'd given a firm nod. "We must get you back to them."

It wasn't long after that that Jones's dreams had started to change. Gibbon had claimed the credit, putting it down to the final surgery he'd performed. Arnold had said maybe, but it was as likely to do with the years Jones had spent with him before that, in Surrey, finally paying off. Jones wasn't sure which of them was right. He didn't much care. All that mattered to him was that the dreams were now much more frequent, longer.

Always full of her.

He'd seen himself at an altar, her faceless form beautiful in white lace beside him. He'd almost wept with joy and grief when he'd woken that time. She was his wife. He had a *wife*. A wife he worshiped, who stared at fireworks in black sequined evening dresses, drank champagne on window ledges, and kissed him endlessly in the sea.

A wife who sat for a photograph, cradling a baby in her sepia arms, the shadows of palm trees playing on her hands, the child's perfect, tiny toes.

His daughter's toes.

He had a daughter, too.

His heart raced with panic every time he thought of her: at how much he'd already missed, and how much he was still missing. The days had an extra cost to them now. Each one he let slip by without getting back to her was another she'd grown up without him.

If only Diana Aldyce would get in touch.

It was Ernest's divorce papers that had given Jones her name. Diana's lawyer had brought them, just the month before, the week after Jones had returned to the King's Fifth. Ernest's aged mother, who might have come, had tragically died in the influenza epidemic at the end of the war. To Jones's sadness, Ernest—without remembering anything—still turned expectantly to the drawing room door every time a visitor came through it. Needing to do whatever he could to help his friend, Jones had knelt beside him when the lawyer had arrived, held his shaking hand and convinced him he wasn't to cry, there was no shame in it but he shouldn't be scared either, he'd be much better off once this was all done with. The lawyer, who'd had the good grace to look mortified at Ernest's distress, had apologized and handed Jones the papers. Jones had taken them and seen the *Diana* right there in black-and-white. He'd felt his spine lengthen, mind moving to his journals upstairs, the name he'd written down the first summer after he'd arrived at the King's Fifth; the only name he'd ever remembered. *Diana's been having a field day.* He'd stared at the ink on Ernest's paper, replaying the one time Diana herself had visited the hospital, living it all over again.

As soon as he'd helped Ernest with his signature, he'd run, straight to Arnold's office.

"I recognized her," he'd said to Arnold, breathless with urgency. "It was why I looked at her twice. And she looked back at me. I thought it was Ernest she was looking at, but it was me. I'm sure she recognized me, too."

"She'd have spoken," Arnold had replied, "surely."

"I think she did," Jones had said, his every muscle straining with adrenaline and fury, remembering how Poppy had walked Diana out; the way she, too, had glanced back in his direction, then behaved so oddly afterward. (*You have nothing to say?* he'd asked her. *Not as much as you,* she'd said.)

It had been Sister Lytton, with her boundless kindness, who'd gone to such lengths to track Poppy down these past weeks, eventually finding her waitressing at a coffee shop in Kingston. She'd persuaded her to admit that Diana had indeed mentioned that Jones looked like someone she'd once known; someone with a wife, a daughter.

But Officer Jones isn't married, Poppy had apparently said, feigning stupidity. *How could it have been him?*

"Selfish girl," said Sister Lytton, when she'd returned to the King's Fifth. "Selfish, unthinking girl."

Arnold had written to Diana directly. He'd telephoned her new husband's house, too. But, to Jones's desperate frustration, there'd been no reply, not that time, or the twenty others Arnold had tried.

They supposed she must be away on honeymoon.

Torturous as it was, all they could do now was wait for her to come back.

CHAPTER TWENTY-ONE

Bombay, 1920

Guy didn't stay with Maddy for long on that bench in the Hanging Gardens. He'd sensed her reserve when he'd asked if he might join her, and even if Peter hadn't warned him of how much she was still grieving, he'd have realized it, just from the sadness sitting like a veil over her slender shoulders; the lost way he'd caught her staring out to sea. He'd known even before he'd said hello that he'd be a fool to rush her. He couldn't rush her, not into . . . anything. So after they'd spoken for just a few minutes—about how it felt to be back in Bombay ("Strange," he said, "wonderful." *You're here*, he yearned to add), then little Iris, who he learned had dark curly hair, and loved drawing, picnics on the beach, "and cake, lots of cake"—he forced himself to say he must leave her in peace.

"You don't have to," she said.

He insisted, hoping he didn't imagine the flicker of regret in her dark blue gaze.

He trod gently after that, very gently. He declined Alice's invitation to dinner, twice, and took her and Richard out to the Taj instead: two perfectly enjoyable evenings where they ate in the chandelier-lit dining room and caught up like the old friends they were—him speaking as little as possible of France and Egypt, because really what was the point in dwelling on all that, and all of them talking about the growing movement toward independence in India, whether it could ever really happen ("I would have said no," said Guy, "but then I've seen so much that I'd have thought impossible happen in the past six years"), and how Richard, now in his mid-sixties (Guy was forty-eight; how had it happened?), was starting to think of retirement, a move to the quieter south. Only one subject remained entirely off-limits. Guy, acutely conscious of his suspicion that Richard had never approved of his interest in his daughter, kept himself from mentioning Maddy. Richard, to his dismay—but not surprise—didn't bring her up either. Alice, treading as gently, Guy suspected, as he was, also remained silent where her daughter was concerned.

By a force of will Guy steered clear of their villa for the week that followed. He didn't go to the Hanging Gardens, or walk by the tiny jungle-rimmed school he'd heard she was teaching at so that he could pick his way through the trees, peek in through the ramshackle windows, catch a glimpse of her surrounded by children, reciting times tables. And when Alice asked him for another dinner, he refused that, too.

"Are you avoiding me?" Maddy asked when he finally went to church and let himself bump into her, leaving the morning service at St. Thomas's Cathedral, ten days after he'd first sat with her in the gardens. Her parents, talking with some of Richard's staff, were still on their way out. Maddy, coming down the steps, stood just inches from Guy in the sunshine, close enough that he could see the sheen of heat on her collarbone, the teasing outline of her silhouette beneath her calf-length blue dress. Beside her, holding her hand, was a child who could only be Iris: a little girl whom Guy had been rather anxious about meeting, and who peeked curiously up at him from beneath her straw boater, as pretty as her father had been striking, and who was in fact the living image of Luke, but that she had her mother's eyes.

"Of course I'm not avoiding you," he said, and was relieved at how relaxed he managed to sound.

"Guy," said Alice, joining them. "Do you have plans for lunch?"

"I was going to work," he said, quite truthfully. He had a stack of papers to go through: research bursary requests from some of the senior surgeons, procurement orders, a proposal he was working on to modernize the theaters.

"Come to us instead," said Alice, not treading so gently anymore. "It's Sunday. You can't work on a Sunday."

"Ahmed works on Sundays," Iris helpfully volunteered. "So does Cook. And everyone, actually . . ."

Guy laughed before he could stop himself.

"Iris," said Alice gently.

"From the mouths of babes," said Maddy.

"I'm not really a babe anymore," said Iris, then made a goldfish movement with her mouth, as though wondering what else might come out.

Guy smiled again. It really was impossible not to.

Iris beamed cheekily back at him, making him glad he had.

"Tell Guy, won't you," Alice said to Maddy.

"Honestly," said Guy. "It's fine."

Maddy looked up at him, eyes shaded by her hat. He couldn't decide whether her expression was affectionate, concerned, or wary. Perhaps a balance of the three.

"Don't spend the day alone," she said at length. "Come."

"Are you sure?" he said.

"Yes," she said, but not without another pause that made him think she wasn't.

He went, though, unable to resist now that he'd stood before her again, back to the villa he'd been so bereft to leave her at in 1914. He filled his cheeks with an anxious breath as he turned his motor in to the driveway, approaching its grand, balconied walls. Welcoming as he knew Alice would be, and yes, bright, delightful Iris, too (she liked him, she really did seem to like him; he felt such a swelling of pride at that), he still wasn't sure he should be coming. It wasn't just Maddy's reticence that worried him. Richard wasn't going to be unreservedly happy to see him either. Would the entire affair be hideously strained?

To his relief, Della, Jeff, and their children were already out on the veranda when Ahmed showed him through, Peter with them. "Hello, you," Della called, lifting the strain with her wide smile.

"Guy," said Jeff, coming forward to shake his hand, helping, too.

"Wine?" said Peter. "It's lovely and warm."

They ate on the veranda, the children with them, drinking and talking until dusk. Guy, relaxing by fractions with each course, made funny faces at Iris, laughed at the increasingly creative ones she threw back at him, chatted with Jeff about their colleagues at the hospital, asked Della how she'd enjoyed her short foray into nursing there ("Not quite as much as I'd

envisaged," said Della. "There's nothing romantic about bedpans." "No,"
Guy agreed, "there isn't"), felt relieved to hear Peter sound so much like
himself again, see him smile, and smiled himself at Maddy opposite him,
whenever he chanced to catch her eye. She was quiet, though, much quieter
than he remembered, and spoke mainly to Richard and sweet Iris, who sat
to either side of her. As the dessert plates were cleared, he hoped Maddy
would get up, come and sit beside him.

But it was Iris who did that, picking her way around the table in her lace
pinafore, black curls bouncing.

"Are you really a doctor?" she said, placing her warm hand on his with
an easy familiarity that he was almost absurdly touched by. It had been
just a few short hours, yet he could already feel himself wrapping—quite
willingly—around her perfect little finger.

"I am," he told her, and fought his smile this time, because she looked
so very grave.

"So you can sew people up?"

"I do my best," he said.

"My doll has a torn tummy," she said.

"Oh dear," he said.

"Suya did it," she added darkly.

He nodded like he understood, despite having no idea who Suya was.
("Our gardener's youngest," Alice enlightened him afterward.)

"Can I bring her down for you to look at?" Iris said.

"Absolutely," he said. "Fetch me a needle and thread, too."

It took him less than a minute to sew the doll's ripped fabric back together. Iris stood next to him as he worked, watching every move he made:
the happiest operation he could remember doing in a long time. Alice came
and sat by them, too, running her hand around Iris's waist. Guy, pulling
the needle, watched her kiss her granddaughter's head and felt a rush of
contentment for her. She'd been lonely too long, suffered too much; it was
wonderful to see her surrounded by family again. She was almost like the
woman he could recall chasing Maddy around the garden. (Not, of course,
that he liked thinking about Maddy as a child.)

"Thank you for coming today," Alice said to him quietly. "Please don't
stay away so long next time."

He glanced at Maddy, who was cradling her wineglass, looking at him, looking at Iris, seemingly lost in thought, and knew that he wouldn't. He stopped stitching, stilled for a moment by the wonder of her attention, the unbelievable nearness of her.

He'd tried to forget her, these past years. He'd fought so hard to do that; dancing with other women in the clubs of Alexandria, almost giving in and proposing to a staff nurse he'd met. Part of him wanted to forget Maddy now: the logical, honest part that brutally reminded him that she'd already had her love story. But as he watched her place her glass absently to her lips, he almost felt the touch on his own, and couldn't forget anything. She was *his* love story. Useless to deny it.

And quite, quite impossible not to hope.

He visited the villa more often after that. He was still being cautious, Alice could tell. He didn't call with the same frequency he had when Madeline had first come back to Bombay and he'd taken her for all those trips around town. (Madeline had long since admitted to Alice how she'd supplemented those excursions with a tour of her own making. "What?" Alice had said, appalled. "You went to the water tank?" "Mama," Madeline had said, "I went *everywhere*.") But he took to dropping by on his way to the hospital, for morning tea. He came again, at Alice's invitation, for Sunday lunch. He agreed at last to the odd supper, too. Each time he came, Iris stopped whatever she was doing—be it eating her tea in the nursery, or playing in the garden—and rushed to say hello, giving him no choice but to hug her (which anyone could see he was delighted by).

On his second visit, he bought her a new doll.

"I find patients always get better more quickly when they have visitors," he said, kneeling down so that Iris didn't have to look up. "Perhaps she'll be friends with your other one."

"Thank you," Iris said, clutching the doll to her chest. "Thank you so much."

"You're very welcome," he said, then laughed as Iris kissed him.

Alice saw the way Madeline watched them both, her expression contemplative, not entirely easy, just as it hadn't been when Guy had stitched for Iris at the table. Alice was almost sure she knew what she was thinking. She'd long thought it, too: that as amusing a godfather as Peter might be, as doting a grandpapa as Richard undoubtedly was, neither of them would ever fill the place of a papa. (Sweet, fey Peter would never be anyone's papa, of course.)

"Wasn't it thoughtful of Guy to bring that doll?" Alice said to her over dinner that night, needing to make sure Madeline really had fully absorbed his generosity.

"Yes," Madeline said. "He's always been kind."

"Iris was so happy," said Alice, not unaware of her own clumsy unsubtlety. "It was almost like looking at Emily and Lucy with Jeff."

"Can you pass the water, please?" said Richard, not unaware either.

He'd warned her against pushing Madeline into anything, back when Guy had first returned. "I know what you've always hoped," he'd said, "but she didn't choose Guy before. I can't imagine making do with him now will do her any good."

"You'd rather she stayed alone?" Alice had asked.

"I'd rather we left her to it," he'd said. "And she's not alone. She has us. Iris. Peter and Della . . ."

"It's not enough," Alice had said, only wishing it could be.

But if it was, then why did she still sometimes hear Madeline crying at night?

She was no fool, though. As the weeks passed into October and Madeline agreed to let Guy take her and Iris for ice cream at the Taj's Sea Lounge, then for lunch at Watson's, even back to the club for polo (since Iris loved the ponies), she saw that, ecstatic as Guy's attention was patently making Iris, there was no true thrill in the tentative courtship for her daughter. Her cream face didn't flush with anticipation when she heard Guy's motor arriving; she never raced down the stairs to meet him, as she'd used to with Luke. But she *did* smile when he smiled. She sat with him on the veranda while Iris played, sometimes for hours at a time, talking and talking. Alice busied herself with sewing in the drawing room and left them to it. She heard Madeline speak of the children she was doing such a wonderful job with at the school, her plans for her Christmas holiday with Iris (which Alice was dreading, and not just for the inevitable silence of the villa; it was the possibility that they might decide to stay); Madeline even managed to draw Guy into speaking of his war.

"I fixed them," Guy said haltingly, slowly stirring his tea. "I kept fixing them, then I'd hear a month later that they were dead."

"Oh, Guy," said Madeline, with such sadness, "I'm sorry."

She loved him, in a way; Alice heard that in her voice. She'd never have dreamed of encouraging anything had she doubted it.

"Of course I love him," said Madeline, "he's a friend. He always has been."

"A friend is good," said Della, who worried about Madeline almost as much as Alice did. "A friend is a start."

"I don't know," said Madeline, brow creased. "I just don't know."

"He'd make you so happy," said Della, "if you let him."

Madeline shook her head. "I want to stop talking about this."

"Let it lie," said Richard to Alice and Della, "please."

"If you're having to push," said Peter, "there's every chance it's not right."

But Alice couldn't accept that. She *couldn't*. Madeline was alone. Guy was alone. He utterly adored her, Iris, too, and Iris was growing ever more besotted with him.

"Because he keeps giving her ice cream and dolls," said Madeline.

"That's unfair," said Alice.

Madeline sighed, knowing it.

"He'd be the best papa any little girl could hope for," Alice said.

"Iris has a papa," said Madeline.

"No," Alice said, cruel to be kind. "She doesn't. She hasn't had a papa in a very long time."

"Mama, please—"

"You could be a family," said Alice. "A proper family."

"Please, don't," said Madeline.

"I need to," said Alice. "You've been sad long enough." She leaned forward, doing what she'd slowly learned to do again, and took Madeline's hand in her own. "I'm begging you," she said, "think about this seriously. You don't have to grieve anymore."

Maddy almost wished he'd never come back. She'd understood her life before he had. It hadn't been easy, but it had been simple.

It had worked.

I feel like I have no one left to talk to now, she wrote to Edie. *Mama and Della never let a day go by without asking about when Guy's next coming, or if he's talked at all of his intentions (he hasn't, and I think I'm relieved about that), Papa constantly tells me not to listen to Mama and Della, Peter that I just have to do what I think is right—but how can I know what's right when everyone else is so full of noisy points of view? Even Iris chimes in, insisting that we drop by at Guy's villa to say hello on the way to school, eager for news of our next outing to the Sea Lounge. Conversely, it's Guy who's the easiest to be with. He's the only one who doesn't try to tell me what I should be doing.*

But I don't think I love him in the right way, Edie. He's wonderful, the warmest, kindest man, yet my heart doesn't flutter when I'm with him. My legs don't shake.

Edie wrote back. *Fitz made mine do that,* she said. *Your mother's as well. Look what happened there.*

Oh no, said Maddy, *don't you start, too.*

She joked, but it wasn't amusing. Nothing felt funny. Somehow, it was almost December and it had been two months that Guy had been calling, and while he might have said nothing, she knew it was only a matter of time. His lingering looks, slow smiles, and all the attention he lavished on a smitten Iris, told her that. She was either going to have to take the plunge, which she didn't feel ready for, or hurt him badly (*again*). She didn't know how she could have allowed herself to get into such a fix. She blamed Guy entirely. She liked him too much to keep him away, even if she couldn't quite love him enough to allow him closer.

Or could she?

Should there even be a question?

"I'm not sure," said Peter sorrowfully, "but I think perhaps not."

And yet, she kept questioning.

She looked forward to her and Iris's holiday even more. Now, the thought of *that* gave her shivers; it gave her thrills. With just a few days left until their December 1 departure, she packed their trunks, folding the thick pinafores and gowns she'd bought at the Army and Navy store. She grew even more excited as she worked, picturing the two of them boarding their liner, seeing their cabin for the first time, eating cake on deck every day, playing quoits, swimming in the new pool P&O had advertised. She saw them docking in Tilbury, walking hand in hand down to the quayside where Edie and Luke's parents would be waiting for them.

I need this, she wrote to Edie, *for so many reasons, not least some quiet to understand my own thoughts. I wish Luke was here, all the time.*

I never had to stop and think at all when he was.

She finished that letter just after she closed the locks on the trunks.

Was she fated, she wondered, to always be getting ready for voyages she couldn't catch?

It really was so stupid of her, what happened next.

She'd warned the schoolchildren endlessly not to do anything but sit on the wobbly chairs they all used. Why she stood on one herself the next morning to hang the tinsel she'd bought as one of her parting gifts for the children, she could never afterward say. But she fell, right in front of all of them, breaking her ankle. It hurt. It shocked her how much. She couldn't help her sobs of pain. Iris, poor little Iris, ran as fast as her chubby legs could carry her, to Della's villa since it was closest, fetching Della and her motor.

"Madeline Devereaux," said Della, breathlessly helping her into the backseat, "what a ninny you are."

Maddy hardly needed to be told.

At her request, Della told her driver to take them to the General Hospital, not Guy's, where Alice had been so ill, and Luke had left Maddy that last time.

"I can't be at that place," Maddy said, through teeth gritted in agony. "All I'll think about is Luke."

"Then the General it is," said Della.

A young British doctor set her leg and prescribed a low dose of morphia, a fortnight in traction since the break was a bad one, then a week after that of hospital bed rest *just to be safe,* several more afterward at the villa.

"You'll be home by Christmas at least," said her mother, who'd arrived clutching the note Della had sent with her bearer, wrought with worry, Richard—who'd raced from his office—with her. "We'll make sure we still have a wonderful one."

Maddy nodded, but couldn't speak; she was afraid if she tried to talk of Christmas, and the longed-for trip she'd now have to cancel, she'd fall apart. She turned to Iris, hating how scared she'd been, stroking her tear-mottled cheeks, trying to reconcile herself to the fact that neither of them were going to be having their holiday.

"I'm so sorry," she managed to choke, "I wanted to take you home so much."

Iris gave her a heartbreakingly wobbly smile. "But this is home, Mummy," she said, which Maddy realized was intended to make her feel better, but somehow made her feel even worse.

She didn't know how she was going to break it to Luke's parents that they weren't coming. She asked her father to wire Edie straightaway, so that that at least was done.

MEND QUICKLY STOP, Edie wired by return. I SHALL VISIT THE DEVER-EAUXS AND TELL THEM STOP BETTER IN PERSON STOP WE WILL ALL STILL BE HERE IN SPRING STOP.

"Spring's not so far away," said Guy, when he came that evening after everyone else had gone, a bunch of hothouse flowers in hand, mince pies from the Taj, too, which he said he knew wasn't the same, but hopefully helped a little.

"I wanted to go now," she said, and really did cry this time. It was the pain in her ankle as well as her disappointment, her crushing disappointment.

"Maddy," he said, setting his gifts down, taking her hand in his, pressing it to his lips before she knew what he was doing. "Please, don't."

"I can't help it," she said.

He moved, drawing her gently to him, not upsetting her leg, and held her close. It was the first time he'd ever done more than brush his cheek against hers. From somewhere deep inside herself, a voice told her to resist. But she leaned her head against his chest, too sad and too shaken not to,

and he stroked her head, kissed her hair, and then she cried even more because Luke had once done that, too, and Guy wasn't him.

"Shh," Guy said, "shh."

And even though he wasn't Luke, she didn't push him away. If she did,
and he went, then she'd be all alone, and she wasn't sure she could stand it.
Not this night.

"I'm here," he said. "If you let me, I'll always be here."

She knew what he was saying. Even through her tears, the fog of morphia, she heard what he meant. Again, that voice whispered: *Stop this.*

You have to stop this.

She didn't stop anything. He kissed her again, resting his cheek against
her head. She felt the weight of him, the companionship of another body so
close to hers, and clung to him, saying nothing.

He asked nothing of her.

Eventually, she felt her sobs subside.

He didn't let her go, though.

He moved back so that his eyes met hers, and touched his fingers to her
damp cheeks. She stared back at him, wondering if he'd kiss her properly,
with no idea whether she wanted him to or not.

His lips found hers before she could decide, and, at the strangeness of
this other man's touch, she closed her sore eyes, still unsure how she felt
about it. He leaned into her, running his hand around her neck, his gentle
kiss becoming firmer, more confident, and she waited for . . . something.

But no flutters came, no shakes.

Just a strange, otherworldly realization—a giving-in, almost—that it
was happening, she'd let it happen.

Nothing could ever be the same between them again now.

It was on a foggy, damp December morning that Arnold came to find
Jones in his room. Jones had been reading through his journals, head in
his hands, pressing his skull, trying to force recollection through his bones.
He looked up, seeing Arnold in the doorway, and stood, pulse quickening
in hope. . . .

But, "I'm sorry," said Arnold, "I don't have anything concrete."

"What do you have?" Jones asked.

"I telephoned Diana's house again, got her maid." Arnold rubbed his spectacles with the edge of his waistcoat. "Diana is indeed on honeymoon. An extended one, I'm afraid."

"How extended?" Jones asked.

"Very. They've gone to Africa, I gather, a mixture of work and pleasure. She said something about them moving east afterward." He frowned. "She really wasn't clear."

"Will Diana be coming back here at all?"

"Briefly. But not until spring."

"Spring?" said Jones in disbelief.

"Don't be disheartened," said Arnold, "we'll get her then, old man. We're not giving up."

CHAPTER TWENTY-TWO

Guy visited Maddy every day of the three weeks she was in hospital, some-times appearing twice a day, calling so often that she really didn't have the chance to become apprehensive about his next appearance. He arranged cover for his own patients so that he could at the very least drop by each morning, if only to say a quick hello and look at her chart to double-check she'd been monitored properly overnight, and given the right dose of morphia.

"They should decrease it soon," he said, "you don't want to develop a dependence on it."

"They've said they're going to," she told him.

"Hmm," he said, flicking through the chart's pages, "I wish you'd let them move you over to me."

"I have a perfectly competent doctor here," Maddy said.

"Is that your way of telling me you'd rather I minded my own business?" he said, looking up from the clipboard with a smile that was as playful as someone as sincere as he could manage.

"Of course not," said Maddy, and was sure it was the truth.

If no one else was in the room, he kissed her when he arrived, making her tense with awkwardness, no matter how hard she tried not to. She only hoped he didn't notice. (He noticed. *Nerves*, he told himself determinedly. *Just nerves*.) He started calling her "dearest." That felt odd, too. No one had ever called her that. Luke certainly hadn't—or darling, or sweetheart, or any pet name. Only, *Miss Bright*.

She'd loved that so much.

"But Luke's gone," said Della, who also called by daily. "He's been gone for ever such a long time now."

"She knows that," said Peter.

"I feel so guilty, though," said Maddy.

"Don't," said Della. "Please. Luke would never have wanted you to stay alone."

"I still feel like I'm betraying him," said Maddy.

"By being with Guy?" said Della.

By settling, she almost said. But she couldn't admit that's what she might be doing; not even to herself.

Often when Guy came, he collected Iris—whom Maddy missed and worried about, every second of every minute—and drove her over with him. On those days, Maddy forgot her unease, her tugging fear that she might be making the most horrendous mistake. She lay waiting for them both in her hot, tiled room, ankle throbbing, her whole being tense with impatience to hold Iris's warm little body close and be reassured that she'd been woken by no nightmares the night before, had enjoyed her breakfast with her grandparents, and eaten all her fruit. She sat up on her pillows, hearing the patter of Iris's approaching steps, feeling a smile of relief and gratitude pull at her cheeks as she listened to the exuberance of Iris's chatter, Guy's indulgent laugh. They sounded like such a team, a perfect duo.

"And they really only met in September?" asked the nurses.

"Only then," Maddy told them.

"Isn't he wonderful with her?" they said adoringly. "What a lucky little girl."

Guy never arrived empty-handed. Her room overflowed with flowers: a veritable garden of bouquets. Their cloying scent filled the air, her throat, a constant, perfumed reminder of how good a man he was; a friend it would be impossible to hurt. If it wasn't flowers, it was cakes, ice cream sped over from the Taj's kitchen (although that was often half finished by the time he and Iris arrived, a deal of it smeared on Iris's rosy cheeks), or books and cards to help her pass the time.

And a ring.

He brought her a ring, the day before she was to go home, two days before Christmas.

She wasn't surprised when he knelt before her and offered up the red velvet box with the emerald inside. She'd known it was probably coming.

Her father had warned her, too, calling late the evening before, smuggling in a bottle of gin and tonic beneath his blazer, saying he needed a drink after the conversation he and Guy had just had.

"He's asked my permission," Richard had said.

"Oh," Maddy had replied, waiting optimistically for a rush of excitement that never came. "I imagine that was rather awkward."

"You imagine correctly," he'd said. "I told him the only person's permission he needs is yours."

"You don't want me to give it," Maddy had guessed.

"I think the world of Guy," he'd said, not answering her question. "He'll treat you like a queen, I have no doubt about it. But I want you to be happy." His face had creased with concern. "I'm so afraid you won't be."

"But what if I can be?" she'd asked. "What if this is what I need? What Iris needs?"

"Iris has you. . . ."

"I think she wants more."

"What do *you* want, though, darling?"

"To not be sad anymore," she'd said, voice fracturing on the pathetic truth.

"Oh, darling . . ."

"I can't spend the rest of my life depending on you and Mama," she'd said. "You'll retire . . ."

"Not yet."

"But eventually," she'd said. "Iris and I, we need our own . . . home. A life."

He'd sighed. "Just think carefully," he'd said, "please."

It was all she'd done through the endless night that had passed, sweaty and sleepless in her narrow single bed, her leg itching horribly in its cast. As she'd pulled at her damp pillows, the sheets, she'd replayed every word, every look and smile she and Luke had ever shared, and tried to imagine having anything close with Guy. She couldn't do it. And wrapped in her memories of Luke, she'd wept at the pain of his silence, her longing for him as agonizing as it had ever been in the black loneliness of her room.

"Why did you go?" she asked him. "Why did you have to go?"

He didn't answer. She pressed the heels of her hands to her eyes, finally starting to accept that he never would, filled with terror that if she said no to Guy now, she'd spend the rest of her days driving herself mad yearning for a voice that couldn't come. Only, she'd be making Guy miserable as well. And Iris. Vivacious, clever, beautiful Iris, whom she'd lay her life down for, whom Guy looked after so wonderfully, and who'd lived almost six years without a papa. *Six*.

Her mother was right: Guy was everything any child could possibly dream of for a father. He was. And a friend, such a decent, true friend.

A friend is good, Della had said.

A friend is a start.

Was it enough, though?

She was still battling to make sense of her own frazzled thoughts when Guy got down on one knee, nervous and handsome in a cream suit, picture-perfect in every way but one. As he raised the box and haltingly told her she'd make him the happiest man living if she'd only agree to be his wife, she couldn't help but reflect on how formal it all was, how different from the easy, teasing way Luke had leaned over the bed, fetching the diamonds she still wore on her left hand, making her cry and laugh with delight.

Sweet, though. So very sweet.

"I know I'll never replace Luke," he went on, with a candor that made her feel like a criminal, "I don't want to try." His serious eyes held hers. "But if you let me, I'll spend every breath I take trying to be as good a husband as you deserve. I'll look after Iris like she's my own." Warmth filled his face. *Love*. "Maddy, she *feels* like my own."

It was that which did it.

That and the sudden kerfuffle at the door; the glimpse of Iris cheekily peeking around the frame, apparently deaf to Alice whispering at her to come back, letting Maddy know they were both there. Guy's smile became rueful. They'd ganged up on her. It wasn't fair. But as Maddy took in Iris's dancing eyes, how she bit her lip in inescapable hope, and Guy asked her once again if she'd let him be part of their family, she knew there was only one answer she could give.

And although she felt a disturbing void of euphoria as the "Yes" left her numb lips, Guy's sweet face transformed in delight, Iris whooped and ran toward them, and it was far too late to do anything about it.

She realized it had been too late from the moment she'd let Guy sit beside her in the Hanging Gardens.

She didn't know if she'd even change it if she could. With Guy pulling her into an embrace, then Iris scrambling onto her bed, throwing her arms around her neck, it was impossible to think straight at all.

"You've made me the happiest man in the world," Guy said.

"Congratulations, both of you," said Alice. Her blue gaze met Maddy's. *I know this wasn't easy,* she seemed to tell her, *well done.* "We'll need to set a date," she said out loud.

"March I thought," said Guy, "before it gets too hot."

"Perfect," said Alice.

Maddy made no objection. Already, she was anxious to be on the other side of the ceremony, safe from any more questions about whether she was doing the right thing.

"Can I be bridesmaid?" said Iris.

"Of course you can," said Guy.

They talked on. Maddy let them. Guy had placed the ring box next to her on the bed. She picked it up, her eyes blurring on the emerald. She turned her hand, looking at Luke's diamonds, sparkling and perfect. It dawned on her that she'd have to take them off, these gems he'd had set into the ring she loved. These gems he'd touched. She'd have to remove her wedding band, too.

So stupid, but she hadn't even thought about that.

"Are you happy, dearest?" Guy asked her.

It took her a moment to realize he'd spoken. "Yes," she said, and nodded, cheeks suddenly straining with the effort of smiling, wishing they'd all just go so that she could give in to the tears filling her throat before they choked her.

They didn't go. Not for several hours. And actually, she was glad in the end that they stayed, because if she'd been left alone with the wave of regret she'd been struck by, it really might have crippled her. As it was, she didn't have the opportunity to dwell on anything, least of all sadness, because everyone else was so very happy.

Guy had brought champagne with him. "Presumptuous, I know," he said with a wry laugh, pulling it from the bag. "Promise me you've had no morphia today?"

"I promise," she said, reaching for a tumbler to catch the bubbles as he set the cork free.

They all drank, Iris talked more about her dress, the flowers she wanted to wear in her hair, and Alice sent word to the civil service office, Della's home, and Maddy's father, Peter, Della and Jeff, even Emily and Lucy came, too, filling the room with congratulations, noise; wonderful, welcome distractions.

No one mentioned Luke. Richard, the diplomat through and through, gave Maddy only one slightly troubled look when he arrived, but otherwise was cordial as he shook Guy's hand, even jovial as he raised a toast to them both, and didn't once betray the concern he'd voiced to Maddy the night before. Although Peter glanced at Luke's rings and quietly told Maddy that he'd buy her a chain for them (making her wonder for the thousandth time what she'd do without him), no one else remarked on how she was still wearing diamonds instead of an emerald. Not even Guy, who left the matter alone with a compassion that just went to show Maddy had been right to say yes to him. Absolutely right.

As dusk fell, Jeff fetched a picnic dinner from the club, the nurses told them they really all did need to start thinking about going home soon, they'd have Maddy back with them the very next day after all, but they all stayed on a while longer anyway, and the whole affair was warm and buzzy and very, very . . . nice.

It wasn't until after they'd all gone, and Guy had kissed Maddy good night, telling her again how very delighted she'd made him, that she sat once more in solitude, her electric lamp flickering, cicadas clacking beyond her window's mosquito screen, and reopened the box he'd given her.

She ran her thumb over the ring, as tentatively as if it could burn her. She took it out, letting the emerald catch the light, throwing green patterns on the whitewashed walls. Drawing a long, deep breath, she raised her left hand, exhaling as she stared at Luke's diamonds.

"Is this all right?" she whispered to the emptiness around her. "Do I have *your* permission?"

Silence.

She sank back on the pillow, looking up at the ceiling. She saw his face. That face she'd loved so much. The enjoyment, the boundless energy and warmth in his teasing smile, his dark, shining eyes. And then she saw Guy. Steady, kind, Guy, who'd worn his heart on his sleeve for every second of the afternoon; his heart, which he'd given so freely to her.

And to Iris.

Slowly, she dropped her gaze once more to her hand. Without consciously making any decision, she set Guy's emerald down and pulled at the rings Luke had placed on her finger. It wasn't easy. Her hands were swollen with the heat, and she had to force the metal over the padding of her flesh, her knuckle. The more they stuck, the harder she pulled, clenching her teeth, grimly determined, now that she'd started, to see it through.

It was only when they both finally came free, leaving a sore, pale indent in her skin, that she realized she was crying. Her tears rolled down her cheeks, on and on: at the fear of what she'd decided, the uncertainty of everything ahead, and most of all the grief, the wrenching grief, of what she and Luke had had taken away, the years she'd wasted fighting to believe they might get it back, and the weight of the rings she held clenched in her hand, the emerald she now needed to put on in their place.

The finality of this long-overdue goodbye.

CHAPTER TWENTY-THREE

Maddy didn't cry again after that night. She didn't allow herself to. Her mother and Della were right; she had to start letting herself be happy instead. Try harder.

Surely it wouldn't be so hard.

She was glad that it was Christmas, and that she could go home. For the week that followed, every day was packed with presents and church and meals; at her parents', at Della and Jeff's. The children tore around in excitement, and she, refusing to rest on the chaise longue Ahmed brought out onto the veranda, infuriated her mother and Guy by using her crutch to hobble around after them, helping Iris set up her new dolls' house, rhapsodizing over the flower patch she'd started growing, teaching her how to play "Jingle Bells" on the piano.

"Oh *no*," Peter could always be relied upon to exclaim, should he happen to arrive while they were at it, "not this again."

"But you love my piano playing," said Iris, quite accurately.

Sometimes Alice or Della would raise the topic of all the things that needed to be done before March (the church that had to be booked—"Not St. Thomas's," said Della. "Of course," said Alice—the reception venue, too, then the band, the gowns . . .), but really nothing could be confirmed until everything reopened in January, so what was the point in talking about it?

"It's exciting," said Della, "that's all. Are you going to wear white?"

"Della," said Jeff, "you're incorrigible."

"That's one word for her," said Peter.

"I'm not sure what I'm going to wear," said Maddy absently, remembering how Luke had made her laugh at St. Thomas's altar by telling her how pure she looked in white. *I might almost be deceived . . .*

"You'll look wonderful whatever you wear, my dearest," said Guy.

Maddy smiled, and wondered when that "dearest" would start to feel normal.

At New Year's, the Yacht Club, which had long since resumed its annual celebration, threw a party. Guy told Maddy he had to go, as most of his staff would be there, Jeff included; Maddy's parents went, too, for much the same reason. Della of course accompanied Jeff. Peter, though, demurred ("The old leg," he told Guy, lying. "It's torture to watch all the dancing"), as did Maddy, who'd gone to the beach at the base of the hill with Peter every New Year's since that first time in 1915, and was beyond relieved to have her ankle as an excuse to do the same again now.

"Surely you can manage to have fun at the club, even with your ankle," said Guy, who had no idea that she'd not set foot through its doors since the war, and was mercifully oblivious to how she'd once stood on its promenade, staring at a stranger in a linen jacket. "I'll keep you company."

"You'll have a better time without me," she said.

"I assure you I won't," he told her. "Come. This really doesn't feel like the most auspicious way to start to the year."

But she was adamant. And he was too kind, too much of a gentleman to insist. It made her feel wretched, and she swore to herself that she'd do better in the future, but she just wanted this one, last time with Peter, down on the balmy sands, staring across at the city's fireworks, *remembering*.

They raised their glasses to Luke as midnight broke; their traditional toast. As they did, Peter once again tipped his fair head backward, eyes on the starlit Indian sky, the heavens Maddy normally always refused to look at.

This time, though, she raised her gaze, too, just as she had at the break of 1914.

Was he truly there, looking down?

She could almost feel the weight of his stare, the touch of his smile. Perhaps he was. She ached to believe his soul was happy somewhere, that he knew how wonderful their daughter was, and that she, Maddy, would join him again one day.

"I wish you'd seen his face when he saw that photograph you sent him," said Peter, as he had many times before. "We were just about to go over the top, and you might as well have given him the earth on a plate."

She smiled sadly, as she had many times before, picturing it.

"Della's right," Peter said. "He'd want you to be happy. He'd want that so much."

"I know," she said, her eyes still on the stars.

"May he know how loved he is," said Peter.

"He'll always be loved," said Maddy, and pressed her hand to her chest, his rings that she now wore on Peter's chain, right next to her heart.

Jones didn't leave his room that New Year's, not even when Sister Lytton tried to drag him down to the inevitable drawing room celebrations. He sat by the light of his oil lamp, going over and over the journals he'd already read countless times; ignoring the vibrations of the gramophone coming through the floorboards, his guilt at Ernest alone and sad in his room, poring over every, tiny detail.

His dreams had flooded his sleep these past weeks, giving him hundreds more glimpses into his past: fragments of memories as precious as they were confusing, none more treasured than the image of those slender fingers holding that tiny sepia foot.

It was all coming back to him. His miracle was just around the corner, he could feel it; in his breath, his bones. Whether it was down to Gibbon's surgeries, Arnold's therapy—or even, as Arnold had also hazarded, a simple diminishment of scar tissue—the dreams kept rushing in, and Jones scribbled down every detail, letting nothing slide away. He was close, so close . . .

But it wasn't happening quickly enough. He turned his journals' pages impatiently, eyes snatching at the words he knew by rote—*toothless man, sailing boat, jungle birds, hammering rain, tears in a hospital, "Auld Lang Syne"*—and, with clarity still stubbornly eluding him, felt his heart race. Perhaps it was the hospital's closure. Maybe the fear that Diana would somehow fail him in the spring.

He didn't really know what it was, but he'd become filled with the most awful dread that he was running out of time.

For much of January, March still felt quite far away, and strangely fantasy-like. Planning for the wedding began in earnest—the banns were read at the local church (not St. Thomas's, *of course*), newspaper announcements went out, guest lists were drawn up—and Maddy played her part in it all, *trying harder,* sitting for the engagement photograph with Guy, nodding along as her mother read through the names of invitees, struggling to make herself believe that it was all really happening. It was. She knew that. She just couldn't *feel* it. Guy helped her hobble around the ballroom of the Taj, holding her arm as the hotel manager pointed out the palatial room's size, its crystal chandeliers, the pillars that had been imported from the selfsame Parisian manufacturer responsible for the Eiffel Tower, and she heard herself agreeing that yes, it would be a quite perfect venue for the reception, and had to remind herself that it was *her* reception she was talking about.

"Are you still on morphia?" Della asked.

"No," said Maddy. "I stopped that a long time ago."

"It'll just be jitters then," said Della. "Don't overthink it. You always think too much."

Did she?

She tried to stop.

But invitations were sent out to more than three hundred people, the viceroy included, and she couldn't help but wonder why she wasn't more perturbed by the vast number, the prospect of saying her vows in front of all of them.

"It's almost like someone else is going to be doing it for me," she said to Peter, laughing, trying to make light.

"They're not," he said, not laughing even a bit. Rather, frowning. Worriedly. "If you're having second thoughts, now would be a good time to say."

"I'm not," she said, "of course I'm not."

And she wasn't. She'd decided. She was going to be *happy.*

With that in mind, she forced herself to do what she'd been putting off, and wrote to Luke's parents about the marriage.

I hope you know how difficult this has been for me, and that no one will ever take the place of your son. I'm so very, very sorry we won't be making our trip to see you this year. She stared at those words, her own sloping handwriting, thinking particularly of how Nina would feel when she read them, and waited for the urge to weep to overcome her.

But nothing came.

It was so odd.

"Good, odd, I think," said her father, who drove her to the GPO on a warm, sunny late January morning so that she could post the letter in person.

"Very good," she said, and was sure that must be right.

"I'd be worried if you'd cried," he went on, overtaking a rickshaw. "I haven't heard you cry in a while."

"I haven't been doing it," she said.

"That's what I'd hoped," he said, a smile creasing his weathered face. "Your mother's told me I should listen to her more often."

"I'm sure she has," said Maddy, and made herself smile, too.

At the start of February, she finally had her sweaty, itchy cast removed, which was a relief beyond relief. Although her ankle was weak, it didn't hurt so much anymore, and she gradually learned to walk more easily on it. It still wobbled, though, especially when she had her dress fittings at Watson's (not the Taj, where she'd gone for her fittings when she'd married Luke, *obviously*). As she watched her intricate drop-waist gown taking shape, she felt so disorientated by her own detachedness that it was all she could do to keep standing.

She struggled even more when, on her thirtieth birthday, Guy surprised her by giving her a motorcar: a silver saloon that sparkled in the sunshine, and was incredible and generous, and far, far too much.

"Of course it's not," he told her, pulling her into an embrace (which she was at least learning to get used to). "I'll teach you to drive." He kissed her (again, it was becoming more familiar). "If you will keep insisting on going out alone," he said, his lips moving to her ear, "at least this way I know you won't be on the trams."

"There's nothing wrong with the trams," she said, closing her eyes, because she truly did want to enjoy his touch.

She agreed to let him take her out that evening. It was all part of being happy. ("Very good," said Della.) They went to one of the jazz-and-oyster suppers the Taj had started to put on each week, in the plush, very hot dining room next to the ballroom the reception was to be in. It was packed; half of Bombay seemed to be there, smoking and dancing and coming by their table to go on and on about their shock that Maddy was out and about after dark.

"Leave her alone, please," said Guy in the end, smiling, but with a steeliness to his voice that reminded Maddy that as well as being gentle and warm, he was also a senior-ranking member of the Indian Army's medical corps. "I'd rather like her to do it twice, and she won't if you don't let her enjoy it."

"You don't need to make enemies on my account," Maddy told him once they were by themselves again (touched as she was that he was ready to).

"No risk of enemies," he said, "they're all too eager to come to the wedding to be offended. Besides," he took her hand, "all I care about is you."

That was the first time that *she* kissed *him*. She moved impulsively, leaning across the table to press her lips to his. There were still no shivers; there wasn't much at all. But, as she pulled away, and saw how his eyes had filled with joy—and yes, relief, too—she swore to herself that she'd kiss him more often.

The waiter brought their silver platter of oysters. The jazz band played on, and the ceiling punkahs wafted sticky air. For once, they didn't speak about the wedding. They drank nice wine, quite a lot of it, and talked of all the things they'd used to talk of: his work, her work, how *of course* he'd support her carrying on with her teaching, just as soon as her ankle was up to her standing on it all day again, but would she consider stopping smoking? He had a theory it might be bad for one's health.

"Well, if that's your theory," she said, stubbing out her cigarette, smiling with an ease she'd almost forgotten it was possible to feel with him, thinking she should perhaps drink wine more often.

"Said no truly content person ever," said Peter, when she met him for coffee the next morning. "How's your head?"

"Fine," she said, even though it was horribly sore and clammy beneath her cloche hat.

"Maddy," he said carefully. "The viceroy will be leaving Delhi in less than a week."

"I know that."

"Once he's here, it will be too—"

"Peter," she said, snapping more than she meant to. (Her head.) "I want to marry Guy."

"And do you still feel like someone else is going to be doing it for you?"

She stirred her milky coffee and said nothing.

It was, though, exactly how she still felt.

At the end of the month, she went with her mother, Della, Iris, and Lucy (also a bridesmaid) to collect their gowns from Watson's. She tried hers on for a final time, listened to her mother and Della exclaim on how perfect it was, laughed at Iris's raptures, smiled at Lucy mimicking Iris, and could have been in a play.

It was the same the week after, when Ahmed and Guy's bearer moved almost all of her and Iris's things down the road to Guy's villa. She stood out on the road amid the screeching insects, watching as the cart disappeared, assuring Iris that yes of course she could come back and see Suya and Cook whenever she wanted, and simply couldn't reconcile herself to the reality that they were going to be living anywhere but where they'd always lived.

"Are you sad?" her father asked, once Iris had trotted off with Alice to inspect her new room. "Iris was a baby here, after all."

"I'm fine, I think," she said, and genuinely didn't know whether it was the truth, or a lie.

She wasn't really anything.

She moved through each day as she'd always moved through her days, but felt . . . mechanical, like a puppet that some invisible person was operating with unseen strings. She spoke as she should, laughed as she should, and since no one asked if she was all right, or looked at her strangely, she supposed she must have sounded more convincing than she felt. She went out with Guy for another dinner, ate and smiled, and even danced with him. He held her close, the lines in his face she'd seen when he'd first returned to

Bombay now faded in his transparent happiness, and really didn't seem to guess how adrift she was.

That was good, at least.

At the start of March, the viceroy arrived in Bombay. They had a huge, formal dinner to welcome him, out on the moonlit lawns of the villa. He twiddled at his mustache, rolled back on his heels, winked at Guy, then kissed her on both cheeks and remarked on what a lucky man his old friend Guy was.

"It's me who is the lucky one," Maddy said, and again had that surreal sense that she was reading from somebody else's script.

It was the next morning, with three days left until the wedding, that she finally started to return to herself. Luke's mother was the one who brought her back, by replying to her letter. It was only when Maddy saw her envelope on the breakfast table that she realized how much she'd been waiting for it. As she picked it up, she *felt* for the first time in weeks: relief that Nina had written at all; fear at what she might have said. She sliced through the envelope, and her heart creaked back into action, her hands trembled. As she read the unfathomably generous words inside, her eyes blurred.

You never need to worry that we think you've ever done anything other than love our son. We wish you happiness, from the bottom of our hearts. And hope that you will still visit us one day. You will always have a home here.

Iris came running out while she was still reading, squealing, "Three more sleeps."

Somehow, Maddy folded the letter away and managed to swallow her tears.

But she stopped feeling so much like a puppet after that. She became quieter, she heard it in herself. She had no appetite for anything.

"Are you unwell?" asked Cook when she apologized for not finishing another meal.

"I'm nervous, I think," she said.

She was.

She was petrified.

She thought maybe she had been ever since she'd agreed to marry Guy, she'd just been so numb with panic, she hadn't realized.

She was relieved that everyone else was too busy to notice her sudden silence. Her mother was fortunately caught up with Della in decorating the church, the ballroom. Her father and Peter were wholly consumed with escorting the viceroy around town; visiting all the cantonments, having lunches and receptions at various clubs and offices, keeping the senior Indian businessmen in the city onside. Guy was at the hospital, working extra hours in theater before their two-day honeymoon, and Iris was frankly too excited to think of anything beyond the cakes she'd been promised, her new bedroom, and whether she or Lucy would hold Maddy's train.

By a force of will, Maddy held her nerve, wading through each baking day and endless night minute by minute; bathing, dressing, listening to Iris, trying to sleep. She almost made it all the way to the wedding itself, certain that if she could just get through the ceremony, everything would be fine.

She was so close to managing it.

Then, the night before, with everyone else in bed, she started to pack for the honeymoon, folding her overnight things into a case so that Ahmed could take it to the Taj suite Guy had reserved. Her shutters were ajar, letting the night noises of the jungle in: cicadas, the whispering leaves, the distant ripple of the sea.

She pulled her stockings from her drawer, the sheer silk catching the golden glow of the lamp, and out of nowhere the thought came to her: *Guy will see these.*

Brow creasing, she tried to shake the alarming prospect away.

But then she took out her negligee, and there it was again: that voice telling her, *He'll see this, too.*

This time, she couldn't ignore her unease. She clutched the barely there item, and imagined him touching it, taking it off. Before she knew what was happening, that was all she could think about. Her mind, so blissfully detached just a few days before, filled with the terrifying inevitability that she would be naked with Guy. *Guy.* The two of them would do what she and Luke had done. Tomorrow.

She placed her hand to her throat. *Tomorrow.*

They were going to do that every night for the rest of their lives.

Every. Single. Night.

"Oh my God," she said. "Oh my God . . ."

She couldn't breathe. She really couldn't breathe.

Abandoning her packing, she ran from her room, as quickly as her weak ankle would allow. Stopping only to check that Iris's ayah was with her, she raced down the stairs out onto the driveway before her parents could hear her and stop her, see her fear. She climbed into the motor she was still learning to drive, clunked it into gear, and, scattering gravel, roared down the driveway, to the only place she could think of to go, not stopping until she reached Peter's small house and was standing, sweaty and shaking, at his door, waiting for him to open it.

He was already in his dressing gown, ready for bed. He pushed his blond hair back in bleary bemusement as he looked out into the night, then, taking the state of her in, blanched and said, "Oh, Christ."

"Peter," she gabbled, "I don't know what I'm doing. I don't."

His eyes widened. "It's too late, Maddy darling. It's too late for this."

"But . . ."

"It's tomorrow," he said. "The viceroy is here. Everyone is *here*. You can't do this to Guy. It would end him. Your father would never be able to hold his head up. Iris . . ."

"Oh God," she said, throat constricting at Iris's name, because of course she couldn't hurt her, or any of them. "Oh God, I'm so stupid. . . ."

He didn't correct her. But he opened his arms and hugged her for a long time, telling her that it was all going to be all right, it was.

"You had so many reasons for marrying him," he said, still holding her close, "let's talk about those."

So they did.

They sat up all night, smoking too many cigarettes, drinking bracing tumblers of brandy, and spoke endlessly of Guy's kindness, his goodness, how lucky Iris was to be getting him, how cherished she'd be.

"How cherished you'll both be," said Peter.

"Yes," she said, sipping more brandy, "yes."

Slowly, steadily, forced to remember all the many admirable things about Guy, not least the perfect papa he was going to make, she felt her alarm over the prospect of going to bed with him (and their *entire lifetime* together) retreat.

Or maybe it was just her exhaustion muffling her panic. The brandy, too.

She didn't question it. It really was too late to go back—she'd known that in her heart even before Peter had pointed it out; it was why she'd been so beside herself—and she would take whatever help possible to move forward.

"Good girl," said Peter, far from easily, as he saw her off at dawn. "I'm always, *always* here."

"Thank you," she said.

"You'll be fine," he said, trying to sound convinced.

"I'll be fine," she agreed, doing an even worse job.

But she let Peter hail her a rickshaw, since she'd had too much brandy and not enough sleep to drive straight. She returned to the villa, where no one had even realized she'd been gone, and was back in her bed before Iris woke and ran in proclaiming, "It's today, it's today."

At nine, the telegraph boy delivered a wire from Edie (HAVE THE MOST WONDERFUL DAY STOP I FEEL SURE THIS IS THE VERY BEST THING FOR YOU ALL STOP) and another from Luke's parents (THINKING OF YOU BOTH STOP). At ten, she removed Luke's rings from around her neck, dressed as a bride for the second time in her life, set off for church in sunshine instead of rain, and at eleven walked down the aisle on her father's arm. Then, in front of more than three hundred people, the viceroy included, she promised a man she'd realized too late that she should never, ever have said yes to that she'd love, honor, and obey him. As he smiled across at her, so smart and proper in his uniform, not teasing, not even a bit (*I might almost be deceived . . .*), she swore to herself that she'd at the very least honor him, and try to make him as happy as he wanted to make her.

The reception passed in a blur, a haze. They sat for more photographs, sipped champagne, smiled and thanked endless lines of guests for coming, and then it was over, and it was dark, and she was holding Guy's hand, and they were climbing the Taj's grand marble staircase toward their room.

"Thank you," he said to her, when he led her through the door, over the threshold, toward the large, four-poster bed. "Thank you for giving me the best day of my life."

"You're very welcome," she said, which was a ridiculous thing to say, but she'd been awake for more than twenty-four hours, could hardly breathe for the consuming fear at what they were about to do, and really couldn't think of anything better.

"Are you nervous?" he asked softly.

I'm terrified, she wanted to scream. *Can we please not?*

"A little," she said.

"You don't need to be," he said. "Please don't be." He leaned down, kissing her neck, her collarbone, reaching to unbutton the clasps on her gown. "I love you so."

He didn't rush her. He took her gown off, then sat her on the bed, rolling her stockings from her legs as though she were the most breakable of china dolls. He unlaced her stays, kissing her chest, running his hands down her waist, around her thighs, and was slow, and gentle, and so very kind.

But all she could think about as he moved on top of her was her fits of laughter as Luke had thrown both of them into the sea that night. All she felt, as Guy's weight pressed her down into the soft, luxurious mattress, was the memory of her excitement, her urgency, as she and Luke had dragged their sodden clothes from one another, making love again, and then again in that tiny, perfect boat.

CHAPTER TWENTY-FOUR

Diana's written," said Arnold, from Jones's bedroom door. "She said she'd prefer not to visit, because of Ernest."

Jones, sitting at his desk, looked up, staring. He'd been waiting so long for this, pinning everything onto it, and now that it was finally happening he was filled with fear.

"What did she say?" he asked, forcing the words from his too-tight throat.

Arnold dipped his white head, studying the letter in his hand, brow denting behind his spectacles. There appeared to be a newspaper clipping folded in the envelope, too. It struck Jones as odd that Arnold didn't simply hand both to him to read. Was he concealing something?

Before he could ask, Arnold said, "Does the name Maddy Bright mean anything to you?"

Jones sat very still, clipping forgotten, waiting for the name to do just that.

Maddy, he repeated silently.

Maddy Bright.

He shook his head slowly, chill resignation seeping through him.

It didn't mean anything.

Nor did the name Luke Devereaux.

Not straightaway.

Crushed by disappointment, he refused to listen to Arnold telling him that he needed to give it time. "This isn't the end," Arnold said, folding the letter and clipping away without having shown Jones either.

Jones made no reply. It felt like the end.

CHAPTER TWENTY-FIVE

High Elms Residential Home, England, December 1975

He never wanted to forget the joy of that moment. The sheer, unmitigated euphoria of finding her, finding everything, all over again. As he sat by one of the home's bay windows, looking out through the steamy panes, over frosted lawns, he felt a constriction in his chest, a burn of such pain and sadness, replaying his own excitement, the hope that had coursed through his entire being.

His desperate impatience to get back to her.

But even as he sat there, his mind began to blur. Confusion thickened it. His breath quickened; that familiar struggle to cling to lucidity.

Within seconds, he'd forgotten he was struggling to hold on to anything at all.

He stared at the window.

He couldn't recall sitting next to it. The shape of his reflection looked back at him: hair that was thick, shoulders that were broad, but lower than they'd once been, frailer.

He'd become so old.

From somewhere in the house, he could smell the scent of a baking fruitcake. On the radio, turned low, classical music played. The living room was barely full. A couple played chess in the upholstered armchairs by the fire. Beside them, a woman and her daughter ate scones and drank tea.

He wasn't alone either. There was an elderly woman sitting, just beside him. She was peering at him, anxiously. Mutely, he looked her over, trying to devise who she was. He tried not to let her see his confusion, sensing she

He declined Arnold's invitation to go with him to his study and talk it all out. When Sister Lytton arrived in Jones's room, cocoa in hand, he sent her away, too. Unable to be where other people would ask him to summon a brave face he couldn't bear to affect, he pulled on boots and a jacket and went out to the forest, breathing fog in the cold March air, beating the trees with a stick, sending leaves scattering. He didn't know how far he walked, but as early spring darkness descended, his energy drained from him; he sank to sitting on the mossy floor, head back against a trunk, and sobbed like a child—for himself, his wife and daughter, his parents, all they'd lost and all he'd lost—overcome by the hopelessness of these years he'd spent trying to find them, ready now, really ready, to finally give it all up.

He was still ready when he returned to the King's Fifth.

You remember what you once suggested, he even thought of saying to Sister Lytton. *Well, I'm ready to start again, be happy enough. I'm tired of this place. I am so very tired. . . .*

He was exhausted. He avoided the dining room, where he could hear dinner taking place, and, before he could say anything he might regret to Sister Lytton, went straight to his room, his bed, falling swiftly to sleep.

And then, he dreamed.

He was in the middle of trees once more, not a cold English forest, but an Indian jungle.

He was in India.

He stood at a gate, looking down a driveway toward a grand villa with bougainvillea climbing its walls. Peacocks strutted on the lawns, palms swayed. There was a porch, and on that porch's steps sat a woman. She was bathed in sunshine; her blond hair and cream cheekbones were shaded by her hat.

In his unconsciousness, he watched her. It came to him that he was waiting for her to look up, notice him.

For once, he didn't wake before she did.

She raised her face to his. He saw, even from a distance, how her face broke into a smile.

It did something to him, her smile.

It gave him everything.

might be hurt—she was, after all, dressed as though she'd gone to some effort: a powder-blue jacket and matching skirt, a pillbox hat placed on her white hair—but from her creased brow, the gentle way she reached for his hand, he supposed he didn't do a very good job.

"Are you lost again?" she said.

"Lost?" he said.

"In Bombay," she said.

He frowned. Bombay?

"Don't worry." She held his hand tighter. "I'm here," she said. "I'll help you." Her eyes shone, with happiness or grief he couldn't quite make out. "I'm here," she repeated.

He felt as though he should trust her.

It would be a comfort, in fact, to do that.

"You'll help?" he said.

"Yes," she said, patting his hand. "But shall we have a cocoa first?"

CHAPTER TWENTY-SIX

Bombay, 1921

After they went to bed on their wedding night, Maddy couldn't sleep, despite her exhaustion. She lay awake until dawn, gritty-eyed and tense by Guy's sated side, listening to the sounds coming through the walls from the hotel's other bedrooms: the creaking pipes and flushing latrines, the coughs and indiscernible voices of strangers. She wanted to go to the latrine herself, but felt too awkward to do that in case she should wake Guy, then full of panic again, because how could she have married a man she couldn't even bring herself to visit the bathroom in front of? She really didn't know, but eventually, as the rising sun tinged the edge of the window shutters with light, she got up, too desperate not to, and crept across the room to the water closet, wincing, sore in a way she'd never been with Luke, not even on her first time. She was as quiet as she possibly could be as she emptied her bladder, then washed her hands, her face, but when she returned to the room again, he was awake, smiling dozily from the bed.

"Come here," he said, sitting up, opening his arms to her. The skin on his torso was much paler than it was on his arms, his neck and face. Luke's had been the same color all over; that light tan he'd got from swimming every day.

Would she ever stop comparing Guy to Luke?

"Maddy?" Guy said, expression becoming concerned. "You look upset. Are you all right?"

"Yes," she said, "it's just . . . I've got the curse." The lie was out before she knew it was coming. She blushed, more at the intimacy of the admission than her dishonesty.

He wasn't embarrassed. He was a doctor, after all. "Oh, dearest," he said (that word again), "you poor thing. Come and lie down."

She went. What else was there for her to do?

He drew her to him, wrapping his arms around her waist, kissing her neck. It was hot, too hot. She started to perspire beneath her nightdress.

"Maybe next month it won't come," he said softly.

"Maybe," she said, and didn't mention that she'd been to see Dr. Tully and asked him for a contraceptive device. As good a wife as she had decided to be—every bit the one Guy deserved—she wasn't ready for a baby with him. Not yet.

He kissed her again, whispering to her that it was still early, she should get some rest before they drove back to the villa, and she closed her eyes, gratefully pretending to fall asleep.

She pretended a great deal in the days and then weeks that followed. She had to. She never knew the (retrospectively blissful) detachedness of being a puppet again. She and Iris moved into Guy's villa, settled into their new rooms with their new paint, and new furniture, and newly polished floorboards, and Iris took to it all like a duckling to water—curling up with Guy for bedtime stories, wriggling into Maddy's bed each morning, just as she always had—and Guy came to and from the hospital with a permanent bounce in his step, which Maddy did her best to replicate, feeling a constant, prickling terror that if she didn't watch her every word and expression she might slip and betray to one or both of them just how very much the opposite of happy she'd become.

When, after her invented monthly had finished, Guy knocked on the door that joined their rooms and asked *if he might,* she told herself that it was now or never, *try harder,* then forced a nod, and made herself breathe as he sat down beside her, pulling her nightgown over her head.

"You're so perfect," he said, kissing her shoulder, pushing her gently so that she was lying down, "too perfect. I can't believe I get to do this."

She closed her eyes, trying not to wince as he moved into her, and couldn't quite believe it either.

It was harder than ever to feel at ease around him, now that their nights were filled with such painful intimacy, and the deceit of her contraception. She hated herself for having to fib again when she *did* get her curse, saying it sometimes came as quickly as every two weeks, even more when he became anxious about her and asked her to see Dr. Tully just in case something was wrong.

"I don't want *you* to worry, though," he said, cupping her face in his hand. "I'm sure it will turn out to be nothing."

"Yes," she said, feeling an utter heel. "So am I."

Resolved to find more to occupy herself, she decided to return to the school, even though Guy was still worried about her spending too much time on her ankle, overexerting herself.

"We've only just had the wedding," he said. "You need to recover."

"From what?" she said. "Della and Mama did all the work."

"But you seem tired," he said. "Rest a while longer. Go to the club, have a long lunch with Della. Get to know some of the wives from the hospital."

She raised a brow at that. "Guy," she said, "you didn't marry that person."

He smiled, then sighed, in a resigned way that made her wonder if he'd started to think it might have been easier if he had.

He didn't protest further, though. He asked only that she drive rather than walk to the schoolhouse, and she promised she would, but it was another lie; she enjoyed the short leafy walk down through the birdsong and sweet muggy heat too much to avoid it.

And she loved being back with the children. So did Iris, who ran to reclaim her spot next to Suya the moment they both ducked into the low-ceilinged classroom. The others all came rushing to Maddy, and she hugged them in turn, laughing at their delight, the feel of their enthusiastic arms around her neck, then clapped her hands and said they should get to it. For the mornings that she taught them—drilling them in arithmetic, singing songs, writing stories, even bringing her mother down to paint—she forgot her nights, her worry. She lost that awful sense that she'd strayed into someone else's life.

But it returned the instant she was in Guy's villa again, shoulders dropping as she and Iris walked into its shadowy hallway, the large, dark rooms with their unfamiliar walls. She felt awful about it. Guy had been nothing but welcoming (all that new furniture, the fresh paint). She resolved to do something for him. He'd spoken about having his senior officers over for a dinner party, saying they were all eager to see Maddy again, and besides, they'd had him over so many times as a bachelor, he owed them. Although she really *wasn't* that person—the type to happily lose hours on table decorations and seating plans—she was also deadeningly aware that it would cause problems for Guy if she didn't eventually start to entertain.

Easing herself in gently, she invited her parents, Peter, and Della and Jeff, for Sunday lunch. Unfortunately, she failed to *ask* Guy's bearer what he thought of the plan, and *told* him about it instead, only realizing this was a mistake when his eyes turned to stone. He refused to discuss the menu and marketing with her, assuring her—with an air even more wounded than Cook's had been when she'd offered to help with his Victoria sponge all those years before—that he was well able to run the villa himself, he'd been doing such work for almost longer than she'd been alive, *memsahib*. Maddy wasn't about to go into battle with him—truly, he was welcome to the running of everything—but did ask that he at least ensure the meat was fresh, since she and Iris had been unwell a couple of times since moving in. Oh, his face. She was sure it was in punishment for her interference that he procured the stringiest chicken she'd ever tasted and, despite the more than one-hundred-degree April heat (even in the shade of the garden's trees where they were to eat), instructed Guy's cook to make lumpy gravy, boiled carrots, and horribly dry roast potatoes to accompany it. No one could eat the meal, not even Guy (who quietly assured her that she really didn't need to bother herself with the domestic side of things in future, the staff were more than capable); they all sweated in the hammering sunshine and picked at the congealing food, setting Maddy's teeth on edge, until Della and Jeff's youngest, Emily, pronounced it horrible, then threw her plate on the grass and, displaying none of her father's sunny tendencies, leaned over and sank her teeth into her sister's unsuspecting arm. It was as Lucy was screaming, inconsolable, and Emily was being carted home in disgrace by Jeff, that the hospital rang for Guy on the telephone he'd had installed, calling him to operate as the surgeon on duty had fallen ill with typhus. As he went, he kissed Maddy goodbye, and it was so public that she tensed in a way she never normally let herself do anymore, moving so that he kissed her clammy cheek and not her lips, then winced, feeling him balk, even more so when she looked around and saw, from the strained way that everyone was suddenly shuffling their napkins, that they'd all noticed the awkward exchange.

"I'm so sorry," Maddy said to Guy, running to catch him as he walked back to the villa. She squinted up at him. "I was just so upset about the meal."

"Of course," he said, relieved, she felt, to be given an excuse.

"I'm no good as a hostess," she said.

"You'll get better," he said, smiling in his kind way, but not correcting her, because he did after all need her to improve. He glanced over her shoulder. "You should get back to the table," he said. "They're all looking." He kissed her again. This time she remembered to let him do it. "Don't wait up for me tonight. If it's late, I'll stay at the hospital."

"All right," she said, relieved herself, then feeling guilty, too, for being relieved.

She returned to the table, braced for the inevitable inquiries as to whether all was well. She assured everyone that it was, the chicken had just made her feel a little sick, and naturally no one took issue with that.

She could tell, though, that they all thought there was more to it. Her father, so mercifully convinced of her well-being throughout her engagement, was once again studying her with concern. Peter, refilling his wineglass, looked rather green. (She wondered if he was thinking of how he'd talked her out of her panic the night before the wedding. "Yes," he said to her later, "it crossed my mind.") Even her mother and Della appeared anxious.

"Is being back at the school too much?" her mother asked. "You've lost weight."

"You have," said Della. "And you seem flat. You were so excited before the wedding."

I had strings, Maddy almost said, but stopped herself.

"Is it the anticlimax?" Della went on. "I've heard that can happen."

"Maybe," said Maddy, seizing on that, "probably." Then, conscious of Iris still and silent beside her, patently listening, she asked if anyone was ready to brave dessert.

"No," they all chorused, hands held up, "no thank you," making her laugh, in spite of their worry.

Loath to risk making it any worse, for the rest of the afternoon she made sure to laugh often, talk more, be *happy,* and was grateful when they in turn seemed to relax again. After Lucy and Iris had run off to play, she even found herself suggesting a birthday party for Iris, who was turning six in just under a fortnight, on the middle Saturday of the month.

"We could make it a surprise," she said, "back at the villa." She looked to her parents. "If that would be all right with you?"

"It would be a delight," said her father.

"A pleasure," said her mother.

"Can we not invite Diana and the new husband, though?" said Peter.

"Diana's back?" said Maddy.

"Only just," said Peter, "with Alfred, or *Alf* as we're to call him." He grimaced. "He came by the office on Friday." He swilled his wine. "Alf is awful."

"Alf makes me miss Ernest," said Richard with a sigh. "Poor Ernest."

"Have you seen Diana?" said Maddy to her mother.

"Not yet," said Alice, strangely tight-lipped. "I'm in no rush to."

"Remind me again why I had to hire her husband?" said Richard.

"It just seemed right to help," said Alice, in that same tense way.

"Well, it's decided anyway," said Della. "No Diana and *Alf* at the party. Iris can thank us when she's older."

"Fine," said Maddy, "we'll keep it small. I'll get the children from the school along. She'll love that."

She would have, Maddy was sure, if that was how it had been allowed to work out.

But Guy, who returned exhausted from the hospital the following morning, proclaimed the party a wonderful idea, and wondered if it wouldn't be the perfect excuse to finally invite all of his colleagues over. So many of them had families of their own, he said, and Iris could make some more friends who were, well, who were . . . like her.

"British, you mean," said Maddy.

"Yes, dearest heart," he said, with a weary smile. "There's nothing wrong with that."

There didn't feel much right about it either, but since he looked so very tired (and she still felt horrible about the way she'd avoided his kiss), she gave in, and tried not to betray her dismay when he presented her with a list of names as long as her arm.

"Well, if we're inviting all of them," said her mother, "we'd better ask everyone at your father's office as well. We can't cause offense."

"It's going to be as big as the wedding," said Maddy to Della.

"What can we do?" said Della.

Nothing, Maddy knew. She began to wish she'd never suggested the party.

She'd wish it even more on the day itself, but that was another matter. Mercifully oblivious to how it was all going to turn out, for the two weeks that followed, if she wasn't at the school, she was in and out of her parents' home, with a frequency that the demands of a child's party didn't *truly* necessitate. But she'd been missing the villa's creaks, its scent of citronella and wood polish, the light-drenched rooms, much more than she'd been prepared for when she'd watched her and Iris's things being moved out. She exhaled each time she stepped onto the veranda and leaned on the balustrade, looking down into the garden she'd grown to love over the years. Occasionally, she stole up to her room and sat on her bed, holding her matches, Luke's golden silk, staring through the window at the sunshine, feeling the knots in her ease. And it was so wonderful to spend time with Cook and Ahmed again, both of whom cackled, delighted, when she told them about the roast chicken debacle. "You should never have been leaving us," they said, and she agreed quietly that she shouldn't, then made them all chai, which they drank as they worked through the recipe books, preparing for the hordes of guests about to descend on them. Iris suspected nothing of what they were doing. She was too caught up reading stories with her grandmama in her old nursery, playing in the garden with Suya and the rest. As her birthday drew closer, she began to resist leaving at the end of the day, crying and begging Maddy to let her please, please just stay another few minutes. In the end, Maddy would carry her home, not admonishing her, but cuddling her tight, because it was clear that content as she'd seemed at Guy's, she missed her home, too. Guy's always felt too quiet by comparison when they got back there, too full of his staff who didn't know them, and empty of him, since another of his surgeons had fallen ill, and he was practically living at the hospital.

Stifling as Maddy found his presence, with him gone, the hours after sunset felt very long. Iris, exhausted from her long days, was always asleep by seven, her quiet snores the only noise in the otherwise echoing house. Maddy was unwilling to invite her parents over, lest she worry them as much as she had at that lunch. She didn't want to bother Della for the same reason; besides, Della was busy with her own family, and an increasingly difficult Emily. Peter, who'd left her in no doubt that she could bother him at any time, had also hugged her for a very long time after that grim Sunday, and would, she suspected, make her talk about things there was no point in talking about if she asked him to come.

So, without ever planning it, she asked the ayah to keep an eye on Iris, and started to go out herself.

Back to Luke's old rooms.

She felt so guilty as she crept from the villa and into her silver saloon. She knew that Guy, who'd bought her the motor she was using to betray him—and who was working so very hard, always helping others—would be crushed if he knew what she was doing. Each time she pulled up outside Luke's sleepy, silent apartment and stared across at the wooden door, imagining the shadow of herself running through it, she told herself that it would be the last. But it never was. Night after night, she slipped from her motor and traced her fingers along the windowsills. She sat on the steps he, too, had touched and clenched his diamond ring in her hands. She leaned her head back against the door, closed her eyes, and lost herself in her memories, sometimes for hours at a time.

She did that right up until the eve of the party.

The party when everything changed.

CHAPTER TWENTY-SEVEN

By one on that Saturday, the celebrations were in full, sun-bathed swing. Richard's and Guy's colleagues filled the large lawn, smoking and drinking in white suits and topees, their heat-flushed wives beside them: laughing, fanning their pink faces, sinking into the grass on their heels. Perspiring children ran everywhere, rocketing from the jugglers to the magician over to the ponies Richard had taken it upon himself to arrange, grabbing at the tables of sweating fairy cakes and sandwiches, the inevitable platters of curry puffs. There *were* far too many people, Alice had to concede that Madeline had been right about that. Well in excess of a hundred had come, and Iris, who'd stuck like a shadow to Madeline's side from the outset, was clearly overwhelmed by all the strangers and not enjoying her surprise even a bit. Richard, resplendent in another of his paper hats, was trying to coax her over to the ponies, but she clung to Madeline, who still looked far too thin, and worryingly tired, with purple shadows of sleeplessness in her cream skin.

Alice let go a troubled sigh. She hadn't expected Madeline to struggle so much in her new life. She hadn't imagined she'd struggle at all. For herself, unable to remain entirely deaf to Richard's initial concerns, she'd watched her carefully throughout the engagement, wanting to be absolutely sure that she hadn't helped push her into something she might come to regret. But Madeline had seemed so . . . fine. More than fine. Almost like her old self. Even Richard had come round, agreeing in the end that the match truly did appear for the best. Alice couldn't think what might have happened since. She'd spoken to Iris, but Iris had assured her there'd been no arguments or cross words at home.

"And does Mummy still smile and laugh?" Alice had asked.

"Yes," Iris had said, distracted by the doll she'd been playing with. "Guy cuddles Mummy, too, a lot."

Alice bit her lip now, studying Madeline as she ran her finger around the neck of her loose, cream lace dress. Peter held a glass of champagne out for her to take, but Madeline shook her head, refusing it. Too hot, maybe. Or—Alice felt her leaden heart lift a fraction—perhaps she was pregnant. She'd been quite poorly with Iris, after all, unable to even smell alcohol. Yes, that really could be it.

Alice turned toward Guy, who was with Della, Jeff, and company by the magician—Jeff holding biting Emily firmly by the hand. Unlike the rest of them, Guy wasn't watching the magician tapping his hat. He was studying Madeline, as though he'd be inside her mind if he could. He looked shattered after his long hours at the hospital, uncomfortable in his suit, and for once every one of his forty-eight years, but not despondent. Far from it. His gaze was . . . protective, almost.

As it would be, if Madeline was with child.

The more Alice thought about it, the surer she became that she might be. She almost started to relax.

And then she remembered Diana.

She'd seen her earlier that week, unfortunate enough to bump into her outside the Gymkhana Club, on her way to meet Richard for lunch. (They'd had lunches a deal more in recent years. With everything so much better with Madeline, she'd managed to stop pushing him away as she once had. It was so nice to have stopped doing that.) Diana had looked much as she ever had: overzealous rouge, a brittle smile, and black hair that she'd had cropped in the new fashion (a mistake in the Indian humidity; it frizzed beneath her hat).

They'd gone through all the pleasantries, both thinking, Alice was certain, of that letter Diana had sent back in 1916. *One never imagines they'll encounter a face like that twice.* Alice, who normally did her best to forget Diana's preposterous suggestion that Luke might have survived, of course hadn't mentioned it.

The last thing she'd expected was for Diana to bring it up.

But she had. "Did you ever tell dear Maddy about it?" she'd asked.

"I told you I wouldn't," Alice had replied, her voice glacial to her own ears.

"It's just there were *developments*," Diana had said, and, to Alice's choking alarm, had gone on, talking of how a Dr. Arnold had written to her, telling her that the man she'd thought she'd recognized as Luke had apparently recognized her, too. "He still had no memory, though. I wrote back to the doctor, telling him that Maddy had married again, and sent the clippings of the photographs, so that this patient could see if he knew her." She'd pouted. "It looked a lovely wedding, Alice. One would have liked to have been invited."

"You weren't here," Alice had said automatically.

"Yes, of course," said Diana. "I knew that must have been it."

"Did you hear from Dr. Arnold again?" Alice had managed to ask.

"Only once," Diana had replied. "He told me that he'd shown his patient the clippings, and I could leave it with him now." She'd shrugged daintily. "Does one assume this man was or was not Luke Devereaux? And is Maddy or is Maddy not a bigamist?" She'd laughed. Actually laughed. "A divorcée rather pales by comparison."

"It won't have been Luke," Alice had said, not laughing. "It can't have been. Peter was with him when he died."

"Well, quite," Diana had said. "You were so sure about that, weren't you? I made mention of that to Dr. Arnold, too." Her eyes had twinkled. Alice, who'd never hit a soul, had been tempted to strike the patent enjoyment from her face. "Are you going to tell Maddy," Diana had gone on, "so she can write to Dr. Arnold herself and check?"

Alice hadn't answered.

She'd thought about it. Endlessly.

She did it again now. She looked from poor, tired Guy, back to Madeline, who was kneeling before Iris, apparently trying to talk her into something, and decided to say nothing. What was the point? That unfortunate soldier really *couldn't* have been Luke. Luke—poor, *poor* Luke—was dead. And Maddy had her family now. A proper family. She needed time, help to adjust, settle into the long years of happiness Alice *knew* were waiting for her, here. In India.

She simply couldn't bring herself to jeopardize that.

Guy stared at Maddy talking to Iris, oblivious to Alice studying him. He smiled at the way Maddy held Iris's cheeks in her hands, head on one side as she attempted to cajole her into having some fun. His wife; so exquisite.

He'd watched her, just a few short hours before, as she'd dressed for the party. He'd just got back from the hospital—where, thanks to some temporary staff being sent from Poona, they'd soon no longer be so shorthanded—and, fresh from his bath, had sat on the edge of his bed to fasten his cuff links. He'd paused, catching sight of her through their ajar connecting door. She'd been wearing just her corset. Her hair had been loose, falling over her bare shoulder. He'd watched the rise and fall of her chest as she'd bent, pulling her stockings up over her calves, and listened to the soft whisper of silk on skin. Her fingertips had skimmed her knees, her thighs, and he'd felt the heat in his own hands. He'd wanted to go to her. He'd felt such an urge to do that. He'd known that he should leave her, that she was busy, getting ready for Iris, but it had been too long since he'd touched her. So he'd stood, unable to help himself, and crossed to her room.

She'd raised her eyes, seeing him.

"Hello," she'd said, and had smiled; that small, slow smile she seemingly reserved for him. "You look like you need to sleep, not go to a party."

"I wouldn't miss it," he'd said, taking her hands in his, kissing her wrists, hearing her breath falter, still so nervous.

He'd pulled her closer, wishing he could help her stop being nervous. He'd lifted her hair, run his lips down the soft nape of her neck, losing himself in her scent, the feel of her, willing her to do the same with him.

She'd demurred, telling him there was no time.

"Let me," he'd said. *Please let me show you how much I love you.*

"Tonight," she'd murmured.

"I can't wait," he'd said, and, in the end, she hadn't made him. He'd been too rushed, though. He hadn't even stopped to give her time to go the bathroom as she'd asked. He'd felt rather ashamed afterward. He'd apologized, for being such a boor.

"You're not a boor," she'd said quietly, already straightening her stockings, and he'd tried not to pay attention to the unwelcome thought that she might have been glad it had been over so quickly.

"We'll see you in a minute," he heard her say now to her father and Peter, as she stood, leading Iris up the lawn.

He frowned, wondering where they could be going.

Not stopping to think, he set off after them.

They were off to have cake with Cook in the kitchen. The gardener's trio had been too shy to come and join the party with so many there, and Iris was worried they'd be upset with her when she saw them again at school, so Maddy had told her they'd find them, too, and bring them in.

"Ahmed as well?" Iris had said.

"Ahmed, too. And Peter will fetch Emily and Lucy . . ."

"I will," Peter had said.

"And I'll get Grandmama," Richard had said.

It was only now, approaching the villa, hearing Guy call her name, that Maddy realized she'd forgotten all about him. She stalled, cursing her own insensitivity.

"Oh no," said Iris, "poor Guy." (From the mouths of babes.)

"Go and tell him," Maddy said, pushing her off with a hand to her warm, clammy back.

Iris trotted away.

Maddy watched her go, saw Guy smile, open his arms to her. "Hello, sweet one."

Then, something strange.

As Guy took Iris in his arms, he stopped, looked over her black curls toward the villa, his attention apparently caught by something on the large shaded veranda. His stare widened in what seemed like alarm at whatever, or whoever, was there.

Maddy didn't hesitate before following his gaze. It came as instinctively as a breath—held, not taken—to look up, toward the cause of his shock. She gave herself no time to pause, to guess what she might see. Even if she had, she wouldn't have allowed herself to imagine that it would be him, hands in his pockets, eyes dark in his unforgettable face. *Did you really think I could miss another birthday?*

She moved, turning her head in curiosity, and raised her eyes. It took a fraction of a second, no more, and then she saw him there. A white shirt. A linen jacket. Dark hair beneath a panama.

A sob rose in her throat. It swelled, choking her, not coming out.

He stood just back from the balustrade, unblinking, staring at her, as though unable to think what was happening either. She watched him— the taut stillness of his jaw, his cheeks—his face that she loved so well, and her tears finally broke free, a strange, strangled sound with them; of elation, overwhelming joy. For a beat, that was all she knew. *He's alive,* she thought, *alive.* The sheer wonder of it flooded her, filling her lungs, her chest, her fingers, her every single nerve. She longed to run to him, to throw herself into his arms. Her muscles screamed to do it.

But she didn't move.

Nor did he.

She couldn't think what was stopping them.

Then he looked past her, to where Guy was of course holding Iris. Slowly, wrenchingly, she returned to the unyielding reality of the garden they were in. She watched Luke (*Luke*) absorb the sight of their daughter in Guy's arms. *Stop,* she wanted to shout, *don't.*

But he'd already seen.

Pain filled his face, and she felt her own chest fracture.

Because he'd come, at last. After six years of waiting, he'd come.

And it was two months too late.

CHAPTER TWENTY-EIGHT

He left the veranda before she could make herself move to stop him, disappearing without a word. It was almost, agonizingly, as though he'd never been there at all. The party somehow continued—the magician blew his horn, people clapped and laughed, the ponies neighed, everyone seemingly oblivious to how the world had just shifted on its axis—and Maddy was dimly conscious that she should be grateful to have had no vast audience, but all she could think about was that Luke was alive, he was *alive*, and she'd let him go.

She needed to get him back.

Legs shaking with urgency, she made to set off.

But, "Mummy," came Iris's voice, cutting through the heat, the garden's noise, stopping her in her tracks. The only voice that could possibly have done such a thing.

Maddy turned. Iris was running toward her, little face wrought. At the panic in her expression, the confusion in her blue eyes, Maddy closed her own, feeling a stab of shame that she'd been about to leave her without a word. She dropped to the grass, opening her arms—fluid with shock—and picked her up, holding her quaking body tight.

"Why are you crying?" Iris asked.

"I'm not crying," said Maddy, biting the insides of her cheeks to stop herself doing it more.

"That looked like my daddy in your photograph," said Iris.

"It was," said Maddy, picturing him already halfway down the driveway, looking over his shoulder, wondering why she hadn't cared enough to follow. "Iris, I need to go after him. . . ."

"No, Mummy, no." Iris clung to her. "Stay with me."

"I'll only be a few minutes."

"You can't."

"Come, too," said Maddy desperately.

"I want you to stay here," said Iris.

"Let's go into the villa," came Guy's voice, letting Maddy know he'd moved to join them. When had he done that?

"Guy," she began, glancing again at the empty space Luke had left, "I need to—"

"No," said Iris, tightening her hold.

"Let's go inside," said Richard, also suddenly present, face drawn beneath his paper hat, a fraught Alice at his side.

I don't want to go inside, Maddy almost shouted. It was Iris, limpet-like around her, who held her short.

"I'm not letting you go," Iris said, in case there was any doubt.

Maddy drew breath, ready to beg her. But before she could, Iris started crying, too.

"Iris," Maddy said in despair, "Iris, you don't need to . . ."

But Iris wouldn't be placated. Not by any of them. Maddy was sure it wasn't just about Luke. She'd been unsettled all day, after all, and her falling apart now was probably as much to do with the overwhelming party—the upset any six-year-old would feel at a birthday gone so very wrong—as anything. It didn't make consoling her any easier, though. Maddy kissed her tears, her hot round cheeks, and felt sick, because the seconds were flooding by, taking Luke away, and she was still here, unable to follow.

"Come along," said her father, propelling them toward the villa.

Somehow, Maddy put one foot in front of the other. She looked over her shoulder as she went, searching the sunny, throbbing garden for Peter. She couldn't see him, only Della, still with Jeff and the girls, watching the magician. Had Peter seen Luke? Gone after him?

She hoped that he had, and that at least Luke wasn't alone. Peter would explain, too, remind Luke how she loved him, how she'd always loved him.

It's you, she told him silently, holding their desolate daughter, following her husband inside. *It's only ever been you.*

He'd known already that they were married. It was why he'd gone to Guy's villa first, only to be sent on here. Arnold had told him of the wedding, the very morning after everything had come back to him in the King's Fifth. He'd shown him the photographs Diana had sent, and Luke had felt his world end all over again.

But he'd come to India. He'd had to come. He hadn't been able to make sense of . . . anything . . . back in England. After the initial, sickening blow of those clippings had passed, he'd grown angry, determined to set right what had apparently gone so catastrophically wrong. If it had been anyone other than Guy whom Maddy had married, perhaps he'd have waited, written to her first—even considered listening to Emma Lytton suggesting that since Maddy *had* married, perhaps it would be kinder to leave her in ignorance. *She thought you were dead, after all.* But Luke had known, even before he'd set eyes on her just now—struck prone by the thousand and one things even his healed memory hadn't done justice to, not least the overwhelming love just the tiniest movement of her hand, her lips, could send flooding through him—that she would never be content with Guy. She'd used to *joke* about marrying him. *As if I could ever do that.* Seeing her so alone on her parents' lawn, so thin, too sad, had confirmed it. He kicked the dusty driveway, sending stones scattering, cursing, as full of rage as he'd ever been, at *her,* for compromising, giving up on her own right to happiness. He couldn't forgive it of her, he *couldn't.*

"She wouldn't accept you were gone," his mother, Nina, had told him, only a fortnight before, as they'd walked Coco along the windswept beach near their house. Coco had kept by Luke's heels, scampering in the sands, delirious with joy. *Loyal.* "I'm so sorry," Nina had said, eyes watering in the wind, the cold, "even I tried to convince her."

"You don't need to apologize," he'd said, hating her guilt, how grief had aged her—how it had aged both his parents—wishing so much that he could give them both back all the years they'd lost.

"Maddy doesn't need to apologize either," his father had said later, sitting by the fire. "You must remember that, when you're there."

Luke had told him it wasn't an apology he was after.

It still wasn't.

He paused at the villa gates, wiping sweat from his throbbing head. It was hot, too bloody hot. And where was she? Not coming after him, that much was certain. Perhaps she was consoling Iris. Iris, whose birthday he'd known it was (he'd bought her a miniature doctor's kit from Hamleys; it was still in his trunk). Iris, who'd stolen his breath with her round eyes and bouncing curls, the living, unbelievable reality of her, and then broken him, by clutching to Guy as she had, like she wanted him to protect her. Afraid. His own daughter. Petrified. Of *him*.

He clenched his jaw, only just stopping the smarting, useless tears, and kept going, onto the quiet, leafy road.

He was almost halfway to the motor he'd borrowed when the call came from behind.

"Luke. *Luke.* Don't make me run. I really can't."

He knew that voice. It penetrated his grief, his anger, and, in spite of everything, he felt his chest swell. As he turned, squinting through the dappled sunshine, he drew a ragged breath—all the happiness he could manage—seeing his old friend ambling lopsidedly along the road's edge, pale eyes brimming with tears that he at least wasn't checking. The last time Luke had seen him, they'd both been shrouded in gas clouds, surrounded by men—boys like poor Fraser Keaton—dying in agony, shells exploding everywhere. He'd thought them about to die, too. When his memory had returned, he'd been terrified that Peter must have. It had been his parents who'd assured him that Peter was not only still alive, but in India with Maddy and Iris. Luke had become desperate to see him, too—to thank him for being by Maddy's side over the years, there for her always—but, in the hideousness of what had just passed, he'd forgotten to look for him.

How could he have forgotten?

He closed the distance between them, pulling Peter into an embrace, overwhelmed by gratitude, the relief, the utter relief, of his being there.

"My God," Peter said, digging his fingers into his back, "my God. Where have you been?"

"It's a long story," said Luke. "I can't tell it here."

"Then let's get you the hell away," said Peter.

"The docks," said Luke.

"Oh, no," said Peter. "No . . ."

"The docks," Luke repeated. "I'm not going anywhere else."

Maddy didn't go back to Guy's. Not at first, no matter how Guy tried to persuade her that they should, saying she'd find it easier to rest there. She didn't want to rest. She certainly didn't need the draft he said he'd mix for her. She needed *Luke*. Her desperation to be with him—hear his voice, hold him again—was growing by the second, overwhelming her. Questions spiraled endlessly in her mind: *Where have you been? Who were you with?*

Do you still want me?

Want us?

They were all she could hear. But by the time she managed to extricate herself from Iris and Guy long enough to even think of attempting to find him, he was long gone, Peter with him.

"Peter's said he'll telephone," her father told her, stealing a moment while Guy was distracted back out in the garden—heroically smiling and saying goodbye to all the guests, despite his own evident shock, the exhaustion that seemed to be aging him by the minute. "He'll do it just as soon as he can." Richard pulled her into a brief hug. "I spoke to him before he went."

"He promised?" Maddy said.

"He promised."

Maddy nodded, feeling a little easier. She didn't tell Guy about that call, or her frantic impatience for it to come. Even in her stricken state, she saw the awful vulnerability in his eyes, the ashen color of his face, and managed to forget the commotion of her own emotions long enough to ache at his fear. She couldn't hurt him more.

But she sat in her parents' baking drawing room all afternoon, ear tuned for the telephone's trill, fists clenched in anticipation of grabbing the

receiver. No one spoke very much. Her parents did have one strained conversation, but it was done out in the hallway; she saw their tense faces, but
heard none of what they said. Her mother was very quiet afterward, obviously upset, and Maddy wondered if they'd been bickering about which of
her husbands she should remain married to.

My God, she thought, swallowing on her bile. *I have two husbands.*

Two.

"Mummy," said Iris, squirming on her lap, "you're squeezing me too
tight."

"Sorry," she said, forcing her arms loose. "Sorry."

She waited for Iris to ask her about Luke. But she didn't. She said no
more at all about her daddy in the photograph, just sucked her thumb in
a pensive way—perhaps thinking of him, maybe fretting over her ruined
day—and eventually fell into a sweaty, exhausted slumber, which at least
gave Maddy a valid excuse for not going back to Guy's.

"I could carry her," said Guy.

"I don't want to disturb her," Maddy said.

"Best not," said Della, who'd sent her girls home with Jeff, as soon as
she'd got wind of what had happened, and knew all about the expected call.
Whenever Guy moved out of earshot—to fetch Maddy more water, or pour
himself a brandy (bracing)—she whispered to Maddy of how wretched she
felt. "All this time, there was me telling you that he was dead."

"You didn't know," said Maddy.

"I still hate myself for it. What on earth are you going to do?"

Maddy had no idea.

She wouldn't until she saw Luke, she was certain. But three o'clock became four, no one other than Della even attempted to talk of what had
happened—least of all Guy—and still no telephone call came to break the
loaded, sweaty silence. Maddy felt the scrutiny of her parents but couldn't
bring herself to meet their worried stares, lest they ask her something
else she didn't know how to answer. Her mother—who didn't appear to
be speaking to her father at all (or perhaps it was the other way round)—
poured endless pots of tea. She spoke about fetching some sandwiches, too,
but never did it. Della remarked on what a shame it was that the party

hadn't turned out better, and suggested they give Iris another birthday the next day. Guy said he thought that a marvelous idea, then asked Maddy whether they shouldn't wake Iris up so that she'd be able to sleep that night.

"Leave her a while longer," said Richard, "she obviously needs the rest."

When she finally woke, she was—to Maddy's relief—more like herself again, squirming down from Maddy's lap, yawning, stretching, and professing herself hungry. The nap had obviously restored her. (If only everything could be so easily fixed.)

"Is it teatime?" she said.

"It is, little one," said Della.

"Teatime?" said Maddy, looking at the clock in alarm. *Five?* How was it already five?

"I'd better get home," said Della regretfully. "The girls will be tyrannizing Jeff."

"We need to go, too," said Guy, standing, not brooking any resistance this time, taking Iris by the hand.

"Yes," said Richard, with a nod to Maddy that seemed to say he'd call with any news. She wasn't sure he expected there to be, not anymore; it was his furrowed brow. She didn't either, not now she'd seen the time and absorbed just how much had passed since Peter and Luke had left. It terrified her, how long it had been.

What had stopped Peter from getting in touch?

"Come on, dearest," said Guy, oblivious to the cold dread filling her. "We'll have some dinner ourselves, an early night. If this little princess permits."

"I'm not tired," said Iris.

She of course wasn't. Fortified by her sleep (and relieved, Maddy suspected, to be on the other side of her ill-fated party), she chattered the entire way home—about the toy dragon Peter had given her, when she could open the rest of her presents, and how she'd paint a card for Suya and the rest to tell them she was sorry there hadn't been any cake—making it impossible for Maddy to try and speak herself to Guy, let alone think what she might say. Just as before in her parents' drawing room, she waited anxiously for Iris to mention Luke, ask . . . anything . . . about him. But she didn't. It was as though she'd decided to forget he'd come. Maddy almost wished she'd bring him up, despite Guy's presence. It killed her that even Iris was pretending he didn't matter. He mattered. He mattered so very much.

She had to see him. She couldn't wait a moment longer. How many places could he and Peter have gone to? *Not many,* she told herself as she followed Guy and Iris into the villa. Once Iris was settled, she'd go out and find him. Surely Guy would understand that she needed to do that. Yes, of course he would. *Of course.*

He'd hate it, too, though; impossible to pretend otherwise. Her voice was taut with apprehension as she told Iris to run along to her nursery so that she and Guy might talk about grown-up things.

She wondered if he heard it, realized what was coming.

She suspected that he did, and that that was why he overruled her, saying that surely Iris could stay down a while longer. "It is her birthday. Let's have dinner together tonight."

"Really?" said Iris, eyes bursting at the treat. "I can eat with you?"

"You'd like that, would you?" said Guy, with a laugh that was as forced as any Maddy had heard from him.

"Can I have champagne?" Iris asked.

"Lime soda maybe," said Guy, and turned to Maddy. "What do you say? Just this once?"

"Please, Mummy," said Iris, looking, for the first time that day, like she was actually enjoying her birthday. "*Please.*"

Maddy hesitated, almost saying no, but Iris appeared to be actually holding her breath in excitement—after all her tears. How could she ruin that for her? *It is her birthday.* And if she did, wouldn't that only make her resent Luke?

They ate out on the veranda, by the light of burning hurricane lamps. Iris, napkin on lap, was like the cat with the cream for the entire meal, and Guy—whose eyelids were becoming ever heavier with tiredness— nonetheless kept going, telling Iris how sorry he was that he'd ambushed her party with all his friends, and asking if they might do as Della had suggested and have another celebration the next day. "I'll make sure to get away from work for lunch, and we can go for ices at the Sea Lounge."

"Really?" said Iris, looking from him to Maddy, checking that she, too, had heard this wondrous suggestion.

Maddy, who'd heard perfectly, was becoming increasingly annoyed. Guy wasn't stupid; he must realize that Luke (wherever he'd gone) might very well want to see his daughter tomorrow. Now if he asked to (*ask,* to see his own daughter; it broke her heart), Iris wouldn't want to. Just as with this dinner, it was almost as though the treat was designed to shut Luke out. It wasn't fair of Guy to be playing favorites. None of it was fair.

"Really," said Guy to Iris. "Shall we take Emily and Lucy, too?"

"Yes," said Iris, clambering onto his lap, "yes please."

Guy kissed her head.

As if on cue, the bearer grudgingly brought out the chocolate cake Cook seemed to have sent over from her parents', resplendent with six sparklers. Iris leaned over them, her ecstatic face illuminated by the glow, and blew them all out. Guy told her to make a wish, and she closed her eyes, lips moving silently.

"What did you wish for?" Maddy managed to ask.

"I can't tell you," said Iris, beaming not at her but up at Guy, "otherwise it won't come true."

Tell me, Maddy wanted to say, hit by the sickening hunch that it involved which father she'd prefer, *I'm not sure I want it to come true.*

It was after nine by the time the endless meal was over. Somehow Maddy convinced Iris into being tired enough for bed and took her upstairs. She bathed her as quickly as her wriggling insistence on making a birthday tea with the bathwater would allow, read her a short story, and tucked her in. Throughout it all, Iris remained disturbingly silent on the subject of her daddy in the photograph. By an effort of will, Maddy didn't bring him up either. She couldn't, *wouldn't,* force things with Iris.

It was only when she bent to kiss her—resigned to her saying nothing—that Iris took her thumb from her mouth and dozily mentioned him again.

"Where did he go, Mummy?"

"I don't know," Maddy said, stroking her hair from her forehead, relieved—beyond relieved—that she'd asked.

"Will I see him again?"

"Would you like that?"

"I don't know," said Iris.

Maddy did her best not to flinch. "I'm sure he'd like to see you," she said.

Iris turned on her side, snuggling down. "His face is nicer in real life," she said.

"Yes," said Maddy, "he has a very nice face."

"But not as happy," said Iris, closing her eyes.

"No," said Maddy softly.

From the mouths of babes.

"Good night, Mummy."

"Good night," said Maddy, kissing her one more time.

Stopping only to pull the mosquito net down and dim the lamp, she left, returning to her and Guy's rooms, determined to tell him that she was leaving directly to find Luke, not let him evade her again.

He was sitting on her bed, watching the door, obviously waiting for her to come through it. He'd removed his jacket, his collar, and had the top button of his shirt undone. Now that he was no longer putting on a show for Iris, he looked beaten. The concaves of his cheeks were gray in the lamplight. His shoulders were leaden. Maddy paused, hand to the doorframe, feeling her impatience dissolve at the pitiable sight of him.

"I don't want to do this now," Guy said, before she could attempt to speak. "Can we both sleep first, please?"

"I don't think I can sleep," said Maddy.

"Then I'll mix you a draft," he said. "You need to rest. We both do."

"Guy," she said, as gently as she could, "I need to see—"

"Maddy," he said, cutting her off before she could say "Luke," "not tonight. I'm begging you." He raised his tired eyes to hers. "I'm not going to give up on us. You're my wife. Iris is my daughter. . . ."

"Guy . . ."

"I'm too exhausted to fight," he said, "and I'll lose if I try, so please don't make me do it now."

"I don't want to fight."

"I meant fight for you." His voice cracked on the words.

She opened her mouth, but didn't know what to say. Her throat felt suddenly very tight.

"Please," he said. "Can we just . . . wait."

She hesitated.

"Please," he repeated.

She stared a moment longer. He stared back, gaze laden with entreaty. It caused her pain, physical pain, to see it. And he really had asked her for so little in their short marriage. For everything he'd given her, one short night of rest seemed the very least she could do for him.

He insisted on mixing her some sleeping granules before he went to his own room. She didn't drink them, but threw the vial down the sink. She bathed, though, got into her nightgown, and climbed into bed, pulling the sheet over her, the mosquito net down. She even closed her eyes.

He didn't come to kiss her good night. He certainly didn't ask if *he might*. She wasn't sure if he took an aid of his own, but before long she heard the low, steady breaths of deep sleep coming from his room. She waited, sheet clutched, until she felt certain he wasn't about to wake and, blood pumping so rapidly she was afraid everyone in the villa must hear, she rose, discarded her nightdress and pulled on a loose gown, then, carrying her shoes, slipped quietly from her room, past Iris's door—peeking in to make sure she, too, was fast asleep, little chest rising and falling, her comfort blanket beside her—and then down the stairs, out into the balmy warmth of the rustling front garden.

She didn't know where in the city she was going to go first. And she didn't take the motor Guy had given her to drive; it would have felt very wrong to do that. Instead, she hastened from the driveway—the crunch of her footsteps the only sound besides the cicadas and night insects—onto the deserted road. She carried on down to the bottom of the hill, which was much busier, lighter, filled by locals still finishing their long days: eating and drinking outside their homes, hanging laundry, sweeping front steps in saris, feeding their tethered cows . . . She passed them all as she made for the tram stop and the line of waiting rickshaws, but it wasn't until she asked one of the wallahs to take her to Peter's house that she knew that was where she was going to go.

But they weren't at Peter's house.

Or at the Taj; not at the Sea Lounge's waterside tables, or in the near-empty bar, the even emptier restaurant. Luke hadn't checked into a room either.

"You're sure," she said to the clerk at reception.

"Quite, memsahib," he said, swallowing a yawn.

Frowning her thanks, she left. Outside the hotel's grand front entrance, she ignored the gleaming saloon motors and carriages, asked the porter to hail her another rickshaw, and climbed into it. She wouldn't worry, not yet. Not when she had plenty of other places to try.

She went to Watson's and scoured its bar and restaurants, too—caring not at all about the looks her hot, sweaty breathlessness was engendering from the staff and handful of late-night guests (*let them look,* she thought)—but he wasn't there either. It was the same at the city's various restaurants, all of which were closing, and the Yacht Club (oh, how it stung to go back there). By the time she'd finished searching the deserted nooks and crannies of the Gymkhana Club—the billiards room, the upstairs bar, the downstairs bar, even the palm-fringed playing fields—she could no longer keep her panic at bay. She stood at the lodge's leafy entrance, clammy fists clenched, teeth gritted on her fear and frustration. Where was he? *Where?*

She didn't know. And she could only think of one more place to try. She walked this time, fast, heedless of the risk she was exposing herself to in being out alone so late, entirely preoccupied with telling herself not to hope, to expect anything. *There's no point. Why would he be there?*

He won't be.

He really won't.

She truly thought she believed her own assurances. She became convinced of it.

And yet, when she arrived at Luke's old rooms and found them as shuttered and abandoned as they'd ever been, it crushed her. She looked from the black windows to the padlocked door and didn't even try not to cry. She'd been swallowing her tears for hours now, was exhausted from her hopeless chase, her ankle so sore, and the sobs broke from her. Gulping on them, she sank down, onto the steps he, too, had touched, head in hands, wishing for so much, and most of all that she'd just run straight to him when she'd seen him on the veranda, *made* him stay.

"Where are you?" she said, again and again, into her palms. "Where have you gone now?"

She wasn't sure how long she stayed there. She was oblivious to time passing, the slow quietening of the surrounding streets as the hours edged into deep night. But eventually her sobs subsided, all her tears dried. They always did that in the end. She rose shakily to her feet, pressed her fingertips to the swollen skin of her cheekbones, and, limping a little on her smarting ankle, left.

She wasn't really conscious of the journey home. She supposed she must have found another rickshaw and paid the wallah to take her to Guy's villa, because she arrived back at his gate. She thanked her driver, fumbled in her purse for rupees, paid him too much (she guessed, from his startled brow), and wearily climbed down onto the soft verge of the road as he bicycled away.

She didn't realize she wasn't alone.

She made to go through the gates and didn't see him waiting behind her on the other side of the road, where the jungle dropped down to the sea.

When he spoke—that voice which she hadn't heard in too, too long, but which was deep, and warm, and his, *his*—it made her jump.

"Hello, Miss Bright," he said.

She caught a sharp breath, spun on the spot.

He stood, just as he'd stood on the terrace: hands in his pockets, stare fixed on her. He was all darkness and shadow, a silhouette beneath the leaves, but breathing, living; real.

Real.

Her sore eyes filled again, her tears not spent after all. "I wish I were her," she managed to say.

"Not Mrs. Devereaux?"

"Her, too," she choked.

They were still a second longer. And then they both moved, fast, urgently. She sank into his hold, just as she'd ached to do every day and every night since he'd left her back in 1914. She gripped onto him, unable to absorb she was really doing it, harder, inhaling his warmth, his touch, his scent of soap, cigarettes . . . She felt his arms tighten around her, his spine beneath his shirt; his every single heartbeat. He held her tighter, so close, as though never to let her go. She never wanted him to let her go. She reached up, kissing him through her tears, feeling the wonder of him kissing her back, crying more because she realized now that in all these years of believing him alive, she really had given up on him coming back. But he had, he *had*, and she'd missed him so very, very much.

"Where have you been?" he asked.

"Where have *you* been?" she said.

His cheeks moved; the hint of a smile. His smile that she loved. "You first," he said.

"I've been looking for you," she said. "Peter was meant to telephone . . ."

"I stopped him," he said, his eyes swimming in hers. "I needed time. I went to the docks, leased my old rooms . . ."

"I was just at them."

"I came here," he said. "I've been staring at Guy's windows, imagining you inside."

"Don't," she said, moving to kiss him again, "please don't."

He pulled away, lips inches from hers. "I'm scared," he said, "of what you've done. I need you, Maddy. I need us."

"I need us, too," she said.

"Peter told me . . ."

"No," she said, and this time she made him kiss her. "I don't want to talk about Peter. I don't want to talk."

She only wanted to feel his touch, his skin, his warmth—become convinced that he truly was alive again—and have that, only that.

Softly, she pushed him, toward the jungle, invisibility. She felt his hesitation, his foreboding, *I'm scared*, and kissed him harder, afraid of his fear. "Please," she said, "please," and exhaled as she felt him give in, give himself over, any protest at an end.

He picked her up, backing her against a tree, kissing her throat, her collarbone, needing to be convinced that she was real, too.

"I'm here," she said, "you're here."

"We're here," he said.

She arched her neck, closing her sore, swollen eyes, and forgot the black villa less than a hundred yards away. She felt his hands on her waist, her thighs, and lost herself utterly in the thrill of his touch, his *being*.

She didn't think about Guy.

She didn't imagine him in his bed, asleep and oblivious, so trusting and good and gentle and kind.

She held on to Luke, telling him how she loved him, hearing him say it back, and blanked her mind to how many times Guy had said the same, too. And his words, just a few short hours before: that she was his wife, Iris his child.

I'm not going to give up on us.

CHAPTER TWENTY-NINE

They were mowing the lawns, that morning. He saw the contract workers out there in the early-spring sunshine, pushing the cutters laboriously up and down the garden's long banks, painting it with dark and light stripes. The scent of shorn grass wafted in through the open windows, filling the room with sweetness; the promise of summer to come.

He'd been writing; he saw that from the notepad on the table before him. The page was half full; the regular slant of a hand he supposed must be his, except he couldn't recall having picked a pen up. And yet, he was holding one. He turned his fingers, weathered with age, and stared at the thin, cylindrical object in his palm, forehead creasing. He looked down, at the words he'd written, and his frown deepened even more.

That night in those trees was one of the happiest and saddest of my life. I almost forgot my dread, my awful jealousy. I believed you when you said that you'd always be with me. I truly trusted that I'd never lose you again.

But I was wrong. You were wrong.

Today is one of my clear days. I remember it all, you see. Every part of our story is with me, and I wish it could always be so, except if I could, I would forget our end.

The part where you left me.

I wish so much that you'd never done it, Maddy. There's so much I wish I could have said. I need you to know that . . .

He stared at the truncated sentence, unable to think what he'd been about to write next.

Or who Maddy was.

She was important. He knew that much from the words he'd written. He *felt* it, too. He closed his eyes, straining to think who she was, what she'd been to him, but no, nothing, *nothing,* came. He clenched his pen, nearly snapping it in his determination, his frustration, but it didn't help. All he had was blackness where the past decades should have been. An awful void that stretched back and back to when he'd first been a patient as a young man in another hospital: a soldier in convalescent blues. He'd written in journals then. He recalled that. He could picture them on the shelf in his room, as vividly as if he'd left them yesterday. Had he been chasing memories then as well? He thought he had. He knew that he'd burned those journals in the end; he and Arnold had done it together, and raised glasses of whiskey to the fire.

What had happened to Arnold?

He didn't know.

And who, *who* was Maddy?

Shaking, feeling a sickening disorientation that was at once familiar and entirely foreign, he threw his pen on top of the notepad, and pushed both away.

"Another letter?" said one of the nurses—a young woman with freckles and a quiet voice—who peered over his shoulder and read his words, then smiled, but with a sadness that made it hardly a smile at all.

"Who is Maddy?" he asked her, and was shocked at how firm his voice sounded when he felt so much the opposite of strong.

She didn't answer, but bit her lip, as though deciding whether to say.

"Please," he said.

"She was your wife," she said slowly, and he could tell she wasn't sure she should be doing it.

"Was?" he said.

But she wouldn't say more. She folded his letter and put it in her apron pocket, and refused even to let him know what had happened to the woman who'd apparently been his wife, or how long he'd been living in this place he found himself in.

"You have to tell me," he said, and to his shame, his voice began to shake.

"You'll panic again," she said soothingly.

"What do you mean, again?" he said.

"Leave it now," she said. "Emma will be here any minute."

"Emma?" he said, heart pummeling now. Who was Emma?

"Yes," said the nurse, "Emma Lytton. Your dear, dear friend. Just wait, she'll explain everything."

CHAPTER THIRTY

Bombay, 1921

Maddy didn't go back to Guy's villa that night. After she and Luke had collapsed against one another, breathless, his head pressed to her neck, her cheek to his hair, *you're here,* they walked slowly, fingers entwined, down to the beach; those silent, white sands he'd taken her to on their very first day out, and where she'd grieved for him on every New Year's.

"I hate the thought of you doing that," he said, pulling her closer.

"Peter was with me," she said.

"I wish he hadn't had to be," he said.

They both wished that.

They sat beneath the palms until sunrise, never letting the other go. Maddy knew she shouldn't stay—that Guy would be worried if he woke and found her not home—but she was in Luke's arms, could feel his breaths going in, out, and nothing, not even the thought of Guy's hurt, could compel her to leave.

They talked, about so much. He asked her to tell him more about Iris. "Every single detail," he said, "I want to know it. Don't leave anything out."

"That's going to take a while," she said.

"I have time," he said. "What kind of baby was she? Did she sleep?"

"Not for months," said Maddy, and went on, pulling everything she could from her memory: first steps, first words, what had made her laugh, cry, favorite meals; all of it. He never lifted his eyes from her as she spoke; she watched the way they moved, hungry, impatient, insatiable for more.

"I love her," he said. "I've never met her, but I've always loved her. So much."

"She'll love you. Just as much."

"She was afraid of me, earlier. She ran to Guy." He tried to keep his voice level, but she heard the hurt there.

She hated it; hated that it had all had to happen like that.

"She's six," she told him, "and was upset anyway before you came. That party was horrendous." She reached up, touching his face—the still unbelievable warmth in his skin—needing to make it better for him. "She'll love you," she repeated.

"I've bought her a doctor's kit," he said. "My mother's idea . . ."

"Thank God for your mother," said Maddy. "No more dolls."

She asked him how Nina and his father had been when they'd discovered he was alive, and he told her of how he'd surprised them at home; a Sunday three weeks before.

"You do like your surprises," she said.

"I wanted to tell them myself," he said, running his fingers up and down her arm. "It was so . . . surreal, being at the house. It was all exactly as I'd remembered it. The garden, the front door, the seagulls on the roof . . . Just the same." He stared out at the black sea, remembering. "My mother, she was in the kitchen, just sitting in a chair and looking at this cupboard I was meant to have fixed."

"I know about that cupboard," she said.

He smiled. (That smile.) "She told you?"

"She said you were drunk when you tried to mend it."

He laughed at that.

She loved his laugh.

"Anyway," he said, "she didn't hear me there. I said to her, 'Why not let me fix that properly for you?' My God, her face . . ." His smile spread, taking over his. "You should have seen her, Maddy."

"I wish I had," she said.

"Then my father came in," he said, "and . . . well, it was . . . incredible."

"I expect they didn't want you to leave," she said, trying to imagine letting Iris go if she'd only just got her back like that.

"They knew I had to," he said, expression becoming serious once more. "I had to come, Maddy."

"Of course you had to come," she said.

There was no question about that.

They talked of the war, of course, what had happened to him, to her, to so many others, not least Fraser Keaton—sweet, young Fraser—whom Luke had thrown his jacket over, and who had been buried all this time with Luke's tags, his photo, so easily mistaken in the chaos of the battle.

"I went to see his family," Luke said, "just before I sailed. It was awful. Beyond awful." He stared at her. "His parents were so . . . grateful, to finally know. I lied to them, told them it was quick."

"I'd have done just the same thing," she said softly, eyes burning at their heartbreak.

They spoke of Ernest, too, still at the King's Fifth, waiting to be moved to his next home. The agony of how narrowly Peter had missed seeing Luke when he'd visited Ernest, three months before Luke had arrived at the hospital back in 1915.

"I can't think about it," said Maddy. "I'll go mad if I do."

"Peter thought he saw me, you know," Luke said. "On the Menin Road, after I was injured." His brow creased. "He told me yesterday."

It took Maddy a second to absorb what he'd said. As she did, and remembered all the times Peter had sworn there was no chance Luke could be alive, she felt her spine lengthen in confusion, disbelief. "He *saw* you?"

"Thought," Luke corrected her. "He assumed it was a hallucination, blood loss." He exhaled a short sigh. "Maybe it was. Your husband helped convince him anyway."

"Guy knew?" said Maddy. "Guy?" She sat up straighter, confusion turning to anger. "He never said. Neither of them *said*."

"Peter hates himself for it."

She almost said, *So he should,* but stopped herself just in time. She recalled Peter's grief when he'd returned to India, the agony ravaging his too-pale face as he'd spoken to her of Luke's death. *Don't make me tell you what I saw.*

"He was always so sure you'd been killed," she said.

"I don't blame him," said Luke. "The way he looked when that shell exploded." His eyes darkened in recollection. "You can't imagine." He shook his head. "I wouldn't want you to."

She stared into his face, imagining regardless. "He still should have told me," she said. "Guy should have told me."

"Guy would have seen more death than the rest of us," said Luke. "Life was what felt impossible out there."

"You're defending him?"

"I don't want to," he said, with an unhappy attempt at a laugh, "believe me. But I don't think there was anything sinister in him keeping it from you."

"And what about Diana?" she said.

He raised a brow. "We really have to talk about her?"

"I'd like to know why she didn't write to me when she first saw you," Maddy said, realizing as she spoke just how much it was needling her. "I'd have come, risked the U boats."

"Well, I'm glad you didn't do that."

"Seriously, Luke." She pulled herself up onto her knees, facing him straight on. "She's always gossiped; why would she have kept this to herself?"

He shrugged, shook his head, with a carelessness she couldn't understand. "I don't know."

"You're not angry at her? I'm angry. . . ."

"I can see that."

"I'm going to speak to her, actually."

"Don't," he said. "Please don't. What can you possibly gain from it?"

"I might feel better. . . ."

"By talking to Diana?" he said, making her smile against her will. "Please," he said, reaching for her, "leave it alone."

"All these years, though," she said, and felt tears pricking once more, through her smile—of sadness, such sadness, at all that could have been. "It feels so . . . needless."

"But done," he said. "It's all done."

"How can you be so philosophical about it?"

"I haven't been," he said. "I wasn't this afternoon, when I saw you in the garden."

"Then . . ."

"I've had time," he said, "weeks to come to terms with it." His gaze bore into hers; so alive, so his. "I was beside myself earlier, and then I remembered . . ."

"Remembered?"

"Why I came," he said. "All the years we've got left." He rested his forehead against hers. "It's what happens now that matters."

"We know what happens," she said. "We start again. You, me, and Iris."

"It's not that simple."

"Why?" she said, pulling back. "Why not?"

"Because you're married."

"To you," she said. "I'm married to *you*."

"No," he said, "to Guy."

"I married you first," she protested, but even as she did, she remembered what he'd said to her before, back at Guy's gate. *I'm scared, of what you've done,* and felt her own fear creep back, trickling through her. "Luke," she said, "we're *married*."

"I died."

"No," she said, "you didn't."

"I did. Legally, I did. I saw a lawyer before I left." He stared. "Guy is your husband, not me."

"No," she shook her head, "no. It can't be right."

The pain in his eyes, his face, told her it was.

"Oh God," she said, pressing her hand to her head, trying to take it in, feeling sick, shaky with dread, because she couldn't see a way out. A divorce would take years. You had to be married at least three. Even then, Guy would have to sue her for adultery, since she wasn't allowed to divorce him, not unless he'd committed a crime. It would all be dragged through the courts, and poor Iris . . .

"It doesn't need to be divorce," said Luke, taking her hand. "We can request an annulment."

"An annulment?" she said. "That's better?"

"Quicker," he said. "Less public, apparently. But Guy will need to give his consent."

"Then I'll ask him for it," she said, and felt her nausea grow at the prospect.

"You're sure?" Luke asked.

"Of course I'm sure," she said. Whatever her dread, she'd never been so certain of anything. She turned, looking out to sea, the horizon she'd dreamed of crossing thousands and thousands of times before. "I want us to go home," she said. "I've never stopped fantasizing about your house in Richmond."

"Your house now. You inherited it."

"Ours, then."

"I gather you refused to sell it."

"I was waiting for the market to improve," she said, and smiled, in spite of herself, as he reached for her and kissed her again, dispelling, for a few short seconds, all of their worries.

She leaned back against him, pulling his arms around her. They sat like that for some time, breathing the thick night air, both watching the rippling sea, both silent. For herself, she couldn't help anymore but think of Guy, and what it was going to do to him when she shattered the family they'd so recently created. Iris, too, would be very upset, of that she was almost certain. But it had to happen, it all had to happen. . . .

"Peter told me you panicked before the wedding," said Luke, breaking into her anxiety, letting her know where his thoughts had been. "I was going to say before, up at the villa . . . I wish you hadn't gone through with it."

"I had to," she said.

"Peter said that, too."

"Everyone was in town," she said, compelled to explain. "The viceroy had come. I don't know what might have happened to my father. As for Guy . . ." She broke off, just picturing how broken he'd have been, then felt worse herself, because it was hardly going to be any different now.

"You had your wedding night at the Taj," said Luke.

"Don't," she said.

"I can't bear the thought of it," he said.

"Then don't think," she said. "Please, just don't think."

"When will you talk to him?"

"Soon," she said. "It has to be soon." And, because she'd been wondering it all night, but hadn't been able to bring herself to ask, "How long can you stay?"

"For however long it takes you to leave," he said, and dipped his head, looking at her. "Please, don't let that be too long."

Inevitably, the horizon lightened, gradually turning from palest yellow to gold with the rising sun. Reluctantly, slowly, Luke walked with her back to the villa. There was nowhere else for her to go. It was impossible to leave him. She kissed him—lingeringly, holding on to his hands for as long as she might—promising to come to his rooms before the day was out.

"Will you tell Guy that's what you're doing?"

"I don't know," she said.

"I don't want to sneak around, Maddy. I can't stand this being furtive."

"I don't want that either," she said. "But I'm so scared of hurting him. . . ."

"Waiting won't make that easier."

She sighed, acknowledging it. "I'll see how he is this morning," she said, "tell him however much feels right."

She had every intention of doing just that. Her resolve hardened with every step she took down the quiet, dawn-lit driveway. *Waiting won't make it easier.* She let herself into the villa's shaded front hall, braced to go straight upstairs to his room, let him know that she'd seen Luke, at the very least.

But there was a note in Guy's hand waiting for her on the porch table. Frowning, loose hair falling over her shoulder, she stooped to pick it up.

Maddy dearest,
All was silent in your room, I didn't want to wake you. Iris is still fast asleep, too, hopefully dreaming of ice cream. I've had to go to work, but have sent word to your parents and Della to meet us at the Taj at noon. Your father can tell Peter. I will see you all there—and hope Iris can contain her excitement, and that you have slept well.
                                        I love you, my dear,
                                                Your Guy

She reread the words, part relieved at the reprieve, but mostly uneasy. *All was silent in your room.* Had he really not checked on her himself?

In his shoes, she would have checked.

Or had he stopped himself, preferring not to know that she wasn't there? She imagined him outside her door, pensive, listening for the sound of her breath, the creak of her mattress, hoping . . . She closed her eyes, lids grainy from lack of sleep, and saw his crushed expression when he heard nothing, feeling the awful hurt he must have felt, the betrayal.

Was that why he'd left so early for the hospital? To avoid running into her coming back?

Deciding the answer was almost certainly yes, she gripped his note, re-playing his happiness these past months—his smiles, his laughter with Iris, his euphoria when she, Maddy, had said she'd marry him—and, thinking of how very long he'd been alone before that, felt herself grow heavy.

I'm not going to give up on us, he'd said. She remembered that now.

And he wouldn't, of course; not on her, not on Iris. Not willingly. Good and kind as he might be, he was also smart, very determined, and no victim.

It had been stupidly naive of her to think that the only difficulty was going to be in *asking* him for the annulment. Torturous as that was going to be—especially given his disinclination to let her talk to him at all—she realized there was a much worse prospect to consider.

The very strong possibility that he wouldn't consent to there being an annulment at all.

Sickeningly dubious on the likelihood of an annulment himself, Luke stared after her as she disappeared into the house, aching to call her back. It felt wrong, deeply wrong, to watch her go anywhere he wasn't able to follow. If he could have, he'd have stayed on that beach with her forever.

He paused a second longer, reliving the moment when he'd realized it was her in that rickshaw. He'd wanted to shout, to punch the air in relief, elation. Even with all Peter's assurances, it had meant . . . everything . . . that she hadn't been inside with Guy, but out, trying to find him, as desper-ate as he was.

He ran his tongue over his bruised lips. He could still feel her kiss. He could smell her scent. She was so much the same—her voice, her smile, her

laugh and every gesture; worth every second of these years he'd spent trying to get back to her. More, much more.

He'd do it all again if he had to.

He turned from the villa, away from its dark windows, its creeping
plants and empty balconies, unable to stand the thought that she was now
in it. Guy's motor wasn't in the driveway. He comforted himself with that.
For now, at least, he had no need to torture himself with the idea of Maddy
with him—or Iris chatting to him, with her voice that he still hadn't heard
beyond his own imagination.

With a long, steadying breath, he set off, not down the hill, but up it,
back to Maddy's parents' house. Much as he wanted to go straight to his old
rooms (he'd hadn't slept since he'd woken on the ship the morning before
and was desperate to collapse on the soft mattress, muted sunlight seeping
through the shutters, the salty breeze coming off the sea), he had to see
Maddy's mother first, and tell her what he hadn't had the heart to admit to
Maddy: that he knew all about the letter Diana had written to her, back in
1916, saying she'd seen a man just like him at the King's Fifth.

I'd have come again myself, Diana had written to Arnold, along with
the clippings she'd sent. *I absolutely would have, had Alice not been so
sure it was impossible Luke was alive. She made me swear not to give his
wife, Maddy, false hope. What could one do? I trust no blame is cast in this
direction.*

Luke had cast rather a lot of blame.

At first.

He'd been incandescent with Alice. He'd gone over and over the endless
days and months and seasons he'd sat alone, waiting—his parents grieving,
Maddy grieving—railing at how they need never have happened, if only
she'd *done* something, told Maddy.

It was Arnold who'd talked him round in the end.

"Do you know how many letters we get from relatives?" Arnold had
said. "Hundreds, more than hundreds, begging us to tell them their sons
or husbands might be here." His eyes had been intent behind his spectacles.
"Their hope," he'd waved at Diana's letter, "this false hope Alice was worried about, it's torture for them."

"But this wasn't just hope," Luke had tried to argue. "I was here."

"Alice wouldn't have thought that possible," Arnold had said. "You weren't reported missing. There was no *presumed*. No one guessed that poor boy's body wasn't yours. They buried *you*. You were dead. Maddy would have had a telegram, probably all your belongings sent to her, a letter from your CO. . . ."

"But Diana . . ."

"Said that she'd seen someone who looked like you. Only that." Arnold had sighed. "You've told me how Alice loves Maddy. Think how hard she'd have found it to see her suffering." He'd paused, giving Luke time to do just that. "In doing this," Arnold had gone on, "she'd simply have been protecting her."

"From me?"

"From more grief," Arnold had said, "which would have been waiting for Maddy if she'd come all this way and found Diana had been wrong."

"She wasn't wrong. . . ."

"Alice didn't *know* that," Arnold had said. "And I'm no gambler, but I would stake a great deal on the probability that she's thought about it every day since, wondering if she did the right thing."

She knew now, of course, that she hadn't. Luke had seen her the afternoon before in the garden, behind Maddy. The shock, then alarm that had filled her face when she'd seen him.

It was why he had to talk to her.

He turned through the gates, squinting in the rapidly intensifying sunlight, feeling the sweat prickle beneath his shirt, and made for the house.

He'd meant what he'd said to Maddy earlier. He had no interest in trawling over the past, all the might-have-beens. They'd been granted this second chance that millions would never have; it was a gift, a privilege.

It really was only what they did with it that mattered now.

CHAPTER THIRTY-ONE

Alice studied Luke from the drawing room window, remembering how she'd used to watch him and Madeline idle down the driveway back when they'd first been courting. Only this time she didn't attempt to tell herself that everything was going to be fine.

Nothing would be now, she was sure.

She was up, dressed for church, not that she could face going. She hadn't slept. She felt wrung out from tiredness, shock. And guilt. So much guilt and fear.

Richard was hardly speaking to her. She'd told him, of course, about Diana's letter, as soon as they'd all come inside from the party.

"And you never thought to speak of this sooner?" he'd said, voice straining with the effort of not shouting.

"I didn't think there was any point," she'd said.

"In telling *me*?" he'd said. "Her father?"

"I'm so sorry. . . ."

"For what part of it?" he'd hissed, anger growing, as livid as she'd ever known him.

"Everything," she'd said, even as her mind had raced, forcing her to face up to the desperate hurt she'd so unwittingly contributed to—not just Madeline's, not just Iris's and Luke's, but Luke's parents' (she couldn't stand it), Peter's, Luke's other friends', his aunts', his uncles'—so fast she couldn't absorb the magnitude of it. She'd fought her tears, knowing she had no right to them, sorry for everything.

"I'd have made you tell her," Richard had said. "Or," he'd stared, "is that why you kept so quiet? Because you knew I would, and you didn't want her going anywhere. . . ."

"No," she'd said, aghast that he could even think it. "*No.*"

"Well, you got what you always wanted, Alice. She married Guy. And look how happy it's made her."

"Richard . . ."

He'd walked away. From her. In just the same way as she'd walked away from him too many times in their marriage.

She might not have done it so frequently had she had the faintest idea how very much it hurt.

She needed Richard to forgive her, to *talk* to her, understand how afraid she was: of what she'd done, how Madeline would hate her for it, and—more than anything—that Madeline would choose Luke, leave India, and take Iris with her. She clenched her cold fingers, feeling the pressure of her terror in her bones, her muscles, overwhelming her.

She couldn't think what she was going to do.

And now Luke was almost at the house. She couldn't stop looking at him. She'd been too blinded by panic to see him properly the day before, but she saw him now. As she did, and absorbed the truth of the life in him—the warmth in his handsome face (that face she'd thought buried beneath the soil of Flanders), the color in his brown curls; the rise and fall of his chest as he jogged the final few paces to the porch—she felt something in her soften, despite everything. She'd grown to love him in the end. In her way. Hard as she'd fought against it, he'd won her over: with his heart, his fun, and how happy he'd always made Madeline. She recalled how she'd wept, back when she'd wired him about Iris's birth, full of grief at what he was enduring, and all that he was missing.

Your family is waiting for you, she'd written, and had only wanted that he should come back.

She was glad that he was alive. She *was*.

But everything had changed. Madeline and Iris had moved on.

Was it so wrong that she wished he'd just stayed away?

He knocked at the door.

She turned, but made no move to answer it.

She knew why he'd come. She'd been expecting his call. Hadn't Diana said that she'd *made mention* of all she, Alice, had concealed to his doctor?

Alice didn't blame him for wanting to confront her. But nor did she feel equal to facing whatever he might say.

She was too ashamed to face him.

She hung back as Ahmed let him in, just as he must have done the day before. She heard—from the warm familiarity with which Ahmed greeted Luke in Urdu, and Luke's own friendly reply (so wrenching to hear that low, vibrant voice again)—where Ahmed's loyalty lay, and felt a familiar tug of pity for poor Guy; he really didn't deserve to come this constant second place.

And now Richard was clattering down the stairs. She sat back on the window ledge as he, too, greeted Luke with a delighted enthusiasm he'd always withheld from Guy—even after he'd grudgingly accepted the engagement.

"My God," he said, "Luke, *Luke*. Come here. . . ."

Alice pictured him pulling Luke into an embrace, slapping his back.

"Richard," said Luke, "it's so good to see you."

"It's bloody marvelous to see you, my boy."

My boy.

Alice shut her eyes.

If only she had it in her to feel such undiluted joy. But then Richard wasn't trapped here in India. He could follow Madeline and Iris if they went. He'd always been able to follow.

Richard invited Luke to take breakfast. To Alice's relief, he declined, saying he couldn't stay long.

"You've seen Maddy?" said Richard.

"Yes," said Luke, and Alice swallowed dryly. Even through the door, she could hear the love in his voice; as true as it had ever been.

They talked on. Alice, hand to her throat, listened to it all: Luke answering Richard's questions about what had happened to him—his lost jacket, his tags, the desperate tragedy of Fraser ("Oh," said Richard heavily, "oh God . . ."), how he, Luke, had come to on the Menin Road, only to black out again—and telling him in turn of how he'd returned to India for Madeline and Iris.

"I can't apologize for it," he said.

"I wouldn't expect you to," said Richard.

She heard Luke ask for her, Alice, and felt a spike of alarm, but Richard said she was indisposed (for which she was cowardly grateful), and that he would gladly take a message.

She wondered if she was imagining it when Luke said what the message was, and that he would never be the one to mention Diana's letter to Madeline.

"You're sure?" said Richard dubiously.

"Quite," Luke said, and went on, saying that she'd been angry enough when he'd told her how Peter, almost dead himself, had only *possibly* seen him back in Ypres. "Alice needs to be able to speak to her about this herself," he said. "And if she doesn't want to, well," he paused, "I'll respect that, too."

"You mustn't feel obliged," said Richard.

"It's not about that," said Luke. "There's been enough pain. I don't want this to come between them. Not more than it has to."

Alice slumped back on the ledge. She'd expected such fury. Her heart pounded at Luke's understanding; the unfathomable generosity of it.

She almost gathered herself sufficiently to get up and thank him in person.

If he hadn't left so quickly, she might even have managed it.

She'd like to think she would have.

"You don't deserve this," said Richard, once he came in to find her. "And whatever Luke says, you have to tell Maddy. You owe her that."

"I know," Alice managed to say.

"Not today," said Richard. "She's got enough to think about."

"I know that, too," said Alice.

Richard gave her a cold look. "I suppose now I know why I have the pleasure of Alf's employment."

She didn't attempt to defend herself. There was no defense.

It made Luke's kindness even harder to understand.

"It's not hard," said Richard, with crippling disdain. "He loves our daughter." Another hard stare. "This is what love is."

"I know what love is," she said, and this time she couldn't help her tears, because it broke her in two that he could suggest otherwise.

"Do you?" he said wearily.

Yes, she wanted to shout, *I know. It's what I have for you, for Madeline and Iris. . . .*

But before she could, he turned on his heel and left.

It was as though he couldn't stand to hear it.

He said no more to her that morning. He didn't suggest going to church either. And although he opened the motor door for her when they left to collect Madeline and Iris for lunch, he did it wordlessly. He kept his eyes on the shaded road for the short drive to Guy's, sighing deeply as they drew to a halt.

Madeline came out to meet them. She looked as weary as Alice felt, her paleness accentuated by the navy dress and cloche hat she wore. Alice wasn't sure why she'd chosen the color. She never normally wore anything dark.

Her mood, perhaps.

She wondered if her meeting with Luke hadn't gone as well as he might have been hoping.

Or was it being back at this villa that was upsetting her?

No. She shook her head mentally. *Stop second-guessing.*

You will run mad.

"Hello, darling," Richard said to Madeline, the affection in his voice a stark contrast to the coolness with which he'd been treating Alice all morning.

"Can we not talk about anything?" Madeline said, embracing him. "Iris doesn't seem herself again, and I don't want to ruin another day for her."

"You have our word," said Richard.

"Of course," said Alice, who had no intention of bringing any of it up anyway. (Her age-old preference for saying nothing when there was too much unspeakable to say.)

"Thank you," said Madeline with a tired smile.

Alice struggled to smile back. She discovered she couldn't quite meet Madeline's eye either. The awful secret she'd kept, and the prospect of admitting it to her, made it impossible.

She looked toward the house instead. "Where's Iris now?" she asked.

"Upstairs changing," said Madeline. "She spilled milk on her dress."

"I'll go and fetch her," said Alice, seizing on the opportunity to escape her guilt for a few minutes.

"There's no rush," said Madeline, as she went. "We're still waiting for the others."

"I know," said Alice.

"Mama," Madeline called after her, "you mustn't mention Luke. She's already been asking why he's not coming today, and I don't want to make it worse."

"I won't say a word," Alice assured her.

She really didn't plan to. All she wanted, as she climbed the stairs, was to give her granddaughter a cuddle. To sit her on her lap and hold her close; she needed the comfort of that so very much.

She peeked around Iris's door, into the beautiful room Guy had furnished with such boundless affection. She soaked it all up: the pictures on the walls, the toys on the shelves—and Iris, in the midst of all of it, not getting changed at all, but sitting on the floor in her petticoat, tongue pressed between her teeth, trying to get the milk stain out of her dress with a wet rag.

"Let's find you another one, shall we?" said Alice, and almost choked on her rush of sadness that if Luke had his way, she might never help this little girl with anything again.

Fighting to compose herself, she went to the closet to fetch her a gown.

You mustn't mention Luke, Madeline had said.

But it was Iris who brought him up.

"Where is my daddy staying?" she asked.

"I don't know," said Alice tightly.

"Do you like him?"

Alice flicked through the dresses. "Yes, of course."

"Does he want to take me and Mummy away?"

Alice went still at the question, the sudden quaver in Iris's voice.

Yes, she yearned to scream. *Don't let him, please.*

"Why do you ask that?" she forced out instead.

"Guy told me."

Alice turned to face her, then stopped short at the anxiety in her wide blue gaze. Moving instinctively, she went to pick her up, cradling her close, just as she'd yearned to on her way upstairs.

"When did Guy tell you that?" she asked.

"Last night," said Iris. "I had a bad dream. Mummy didn't come."

Alice's heart juddered. She'd been with Luke. She must have been.

"Did Guy try to wake her?" she asked Iris, somehow managing to keep her voice at a normal pitch.

"I don't know."

"And have you told your mummy about your nightmare?"

"Guy said I shouldn't."

Alice nodded. "And what else did Guy say?"

"That he wouldn't let anyone take me anywhere, and I'm safe, and I should tell Mummy how much I want that." Iris looked up at her, hot little face creased and horribly confused. "He said she'd do anything for me."

Alice closed her eyes. "Did he?"

"Would she?" said Iris.

"Yes," Alice said, "of course. That's what mamas do."

"So I should tell her I want to stay here?" Iris said, bottom lip wavering, perilously close to tears.

Alice hesitated before answering.

Then she kissed her again, and slowly, the words seeming to create themselves, said to her what she realized she must.

"You promise me?" said Iris.

"I promise," said Alice. "But you must do as I've said, and never tell your mama that Guy told you to do this."

"I won't," said Iris solemnly.

"Good girl," said Alice, already half tempted to take back all she'd said. But it was too late. She couldn't turn back. Not now.

She talked on, telling Iris to come and see her, any time she needed to. "I will always help you, my darling."

Iris nodded.

Alice held her tighter.

This, she told herself, *this is what love is.*

CHAPTER THIRTY-TWO

Guy was waiting at the large seafront table he'd reserved when the rest of them arrived for the lunch and ices he could truthfully do without. He glimpsed Della first, leading the way out through the hotel's glass doors with the menace that was Emily contained in her viselike arms. With a sigh, he tucked the note he'd been reading away—the one his bearer had left for the maître d' to hand to him—and, still trying to make out what he thought of the contents, ran his hand down his face, assumed a smile, and stood to greet them all. His legs were unsteady. His entire body was shaky with fatigue. Exhausted as he'd been when he'd blacked out after dinner, he hadn't been able to sleep again once Iris had woken and he'd found himself manipulating her as he had. He'd lain awake in his hot bed, bloodshot eyes on the mosquito net, sickened at himself for involving such a small child, even more so because he'd known already that he wasn't going to take any of what he'd said back.

He touched his hand to the note in his pocket and feared he'd say it all again if he needed to.

As the hours had ticked by until dawn, he'd kept glancing at the door to Maddy's room, willing a noise to come from it and convince him that she only hadn't run to comfort Iris herself because of the draft he'd given her. It had been a strong one, after all.

He watched her now. His wife. She was with Peter, as she so often was, her blond head dipped toward his, her hand on his arm. Peter was holding her gloved fingers, nodding as she talked, looking quite wretched. Guy had a good idea as to why. Their long-forgotten conversation in the Quai d'Escale had returned to him forcibly. It was another thing that had kept him awake the night before: how he'd assured Peter that his sighting of Luke on the Menin Road must have been imagination—and how that nurse had tried to convince him in turn that it mightn't have been. *In all this hideousness, wouldn't it be nice to think there might still be some good surprises left?* God, but he'd been so certain she was wrong. It mortified him now, how readily he'd dismissed her optimism as fantasy.

But he hadn't ignored her. He stole comfort from that. Even in spite of that naik's assurances that he'd seen Luke buried, he'd tried to call at that CCS she'd told him about. He had tried.

What more could he have done?

Nothing, he'd told himself again and again.

Nothing, he told himself now.

He pushed the matter determinedly from his mind, before it drove him to distraction.

He had plenty else to think about, in any case.

"Maddy," he said, as she drew closer.

She looked up, toward him, her irresistible eyes concealed by the rim of her hat. He couldn't make out whether her lips turned in a smile that was nervous, or guarded. Tired, certainly. Much more so than he might expect from someone who'd been knocked out for the night by sleeping salts.

Shaking the unwelcome thought away, he went to meet her.

"Hello, dearest," he said, pressing his lips to her warm cheek, feeling himself stir despite his worry. "Can we have a quick word, before we join everyone else?"

He led her back into the hotel, out of sight of everyone else in the main foyer, behind an ornamental potted plant. Through the leaves, Maddy could just see Della's hat, Peter's fair head, both of them craning their necks from beneath the table's large parasol, trying to see where she and Guy had gone. She hadn't had long to speak to either of them. Only a snatched minute to tell Peter he wasn't to blame himself, not even a bit, *you've done that more than enough,* and to quietly let Della know that yes, she had seen Luke.

"And?" Della had mouthed, as Emily had begged her for a carry. "What happened?"

"Later," Maddy had mouthed back.

"Maddy," Guy said, drawing her eyes back to him. "Are you listening?"

She stared up at him. She had been.

"You've seen a lawyer," she repeated flatly.

His face softened. "Please," he said, "don't be like this. . . ."

"You're asking too much," she said.

"Too much?" he said. "I'm your husband. You vowed to—"

"Don't," she said, louder than she'd intended, so loud that even the punkah wallahs—drilled in the art of being wallpaper—turned to look. It was the long night, her nausea at everything he'd just said. She couldn't contain it. "Please," she said, "don't say obey."

"I was about to say love me," he said, with such awful distress that she had to look away. "Like I love you. And Iris. It's why I want this."

"Guy," she said, "be reasonable. Luke is Iris's father. He's missed . . . everything, *everything* he should have had with her. He is not going to let you be chaperone when he meets her. *I* am not going to let you."

"I don't need your permission."

"You certainly don't have it," she said. "I can't imagine what you're thinking."

"It will be better for her this way."

"Please don't try and tell me what is best for my daughter."

"You need to listen," he said, taking a step toward her. "Please, just listen to me."

She took a step back, knocking awkwardly against the plant. "I won't listen to this."

"Have you even asked Iris what she wants?"

"She's a child," she said, moving to set the plant straight before it fell.

"You should ask her," he said.

"Like you've asked me?" she said, her gloves now covered in soil.

"I don't think you know what you want."

"Guy," she said, giving up on the plant, "I *know*. I am so sorry, but I do."

"How can you?" he said, eyes wide, imploring. "It's been five minutes."

"A little longer than that. I—"

"No," he shouted, making the punkah wallahs turn again. He took a breath, appearing to calm himself. "I won't talk about this now," he said. "I've told you, I need you to give me this month."

"A month is too long."

"A month is barely any time at all," he said, taking another step toward her. This time she had nowhere to go. "Let me prove to you how happy I can make you." He reached for her soil-dusted hands. "Promise that you won't see Luke alone, that you'll try with us."

"Guy . . ." She shook her head, unwilling to make any more promises she couldn't keep.

"One month," he said, grip tightening. "At the end of it, we'll talk again, I swear."

"Please," she said, "I—"

"We'll see what you want," he said, "ask Iris what *she* wants. If you both tell me it's to go, then," he swallowed, averted his eyes, his entire face tense with reluctance, "I'll stand aside."

"I need to be with Luke," she said, as kindly as anyone could say such a thing. "I've always needed that. Iris will be happy one way or another." Still he didn't look at her. "Guy," she pressed his arm, urging him to, "please don't do this. A month won't change anything."

But he wouldn't be moved.

"We'll see" was all he said, turning to go back outside. "We'll see."

Somehow, they got through the sweltering two hours that followed: the curled sandwiches and warm champagne, the sundaes that were already half melted by the time the waiters brought the glasses to the table.

"I don't mind," said Iris, who at least seemed happier again, perched on her grandmother's lap, the sea glistening behind her, her grandfather on one side, lovely Lucy giggling on the other.

Maddy sat just along from them, between Peter and Della, as far away from Guy as she could manage. She refused to look at him, certainly not as much as her hot, prickling skin suggested he was looking at her. She wanted only to leave, find Luke in his rooms and tell him all of it so that he needn't be in the dark a moment longer. She was so angry at Guy, more so the higher the sun climbed, and the grittier her tired eyes became: for exploiting the archaic laws that trapped her to give her such an ultimatum, but mostly for even suggesting it would do Iris any harm to see Luke without him.

How dare he suggest that?

"He's desperate," whispered Della. "That's how he dares."

Maddy gave an agitated sigh. "Don't," she whispered back, "I *cannot* feel sorry for him."

"Well, you've never been able to help that," said Peter.

Another truth. It was one of the reasons she wasn't meeting his eye. If she did, and allowed herself to see the inevitable concern there, she knew she wouldn't find it so easy to maintain her fury. And she wanted her fury. She *needed* her fury.

It would be so much harder to keep battling him without it.

"You're not really going to let him be there when Luke meets Iris, are you?" said Peter.

"Of course I'm not," she hissed.

She had no intention of complying with any of Guy's conditions. Not only would she simply *make* him accept that Iris had to be allowed to get to know Luke unobserved, she'd continue to see him alone herself. Every opportunity she could find.

She'd just be very careful not to let Guy discover that's what she was doing.

She pushed her untouched sundae away uneasily. She couldn't help it; the thought of the deception didn't sit easily on her. Not at all. Badly as Guy might be behaving, he *was* still Guy. She didn't need to look at him to remember that. Or how he'd loved her all these years.

And how long he'd fought to make her happy.

"Darling Maddy," said Peter, who of course understood.

He'd always thought the world of Guy, too.

She stared out at the blinding sea, the fishermen in their colorful boats, thinking of Luke's words earlier. *I can't stand this being furtive.* She really couldn't either.

But Guy had all the cards in his hand. And he had asked for this month.
What choice did they have but to give it to him?

"None, apparently," Luke said when, much later that same day—after Guy
had gone back to the hospital, and Iris to Della's—she finally managed to
get over to his rooms.

She couldn't stay for long. Guy had said he'd be home for dinner, and
the sun was already dipping toward dusk. She could see it through the back
windows, drenching the glassy Arabian Sea in color: that view she remembered so dearly. Luke hadn't lit any lamps; the apartment's white walls and
mosaic floors were darkening by the second, bathed in the last pink rays.
She didn't want to leave it. She rested her head against Luke's chest, and
once again couldn't think of leaving him.

"I want to go over to the hospital," Luke said, "tell him what I think of
him."

"You can't," she told him, in much the same way as she had her father
earlier, after they'd dropped Iris at Della's and she'd enlightened him and
her mother as to what Guy had said.

I'll talk some sense into him, Richard had said, gripping the steering
wheel.

You think I didn't try? Maddy had replied.

"We need him," she said now to Luke. "Otherwise it will be years of
fighting, scandal. Even then, he might not ever agree to end the marriage.
Iris would always be that child . . ."

"I know that," Luke said, and she saw the reflection of her anger in his
dark gaze. "I just hate that he does, too."

"It's only a month." She said it to herself as much as to him. "Just a
month."

"A lot can happen in a month," he said.

"Not this one," she said. "We'll get through it, go home married, like
we've always been. And you'll have time to get to know Iris here, before we
take her anywhere."

It was Alice who'd helped Maddy see that particular silver lining. While she, unlike Richard, had been very careful not to cast any actual blame in Guy's direction (naturally), and quietly insistent that it would be a good thing for Maddy not to be hasty in making any *decisions,* she hadn't said a word against Luke either. Never once had she tried to make Maddy feel guilty for talking about going with him back to England, in spite of the awful terror Maddy knew she must be feeling at their leaving.

And she'd only seemed shocked by Guy's suggestion that he should play chaperone to Luke and Iris here, in India.

"I can't imagine how I'd have felt if Edie had done that to me," she'd said.

"She never would have," Richard had said quietly.

"No," Alice had conceded, quieter yet, the two of them still being so inexplicably stiff with one another. "But," she'd gone on, speaking once more to Maddy, "you need to remember that you're talking about upending Iris's entire world. It's not something that should be rushed."

She'd suggested then that Luke meet Iris at their villa. *Neutral ground.* "I'll speak to Guy about it," she'd said, with a sigh that made it obvious she didn't relish the prospect. "I'm sure he'll see it will be kinder on Iris this way. And it might make him feel better that I'll be there."

Richard had looked at her askance, clearly as taken aback as Maddy felt at her apparent impartiality. He, like Maddy, had obviously assumed she'd be wholly in Guy's corner.

It had touched Maddy, so very much, that in spite of everything, the only side her mother seemed to be picking was her own.

"Come over tomorrow," she said to Luke now. "See Iris after school."

"You're sure she's ready?" he said.

"I don't know what ready might even look like," she said, truthfully. "But she's been asking after you, wanting to know where you are."

"I'm terrified she'll be scared of me again," he said.

"No," said Maddy. "*No.* We won't let that happen. It will be different. And my mother will help."

"I wish she didn't have to," he said. "I wish . . ."

"I know," she said, reaching up, taking his face in her hands, pressing her lips to his, as though it could be possible to kiss his anxiety away—her own, too. "It will get easier," she said, pouring the conviction she was desperate for them both to feel into every word. "You'll see. One day it will be as though none of this ever happened."

He nodded slowly. She could see how much he wanted to believe her. She could *feel* his need.

Believe, she thought, kissing him again, *please believe.*

Then I can, too.

She'll never believe in us, unless we do.

She left it too late to leave, of course. She barely had time to race over to Della's to collect Iris, and then quickly bathe herself—clear any trace of her stolen hour with Luke from her skin—before Guy returned to the villa, too.

He found her in her bedroom, just as she was finishing pinning her hair for dinner. She looked up at his weary reflection in her dressing table mirror, and saw to her dismay that he had a bunch of flowers in hand.

He told her, as he crossed the room and offered them to her, that Alice had indeed been to see him. "I'll stay away when Iris and Luke are together," he said, "if that's truly what you want."

"It is," she said, turning to face him, but not thanking him, despite her rush of relief. She refused to be grateful for this.

She certainly didn't feel it when he went on, telling her that if he wasn't going to be present for the meetings, someone else had to be.

"*Guy,*" she began, ready to protest.

"It has nothing to do with me not trusting you," he said, which was enough to silence her. He took a step closer, still holding the flowers, his forlorn expression at once contrite and begging for understanding. "I just don't think I can stand to be in surgery, thinking of the three of you out alone." He stared. "I feel sick, actually, Maddy, at the thought of it."

At the anguish in his eyes, his voice, she felt her heart soften, entirely against her will. It was the very thing she'd feared happening at lunch. She fought to cling to her anger, and didn't entirely fail—there was still far too much to be furious about—but, as he proffered the flowers once more, she found herself taking them, too sorry for him not to. *Well,* came Peter's voice, *you've never been able to help that.* She sat quite passively while he leaned forward and brushed her cheek with his lips; the cheek Luke had so recently kissed with rather more urgency, her back pressed to the wall, her body wrapped around his. She nodded when he said he might go and read Iris a bedtime story, and didn't interrupt them, not even when she heard them both chatting and started to worry that he might become suspicious if Iris happened to tell him of her protracted play over at Della's.

If Iris did mention it, he said nothing of it to Maddy over dinner. They talked of very little as they ate the meal out on the dark, leafy terrace, and only then in murmured incidentals (the weather, Iris's reading, staffing at the hospital) that Maddy forgot as soon as the words left either of their lips. She, thinking of Luke, imagining what it would be like if she were to get up, leave the table—the flickering lamps, the frying mosquitoes—and go to him, as she was so very desperate to go to him, had no idea how she managed to keep playacting with Guy at all.

She supposed she rediscovered her strings.

She could only let them take her so far, though.

As she and Guy walked upstairs to bed, she turned to him, telling him—before he could even think of asking *if he might*—that she'd prefer to be left alone that night.

"For all of this month, actually," she said. "I need time."

He didn't protest. He nodded, in apparent understanding.

"I want you to have it," he said, every bit his old, gentle self again. "Maddy, my dearest," he kissed her softly on the forehead, "time is all I ask."

CHAPTER THIRTY-THREE

Guy got his time. Twenty-nine days of it.

Maddy and Luke couldn't be alone for every one of them. Guy, without ever suggesting it was what he might be doing, made it as hard as he possibly could for Maddy to escape anywhere by herself. Liberated by the Poona staff who arrived to help at the hospital, he came home earlier each evening, always with flowers in hand, ready to read Iris more stories, have a *nice long dinner* with Maddy. Sometimes, he appeared without warning at the school (which Maddy had now given notice to, wanting to leave them as much time as possible to replace her), or at Della's (if Maddy had mentioned she might take Iris there), *just to say hello*. With his movements so unpredictable, Maddy didn't dare risk hailing a rickshaw to Luke's rooms nearly as often as her longing compelled her to.

But Guy couldn't be present all the time. He still had surgeries to perform—the steady round of appendectomies, splenectomies, and fixes to injuries sustained on the drill grounds and polo fields that kept the hospital so busy—and the odd, unavoidable night shift. Maddy didn't waste any of them. Every minute, every second she could grab with Luke, she took it. He was always waiting on his steps for her when she arrived, his hair often damp from a swim, his skin darker by the day under the intensifying summer sun. She lived for the moment when he'd see her at the end of his alleyway, and stand, smiling (that smile), opening his arms, ready to scoop her close and warn her that this time he wasn't going to let her go.

"Don't," she'd say, "please don't."

As she sat each evening with Guy, picking at her food, she'd fantasize about being back in Luke's bed, her head in the crook of his neck, his fingers moving up and down her spine, both of them sweating, breathless; *together*.

She worried about him, though, so much. She saw the shrapnel scars on his chest, his back and neck, and never forgot what he'd been through. Sometimes, when they were talking, he'd stop in midsentence, forehead creasing on one of the sudden pains he'd admitted had started to plague him since he'd returned to the heat, the mayhem of India. She'd wait, gripping his hand, staring at his agony, holding her breath for the time it took to pass, kissing him when it did, hating that there was so little else she could do.

She never let herself fall asleep when they were together; no matter how tired she was (and she was so very exhausted), she always kept one eye on the time. But occasionally he slept, and she'd lie next to him on the pillow, staring at his flickering eyelids, picturing his dreams, flinching as he flinched—when a distant exhaust banged, or a firecracker went off—horribly aware that he was back there, in the trenches she couldn't follow him into, and which he'd so recently remembered.

"It's like I only just left," he told her, early in their first week together. "It seems like it must all still be going on. It doesn't feel real that it's not, especially here. I keep thinking of Richmond, the river, its peace . . ."

"We'll be back by summer," she said, loathing the uselessness of her own words in this, their endless present. "I wish we could go tomorrow."

"And what would Iris think about that, I wonder," he said.

She had no answer for him there.

In those initial days, Iris continued to be a worry they both struggled to know what to say about.

The first meeting was strained, as Maddy supposed it was always going to be. It didn't help that Guy took it upon himself to tell Iris it was happening, before Maddy had even come down to breakfast that morning.

"Why did you do that?" she asked him as she left Iris at the table and followed him out to his motor, not even trying to contain her irritation. "Have you seen her face? She's going to be anxious about it all morning. . . ."

"Maddy," he said. "You couldn't just spring it on her."

"I wasn't going to," she said. "I was going to talk to her after school. . . ."

"Well, now you don't have to," he said, quite as though he'd done them all a favor.

Iris assured her, as they walked to the schoolhouse, that she wasn't worried. "I'm going to do my best to like him," she said, which seemed such a strange thing for a child to say.

Frowning, Maddy asked, "Did Guy tell you to say that?"

Iris shook her head. Then again when Maddy pressed her.

But she was once again uncharacteristically quiet all through morning lessons. And she clutched onto Maddy's hand afterward, as they went up to her parents', undoubtedly nervous.

Maddy was nervous herself. Her mouth felt uncomfortably dry as she tried to distract Iris by pointing out the various birds up in the leaves, the monkey who sat on a high branch, peering down at them. Her hands were clammy in her gloves. They were *all* too nervous, of course, too mindful of how well they needed the meeting to go. Alice especially was awkwardly stiff. For all her talk of being there to help smooth things over, she was, to Maddy's despair, as reserved as she'd ever been with Luke, flushing scarlet when he arrived, and whispering what sounded like thank you when he kissed her hello (another incredibly odd thing for someone to say). She remained very quiet as they took tea on the stifling veranda, pulling at the collar of her cream tea dress, looking everywhere but at Luke and Maddy, until even Iris—glued to Maddy's lap, her new doctor's kit clutched in her chubby hands—felt compelled to ask her if she didn't feel very well.

"I'm just hot," she said.

They were all that.

Not even Peter, who'd taken the day off work at Richard's suggestion, ready to lend his support to the proceedings, could lighten the fraught atmosphere. He kept up a steady enough patter of conversation—telling Iris that her daddy was an expert polo player, didn't she know, asking Maddy how school had been, saying what a luxury it was to be at his leisure on a Monday, forcing a laugh when Luke smiled and said that it was possible to have enough leisure—but struggled, like they all struggled, not to keep casting anxious looks at Iris, wondering when she might come out of her shell.

Luke at least realized that he mustn't push her. He didn't take his eyes off her either. Maddy watched the wonder in his gaze as he soaked up her bowed head, the quiet way she examined each of her miniature doctor's instruments in turn, and knew she was seeing something she would never, not ever, forget.

"I kept thinking of her little sepia foot in that photograph you sent me," he told her afterward.

He asked Iris just a very few questions: about her friends ("Suya and Lucy," she whispered), what she liked to do at school ("Painting," she said, eyes fixed on her kit), at the weekend ("I don't know," she whispered again), and almost, *almost*, made her smile by inquiring if Suya had taught her how to terrorize the peacocks.

"Yes?" he said. "It's a yes, isn't it? I can tell. Those poor peacocks."

But it was only as he and Peter left that he did what Maddy was certain he'd been desperate to do from the second he saw her, and got up, coming to crouch by their side.

"Iris," he said, "am I right in saying you feel rather shy?"

She said nothing, just looked up from her toy, warm body tensing on Maddy's lap: an obvious yes.

"That's all right," Luke said. "You don't know me yet. You can be as shy with me as you like."

More silence.

He smiled at her. Maddy had no idea how he managed it.

"Do you like horses?" he asked. "Is that why Peter told you I play polo?"

This time, she nodded. Her sweaty curls bounced.

"Well then, how about we go to the cantonment tomorrow?" he said. "I happen to know a few of the cavalry officers there. We can see if we can arrange a lesson."

Maddy felt her heart lift at the suggestion. It was a good one, she thought.

She had high hopes that it would be a better day.

Especially when Della said she and Lucy would come along, *hopefully help take some of the pressure off everyone.*

❋

Maddy stood with her at the edge of the sand paddock, watching as Luke and a couple of lieutenants helped the girls into their saddles and led them around in the blazing sunshine, coaxing them into slow trots. Lucy laughed the faster they went, squealing at Della and Maddy, asking if they were watching.

"We're watching," Maddy assured her. "Don't you worry about that."

She willed Iris to squeal, too. But while she smiled, a couple of times, and even—wonder of wonders—laughed, for the shortest of seconds, she didn't squeal at all. Not once.

"I see what you mean," said Della, eyes narrowed beneath her hat. "She's not herself."

"I just don't understand it," said Maddy, thinking of her normally exuberant chatter, her ready affection. "I feel like I've looked away and found another child in her place."

"She'll just be taking her time with it all," said Della.

"But when Guy came back to India, she didn't hesitate. She was ready to adore him from the start."

"There was no reason for her not to," said Della, gently. "She couldn't have had the faintest idea how much everything was going to change for her. The poor little thing probably didn't think past her next sundae at the Sea Lounge."

Maddy sighed heavily, acknowledging it.

"She's hardly had a second to get used to things at Guy's," said Della, "and now all this. She must be overwhelmed."

"I think there's more to it," said Maddy, studying Iris's pensive, rosy face beneath her cap, the wary way she listened to whatever Luke was saying to her. "It's just not *like* her to be this . . . withdrawn. With anyone."

"Has Guy said anything?" asked Della.

"He thinks she's scared," said Maddy, recalling his words the night before, after he'd arrived home with a fresh bouquet of flowers and asked how the meeting with Luke had gone. She'd admitted how quiet Iris has been, still cross enough at his interference at breakfast to want him to own his part in her upset.

He hadn't.

"This is all very unsettling for her" was all he'd said. "I'm not at all surprised it was difficult."

"She'll come round," Maddy had been quick to assure him, assure them both. "Children are adaptable. Apparently I was beside myself when I first went to England—"

"I'll go and see her," he'd said, cutting her off, not wanting to hear it. "I'm sure she'll be happier for a story."

He'd taken so long about it that she'd gone up, too, to see if everything was all right; she'd found them both asleep on Iris's bed, and had wanted to weep at how content Iris looked in the crook of Guy's arm.

"Have you spoken to Iris?" Della asked her, drawing her back to the paddock.

"I've tried," she said. "She keeps clamming up. It's almost like she's worried about what she might say."

"Does she talk to Guy?"

"I'm not sure," said Maddy, mind moving back to the sight of them asleep, much as she might probe at a bruise. "Honestly, I can't bring myself to ask."

She never did.

There's no point, she wrote to Edie, in a letter that she penned over the course of the month, but never actually sent; it became more a diary than anything, a way to keep her sanity when she was alone in Guy's villa, holed up in her bedroom listening to him in his, desperate for someone to talk to. *He'd only make me feel guiltier than I already do for putting her through all this. Besides, I can't help but suspect he's relieved Iris hasn't become instantly smitten with her daddy. I'm not sure he'd have been able to bear it if she had. And of course he has his conditions for letting us go at the end of this ridiculous limbo, one of them being that Iris must want it, too. I'm certain he's counting on her support.*

How can we even ask her what she wants, though? She's barely more than a baby, far too little to be involved in such a matter. I've tried to tell Guy we must leave her out of things, but he doesn't listen. He still won't speak to me about any of it at all. He just keeps coming home with more bunches of flowers, new books for Iris, determined to prove how happy we can be.

Another day, she wrote, *Iris has started to become quieter with him too now, though.* Her hand stuck to the humidity-dampened paper. *I think she feels as wretched as I do about making him sad.*

Maybe that's why she's forcing poor Luke to work so hard.

But, he's doing it, she continued on another evening, *I wish you could see him with her, Edie. He's always coming up with something fun to do—fishing down at the beach, picnics, tennis at the Gymkhana Club, back at the cantonment for more riding lessons—and even though we have our cycling rota of chaperones, it really is starting to feel like we're becoming a family. At last. Mama tags along most of the time, and I feel terrible because I can see how much she's dreading us leaving (she's almost as quiet as Iris, but has reverted to her old habit of bottling everything up, refusing to admit that there's anything wrong—even between her and Papa, when anyone can see they're still not speaking); sometimes I feel like she might be on the edge of saying something to me, but she never does. I want to assure her that we'll visit, that I haven't given up on getting her on a ship again (I haven't, by the way; in fact, I feel very determined. It's been years since she last tried, and she's not as alone as she was then), but I don't want to make her any more upset.*

However, she went on, several days later, *I have to say she really does seem to be relaxing with Luke now. He hasn't given her much choice, of course (he's always chatting to her, smiling, asking her opinion about what we should do tomorrow), and it appears to have worked.*

And so, Edie, has it with Iris! I didn't want to tempt fate by writing anything before, but I really, truly, absolutely, unilaterally think it's safe to say that he's winning her over—by pure, grit-toothed determination. I didn't even notice it happening at first, but she's laughing so much more again, especially when he laughs. More often than not, she forgets to bite her lip when she smiles at him. I cannot tell you how happy I am that she's stopped doing that. She's always been such a smiler. And she's started chatting to him, truly, properly chatting. It's as though he's finally worn down her defenses and she simply can't help herself anymore. She seems especially keen to know about his lost memory: what it felt like, why he was in hospital for so long, whether the doctors and nurses were kind to him. Only today, she asked him if he was ever sad. "I was sometimes," he told her, *"because of how much I was missing you and your mummy,"* and she looked so sad, too, until he told her that she mustn't be, that it was his job to *make sure that didn't happen.* "Because you're my daddy," she said. "Because I'm your daddy," he said. "It's the only job I have at the moment."

Oh, Edie, is it possible that I love him more than ever? Since you can't answer, I shall for you.

I think it might be.

No, I don't think. I know.

Her love for him grew again that same afternoon, the twenty-ninth of Guy's thirty days. She'd just finished her final set of classes at the school, and they'd come, at Iris's request, down to the beach with Richard to catch dinner.

Maddy didn't join in with the fishing herself. Nor did her father. They sat back beneath the palms, leaving Iris and Luke to it, talking quietly between themselves as Luke rolled up his trousers and told Iris to get rid of those ridiculous boots, then led her down to the shore. Maddy, who'd been trying once again to get her father to admit what the matter was between him and her mother, gave a short sigh, because he was (once again) being as tight-lipped as Alice.

"You have enough on your plate without worrying about us," he said.

"And yet," she said, "I'm still worrying."

He smiled, rubbed her hand. "Don't."

"Is it worth it, Papa?" she asked him. "Whatever it is, is it really worth any more upset?"

His smile became a little sadder. "Maybe not," he said.

She waited for him to say more.

But he didn't.

Accepting, reluctantly, that it was hopeless to push him, she gave up, returning her attention to the shore.

The sun beat down, bathing the sands and sea in gold. Luke knelt on one knee, the sea lapping his foot, preparing the rod while Iris watched. Overhead, a bird swooped, into the water, finding a catch of its own. Iris didn't look at it. She appeared entirely engrossed in Luke threading the hook. Seemingly without thinking, she leaned closer to him, curls dipping, and placed her hand on his shoulder.

It took Maddy a second to absorb she'd done it. She caught her breath, scared she might be imagining it.

But, "Now look at that," said Richard, voice hushed, "she's just made his whole world, and she doesn't even know."

Luke didn't react. Somehow, he carried on working as though nothing out of the ordinary had happened. Maddy heard his voice as he spoke to Iris, although not his words. She watched Iris nod along, still holding his shoulder. Her hand didn't move at all. Then she giggled, splashed him with her foot. Actually splashed him.

He laughed. It made Maddy's heart sing. More when Iris giggled again. Luke stood, handed Iris the rod, and helped her to cast out.

Then he turned, he looked over his shoulder toward Maddy and Richard, and smiled; a smile, of pure, undiluted joy.

A smile Maddy would never forget.

A smile that said, *This really is going to be all right.*

She believed it herself.

In that moment, looking at the pair of them side by side, dark curls glinting in the Indian sun, she had absolute faith in what their future was going to be.

And then, that evening happened.

The one where it all unraveled.

She'd suspected what was happening inside her body. She'd been through it once before; it was all very familiar. She'd been so much more tired than normal, falling into bed straight after dinner, and sleeping very deeply. Just lately she'd had that strange taste in her mouth, and had needed to visit the bathroom more often. Then, she was two weeks late with her curse. (Her curse, which, contrary to what she might have told Guy, normally came like clockwork.)

Even given all that, she hadn't been sure. Or, she hadn't *let* herself be sure. In fact she'd tried, quite stubbornly, not to think about the possibility of another baby at all. She would have been happy to think about it, had Guy not insisted on that rushed, far from comfortable, encounter before Iris's birthday party. If she'd only had time to use her cap back then, she'd have been over the moon at the prospect of the little life within her. She wouldn't have hesitated to tell Luke that a tiny brother or sister was on his or her way for Iris. She'd have been beside herself at the prospect of hearing his sharp intake of euphoria, seeing his face transform in disbelief and wonder, the happiness she'd been robbed of back when she'd only been able to wire him about Iris.

But she hadn't had time to use her cap.

So even though she'd been with Luke countless times since—all wonderful, all incredible, all every bit the kind she longed to believe a life would choose to begin in—she couldn't know for certain that this baby was his.

She had no idea what to do about it. Pretending it might not be real had felt like the only thing *to do.*

Until she couldn't pretend anymore.

Her mother was with her when it happened, on that twenty-ninth evening.

She came over just as night was falling, turning the jungle and Guy's already dark villa even darker. Maddy was on her way upstairs to get Iris ready for bed when she heard the knock at the front door. Moving gingerly, already feeling a little dizzy, she went to open it, and felt too shaky to even wonder why her mother was standing there in the shadows, hands clasped, face pinched, looking as though she'd rather be anywhere else.

"Where's Iris?" Alice asked.

"Upstairs," said Maddy, and the insides of her cheeks stuck as she spoke. "Guy?"

"Not home yet," said Maddy, leaning against the door. They were cooking rice in the kitchen for dinner. She could smell it.

It was rice that had undone her with Iris too.

"I just need a quick word," said Alice.

"Do you want to come in?" said Maddy, pressing her hand to her watery stomach.

"It's all right," said Alice. "It's only I saw Diana today . . ."

"Diana?" said Maddy confusedly.

"Have you seen her?" said Alice.

Dimly, Maddy registered the tension in her mother's voice. The strange flush to her cream skin, too. She couldn't think about it, though. The scent of rice was overwhelming her; she felt sweat prickling on her forehead, her chest . . .

"Maddy?" Alice prompted.

"No," said Maddy, "I don't really want to see Diana."

"She said she might call on you, though," said Alice, and, to Maddy's horror, burst into tears. "I have to tell you," the tears kept coming, "your father said there's no need after all . . . but I think he was right before. I should have done it long ago. . . ."

Maddy had no idea what she was talking about. On some level it occurred to her that it might be to do with whatever her parents had been arguing about, but she didn't stop to find out. Distraught as she was to see her mother crying, she couldn't contain her nausea a second longer.

She pushed past her, stumbling through the porch to the front garden, where she vomited into the rosebushes Guy's bearer was so proud of cultivating. For a few seconds, she forgot everything but the hideousness of her bile, her own heaving stomach, and the tears now streaming down her own cheeks (she always did cry when she was sick). She wasn't really conscious of her mother's hands, reaching for her shoulders. Or the motor that came through the gate; the slammed door, then the footsteps running across the loose dirt driveway.

It was only when her convulsions subsided that she became properly aware that any of it had happened, and that Guy as well as her mother was now with her.

They'd both been present when she'd realized she was pregnant with Iris, too.

Pressing her shaking hand to her mouth, she recalled how easily Guy had guessed back then. She had no doubt he'd do the same this time. It came to her that he'd been watching her for days, observing her yawns, early nights, and frequent trips to the latrine.

Again, it was something she'd fought to ignore.

She couldn't bring herself to face him. She swallowed on the last of her bile, trying to absorb the irreversibility of what she'd just allowed to happen, failed utterly, then (knowing she'd have to do it sooner or later), forced herself to turn.

He stood just a few paces from her, still in uniform from his day at the hospital. His eyes, his good, kind eyes, were fixed on her: exhausted, worried, but hopeful, too.

And smiling.

He smiled.

A smile that Maddy would never forget.

A smile that said, *I won't ever let you go now.*

A smile that said, *A lot can happen in a month.*

CHAPTER THIRTY-FOUR

It was chilly for summer, and raining, too; a misty smattering that coated High Elms's lawns, its leaves, and bursting flower beds with a sheen so fine, Luke felt he was breathing it.

Hardly rain at all, is it?

Arnold had said that to him once. He remembered. They'd been in the old orchard at the King's Fifth. He smiled sadly, thinking of his doctor, and that corner of the hospital's grounds he'd grown to love: the windfall apples, that trickling stream he used to find so grounding (it had reminded him, he supposed, of his riverside garden in Richmond), all those hedges packed with berries. And the guns. His smile fell, recalling them, and how he and Arnold had listened to the grim rumbling from the Somme; a bombardment so intense it had traveled across the Channel.

He could hear the pounding, even now.

It was not a noise one forgot.

He remembered, too, how he'd wanted to compare the rain to something else that day. Exactly what had eluded him, as so much had back then.

As too much still did.

But he could guess now what the comparison would have been. He tipped his head back, looking into the endless sky, feeling the rain whisper on his cheeks, his lips, and thought of India, the rains there, and how different they'd been that summer before the war.

That incredible summer he'd married her.

The last Bombay summer he'd ever known.

He had his letters with him in the garden, tucked beneath his jacket: all the letters he'd written to her since coming to this place. The staff kept them from him (quite at his own request) when he slipped into one of his bad times, his lost days; the episodes when his own words meant nothing, and he feared he might destroy the pages he'd written in his panicked attempts to understand. He couldn't do that, not as he'd burned his journals with Arnold all those years before. His battered mind was giving up on him again, and he feared that all too soon his letters would be all he'd have left of the memories he was so terrified to lose.

A child's shout startled him, bringing him back to the moment. He turned in the direction it had come from, over by the hydrangeas. He wasn't the only one who'd braved the weather that afternoon. One of the other residents at High Elms was out walking, only she had her family with her: the little boy with the ball who'd shouted, his brothers and sisters; so many children, grandchildren and great-grandchildren.

Miriam, the lady was called.

She'd had a very hard life. She'd told Luke—many, many times now—of how she'd fled Vienna just before the Anschluss, leaving almost all of her Jewish family behind. She wept whenever she spoke of them all: the lost sisters and brothers, parents and grandparents; the children, who'd never grown up. He always held her hand when she did, listening, not trying to speak. Not when there were no possible words.

But today . . . Today she was smiling, and he smiled, too, in spite of everything he'd been recalling, because it was so wonderful to see.

It was her birthday. She was eighty. *A spring chicken,* he'd said as he'd congratulated her that morning, giving her his gift of the Austrian biscuits he'd asked Emma to collect from their old local bakery. They were going to have a party that afternoon: the usual diluted cordial and poppers that didn't make bangs. Emma had said she would come.

Sweet Emma.

The boy kicked the ball high into the sky, then caught it with the side of his foot. Luke watched the way his flushed face lit up, how he looked around to see if his parents had seen the feat, and felt his own chest ache, remembering, remembering. . . .

Miriam laughed with the boy, telling him, in her lightly accented voice, to do it again. She was arm in arm with her oldest daughter, hand holding her hand. He saw how happy she was, how content.

He drew a shaky breath, mind moving—almost against his will—back to Maddy.

Would she look like this now, if she were walking here with their Iris?

He breathed deep, trying to picture it. He blanketed his mind of the garden's noise, its rain, its laughter and other people, needing them with him instead.

But they didn't appear.

Or at least, not in the way he wanted to imagine them.

Instead, they came to him as they'd been when he'd looked down at them on the frantic Bombay quayside, from that ship's deck, about to leave India for the very last time. He saw Maddy clutching Iris's hand, little Iris waving up at him; their bright blue stares glued on his.

He raised his hand, ready to wave back at them, here, in this garden. That was how vividly they appeared to him. He watched Maddy's lips move, read the words that she said, and felt his throat tighten, until it was all he could do to breathe, just as it had back then.

He stumbled toward a nearby bench, needing to sit down. He felt his way. He couldn't look.

His mind flooded with memory, and his eyes—his stinging, weary eyes—were suddenly too clouded by tears for him to see anything at all.

CHAPTER THIRTY-FIVE

Bombay, 1921

Maddy told Guy that he might not be the father, right there in the driveway. She didn't hesitate. It was at once the hardest and easiest thing she ever did, because although it crippled her to snatch his happiness away so quickly, so cruelly, his smile terrified her enough that she simply couldn't allow it to remain a second longer.

"This is not as simple as you want it to be," she said, feeling her eyes well all over again as, through the dusky darkness, she watched his elation drain from him.

He knew what she was telling him. It was painfully obvious from his fallen face that he realized it all.

But, "Of course it's simple," he said, and even held out his hand, reaching for hers.

She didn't blame him for trying to pretend. (Hadn't she been doing the same thing?) She felt no resentment toward him at all; none of the anger she'd held on to this long month. Just heartbreak at the wrought vulnerability in his pleading gaze.

She didn't give him her hand, though. She held it back, fist clenched, knowing that she mustn't attempt to be kind. Not this time.

There could be no more hope.

Instead, she took a step away from him. As she did, she felt her mother move toward her, touch her arm. She drew a shaky breath, strengthened, just a fraction, by the gesture, the almost unbelievable reassurance that Alice didn't blame her, she wasn't appalled. Just there. *On her side.*

"You asked me for a month," she forced herself to say to Guy, "it's time to let it be over now. I promise you, we won't shut you out. You'll have a place in this child's life . . ."

"A place?" He stared, expression hardening. "A *place*?"

"Guy, there's every chance you're not—"

"No," he said, cutting her off, just as he had so many times. "I won't hear it."

"You have to," she said, voice raised in growing despair. It made her franker than she might otherwise have been able to be. "I want to be with Luke," she said. "I *love* Luke. He is Iris's *father*, very likely this baby's—"

"Enough," he said, turning so that she couldn't see his face anymore (or, perhaps, so he didn't have to look at hers), "it's enough."

Before she knew what was happening, he was striding away from her to his motor.

"Where are you going?" she called.

He didn't answer. Without even a goodbye to Alice, he left, too fast, his wheels scattering clouds of dust over the black lawn.

It hit her that he might be going to confront Luke. She felt her panic intensify at the possibility. She hadn't even spoken to Luke herself. He couldn't hear about this from Guy . . .

"Go," said her mother, as though reading her mind, "I'll look after Iris."

"Don't tell her."

"Of course I won't *tell* her. Go."

Maddy didn't need to be pushed a third time. She went, taking her own motor, so preoccupied with getting to Luke that it didn't occur to her until after she'd sped away how bloodshot her mother's eyes had still been.

Her mother, who'd been crying, too.

Maddy hadn't even asked if she was all right, or what had made her so upset in the first place. *It's only I saw Diana today . . .*

She gripped the steering wheel, trying to think what on earth she could have been talking about, cursing inwardly because she had no idea. She couldn't turn back now, though. She accelerated on, through the black jungle, and told herself she'd talk to Alice as soon as she got back.

For now, there really was only so much desperate worry she could take.

Guy wasn't at Luke's.

Luke almost wasn't at Luke's. He'd been about to go out, over to meet Peter for drinks, still riding high on the afternoon he'd spent with Iris at the beach, and the thought of all he could finally see opening up ahead of them: the years and years he was starting to believe the three of them might truly have.

Iris had let him carry her back up from the beach on his shoulders.

He'd held his daughter on his shoulders.

He smiled, just thinking about it as he did up his collar; the laughing way she'd grasped her salty palms to his cheeks, his hair. He was still smiling when he opened the door to Maddy.

And then he saw her face.

"What's wrong?" he asked, dread cooling his veins. "What's happened?"

"Everything," she said, and as he pulled her inside, she told him, all of it, swollen eyes fixed on his, the words spilling from her, as though she was afraid that if she stopped talking, she wouldn't be able to start again.

He didn't interrupt her. He heard everything she said—about the baby she was so desperate to be his (*Yes,* he thought numbly, *I want that, too*), how Guy had reacted just now, her own fear that he'd give them no annulment—and couldn't speak at all. He held on to her, more from instinct than decision, and hardly knew what he did. It was all too much, too sudden; it was like it was happening just beyond his reach.

It was only when she started telling him how sorry she was, how desperately sorry, that something in him clicked, bringing him back to her, to himself.

He didn't want her to be sorry, not for this.

What did she have to be sorry for?

"I tried to put him off before the party," she said. "I didn't want it, I swear to you. . . ."

"Maddy," he said, finally rediscovering his voice, "you think that makes me happy?" He stared at her distraught expression, shaking his head, appalled that she might. "It doesn't make me happy." Just thinking about her . . . *putting up* . . . with that. It killed him.

In that moment, he wanted to kill Guy. His anger, intense enough where his wife's husband was concerned, exploded within him. Guy must have sensed her reluctance back then. He *must* have.

And yet he'd kept going anyway. Asked it of her.

"Where is he now?" he said.

"I don't know," she said. "I thought he might be here."

"I wish he was," he said. All month, he'd been on the edge of confronting him. He'd lost count of the number of times he'd battled, only just successfully, with the urge to go into that hospital and ask him what the hell he thought he was about, putting them all through this.

We need him, Maddy had kept saying. *He'll come round.*

He will, Peter and Richard had assured him, time and again.

Now, though, now . . .

"I am so sorry," came Maddy's voice, breaking into his fury.

"Why do you keep saying that?" he asked, softer now.

"I should have told you."

"Yes," he said, since it was undeniable, "you should."

"And the baby . . ."

"Will be loved," he said, without hesitation, realizing, as the words left him, how undeniable that was, too.

"Yes?" she said, smiling—albeit very tentatively—for the first time since she'd arrived.

"Yes," he said, feeling the truth of it in his chest. He didn't question it. It wasn't a choice to be considered. Of course he hoped that the child was his, but he knew that it would be anyway, in every way that mattered.

How could it not be, when it was hers?

"Guy, though," she said.

"I know," he said, since (even in spite of his own intense anger) he couldn't remain cold to how much pain they were going to cause him. He saw how he loved Iris—just the way he'd hugged her, back at her birthday party, had been enough to show him that; he realized part of why he'd been behaving as he had was because of how scared he was of losing her as well as Maddy. It didn't excuse him, nothing could, but Luke would have to have been inhuman not to understand it.

And now they'd be taking this baby from him, too.

"We're not going to disappear," he said. "Iris will need to see him, write." He'd long since learned to make peace with that. "We'll have to come back to see your mother. . . ."

"I don't know," she said distractedly, "I'm determined to get her on a ship."

"So you keep saying."

She sighed deeply, and leaned against him. He rested his cheek on her head, leaning on her.

"Is this going to be all right?" she said.

"It has to be," he said.

"He's a good person," she said. "I want to believe he'll do the right thing."

So did Luke.

"We'll manage, though," she said. "Even if he holds back the annulment. We have a home, family. You have your work waiting—" She broke off, looked up at him.

He saw the question in her eyes.

"No one will take my work away," he assured her, hoping that he was right. "We won't be destitute. Not everyone will judge."

She nodded slowly.

Plenty would, of course. They both knew that.

But, "We'll be together," she said. "We're going."

"We're going," he echoed. "No one can stop us doing that."

"You absolutely can stop them," said Guy's lawyer: an old school acquaintance by the name of Henry Parsons who, while not a close friend, was familiar enough that Guy had felt able to call on him at home, even so late in the day.

He'd been very good the month before when Luke had first returned, assuring Guy that not only was his marriage to Maddy valid, but he and he alone had the power to end it, be it by annulment or divorce. "She's simply not allowed to sue you," Henry had said, "not unless you give her grounds for suggesting you've raped another woman, or committed incest."

"Well, I'm not going to do that," Guy had said, appalled.

Henry had laughed, like it was a grand joke.

He was just as relaxed this time, swilling his Scotch, telling Guy he had nothing to worry about, *nothing*, the courts would absolutely recognize his right as father to this baby. He was Maddy's husband, no one else.

"We can get a ruling to keep Maddy in India while she's enceinte," he said. "As the father, you're the legal guardian of the child. You can seize full custody as soon as it's born, without question."

"Well," said Guy, shifting in his chair, "I wouldn't want it to come to that. . . ."

"Of course, of course," Henry replied, reaching for a cigar, "but don't tell her that, for God's sake. None of this needs to end up in court at all. Just have a little chat, make sure she understands what the consequences will be if she keeps up this nonsense. She doesn't strike me as the kind to put herself before her children. As I've said before, you've a case for claiming custody of Iris, too."

Guy stared into his own whiskey, baffled by how it could have come to this. They'd all been so happy, such a short time before. He'd been so happy. . . .

"Don't look so concerned," Henry said. "Maddy's going nowhere, and nor are the children. Your family's safe, my friend."

Guy nodded, starting to feel safe, despite his ill ease. Henry's words, spoken with such assurance, seemed . . . rational . . . to him, sitting in his paneled study full of law journals; almost reasonable.

They continued to feel so all through his drive back to the villa.

Even when he pulled up and looked toward Maddy's glowing window— realizing, with a mixture of relief and apprehension, that she was not only home, but still awake, despite it being well past eleven—he was sure that it was right to go and talk to her, have that *chat*.

When all was said and done, what choice had she given him?

He *was* her husband. She'd chosen to marry him, given Iris to his care, and was carrying his baby. (It *was* his baby, he was certain of it. Absolutely certain. Definitely certain. Quite, entirely, conclusively . . . certain.) He could almost hear the little thing's flickering heartbeat. He'd already imagined what it would be like to hold it for the first time. He could not, would not, let her take any of that away.

And yet, as he climbed the stairs slowly, then stood outside her room, hand raised to knock, thinking, really *thinking* about looking into those eyes of hers and saying everything Henry had suggested he say, he found himself hesitating.

Out of nowhere, he remembered the note his bearer had left waiting for him at the Sea Lounge, back at the start of this whole sorry affair, before Iris's birthday lunch. Alice had sent it, insisting Guy's bearer hurry to deliver it ("In the noon heat, sahib," his bearer had said indignantly afterward), apparently anxious that Guy should receive her telling-off before everyone else arrived.

It hadn't been the easiest start to that torturous lunch.

I'll say nothing to Madeline, she'd written. *I don't need to tell you that she would never forgive you for trying to use Iris against her. I'm struggling myself. I understand why you did it, though. Guy, I'm scared, too. But I've promised Iris you won't again, and that there'll never be a world in which she won't see any of us. I've told her that whatever happens, her parents will make sure she's happy, never sad.*

Don't make her sad again, Guy. If you love her as much as I believe you do, find a more honest way to convince my daughter you deserve her.

Please don't become something less than you are.

She'd said it to him again, later that same day when she'd found him at the hospital, ready to convince him of how unfair he was being by trying to come between Iris and Luke.

"A chaperone, Guy?" she'd said, making him feel like an animal. "Have you forgotten what Luke has been through? All he's missed? Can't you see how this will push everyone away?"

She'd still wanted Maddy to choose him, back then. He'd been sure of it. *I'm scared, too.* It was why he'd listened to her, about not supervising Luke's time with Iris at least.

Iris, who despite his own demeaning efforts to keep her on side—with all his talk of how she must do her best to be polite to Luke, no matter how frightened she might be; his assurances that he'd keep her safe, always look after her, *how could I bear it if I didn't get to do that?*—had started to fall under her father's spell, too.

He turned, looking wearily down the corridor toward her room. He pictured her asleep on her side, lips moving in a dream, dark curls sticking to her rosy cheeks, and dropped his head, replaying the cautious way she'd started to look at him lately. The uncertainty in her. She'd started to doubt him, this sweet child who'd once run to him so eagerly. Become afraid of what he might try and tell her next.

A cough from behind Maddy's door made him turn again, and remember how sick she'd been before. He felt his heart pinch in concern as he heard her run toward her bathroom. He wanted to go to her, hold her shoulders. Be there.

He only ever wanted to do that.

He hesitated a second longer, staring at her wooden door. He stepped toward it and pressed his hand against the warm, damp paneling, his forehead, too.

They'd lost their way, the two of them, too quickly. They hadn't had enough happiness. Not nearly enough time.

He closed his eyes, mind filling now with everything he must say to her.

He'd never be able to make himself do it. He knew he wouldn't. So he didn't try.

He turned slowly and went into his own room, where he wrote it all in a letter instead.

CHAPTER THIRTY-SIX

Maddy was awake when Guy pushed the envelope under their connecting doors. She'd been awake all night, listening to him pacing, sighing, scribbling at his desk. She'd felt almost tempted to get up, go and talk to him. *Please, can we just do that at last?* But she'd felt too sick—too drained by the emotion of the day—to do much beyond lie on her bed, her hand to her stomach, going over the hundred possible forms whatever was coming next might take.

She'd been worrying about her mother, too. She hadn't been fair to her, when she'd got home from Luke's and found her in the nursery, watching Iris sleep with a look of such abject loss on her pale face.

Luke had been with her. He'd insisted on driving her back after she'd had to be sick again at his apartment, saying he didn't want her going anywhere alone. It was as they'd reached Malabar Hill and she'd started telling him about her mother's earlier upset—realizing (from the entirely unshocked way he'd frowned at the road) that he at least seemed to know just what it had all been about—that she'd paused, hearing her mother's words once more, *it's only I saw Diana today,* and finally, creakingly, felt everything fall into place.

She'd turned in her seat, reeling at how much suddenly made sense: her parents' long row, the awkward way Alice had thanked Luke when she'd first seen him, Alf's new job, Luke's determination that she, Maddy, shouldn't confront Diana . . . She'd placed her hand to her spinning head, wondering how it could have possibly taken her so long to realize, fighting to make sense of how she felt about . . . any of it.

"Why on earth didn't you tell me?" she'd asked Luke.

"I wanted her to be able to," Luke had said, pulling over on the dark, leafy verge. He'd gone on, repeating all Arnold had said to him, rationalizing her anger away before it had a chance to take proper hold. He'd made her remember how desperately worried Alice had been over her grief, for so long; how convinced she'd been that he was dead. As he'd talked, warm eyes never leaving hers in the dark cabin, she'd found herself picturing her mother as she'd been back then, after that life-ending telegram had come: the torture in her face all those thousands of times she'd held her, Maddy, trying to console her as she'd wept. *You're my Iris.*

"She's wanted to tell you," Luke had said. "I've spoken to her, I don't know how many times now, when we've been out. She's been terrified, Maddy, of losing you all over again."

Maddy had leaned back against the seat, unable to stand the thought of that either. Her own words, spoken to her father on the beach, had come back to her.

Is it really worth any more upset?

She'd heard her father's reply, *maybe not,* and closed her eyes, knowing, deep down, that of course it wasn't.

She'd meant to be kind to her mother when she saw her. In spite of her grief, her unshakable sadness at how much time had been wasted, she really had meant to tell her that it was done, all over.

She hadn't for a second considered saying what she did to her. It had been the awful way Alice had been looking at Iris that had made her do it. The idea of yet more needless grief.

The words had been out before she knew they were coming.

"Make it up to us," she'd told her. "Prove how sorry you are."

"Yes," Alice had said, half standing, "yes. Just tell me how."

"Sail with us to England," Maddy had said. "If you don't do it with us, you'll never be able to. You don't have to lose anyone. Papa's desperate to retire there, I know you are, too. It's the last voyage you'll ever have to take. Come, and I'll forgive you."

She'd watched Luke's eyes widen. *Are you being serious?* he'd seemed to say.

Alice had simply stared, horrified.

It *had* been unfair, Maddy knew that.

But as she stood from her bed, swallowing on yet another wave of nausea, and crossed the room to pick up Guy's letter, she couldn't regret it.

She wouldn't take it back.

She forgot about it all in any case as she opened Guy's letter and saw what was inside.

Her eyes moved, taking in everything he'd written: the talk of parents never putting themselves before children, how sorry he was, how very, very sorry . . .

Her hands shook. She turned the paper, reading it all over again.

You used to smile when you saw me, I need to be able to hope there'll come a day when you'll do that again. When we'll both do that.

She stared, tears rising.

Please, don't make me talk to you about this. Not now. I can't.

Paper clenched, she looked up, toward his door.

Don't make me talk about this.

She wasn't going to give him any choice.

Not pausing to think twice, she reached for the handle, opening it, and was wholly unsurprised to find him on the other side, still in the uniform he'd obviously been wearing all night, leaning against the wall, as though he'd been listening to her reading, replaying his own words in his head, hearing them in hers.

"You mean this?" she said, holding out the paper, her voice trembling even more than her hands.

"I wish it could be different," he said, just as shakily, "but yes, I do."

Her eyes blurred. She looked down at the page once more, tears dropping on the requests he'd made.

That he be allowed to say goodbye to Iris in his own way. *I need her to not feel guilty. I need her to never be too sad, or too worried to want to see me.* That they go quickly, as soon as possible. *I would be so grateful if it could just be over.* And that he always know Iris, and that the baby be told that it might belong to him. *I'll never marry again, Maddy. I know that in my heart. You've given me the only family I'll ever want, and I can't entirely give up these children who feel so much my own.*

She raised her head, meeting his gaze once more; his kind, gentle gaze.

"Thank you, Guy," she said, pouring her whole heart into the words, wishing so much, so very, very much, that it could all have been different, too.

They left India two days later, on a packed P&O liner to Tilbury that steamed out of Bombay's heaving, sun-drenched docks late in the afternoon. Luke's parents would be waiting for them when they arrived in England, Edie, too; Maddy and Luke had wired them, just as soon as they'd reserved the passage, taking Iris to the telegraph office with them, wanting to keep her close, safe, and cherished through the tumult of their hasty departure, as happy as they could make her. Luke had lifted Iris up at the telegraph counter, helping her peer through the metal grille so that she could watch the clerk punch out their messages. ON OUR WAY STOP. Maddy had smiled at Iris's wide eyes, her wonder that the wires would arrive in England in a matter of minutes, agreeing that yes, it was very like magic, relieved—as they were all relieved—at her excitement, determined not to mar it by giving away how sick she felt in the sweaty press of the room.

After that, they'd barely stopped, getting everything ready to go, saying so many farewells. They'd made one last, bittersweet visit to the school—taking cakes, stopping long enough for Maddy and Iris to hug the clamor of children, many times—and, amid all the frantic packing, they'd stolen an hour for a lingering walk up to the Hanging Gardens, another down to the beach. The evening before, Della and Jeff had thrown them a farewell dinner, and they'd let the children stay up well past their bedtime—the gardener's trio included—reluctant to cut into their running and laughing and games of chase on the moonlit grass, or end the night any sooner than they had to.

"I'm not sure I can stand it," Della had said, setting down her wineglass tearfully. "Can we not convince you to stay, after all?"

"Not this time," Maddy had said, reaching for her hand. "I feel I've missed enough voyages."

"You look terribly green, though," Della had said.

"You do, Maddy darling," Peter had agreed. "Here, have another lime to suck."

It had been hard, so very hard, to leave them all, but made just a little easier by the promise that they'd be back to visit, in the cooler winters, just as Guy would visit them. There'd be other meals, play times for the children. It was not going to be the last time Iris saw her friends, or her ayah (who'd already moved in with Della and Jeff, ready to help encourage some sunnier tendencies from Emily), Suya, Cook, Ahmed, or any of the people she loved.

She didn't have to say goodbye to her grandmother at all.

Maddy had seen to that.

Luke, waiting on the baking starboard deck, glanced over his shoulder, toward the cabin Alice was already in. Richard had spoken to the captain, an old friend of his (as so many people were), and the captain had escorted her on board that morning, through his own private entrance, ahead of everyone else. They'd all helped her—Maddy, Iris, Peter, Della, the girls, all of them; Richard hadn't left her side since. He was coming with them, just for a short stay this time, until he could arrange his retirement.

I can't do this without you either, Alice had told him.

Maddy and Iris had had to leave, just for an hour—Maddy clutching a bag of the ginger biscuits Cook seemed to think would help with her sickness (Luke hoped to God he was right)—off for the final farewell Guy had requested: ices at the Sea Lounge.

But they were back now, the two of them hurrying hand in hand through the shouting porters and luggage carts, pushing their way to the front of the hundreds of British and locals packed onto the clamoring quayside. Luke leaned forward, hands on the ship's warm, salty railings, watching them. He'd been worried that Iris would be upset after leaving Guy. He'd been afraid there would be tears, a struggle. But to his relief, she was laughing as she ran beside Maddy for the gangplanks. His little girl with the sepia foot was laughing, on her way to him.

"You're here," he shouted, making them look up, their bright blue eyes meeting his.

Iris waved.

He waved back.

"We're here," Maddy called, "we're going home," and as her words reached his ears, the truth of it washed through him, and he felt his throat tighten in joy, such elation.

A happiness so overwhelming that it was all he could do to breathe.

EPILOGUE

A Letter to Maddy, from Luke

Today, I recall what year it is. I know that I have been living here for two years, in this home that's less than a mile from our old house by the river; our house which became so full in the end that we sometimes talked about moving, always knowing we'd never, ever be able to bring ourselves to do that.

It was my decision to come here to High Elms, after you went. I couldn't let any of the children have me to live with them, no matter how they insisted. They visit so much—much more than my temperamental memory is prone to give them credit for—and that is all I ever want to ask of them.

It hurts them so, when I forget.

I am forgetting too much, these days. Our time together is slowly slipping away from me, and I have written almost as many letters to you now in confusion—such panic that I never found you—as I have remembering all the thousands of memories we made after we found each other.

These letters, the letters of our life, are the letters I keep. They are stacked beside me. Some are just notes, scrawled to you in haste; others much longer. All of it is here.

Our wedding, that first frozen Christmas after we got back from Bombay, in the small candlelit church at the end of our road. You were so pregnant, and very ready to not be anymore. You laughed when you met me at the altar and I told you how beautiful you looked. You are, *I said*, you must trust me on this, Miss Bright. *Owen arrived just a week later, confounding us all by looking only like you, and demanding to be loved—as he was always going to be loved—from the second he opened his dark blue eyes.*

Less than two years later came the twins, Ben and Will, giving us the most sleepless of summers, until Iris asked if we could send them back. She'd wanted a sister, of course. But Jacob came, in the spring of 1926, destroying her last hope of that.

She didn't hold it against him, though. How could anyone have held anything against such a child? She doted on him, as we all doted on him. I can see him now, laughing in the garden, trying to keep up with the rest of them, wait, wait, *his arms and legs pumping, always chasing a football.*

Those years when they were small, they were wondrous. All the hot summers when the five of them tore up and down the lawn, in and out of the river. Our walks in the park, fireworks in the freezing cold (what I would give to watch them with my arms around you, just one more time), birthdays and Christmases with your parents, my parents, Edie, Guy, Peter and Della—whom we visited just the once in India, before they followed us back—and Emma, of course. Emma, who came to our wedding with Ernest and Arnold, then to Owen's christening, then again just because she happened to be in the neighborhood, and so on, until she chanced upon a job in the local hospital, you said she'd better take it, and be godmother to Will, too, and after that she never missed another birthday or Christmas again.

It all passed so quickly, though. It took us by surprise that the days, which felt so long at times, vanished in years that went in the blink of an eye. One morning, we were taking Iris to her first day at her new school, the next up to Somerville for university, so nervous in the new duffel coat you'd insisted she'd need, so determined to not appear nervous.

And so cross at her brothers for being too noisy when we all saw her into that tiny room we couldn't bear to leave her alone in. Crosser yet when Jacob, just eight, ran onto the quad to fetch his escaped football, and came haring back, eyes wide in terror and laughter, after he was shouted at by the porter.

"I hate that I ever told him off," Iris said to me, just the other day.

"You didn't know," I assured her. "And he worshiped you."

We never thought any of them would go into uniform. All of us were terrified of a second war. But it happened. We couldn't stop it. No one could.

Iris went first, with the air force to Cairo, Della's girls with her, and seeing them off was one of the hardest things any of us did. But they came back. Iris came back, married and so happy, the first of our grandchildren, Megan (about to be a mother herself), already a month old.

Owen, determined to become the surgeon he now is (much to Guy's and my mother's delight), joined the Medical Corps and somehow stayed safe, too, in the Mediterranean, the Pacific. So, miraculously, did the twins, our pilots, but not without giving us hundreds more sleepless nights.

It was only Jacob, eighteen just in time for the Normandy landings, who we've never been able to stop waiting for.

More than thirty years on, and I cannot write those words without my heart breaking.

You told me you would look for him. When you went—leaving me as you promised you would never leave me—I think it was the idea of that which gave you such peace.

I hope you are together, but I still cannot stop wishing that you were here. You became ill so fast, and it wasn't until after you were gone that I realized how much I had left to say to you: countless things that I wanted you to know, all of them about how much you gave me.

These letters, I suppose, have been about my telling you that, too.

I need to stop writing now, though. I am growing tired. The pen feels heavy, and I need to sleep.

I want to sleep.

When I sleep, I dream. And my dreams are all I have left of that other world.

The one I know I once belonged to, with you.

ACKNOWLEDGMENTS

There are so many people to whom I am hugely grateful for their help and support in writing this book. As always, a very big thank-you to my amazing agent, Becky Ritchie, as well as the rest of the team at AM Heath, and of course to Deborah Schneider. Thank you, too, to my wonderful publishers, in particular, Leslie Gelbman at St. Martin's Press, and all the team—Tiffany Shelton, Danielle Fiorella, Adriana Coada, Lisa Davis, Marissa Sangiacomo, Jessica Zimmerman, Devan Norman, Brant Janeway, Dakota Cohen, Kathryn Carroll, and Drew Kilman—and Viola Hayden, Darcy Nicholson, Stephie Melrose, Gemma Shelley, Thalia Proctor, Lucy Malagoni, and Cath Burke at Little, Brown in the UK.

In writing this book, I went on an incredible research trip to India and am very grateful to everyone who welcomed me there. I would especially like to thank the staff at The Royal Bombay Yacht Club, then Pranav at Grand Mumbai Tours—for meeting me at the crack of dawn and tailor-making an itinerary that transported me back in time to colonial Bombay, immersing me in the world that Maddy and Luke inhabited—and last, but by no means least, Renjen at the Bombay Gymkhana club, who not only invited me into the club, but took me on a guided tour of its verandas, facilities, and rooms, giving me a morning I will never forget.

Thank you to all my amazing friends, and a group of writers I couldn't imagine doing this without: Iona Grey, Kerry Fisher, Sarra Manning, Lucy Foley, Kate Riordan, Katherine Webb, Cesca Major, and Claire McGlasson. Thanks to my brilliant parents, my brother and sister, and, always, to my husband, Matt, and our children, Molly, Jonah, and Raffy—I don't know what I'd do, or where I'd be, without you!